Jo Walton won the John W. Campbell Award for Best New Writer in 2002, and the World Fantasy Award for her novel *Tooth and Claw* in 2004. Her last novel *Among Others* won the Hugo and Nebula Awards in 2012. A native of Wales, she lives in Montreal.

Praise for the Small Change Trilogy

'If le Carré scares you, try Jo Walton. Of course her brilliant story of a democracy selling itself out to fascism sixty years ago is just a mystery, just a thriller, just a fantasy—of course we know nothing like that could happen now. Don't we?'

Ursula K. Le Guin

'A stiff-upper-lip whodunit boasting political intrigue and uncomfortable truths about anti-Semitism.'

Entertainment Weekly

'A beautifully-written alternate history thriller by World Fantasy Award-winner Jo Walton, *Farthing* is a smart, convincing tale of a country's slide into fascism that's sure to entertain casual and genre readers alike.'

Cinescope

'Stunningly powerful…While the whodunit plot is compelling, it's the convincing portrait of a country's incremental slide into fascism that makes [these novels] a standout.'

Publishers Weekly

'*Farthing* starts out as a cozy period house party mystery, becomes a brilliant alternate history yarn, and at last reveals itself to be a chilling political thriller. It's smart, riveting, and deeply moving. Once you start reading, don't plan to put it down.'

Emma Bull

'[*Farthing* is] a wonderful book, simultaneously a gripping mystery and a harrowing cautionary tale. Walton's credible – and entirely convincing – alternative history becomes a terrifying meditation on class, power, and persecution.'

Susan Palwick

'Haunting... Like meticulously nested Matroyshka dolls, both *Farthing* and *Ha'Penny* reveal complex arguments layered in their elegantly structured narratives.'

Sarah Weinman, *Los Angeles Times*

'[*Farthing* and *Ha'penny*] are compulsively readable for their characters and plots. But it's [Walton's] observations about power that make them hard to put down."'

Baltimore City Paper

'Stellar...Horrifying and all-too-possible.'

RT Book Reviews

Novels by Jo Walton

The Sulien series

The King's Peace
The King's Name
The Prize in the Crown

Tooth and Claw

The Small Change series

Farthing
Ha'penny
Half a Crown

Lifelode

Among Others

JO WALTON

HALF A CROWN

corsair

Constable & Robinson Ltd.
55–56 Russell Square
London WC1B 4HP
www.constablerobinson.com

First published in the US by Tor®,
a registered trademark of Tom Doherty Associates, LLC, 2008

First published in the UK by Corsair,
an imprint of Constable & Robinson Ltd., 2014

A copy of the British Library Cataloguing in
Publication Data is available from the British Library

ISBN: 978-1-4721-1299-6 (paperback)
ISBN: 978-1-4721-1302-3 (ebook)

Printed and bound by
CPI Group (UK) Ltd, Croydon, CR0 4YY

1 3 5 7 9 10 8 6 4 2

This is for Patrick Nielsen Hayden, for keeping the faith.

ACKNOWLEDGMENTS

I'd like to thank Mary Lace for reading this as it was being written, and Emmet O'Brien, David Goldfarb, Janet M. Kegg, Sherwood Smith, Clark E. Myers, Naomi Kritzer, Alison Scott, Jennifer Arnott, Naomi Libicki, Madeleine Kelly, Lila Garrott, Melissa McDowell, Laura Tennenhaus, Mary Ellen Curtin, Sylvia Rachel Hunter, Mary Kay Kare, Bob Webber, Rivka Wald, and Anne Gwin for reading it when it was done.

I'd like to thank my father-in-law, Tony O'Brien, for rescuing 1,500 words from the hard drive of my deceased laptop, Caliban. (Always back up!) Grande Bibliothèque du Québec, Fraser-Hickson Library, Cardiff Central Library, and the Montreal library system were all generous with books for research. Of all the books I used, I'd most especially like to mention the work of the biographer Anne De Courcy. I couldn't have written this without *1939: The Last Season,* but all of her books have been reliable, readable, and so relevant she couldn't have done better if she were my personal researcher.

Emmet O'Brien and Sasha Walton put up with me while I was writing, even on days when dinner was late or forgotten altogether. Alter Reiss helped immeasurably with depressing statistics, odd facts, seder details, and general encouragement.

My LiveJournal correspondents provided useful corroboration, information, and support (papersky.livejournal.com). Zev Sero gave me one perfect comment, which appears in chapter 25. Thanks to everyone at Tor, especially the hardworking production department.

This book is the third and last in my "Still Life with Fascists" or "Small Change" series. The earlier volumes are *Farthing* (2006) and *Ha'penny* (2007). I've always been a very hopeful and optimistic person. That's why I wrote these books.

Those who would give up essential liberty to purchase a little temporary safety deserve neither liberty nor safety.
—Benjamin Franklin (1759)

The only thing we have to fear is fear itself.
—Franklin D. Roosevelt (1932)

HALF A CROWN

1

A week before she was due to bring me out, I overheard Mrs. Maynard saying I was "not quite . . ." That's just how she said it. "Elvira's not quite . . ."

When she let her voice trail off like that I knew precisely what she meant. I knew it in the pit of my stomach. I had been coming down the stairs to join them in the drawing room when I heard her speaking, and stopped dead, clutching the handrail in my left hand and the bunched seersucker of my skirt in the other. It was 1960 and skirts in the spring collections were long enough that they had to be lifted a little to avoid stepping on them on the stairs.

Mrs. Maynard's friend, Lady Bellingham, made a little sound of inarticulate sympathy. There could be no question what Mrs. Maynard meant, no way that I could think—or that anyone could think—she meant not quite ready, or not quite well, though I knew if I challenged her that's what she would say. "Not quite out of the top drawer" is what she really meant; "not quite a lady." I was still "not quite up to snuff," despite eight years in the best and most expensive girls' schools in England and a year in Switzerland being "finished." At eighteen I still had two distinct voices: the voice that went with my clothes and my hair, the voice that was indistinguishable in its essentials from Betsy Maynard's, and then the much less acceptable voice of my childhood, the London Cockney voice. My past was never to be forgotten, not quite, however hard I tried.

"Then why ever are you bringing her out with Betsy?" Lady Bellingham asked, her voice positively oozing sympathy the way an eclair oozes cream.

"Well her uncle, you know," Mrs. Maynard said. "He's the head of the Watch. One doesn't like . . ."

Spending time with Mrs. Maynard, you get used to trailing sentences with everything explicit but nothing spelled out. I could have run down the stairs and pushed into the drawing room and shouted that it wasn't anything like so simple. Mrs. Maynard was bringing me out because her daughter Betsy had begged me to go through with it. "I can't face being a deb without you!" she had said. Betsy and I were friends because, in the alphabetically arranged classroom at Arlinghurst, "Elizabeth" and "Elvira" happened to fall next to each other, and Betsy and I had both felt like misfits and clung to each other ever since. I didn't give more than half a damn about coming out and being presented to the Queen. What I wanted was to go to Oxford. You may think it was an odd ambition. Half the people I met did. Going by my born social status rather than my acquired one I couldn't even hope to be admitted. Still, I had been interviewed and accepted at St. Hilda's and had only the summer to wait before I went up. It was April already. Most girls I knew would have hated the idea of grinding away at their books, but I'd always found that side of things easy; it was parties that bored me. But Betsy and Uncle Carmichael had set their hearts on my coming out, so I had agreed I would do that first.

Besides all that, Mrs. Maynard was bringing me out because my uncle, who wasn't really my uncle at all, was paying for me and subsidizing Betsy. However County the Maynards might be, they never had much money to spare, at least by their own standards. By the standards I'd grown up with they were impossibly rich, but by those of the people they moved among, they were struggling to keep up appearances. Anyway, people with money are often horribly mean; that was the first thing I'd learned when I'd started to move among them. But, sickeningly, none of that got a mention. Mrs. Maynard's trailing off made it sound as if she was bringing me out despite my deficiencies because she was afraid of my uncle.

"Might I trouble you for a little more tea, dear?" Lady Bellingham asked.

The banisters were Victorian and rounded, like chair legs, with big round knobs on the newel posts. Between them I could see down into the hall, the faded cream wallpaper, the top of the mahogany side table, and a crystal vase of pinky-white carnations. The house was narrow, like all Victorian London houses. I could see the drawing room door, which was open, but I couldn't see in through it, so I didn't know if Betsy was sitting there too. It seemed terribly important to find out if she was listening to all this without protest. I let go of my handful of skirt and slipped off my shoes, feeling absurd, knowing that while I was fairly safe from Mrs. Maynard, the servants could come out of the back part of the house at any time and catch me. They probably wouldn't give me away, but it would still be frightfully embarrassing. I ran one hand lightly down the banister rail and tiptoed gingerly down the strip of carpet in the center of the stairs to the half-landing, where I could see through the drawing room door if I stretched a bit.

I took a good grip, leaned out, and craned my neck. Mrs. Maynard was eating a cream cake with a fork. She was not seen to advantage from above, as she had a squashed-up face like a pug and wore her graying brown hair in a permanent wave so rigid it looked like a helmet. Her afternoon dress was a muslin patterned with roses, that made her stocky figure look as upholstered as the chair she sat in. Lady Bellingham, on the sofa and reaching towards the tea trolley for a sandwich, looked softer, thinner, and altogether more fashionable. I had just determined to my satisfaction that they were alone, when with no warning at all the front door opened.

Of course they saw me at once. They couldn't help it. Mr. Maynard, Betsy's father, took me in with one rapid glance, raised his eyebrows, and looked away. The other man with him was a complete stranger with a dark piratical beard and a perfectly normal bowler hat. I felt myself turn crimson as I pulled myself back onto the half-landing and slipped my shoes back on.

"Ah, Elvira," Mr. Maynard said, with no inflection whatever. I didn't know him well. He did something boring and diplomatic to which I'd never paid much attention and which seemed to take up a great deal of his time. On holidays I'd spent with Betsy he'd never paid much attention to me. "Sir Alan, this is my daughter's friend Elvira Royston, whom my wife is bringing out with Betsy this summer. Elvira, this is Sir Alan Bellingham."

"Delighted to meet you," I said, coming down the stairs and extending my hand as I had been so painstakingly taught.

Sir Alan ignored my fading blushes and shook hands firmly. He was almost exactly my height, and looked me in the eye. "Charmed," he murmured. "I don't suppose you know if my mother is here?"

"She's taking tea with Mrs. Maynard in the drawing room," I said, blushing again.

"And Betsy?" Mr. Maynard asked.

"I don't know where she is," I said, honestly. "I haven't seen her since lunchtime."

"See if you can rustle her up, there's a good girl. I'm sure she'd be glad to see Sir Alan. You'll take a cup of tea, Sir Alan, while you wait for your mother to be ready?"

Sir Alan smiled at me. Because of the beard, I couldn't tell how old he was. At first I had thought he was Mr. Maynard's age, but when he smiled I thought he was much younger, maybe no more than thirty.

"I'll find her if she's at home," I said, and turned and went back upstairs to look for Betsy.

I tapped on her door.

"Who is it?" she called.

"Me," I said, opening the door. Betsy was lying on the bed in a green check dress that looked distinctly rumpled. "Your father wants you to come down and drink tea, but you'd better tidy yourself up first."

She sighed and sat up. "Who's here?"

"That bitch Lady Bellingham, and a mysterious stranger called Sir Alan who seems to be her son."

Betsy lay down again and put her pillow on her head. "He's not a mysterious stranger, he's my father's idea of a suitable son-in-law," she said, her voice rather muffled. "Do go down and tell them I'm mortally wounded and not likely to make it."

"Don't be a ninny," I said, pulling off the pillow. "They can't make you marry a man with a beard."

"Ghastly Lady B. is Mummy's best friend, and her son's frightfully rich and doing things with the government that seem likely to make him even more frightfully rich, and powerful as well. And he's very polite, which makes him perfect in Mummy's eyes. You don't know how lucky you are being an orphan, Elvira."

In fact, my mother was alive and well and running a pub in Leytonstone, but I thought it better never to mention her in my daily life. She certainly wasn't going to interfere. She hadn't wanted me when she ran off with her fancy man when I was six, and she hadn't wanted me when my father died when I was eight, so she wasn't likely to want me now. I hardly remembered her, but my aunt Ciss, my real aunt, my father's sister, kept me up to date with gossip about her. Aunt Ciss would have taken me in, even though she had five children of her own, but she thought having Uncle Carmichael take an interest in me and offering to send me to Arlinghurst was a great opportunity for me to make something of myself. I'd thought it a funny phrase then, like making stew of a neck of lamb, or a fruit cobbler of two bruised apples and a squashy pear. What they had hoped to make of me was a lady, and I'd been too young to question why anyone thought this would be better than what I would have grown into if let alone. It was only in the last year or so I had wondered about this at all, as I'd grown old enough to consider what they had made of me so far and what I might want to make of myself, given the opportunity.

"Put on a clean dress and come down, do," I said. "I'll do my best to draw the cross fire."

That made her smile. It was, of course, Bogart's famous line from the end of *The Battle of Kursk*. She stood up and pulled her dress off over her head. "I met Sir Alan the other night when you were having dinner with your uncle," she said. "Oh, how I loathe this whole dreary business. Men. Dancing. Coming out. And on Wednesday, fittings for our Court dresses, which cost a fortune and which we'll wear for one night next week, to make our curtsey to the Queen, as if it makes any difference at all to anything." She dropped the green dress heedlessly on the floor and opened her wardrobe. "What should I wear?"

"What do you want to look like?"

"I want to look like Elizabeth instead of Betsy." This was her newest enthusiasm. I found it very hard to comply with, and nobody else tried at all. "And I want to look like someone who doesn't need to have her parents drag home a husband for her. I swear Daddy's expression is just like Tigrath's when she's dragged home a mouse and dropped it proudly on my pillow."

I laughed. "Why not the cream seersucker thing with the gold ribbon we bought in Paris?"

"Because we don't want to look like twins," she said. "It only makes me look worse."

I smoothed the ribbon at my neck self-consciously. I can't help being prettier than Betsy. She never cared before Zurich.

She pulled out a forest green dress patterned with leaves so dark you could hardly see them except when the light was angled just right, another of her Paris purchases. Somebody, probably her mother, had once told Betsy that redheads ought to wear green. In my opinion it did nothing for her. "What about this?" she asked.

"What about the gray one?" I countered. It was the same cut, and almost the same fabric only in gray with the leaf pattern in black.

"I hate the gray one," she said, pulling it out. "All the same, I'll wear it, because I hate Sir Alan too. He's such a fascist."

"We're all fascists now, surely?" I asked. "And anyway, what's wrong with fascism? It's fun!"

"I find fascists just too sick-making," Betsy said, pulling on the gray dress and belting it viciously tight. It fell precisely just above her ankles. She looked all right. Most people are neither beautiful nor ugly, they fall somewhere in the range of the middle. If I tried, and trying was what we'd been taught at our expensive Swiss finishing school, I could get into the top end of that range. All right was about as good as poor Betsy could manage.

I passed her her hairbrush, silver-backed with her initials engraved, a present from her father when she turned eighteen. "You're just saying that to be shocking. It's your mother makes me sick. She said I was 'not quite.'" I tried to say it lightly, but my voice let me down.

"That's ghastly. To Lady B.?" Betsy asked, dragging the brush through her hair much too hard.

I nodded. "Just now. I'd finished studying for the time being and I was coming down the stairs in search of tea and I overheard them."

"She was probably trying to make sure Sir Alan didn't fall for you instead of me," Betsy said.

"Oh Bets— Elizabeth!" I said. "That's ridiculous. As if he'd look at me when I'm nobody, and about to be an undergraduette too. And anyway, he has a beard!"

"I believe it doesn't impede one's sex life," Betsy said, and we both giggled. "Do my necklace up?"

She ran her hands through the little silver box on her dressing table and fished out a thin gold chain hung with a half circle of seed pearls. I lifted her hair and fastened the clasp. It sat nicely on her skin above the neckline of the dress. "That's pretty," I said. "Where did you get it?"

"My aunt Patsy gave it to me. It was hers when she came out, and she felt it brought her luck. It's a funny length, but I like it." She straightened it. "Do you want something?"

"I'd better not; I can't trust your mother not to say something if I borrow your jewelry. Besides, there's this ribbon." I smoothed it again.

"I'm sure your uncle will give you something of your own soon now," Betsy said. "I expect that's what he's going to do when he takes you out on Thursday, take you to Cartier and let you choose."

"I don't think he has any idea I ought to have something. He has no wife, no daughters of his own, no sister even. I can't really tell him. He's been so good to me already, paying for all this nonsense, and for Oxford too," I said. "But I'm sure that's not what we'll be doing on Thursday. That's our annual date to go down to Kent to look at the primroses, in memory of my father."

Betsy hugged me. "I'd forgotten," she said. "Well, you're welcome to anything of mine any time, whenever Mummy isn't looking. Come on. We'd better go down, or they'll be sending out search parties."

We went down to the drawing room together. There was a much better than normal selection of tea, several kinds of sandwiches, and a whole plate of cream cakes from Gunter's, as well as the usual fruitcake and digestive biscuits. I took an eclair and a cup of tea and retreated towards the wing chair by the window. Sir Alan was on the sofa by his mother, and Mr. Maynard on the other wing chair. "Cross fire," Betsy mouthed, as she cut me off from the wing chair, leaving me the place that had clearly been left for her, at the other end of the sofa. I sat there and sipped my tea. No matter how hard I tried, I thought, these people would never truly accept me. If they did, if I managed to fool some of them for a little while, someone who knew, like Mrs. Maynard, would be sure to tell them that I wasn't "quite." This was why I wanted to go to Oxford. Even in the little glimpse I'd had of it so far, I could tell that standards were different; intellectual attainments still mattered more there than who your parents were.

But "not quite" had stung. I might want to turn my back on this world, I didn't want to be rejected by it as not good enough. I'd made so much effort already, worrying about clothes and hair and jewelry. It was just over a week until we made our debut, and then there would be a round of balls and parties over the summer. April, May, June, July, August, September. Then, in October, I could begin my real life. Six months.

The silence in the drawing room now everyone had settled was a little uncomfortable. I leaned towards Sir Alan. "So, Sir Alan, Betsy tells me you're a fascist?" I said.

"Betsy's too kind," Sir Alan replied. "And you, Miss Royston, are you fond of fascism?"

"Oh yes, I think it's the most terrific fun," I said.

Mrs. Maynard winced a little and exchanged a sympathetic glance with Lady Bellingham. The thing was that fascism, while all very well in its place, was in Mrs. Maynard's eyes something to look down on just the tiniest bit, as being very useful of course, and something that did very well for keeping Them in place, but was actually not quite . . . After all, it was open to everyone, except Jews of course.

My reply seemed to please Sir Alan, who nodded and smiled. "Fun, yes, absolutely. Have you ever been to an Ironsides rally?" he asked.

In fact I had, when I was very young. It had been a march through Camden Town, where I lived then, and my father had taken me. I remembered the uniforms and the bands, the fireworks and the tremendous spirit of fellowship. "No," I said, regretfully. "I never have. Only on television."

"Not the place for a young lady, perhaps, Alan," Lady Bellingham said, carefully, her hands fluttering in her lap.

"Nonsense, Mother," her son corrected her robustly. "Certainly not the thing unescorted, but if Miss Royston and Miss Maynard would like to join me, I could see that they had a good time without being near any trouble. You hear much more about trouble than you see these days; the Jews and communists don't try to break up our marches anymore, the Watch have cracked down on them too hard. It's been years since there was any trouble of that kind. There's a torchlit march to Marble Arch tomorrow night, what do you say, ladies?"

Mrs. Maynard was looking like a pug with a stomachache. "I'm not sure it would be quite . . . ," she said, looking at her husband, who was staring at the faded pattern on the rug as if it interested him extremely.

I hadn't quite made up my mind how far I wanted to push this, but Betsy, for all her saying fascism made her sick, decided for me. "We'd love to, Sir Alan," she said, shooting a burning look at her mother.

"Oh yes," I agreed, following her lead. "We'd love to. I've always wanted to see a torchlit parade close up."

"As long as it's quite safe, of course," Betsy added.

"Quite safe these days," Sir Alan reassured everyone, turning around the drawing room with a smile that made him look more than ever like a pirate.

So that's why we were right there when the riot happened.

2

Watch Commander Carmichael glared down at the logistical nightmare on his desk. He quite understood that there had to be a peace conference for what the Germans were calling the "Twenty Year War," but he couldn't understand why anyone thought it was a good idea to hold it in London. All these heads of state and foreign ministers, all these meetings, all these security services with their own ideas who would need to be treated carefully, while the actual security for the whole event fell heavily onto the shoulders of Carmichael and the Watch. He looked up with relief when Lieutenant-Commander Jacobson came in, a parcel neatly wrapped in plastic in his hand.

"Sergeant Evans was on his way to bring you this, and I intercepted it on my way," he said, putting the parcel on the corner of Carmichael's desk.

"Just some books," Carmichael said, not reaching for the parcel. He had sent Evans down to Hatchards to pick up anything new on Byzantium, in the hope it would be some consolation for Jack. Jack was unhappy, as usual, because Carmichael didn't have enough time to spend with him and because they never got to do anything together. Jack was especially unhappy because he wanted a holiday in Greece or Turkey, to see his precious Byzantine remnants for himself. Carmichael had been forced to say he couldn't get away until September at the earliest, and then had offered him Italy, which was safer, and possible. Jack had objected that they had been to Italy before. To Carmichael it was all the same—sunshine, Mediterranean food, dusty ruins, rough wine, olive trees. Only Jack cared which ruins they were. Carmichael sometimes thought they lived in different worlds. In his world, there was an insurrection going on in Greece and the Turks had done an awful lot worse than sacking Byzantium since.

"I don't want to interrupt, but there are a few things," Jacobson said.

"I'm glad to be interrupted. I'm working on the blasted conference, and I can't see how to do it without more men—and that's with calling in the Met. And the Met are being irritating, as usual. Close the door and sit down."

"Yes, sir," Jacobson said, and turned to the door. It was a heavy oak door, like all the doors in the Watchtower, designed to swing on a touch and not to let sound escape. Like many things about the Watch, they were designed to intimidate but had more than one use. Once you were safely inside, you knew nobody outside the room could listen.

"Irish consignment get off all right?" Carmichael asked, once the door was safely shut.

"Like clockwork," Jacobson assured him, sitting down on the other side of the desk. "Biggest one yet, and not a ripple."

Carmichael smiled with relief. "Every time I worry—"

"Oh, the Irish will do anything to stick it to the Brits," Jacobson said. "Anything up to and including accepting our unwanted Jews, anti-Semitic though they might otherwise be. And we have the transport down to a routine by now. But it's going to be a damn sight harder when the Gravesend facility gets finished."

"I kept saying that it wasn't economic for us to have our own death camp, which is an argument that usually gets their attention, but the Prime Minister himself was insistent that we needed it. He winced at the word though, kept saying *prison for intransigents* and *facility.*" Carmichael sighed. "I don't know how we're going to get around it."

"Do you think Normanby's envisioning an increase?" Jacobson asked, looking worried. "A general roundup, like in 1955?"

Carmichael shook his head. "He'd be bound to mention that to me, and when I saw him on Friday it was nothing but the conference. He didn't even mention the Gravesend facility until I brought it up. They couldn't do a roundup without us. We'd have warning, like before, for what good it did. I think it suits him to have the good quiet Jews right there as targets. It keeps everyone a little bit afraid. Same as having me on television. He knows it increases the numbers of people taking potshots at me, and he doesn't care. He wants people scared. He doesn't even have to bother making things illegal if people are voluntarily not doing things because they know the Watch wouldn't like it, and the Watch is watching." Carmichael's voice rose in vicious imitation of the advertisement as he parroted the slogan. "If he's expecting an increase in deportees I think it's the strikers and marchers he's aiming it at."

"It won't be deportations though; they'll have to call it something else when we have our own facility."

Carmichael observed the distress in every line of his subordinate's expression and hastened to reassure him. "You're safe, anyway, Jacobson. You're useful to them because they think they have something on you. And your family—"

"My family are safe in Newfoundland with impeccable papers, except my wife, who just won't go," Jacobson said, quickly. "No, that's not what I'm worried about. It's just—how many Jews have been massacred now, in Europe? How many are left? And in a way, they're all my people. Oh, we get some away—"

"It would be a lot worse if not for us. We get a lot away. Twenty percent this year." Carmichael did not want to mention 1955 again, did not even want to think of it. He dreamed about it, sometimes.

"Twenty percent of those innocents we arrested in this country we managed to save. They weren't all Jews."

"They were all innocent," Carmichael said, vehemently. "We do as much as we can without risking being found out—because if we are, that's the end of it, you know that; it would be as bad as it is on the Continent. The Inner Watch does as much as it safely can, and we're increasing that all the time. Now that document issue is in your division instead of Ogilvie's, we can increase what we're doing there. We do have to keep being careful about who we recruit. We can't slip up there or we can lose everything. And it's such a lot to ask. Not everyone is prepared to live with death in their mouth." Carmichael touched the side of his jaw where his false tooth was concealed.

Jacobson reflexively touched his own cheek. "It all feels so futile in the face of—"

Jacobson fell silent as the door swung open and Carmichael's other Lieutenant-Commander, Ogilvie, came in. Carmichael didn't like Ogilvie. He never had, though over the years he had learned to appreciate his efficiency. He was gleaming this morning; his balding head seemed to shine, his teeth flashed, and the effect was set off by a thin gold stripe in his tie. "Good morning Chief, Jacobson," he said. "Heard the news?"

Carmichael knew from experience that nothing could repress Ogilvie. Nevertheless, he replied with the morning's *Times* headline, " 'Factory Owners Gun Down Strikers in Alabama'?"

Jacobson choked, but Ogilvie sailed over it as Carmichael had known he would, with another flash of his teeth. "No, that the Duke of Windsor wants to come to the conference," he said, taking up a position leaning on the wood paneling at the side of the door.

"Edward the Eighth?" Jacobson said, twisting in his chair to look at Ogilvie. "He can't!"

"I don't think the terms of his abdication actually included exile," Carmichael said, slowly. "Certainly he hasn't been back to Britain since, though. Why does he want to come now?"

"He wants to come to the conference because he feels he has something to contribute to the peace of the world, or so he apparently says," Ogilvie said. "He, or rather his minder, equerry, or whatever, Captain Hickmott, contacted the Home Office, the HO contacted us, and the flunky they spoke to had the sense to kick it up to me. I got on the blower to them, and so now I'm kicking it up to you, sir." He stepped forward and handed Carmichael a piece of paper with Captain Hickmott's name and number written neatly.

"What did the HO say?" Carmichael asked, waving Ogilvie to the other chair.

"Said they wanted to know about the security aspects of it before making a political decision," Ogilvie said, pulling the chair closer to the desk. "Don't want to get caught with a hot potato, if you ask me."

Carmichael sighed and looked down at the drifts of papers. "It was going to be a nightmare anyway. Adding one spoilt Royal Duke won't make much difference from a security point of view. It's the political side they need to think about, bringing him back, how people are going to react. The abdication is still an emotional issue for a lot of people."

"He shouldn't get any special security, or special attention either. You can't pack in being king because you're sick of the responsibility and then expect everyone to treat you just the same," Jacobson said, with a vindictiveness that surprised Carmichael.

"Hark the herald angels sing, Mrs. Simpson's pinched our king!" Ogilvie put in, musically.

Carmichael remembered that being sung in his school in 1936, the year Edward VIII had, astonishingly, preferred to marry an

American divorcée to being King of England. Wallis Simpson was twice-divorced, older than the King, and not even pretty. "He isn't planning to bring her, is he?"

Ogilvie shrugged. "Don't know, sir. Captain Hickmott didn't mention her. But the conference starts next week, so they'd need a pretty quick answer."

Wallis? Carmichael wrote on the paper Ogilvie had given him.

"Anyone asked the Palace how they feel?"

"Not so far as I know, sir," Ogilvie said.

"Well, your instinct to kick it upstairs seems sound, and I'm going to do the same. I'll speak to the Duke of Hampshire about it today, and if necessary get him to talk to the Palace," Carmichael said, making another note and underlining it. "Anything else? Anything else important?"

"No, sir," Jacobson said, getting to his feet. "I'll get on if that's all right with you."

"Thanks again for bringing up my parcel," Carmichael said, as Jacobson slipped out. "Ogilvie?"

"Couple more things on the conference front. Thought you might like to know that the Spanish security people have joined the Eye-Ties and the Gestapo in poking around London already." Ogilvie rolled his eyes. "They came in on the regular airship from Rome yesterday. I had a meeting with their top fellow last night. The Japs are arriving today, so no doubt we'll have them underfoot as well. Fortunately, everyone else seems happy to trust us or doesn't have much choice about trusting the Jerries." He laughed heartily, and didn't seem to notice that Carmichael didn't join him. "The Frogs aren't sending anyone except a few guards with Marshal Desjardins, and the same with the other Continental states, King of Denmark and so on. I suppose they're right thinking that there are enough Gestapo around to look after the pack of them."

On Carmichael's desk sat three black telephones, heavy with

authority, one of them half buried in the drifts. He put out a hand to the nearest of them, then thought better of it and looked back at Ogilvie. "You're doing well with all this," he said. "Here's another job. After the state opening of the conference—the procession and all that—it's just a case of getting everyone from their embassies and hotels to St. James's every day. The top people won't be staying the whole course. Franco, Hitler, and so on, they'll stay a few days and party, then come back to sign the treaty when it's all settled. I expect the Japanese will stay, as it's such a long way for them. I've been working on that regular conference security, but I'd like to delegate the procession to you. Make plans that'll let the people out to cheer and wave flags but prevent assassins from being among them."

"Yes, sir," Ogilvie said, beaming. "Can I alter the route, if necessary?"

"Do what you need to. Set up as many checkpoints as you like. Cooperate with the foreign security people if you can, while keeping a discreet eye on them. Talk to the FO about precedence, they've hammered something out. I've got a list here." Carmichael fished on his desk and came up with it. "Here you are. The Queen goes first, then Herr Hitler, then Mr. Normanby, then the Japanese; after that it gets complicated."

"Worse if the Duke of Windsor comes," Ogilvie said, taking the paper and rapidly glancing down it. "What, the South Africans are coming after all? And President Yolen is actually deigning to care about the affairs of the world outside America sufficiently to send a representative? Wonders will never cease. Though since we've put his man in between the Indians and the Ukrainians, it won't help their good opinion of us. Still, ours not to reason why, eh? Oh, what about the Met? Are they cooperating with us?"

"As usual, they're dragging their feet," Carmichael said.

"Whose side are they on, anyway?" Ogilvie asked. "When this

flap is over we ought to have another go at getting a mole into their top levels. I heard that Penn-Barkis will be hiring a new secretary this year. We could try something there."

"Make a note of it," Carmichael said. "But be careful. And with the procession business, be polite. They do have nominal supervision over us, after all."

"I'll be polite." Ogilvie grimaced. "Better get on with it, then."

He stood, nodded at Carmichael cheerfully, and went out. Carmichael stared for a moment at the print he had selected for the wall opposite his desk: Grimshaw's painting of a deserted London street. The bare trees and single figure struck some people as bleak, but they reminded Carmichael of days investigating simple crimes with clear solutions.

He sighed and reached for the nearest telephone.

3

Betsy knocked on my door on her way back from the bathroom and caught me standing in my bra and pants with all the dresses I'd brought back from Paris the week before spread out on the bed. "So you don't know what to wear either!" she said.

"Well, what does one wear to a rally that starts at sunset?" I asked. "An evening dress? An afternoon dress? Leni always said you should make up for candlelight by candlelight, but what about torchlight?"

Betsy was wearing an old toweling dressing gown that had originally been pink and was now so faded as to own no color at all except at the seams. "It's such a pity we can't wear black," she said. "From what I gather we'd blend into the crowd if we could."

"Young ladies neffer neffer wear black," I said, but Betsy didn't so much as smile.

"I made you this," she said, and handed me a blue silk lavender sachet, just the right size to go inside my bra, embroidered with an exquisite *E* in the style we had both acquired over many hours in Arlinghurst. Though it was only April the bag brought the faint smell of summer.

"Thank you! But what's it for? It isn't my birthday until May."

She sat down on the end of my bed, tucking the dressing gown around her. "I just wanted to give you something. To thank you for drawing the cross fire, and for being here. And because Mummy's a pig about me lending you jewelry, which seems so stupid after Switzerland, and well, for Zurich and everything. I just felt fond of you and—it's only a little lavender bag, but I know you like them."

"Love them," I said firmly, tucking it into my bra right away. I didn't want Betsy to get started on Zurich and what she owed me. She needed to put that out of her mind, and dwelling on it was the worst thing. "That's really sweet of you, Elizabeth. Thank you. Now tell me what to wear?"

"We'll be wearing raincoats, because it's a chilly evening and we'll be outside, so you want something that works under that," Betsy said. "And we should wear comfortable shoes, because we might have to stand about or even walk. Mummy always says if you're not sure what to wear you can't go wrong with tweeds."

"But tweeds are for the day! What if he suggests a nightcap afterwards somewhere dressy?"

"We could always say no," Betsy said, fervently. "Besides, did Sir Alan look to you like a nightcap-at-the-Ritz sort of man?"

"He looked like a pirate," I said, honestly. "But if you're so off him, why are we going again? You were the one who wanted to."

"I put the immediate pleasure of annoying Mummy yesterday above the disadvantages of this evening," she said, picking up one foot in her hands and examining the sole. "I'm sorry. But it'll be an experience, anyway."

"How about being twins for once and both wearing tweed skirts, with silk shirts and cashmere sweaters?" I asked. "If we go anywhere dressy later, we can take the sweaters off and leave them with our coats. And you could wear that pretty seed pearl thing you wore yesterday, and I could wear your pearls, and your mother wouldn't know because she wouldn't see us. You could put them in your pocket and we could put them on in the bathroom."

"Genius!" Betsy said.

I picked up my pale pink silk shirt and pulled it over my head. "Do me up," I said, turning my back to Betsy. She began to hook me, then stopped.

"Mummy wants me to get a proper maid. She's sick of us borrowing Olive and Nanny to do our hair or button us up."

"Well, you do what you like, but I'm sure I don't want one."

"I don't want to either, Mummy'd be sure to get me one who'd spy on me to her," Betsy said, her fingers resuming their work on my hooks. "I'm better off with Nanny if I need to go away anywhere."

"I don't know what I want. I don't even know if I want to come out, really. I'm not really a deb type. It's such a waste of time for me."

Betsy leapt up from the bed and came around in front of me. "You have to come out!" she said, taking my hands. "You promised. We're doing it together! That's the only thing that makes it endurable. Or affordable, for that matter. It's only a week until the Court. You can't back out now, Ellie!"

"I won't abandon you," I said. Her dressing gown had fallen open, revealing one pink-tipped breast and the curve of her stomach below it. "I'll go through with it now I've gone this far, have my season and be presented and all that. All the same, I'm not going to make a respectable alliance, and there's no point pretending I am."

"You might," Betsy said, letting go of my hands and refastening her shabby dressing gown. "You're awfully pretty, and your uncle is awfully powerful. He's part of the new nobility, practically, and that means you are too. Your parents might have been working people, but your father died a hero, almost a war hero. He got a medal, didn't he? You're not going to marry a duke, but neither am I, and I think there are lots of men who would overlook the disadvantages and want to marry you, especially once they knew you and saw how terrific you are."

"But I'm not at all sure I want to marry someone that way," I said. "I want to graduate from Oxford and then take up a profession. But what is there? Teaching, ick, and nursing, double ick. Unless I could stay on in Oxford, or maybe become a journalist."

"I wondered about doing a secretarial course and then asking your uncle Carmichael to find me a job in the Watch or for the government," Betsy said. "But my parents would have piglets at the thought of me working."

"I expect he'd find you a job, but it sounds deadly. Your parents would cast you out, when they saw you really meant it. The job would be nine to five, and perhaps you could afford a little flat, which would be nice, but not forever, and who would you meet? They never pay women a proper wage, to discourage us. I think I would like to marry and have children, eventually, but to marry someone I know and love, and someone who really wants me, not someone who sees an advantage in marrying me and is prepared to overlook the disadvantages."

"Well, me too," Betsy said, emphatically.

"You're not still . . . ," I asked, letting my voice trail off almost like her mother.

"Not still pining for Kurt? No, I'm not. How could I be, after all the lies he told me? But the one thing Zurich has taught me is that I don't want to go through life with my eyes closed, just accepting."

"That's no way to be," I agreed. I pulled on a slip, and then my tweed skirt over it. It fell halfway down my calves, because I'd grown since I had it made. Only my Paris clothes were the right length. I hoped I was finished with growing now, at five foot ten and almost nineteen. My father had been tall, I remembered, with a child's memory of a giant.

"You don't think anyone can guess, about Kurt?" Betsy asked.

A debutante is an upper-class daughter trying out for a career as an upper-class wife. She might have a settlement, which means a dowry like a Jane Austen heroine, and in fact Betsy did, though she was by no means an heiress. While married people are allowed to be as promiscuous as they like as long as they don't make a scandal, virginity is supposed to be a debutante's most prized possession, absolutely the most significant thing she has to bring to a marriage. This is only for the girls. Men can have as much experience as they want, of course. The hypocrisy is shocking. "Nobody can tell," I said, as reassuringly as I could, though of course I didn't know any more about it than she did—less. "Try to pretend none of it ever happened. Nobody knows except you and me, and Leni, but she'd never tell because it would destroy her own reputation. Nobody need ever know."

Betsy grimaced and nodded. Then she took a deep breath and changed the subject. "I don't suppose Sir Alan will take us out for drinks," she said, getting up and drifting towards the door. "No chaperone. And he's my father's friend, so he's probably frightfully proper."

"We chaperone each other, don't we? And he doesn't seem all that proper to me, not with that beard. He must be a bit of a pirate, surely?" I looked at the dresses strewn on my bed and decided to leave them for Olive to hang up.

"Mummy says his mother says he has a skin condition which makes him get pimples when he shaves," Betsy said. "Doesn't sound very piratical to me."

We both laughed. "Come and do me up when you're ready," she said.

I took my watch off the bedside table and looked at it. "I'll come now. He'll be here any minute." The watch was slim, golden, and Swiss. I fastened it around my wrist. Uncle Carmichael had given me the money to buy it, and then more money when I told him it needed mending, when we'd needed money for Betsy's operation.

I helped Betsy dress. She gave me her string of pearls, which I slipped into my bag, while she put her chain into her skirt pocket. We both pulled on our sweaters and did our hair and our faces in Betsy's room, where the mirror wasn't so flyspecked as the one in my room. We were lingering over our makeup when Nanny came to say that Sir Alan was here and waiting for us. We snatched up our handbags and went down.

"Miss Maynard," he said, very correctly, as Betsy preceded me into the drawing room.

"Sir Alan," she replied, shaking his hand without undue cordiality.

Then he turned to me. I couldn't help noticing again that his eyes were at precisely my own level. "Miss Royston—but I will always think of you as Cinderella."

"It was a pair of shoes, not a slipper," I said, disconcerted.

"Don't keep them out too late," Mrs. Maynard urged.

"All mothers have said that to young men since we were living in caves," Mr. Maynard added, smiling.

It didn't surprise me that Sir Alan had his own car; it did surprise me that it was a sleek new Skoda Madame, in cherry red. "This is my new toy," he said, opening the back door for me. "Fruits of the peace. Two years ago they were building nothing but tanks. Now the Russians are flattened, they can turn their attention to gentler things. I had a boring old Bentley until the first of these were imported."

He drove us smoothly through the streets of London, talking to Betsy about cars. He parked neatly in a side street near Cavendish Square. "I have a friend with a flat here with rather a good view onto Wigmore Street," he said, escorting us out of the car and down the street. "We'll be able to see the procession coming down Portland Place, coming round the corner, and then passing right in front of us and going down Wigmore Street, and all without being crushed in the crowd. Then we can come out, hop into the car, and drive down to Marble Arch to see the end of it—we'll have to be in the crowd then, but that's part of the fun. There'll be singing and speeches and I hear there may be a bonfire!" He knocked on a door, which was opened by a footman, or manservant of some kind, who clearly recognized Sir Alan.

"Come in, girls," Sir Alan said, and led the way up a steep flight of stairs. "Then afterwards," he continued, as we followed him, "I thought I might give you a spot of dinner at the Blue Nile."

Betsy turned around and raised her eyebrows at me. I shrugged. You can go anywhere in a silk shirt with pearls, I thought, even a nightclub more sophisticated than we'd ever visited.

By this time we were at the top of the stairs. The footman opened a door, letting us in to what was obviously a party. The room seemed full of people—a flutter of women in jewel-colored afternoon dresses and men in tails. They were all holding glasses and talking and laughing.

"Did your mother know?" I murmured to Betsy as a man who was obviously the host came up and shook hands with Sir Alan.

"She can't have," Betsy said, then she stepped forward to be introduced.

"Sir Mortimer, Miss Maynard, Sir Mortimer, Miss Royston," Sir Alan said. Sir Mortimer Whatever was fat and looked a little drunk. His palm was moist and fleshy.

"Drinks are on the sideboard, put your coats in the bedroom," Sir Mortimer said to Betsy, and to me, "Where has Alan been hiding you?"

"Thank you so much for inviting us," Betsy said.

I just smiled, and looked aside. Aside happened to be at a blond woman in peacock blue silk, who was looking at me as if she wouldn't have offered tuppence for me. I looked back at Sir Mortimer, but he had drifted off.

"Coats in the bedroom," I said, grimly, to Betsy.

"No, hold on to your coats," Sir Alan said. "We'll be dashing off after the parade has passed, remember. Let me get you some drinks."

It was the middle of April, and the bow window that gave onto the square was open, but there was a cheerful fire in the grate and I felt too warm in my sweater and raincoat. I took the coat off and folded it over my arm, with my bag dangling. Betsy copied me, grimacing. "We should have worn some of our Paris dresses," she said, through gritted teeth.

"They're all strangers, it doesn't matter," I said. I wished we could have gone into the bedroom and put on the pearls. I felt dowdy in my mauve sweater and heather tweed skirt.

Sir Alan returned with two drinks, cocktails. I sipped mine as he went off to fetch another for himself. I wasn't sure what the mixture was, but I could definitely taste gin, which meant Betsy wouldn't like it. I didn't drink much, but I much preferred cocktails to beer. The smell of beer always made me feel slightly sick. It reminded me of the way my mother had smelled the last time I had seen her, when she had come home briefly to tell us she was leaving for good.

"This is jolly," Sir Alan said, coming back. "Let's see if we can see anything yet."

We made our way to the window, and I leaned out. The sun had set, and presumably the parade had started off, but all I could see was the crowded pavement below, where people were waving Union Jacks and Farthing flags. People were calling out that they had candyfloss, wet sponges, marshmallows. Across the street, there were parties at other windows. The sky was fading behind the roof peaks and chimney tops, which stood out like cardboard cutout silhouettes, and I looked from them to the lit windows, and back again. A flock of birds, pigeons probably, wheeled across the sky, heading home before dark.

"A penny for them, Cinderella," Sir Alan said.

"My thoughts are worth much more than a penny," I said, flirtatiously.

"Well, half a crown for them, then?"

"Not worth as much as that. I was only wondering where city birds sleep," I said.

Just then I heard the first strains of the band, and turned to look out again. I could just see the torches coming into sight.

"Oh look!" Betsy said, pressing forward.

I could hardly hear the bands over the cheering. I'd somehow expected everyone to have a torch, but of course the bandsmen playing instruments didn't. Torchbearers walked to both sides of the bands, making a stripe of light. Sir Alan was right that the best way to see the parade was from above, because that way you could make out the patterns, especially in the sections where people were dancing and making shapes of fire. A few celebrities rode on floats, all dressed up as famous scenes from history. There was Britannia with her shield done in flowers, Nelson with his telescope, one done up like a bowling alley, which I didn't get at all until Betsy said something about Drake and then it was obvious. The Ironsides themselves came along between the bands and floats and shapes of flame, young men puffed up like pigeons and marching like soldiers. They carried decorated banners with the names of their local groups. The floats got the biggest cheers, especially when the people were well known. When Mollie Gaston, as Queen Victoria, threw toffees to the children in the crowd, you'd have thought she was the real queen, not just the grand old dame of British theater. Most popular of all though were the Jews, roped together in groups, who the crowd could pelt with wet sponges they'd bought for the purpose. When I was a child, people used to throw rotten vegetables and bad eggs, but that had been stopped because it made a mess of the streets. Sometimes people threw them anyway, of course. When the last of the bands passed us, playing "Knees Up, Mother Brown," Sir Alan said it was time to go.

I drained my glass, which was mostly ice-meltwater by now. It was strange turning from the parade back to the room. I'd been half leaning out of the window, entirely caught up in the jolly fun of it, mingled with childhood memories and general patriotic enthusiasm. Now the cynicism and sophistication of the party seemed stifling. I was glad we were leaving. These people didn't seem moved by the rally at all, they didn't really care. Like Mrs. Maynard, they thought it a good way of keeping people they despised occupied. I said good-bye to Sir Mortimer politely, and almost slipped in my haste to get down the steep stairs.

The main streets were crowded as the spectators followed after the parade, but Sir Alan knew the backstreets and raced along them. "What did you think of it?" he asked.

"I thought it was great fun," I said, when Betsy hadn't answered after a moment.

"I didn't like the Jews," she said. "That family they had in the last group upset me. I could see the little girl bleeding."

"You have too tender a heart, Betsy," Sir Alan said, condescendingly. "They're only Jews. A little water doesn't do them any harm, and nor do a few shouted names. Even if people throw the odd stone or rotten tomato, it's much less than they deserve. Think how they sabotage the economy when they get the slightest chance, and what they'd do to us if they could!"

There was a huge bonfire outside Marble Arch, and I could already hear the bands playing in the distance. "I hope you girls aren't too tired," Sir Alan said.

"Will there be speeches?" Betsy asked cautiously.

Sir Alan laughed. "Not very many, don't worry."

He parked the car and we made our way through the cheerful crowds. There was a bonfire, there were torches, there was band music, I could smell candyfloss and wished we could have some, though I knew it would be impossibly lower-class of me to ask for it. I was lower-class, and I knew it. I felt a deep camaraderie for all these people, marchers and watchers, the barefoot children cheerfully begging. London had not changed much since Dickens's day, I thought, giving one of them half a crown.

And that's how it was; we were walking through the crowds and the people all seemed to be smiling. Sir Alan said something to Betsy that I didn't catch, and then we were in front of a rostrum next to the bonfire. "This is where the singing will be," Sir Alan said. I could hear band music in the distance, and nearer, an orator addressing part of the crowd from another rostrum.

There was a group of Jews directly under the rostrum; two men, four women, and a little girl. They might have been the ones Betsy had seen before, because the child had blood running down her face from a cut on her temple. They all looked terrified. The ones I'd seen earlier had looked a little resigned to what was happening, and even exchanged some banter with the crowds. These kept looking from side to side and flinching, though nobody was taking any especial notice of them.

"What happens to them after?" Betsy asked.

"Mostly they're let go again, sometimes they're handed over to the police to be sent off to the Continent where they know how to deal with them," Sir Alan said.

Just then a young man in a black shirt jumped up onto the rostrum and shot out his hand in the Continental fascist salute. The crowd responded, of course, copying him and cheering. He was very good-looking, with such an air of health and vitality that you didn't really notice the details of his appearance. He seemed very young. I thought him my own age and the age of the young men I was used to dancing with at parties. There was something appealing about that. "Are you proud to be British?" he called. He had an unusual accent; not a foreign one, but not London either. The crowd roared. He leaned down into the crowd and took something from one of the men to the side of him, then straightened up again with a guitar. He started to play almost immediately, not waiting for the crowd to quiet, so I didn't catch the beginning of the song. The tune was lovely, but the words were the usual stuff about patriotism and motherland, with a chorus we soon started singing along to that went "Power, power, British power."

When he finished the song, he handed the guitar back down and called again, "Are you proud to be British?" The shout of affirmation seemed louder this time, maybe because I was part of it. He quieted us by lowering his hand. "Are you proud to be fascists?" he asked next. Another great roar. I was still roaring with them. I noticed Betsy wasn't shouting; she was looking at the cowering Jews again. "Are you proud of your country, your Empire, your leaders?" We cheered more heartily than ever. The young man lowered his hand again and spoke quite quietly into the hush. "Then why are we giving the Hitler salute?" He gestured downwards. "Why are these Jews waiting to go to Germany to be dealt with? Why do we call ourselves Ironsides, instead of Blackshirts as we used to?" He paused, and the hush of people listening to him spread. I could no longer hear any other orators. "Because Germany has a proper leader, and we don't!" he shouted. "What kind of a leader is Mark Normanby? His main claim to fame is that he was crippled when sitting next to Hitler! He's a fraud and a cripple! He's no sort of man, no sort of leader. He's a politician, he politicked his way to power, he didn't rise on a wave of belief like Hitler, like Mussolini, like Franco. He took Hitler's name for us and called us Ironsides. He's a lapdog! Who believes in him and his Farthing elite? Who wants second-rate watered-down fascism, as if the British Empire wasn't the greatest state the world has ever known? British power!"

A group of men in black shirts with a banner to the side of the rostrum began singing the chorus line over and over, "Power, power, British power!"

"Normanby!" others in the crowd were shouting, in a much less organized way.

I looked at Sir Alan. His smile seemed uncomfortable. Betsy was biting her lip. "I think we should slip away now," Sir Alan said, taking my arm, and took a step backwards through the crowd. I followed him.

The "British power" chanters quieted when the young man spoke again, but the others did not, and kept shouting as if to heckle him. "What are we going to do with these Jews? Send them off to Germany because we're too weak to deal with them? Throw them on the bonfire!"

"Oh no!" Betsy said, turning back. The crowd around us was very dense, and surging forward. Nobody seemed to be smiling anymore, and everyone seemed to be shouting.

"Normanby! Farthing!"

"British power!"

"Come on!" Sir Alan said, tugging Betsy's arm and letting go of mine.

"Jews on the fire!"

"Farthing! Normanby!"

I don't know which side started the fighting. I was swept away from Betsy and Sir Alan immediately. I had trouble keeping on my feet. Nobody was trying to hit me, but it was sometimes hard to dodge badly aimed blows. I'd made it almost to the edge of the melee when a glancing blow caught me on the side of the head and I felt myself falling. "British power!" I heard, as I went down.

4

"Are you sure the riot wasn't incited by communists?" Carmichael asked.

"As sure as it's possible to be at this stage, sir," Ogilvie said. His frown made his flat face seem very dour. "I could ask what communists, because with Russia collapsed communism seems rather old hat to most of the young troublemakers today. But what communists there are, we're keeping a close eye on them just like we're supposed to and I didn't hear a whisker of anything from them about this march. I knew you'd want to see me about this so I came in early and checked back through, and there's sod all there, sir, excuse my French, not a mutter, not even a mention."

Ogilvie was painfully thorough and conscientious, as Carmichael had cause to know. He sighed. "So if you're right, how did it happen? We have nine deaths, twenty-seven people in hospital, three hundred and ninety-two rioters in the cells, and a lot of broken windows along Oxford Street. Something set them off."

"I haven't had time to look into it in detail, but from what I know so far, it seems as if they started fighting among themselves. The Mets on duty just started slinging everyone into the Black Marias as soon as they could, indiscriminately, and practically everyone they scooped up is an Ironside, so far as I've had a chance to see. Maybe there were two groups of them with a grudge against each other for some reason—these city boys can be a bit thuggish you know, sir. Or something small touched it off maybe, the wrong word, and once fists started swinging the rest of them just joined in for the fun of it."

"I want a proper report sharpish," Carmichael said. "Get it to me by five this afternoon. I want to know exactly what happened and why, and how we can prevent it happening again. And check the communists again too. We can't have this sort of thing."

One of Carmichael's telephones rang, sharply insistent. "Five past nine," Ogilvie said. "Someone's eager."

"My turn to be on the carpet," Carmichael said, reaching for the receiver. "Go on. Find out as much as you can, Ogilvie, and get back to me."

Ogilvie left, leaving the door open behind him. Carmichael took a deep breath and answered the phone on the fourth ring. "Carmichael here."

"Hold for the Prime Minister," said a young female voice, and then almost immediately, the familiar silky tones Carmichael knew and hated. "Are you there, Carmichael?"

"Yes, sir."

"Well, how about if you stop being there and start being here right now and tell me how that happened?"

"I don't have enough information yet, but I have a man preparing a report on the riot now, Prime Minister, and I should be able to give you full details by this afternoon," Carmichael said, keeping tight control on his voice. "Shall we say five o'clock?"

"No, we shan't, because I shall be expected to speak to the Commons at three. We shall say *two* o'clock, directly after my luncheon, in my office at the House. I don't expect you to waste time lunching."

"Yes, Prime Minister." Carmichael suppressed a childish urge to stick out his tongue just because Normanby couldn't see him.

"And you'd better have what I need by then, Carmichael. We just can't be having this kind of thing happening the week before there's a major international conference. It looks bad. There are foreign journalists here already."

"Yes, sir. I know."

"And since you're coming round, I want a report on the Japs as well. Guy seems to think they're the biggest threat to the British Empire, now the Russians are out of it, not to mention that they now have a direct border with the Reich." Normanby sounded peevish.

"What do you want on the Japanese, sir?"

"Oh, just a general overview, whatever's getting Guy's knickers in a twist, whether they're actually a potential threat to Burma and Malaya or whether that's all hot air. This Scythia thing. Bring it along at two."

"Yes, Prime Minister. Sir Guy hasn't spoken to me about the Japs, but I'll—" Carmichael realized he was talking to the empty air; Mark Normanby had hung up. He put the phone down and gritted his teeth. He picked up the left-hand phone, the internal Watch Offices line, and dialed.

"Ogilvie," Ogilvie said brightly.

"Carmichael, Ogilvie. Big Wheels himself has taken an interest; I have to present your report to him at two. So see I have it by half past one, could you?"

Even through the phone line, Carmichael could hear Ogilvie's sharp intake of breath. "But I have to interview!"

"Take as many people as you like to help you this morning, just concentrate on this and let me have as much as you can. I know I can count on you."

"Yes, sir. I'll do my best."

"I know you will. I'll stop wasting your time and let you get on with it."

Carmichael clicked the receiver down and stared at his Grimshaw print, the one bit of light and color in the room, which was otherwise all maroon leather and dark wood. He dialed again.

"Fanshaw, Foreign."

"Ah, Inspector Fanshaw. Carmichael here. I want a general précis of the Japanese situation, with especial attention to whether they pose a threat to the Empire in the East and the Scythia thing. I need it on my desk by one-thirty."

"The Scythia thing?" Fanshaw echoed. "You mean the proposed buffer state? That's very controversial."

Carmichael hadn't heard of it before. "Prepare me a detailed brief on it, and on the Japanese threat to the Empire, by one-thirty."

"Yes, sir," Fanshaw replied.

As he put the receiver down, Carmichael guessed that Fanshaw would be cursing him for the disruption of his ordinary Wednesday morning routine much as he was cursing Normanby. Fanshaw would no doubt get his Far East bods to write the reports, and he would curse Fanshaw and that, he supposed, was the secret of a chain of command. Having put out the morning's fires, Carmichael settled down to a steady morning's work on the conference.

Fanshaw brought his reports up himself, while Carmichael was just finishing an egg sandwich at his desk.

His secretary, Miss Duthie, peered around the door. "Mr. Fanshaw, sir," she said. "Shall I bring tea?"

Carmichael hastily stuffed the remnants of his sandwich into his mouth and stood to greet his subordinate. "Tea would be lovely," he mumbled, swallowing. "China tea all right for you, Fanshaw?"

"Thank you, sir, yes, and I'm sorry to interrupt you," Fanshaw said, coming in. He was a neat little man with a walrus moustache. He had two folders under his arm, one beige and one blue. "I thought I'd better come up myself."

"Well, sit down and tell me about it," Carmichael said, pushing away his papers. "Tea for two, Miss Duthie."

Miss Duthie vanished. She had come from a very respectable agency at the time when Carmichael had been promoted to his present post. Her skills at shorthand and typing were only adequate, but Carmichael had selected her because she was from outside the police, because she was older than most of the applicants, and most of all because she had made the best cup of tea. She fended off unwanted callers, selected the day's watchword from a *Golden Treasury of Verse* on her desk, and in all ways performed her duties adequately. Carmichael liked her.

"The threat question is fairly simple," Fanshaw said, settling himself. "The short answer is that they probably aren't a threat unless something changes. They'd probably like Singapore and Hong Kong, but they know there are easier pickings. We've never given up an inch of land, and they know it. We cleared out of Shanghai, of course, but that's a different kettle of fish. I don't think we should relax and take our eye off the ball there, but they have an awful lot on their plate with China, and I think they'll leave us alone."

He offered the beige folder to Carmichael, who took it. "Is this different from the FO view?" Carmichael asked. "The PM said that the Foreign Secretary was concerned about it."

Fanshaw blinked. "I don't know how Sir Guy feels personally, but I'd say that on the whole the FO would agree with our assessment."

"Thank you," Carmichael said. "And Scythia?"

"Now, that's the sticky one," Fanshaw said, as Miss Duthie came back into the office with a small brass tray bearing a teapot, milk jug, and two cups, in Royal Albert Orange Tree pattern, Jack's choice. There was also a plate with digestive biscuits. Fanshaw jumped up and took the tray from her and set it down on the edge of the desk.

"Shall I pour?" Miss Duthie asked.

"If you would," Carmichael said, glancing at his watch. It was a quarter past one. He had half an hour before he had to leave if he was to be on time for his appointment with Normanby. He took his tea, milkless as always, and set it down. Fanshaw took his on his knee, fussily, thanking Miss Duthie.

"So, Scythia. It's a proposal Japan and the Reich are squabbling over in the peace negotiations, and likely to be a difficult one. With Russia gone, the Reich are advancing into the vacuum from one end, and Imperial Japan from the other. The Scythian proposal is to establish a buffer state between them on the Steppes. We don't have an official position on it. The FO seem to be strongly for it, I can't think why, as it's nothing to do with us or our sphere of influence at all. But the FO have been meddling, which is what I wanted to say to you directly, sir, and not put in the report." Fanshaw set the blue report down before Carmichael, then sat back, sipping his tea.

"Do you think that's what the PM wants to hear?" Carmichael asked, ignoring his own tea.

Fanshaw shrugged. "It depends how much he approves of Sir Guy stirring up international policy. I said Japan isn't a threat, but they easily could be if they thought we were about to put the boot into them. And then it would be watch out Singapore—since they mopped up the old Dutch colonies we're vulnerable. A war could be long and messy, considering how far away they are, and there's the question of whether the Americans would let us use the Panama Canal."

"Thank you, Fanshaw, I'll pass all this on." Carmichael stared at the folders.

"Well, not the job of the Watch to be popular, is it, sir?" Fanshaw said, cheerily.

Carmichael smiled, liking his subordinate. "Fortunately not. Thank you for doing the reports so quickly. I'd give you a bit more warning if they gave me more warning."

"If you like, sir, I could get a few of the boys working on the threats one in a bit more detail, with projections on what might happen if the Japs don't like the FO meddling?" Fanshaw took another swig of his tea.

"Yes, do that over the next few days, that might be useful," Carmichael said. "Do you have copies of these briefs?"

Fanshaw set his empty cup and saucer back on the tray. "One copy of each. Shall I send another copy up?"

"That might be a good idea," Carmichael said. "I'm not going to have time to give them as much attention as I'd like before I pass them on to the PM."

"I'll get on with it then. Thanks for the tea, though it's awful dishwater, I don't know how you drink that stuff."

"You're not supposed to put milk in it," Carmichael said.

Ogilvie tapped on the door as Fanshaw stood up to go. "I've got your report, Chief. Sorry I'm late, but I practically tore it away from the typewriter as she finished each page as it is," he said, coming in, waving a large buff envelope. "Oh, hello, Fanshaw!"

"Looks like the Chief has got us all on the hop today," Fanshaw said, and left.

"So what's the short version?" Carmichael asked, drinking his own neglected tea. "Make it quick, I have to go in a minute."

"Clash between two groups of Ironsides, like I said. It doesn't make much sense, if you ask me. Lot of nonsense, probably. Of your nine deaths, six of them were only Jews, and so were ten of the casualties. Some lad from Liverpool, here for the march, stood up and started saying that Normanby wasn't tough enough on the Jews. People who didn't like that started breaking heads, and his boys hit back. Or, to listen to the other side, he said some words against the Prime Minister and then when they replied verbally, fists came out. There was nothing worse than fists and improvised weapons. Lots of the injuries were fire-related. The deaths that weren't Jews were from trampling."

"Charming," said Carmichael. "I take it we have the agitator from Liverpool in custody?"

"Regrettably not," Ogilvie said. "We do know his name. Shall I send someone around to pick him up?"

"Might be for the best. And don't let anyone go until I have a policy decision on all of this. The Prime Minister is taking an interest and making a statement in the House. We don't want to get caught with our trousers down." He reached for the envelope. "What's in here?"

"A summary of the interviews, a few photographs, and a report," Ogilvie said. "That enough?"

"It'll have to be. Walk up with me."

In deliberate contrast to the way New New Scotland Yard was arranged, Carmichael's office was in the bowels of the Watch building, underground in a bombproof cellar supposedly proof against anything but a direct hit—though with the new Atomic Bomb in consideration, he doubted it was any safer than anywhere else. Carmichael took his hat and coat from the hat stand in the hall, nodded good-bye to Miss Duthie, who was perched at her desk, and walked down the hall, Ogilvie at his side.

There was a lift to the upper levels. Carmichael preferred to walk up the green-painted stairs. The introduction of concrete and steel as a major building material in the last twenty years had led to many interesting new styles, of which the Neo-Assyrian of the New New Scotland Yard, with its flattened sphinxes, was by far the ugliest. In contrast, the Watch building was a pillared reminder of Palladian elegance, with the front sporting pillars four stories high. Wags had immediately dubbed it the Watchtower, naturally, and the name had gone through the usual stages of changing from joke to almost official status. The stairway brought Carmichael and Ogilvie out at ground level, between the bases of two pillars. It was raining heavily. A guard standing under the portico nodded to them.

"I'll have that agitator in custody before you get back, sir," Ogilvie promised.

"It's a stupid waste of our time," Carmichael said. "Charge him with being a communist; that should wreck his credibility with his friends."

Ogilvie laughed and retreated back inside. Carmichael hurried down the steps, nodding to one of the waiting unmarked black cars. "Just down to the Palace of Westminster," he told the driver as he got in.

In the back of the car he looked through Ogilvie's envelope, finding it well arranged, as he had expected.

At the Victorian Gothic monstrosity of the Houses of Parliament he told the car to wait. He hurried past the statue of Cromwell, turning up his collar against the spring rain, and hastened inside.

Mark Normanby was alone in his office when Carmichael was shown in. He sat behind his desk in his great humming wheelchair. A plaid blanket covered the Prime Minister's useless legs, paralyzed since an assassination attempt in 1949. Carmichael had saved his life but not his legs, and Normanby had never forgiven him.

It was such a commonplace of political cartoons to portray Normanby as a spider that Carmichael was surprised every time he saw him how apt it seemed. Normanby had never been a very big man, and now he was shrunken in the huge powered chair. He had been good-looking; now he was like some ruined Byron. "So here you are at last," he greeted Carmichael, though he was exactly on time for his appointment. "Have you finally got me some information?"

Carmichael knew better than to answer his barbs. Normanby could still be smooth and pleasant when he needed to be, but it seemed he needed to be less and less often, and he had always delighted in tormenting Carmichael. There were no chairs in the room. Carmichael could not feel comfortable standing, and he knew Normanby relished the psychological advantage it gave him. He stood at the modified parade ground attention he had mastered in the army so long ago. "The riot seems to have been an odd affair of different groups of Ironsides clashing," he said. "I have a report here for you. It seems some of them were shouting for a stronger policy on the Jews, and others supported you."

"Let me see," Normanby said. Carmichael walked over to him and gave him the envelope. He stood near while Normanby flicked through the photographs and read the summary. The Prime Minister looked bored, until something made him whiten, his hands tensing on the papers so that they shook in his hand. "Cripple?" he asked. "Cripple, is it? Weak and a cripple?" He set the envelope down and looked up at Carmichael. "Let those who were fighting for me go, and send the rest off with the next lot of deportees. That'll teach them who's weak."

"Is that wise?" Carmichael dared to ask. "They're not Jews, and not communists, and they will have connections."

"Oh yes, connections," Normanby sneered. "They're Mosleyites, calling for British power and using the old name Blackshirts. Send them off; they're no good to us and no good to the country. I'll get you to deal with whatever connections they have too, nip it in the bud. Report directly to me if there are any inquiries about them—especially ones from high places."

"Whatever you say, sir," Carmichael said. He made a note. "About the other things you asked about—"

"I don't have time now. Leave me the briefs," Normanby said.

"Here you are." Carmichael handed over the folders. "There was one thing my chap said which isn't in the report in so many words, which is that our people feel that the Foreign Office have been meddling with this Scythia thing and that this could cause problems with Japan."

"Guy's been meddling?" Normanby's eyes were sharp. "I'll look into that. That's useful. Good that they're all going to be here for this wretched conference, it'll give me a chance to sort things out for myself."

Carmichael moved towards the door. "Have you still got that good-looking valet?" Normanby asked.

"You know I have, sir," Carmichael replied calmly, though his heart had jumped, and he suspected Normanby knew as much.

Normanby laughed. "Just checking," he said. "Go and get on with it, Carmichael. And I'm going to say the rioters were communist saboteurs, so you can write them down that way when you send them off to the camps."

"Yes, sir," Carmichael said, and left. He stood in the corridor for a moment waiting for his heart to stop racing, and only too glad to be out of the room. Normanby needed him, he thought. It was why he was alive, how he could get away with what he did get away with—Jack, the Inner Watch, all of it. He won what he could by being useful to Normanby. If it suited Normanby to torment him, it was a small price, really. He was sure Normanby knew how much he hated him, knew it and relished it. He shook his head and walked back to his car.

5

Farthing! Normanby!"

I wasn't down for long, a few moments only, but it felt like a century. I was terrified that I'd be trampled. I put one arm over my head and tried to struggle back to my feet. It was like those dreams of walking through treacle. The crowd pushed against me, and someone did tread on my leg. Then somebody helped me up, a complete stranger, a burly middle-aged man in a cloth cap. "Thank you!" I said, and heard myself saying it in my old voice, my Cockney voice.

"You're welcome, love. This is no place for a lass," he said, and turned back to pummeling his neighbor.

I took a step away from him and tried to run, realizing immediately that it was impossible because when I'd fallen, I'd lost a shoe. Absurdly, I thought of Sir Alan calling me Cinderella. The pressure of the crowd was holding me up, but if I tried to run I'd fall. The sensible thing would have been to take the other one off, but I didn't want to bend down, either. Being under the level of the surface of the crowd had scared me too much to risk it again. I looked around for Sir Alan and Betsy but couldn't see them anywhere. I did see the young guitar player, who was abruptly next to me as the crowd swayed. He gave me a lovely smile as he passed, singing out, "Power, power, British power!"

Then I thought I was saved. On the edge of the crowd I could see a policeman—not a Watchman, but an ordinary London bobby. I staggered as best I could in his direction, ducking blows.

He was the edge of a big police operation. There were police cars and big black vans. I was comforted by the sight of them. I thought they'd help me. It's hard to believe I was that naïve. I'd known as a child not to trust the rozzers, even though my father was Scotland Yard, and as proud of it as a dog with two tails. In the last ten years I'd got used to seeing the police as a kind of servants.

"Police!" someone more sensible shouted, and the crowd started to move away from them. It was hard for the crowd to go anywhere, because they were so tightly packed and because there was more crowd beyond, people who had been listening to the bands and the other speakers, who had also begun to fight now. The police were grabbing everyone they could, quite indiscriminately. I still thought they'd help me, right up to the point where they grabbed me and threw me into the Black Maria.

I landed on my stomach with all the wind knocked out of me. By the time I struggled onto my knees, the van was almost full and had started to move. It was very dark, lit only by whatever light came in from streetlights through the cracks around the door. "What's happening?" I asked. "Where are we going?"

"Little trip to the cells," someone said, a man with a Northern accent, perhaps the one who had helped me up before. "Don't worry, they'll check us over and let us go. Like old times, this is."

Someone put an arm around me, which I welcomed for the comfort until he started groping my breast, whereupon I poked him in the ribs, hard. This had always worked with men at parties and in Switzerland, and it worked now, though perhaps only because the van stopped abruptly at that point, knocking me off balance again and jerking my would-be assailant forwards.

The van doors opened. Three policemen stood there, one with a torch and two with leashed dogs, big beautiful German shepherds with smooth well-cared-for fur.

"You're in Paddington Nick," one of the policemen said. "Come out quietly one at a time and let's have no trouble, or Betsy here will have to have a word with you." His dog growled. How strange it was that she should be called Betsy. I wondered where my Betsy was, if she had got away or if she and Sir Alan were in another such police station. I hoped they had made it back to the car.

I came out when the torch shone on me. I limped quietly into the station on my one shoe. When I stooped to try to take it off, the bobby hurried me on. The station seemed very bright inside. It smelled strongly of disinfectant. "Papers," the man inside the door demanded.

I took my card from my bag, very grateful that it had remained on my arm through all of that. He glanced at it, and then back at me, checking the photograph. He hesitated for a moment, looking back at the photograph, where my hair was neat, not draggled around my face, and I wore no makeup. My features must have reassured him, because he nodded. "Bag," he said. I held out my bag, and he rummaged through it, pausing twice, at what I guessed were Betsy's pearls and my purse. Nothing else seemed to disturb him. He stuck a numbered label on it, and another on my papers, and put them both on wire racks, with stacks of other cards and assorted possessions.

"Stand up," he said.

I stood, and he patted me down in a bored and professional way, finding nothing.

"Go through, you'll be called when it's time to be booked," he said, clearly his routine speech.

"Can I have my things back, please?" I asked, as politely as I could, and quite deliberately in my best Arlinghurst accent.

"You'll have them back when you're released, miss," he said. "Purse too. We don't allow papers or money in the cells."

I went in. I'd surprised a "miss" out of him, but if my modulated voice wasn't good for more than that, I could see that it would be better to use my childhood voice in the station, as I instinctively had with the crowd. I'd had more than enough of being picked on for my accent.

I went through, as the policeman had indicated, into a room with three walls with benches along them, and bars separating it from a corridor. This room, I was relieved to see, contained women only— about a dozen of them. Most of them were respectably dressed, but one or two wore men's raincoats over underclothes, the uniform of the London streetwalker. "Was you in the riot up Marble Arch?" one of these asked me.

"Yes," I said, back in the voice of my childhood. It was strange how unnatural it seemed to use it deliberately. "I got separated from my boyfriend and dragged off by the rozzers. I hadn't done nothing, they can't book me, can they?"

"Don't worry," said a middle-aged woman in a headscarf and a wool coat. "They always used to do this when there was fighting, in the old days, when the communists would come out and provoke us. They scoop everyone up, then they sort through and let the Ironsides go. They didn't used to charge us or nothing. We'll only be here an hour or so, I should think, love. Come and sit down."

I walked over to where she was sitting and sat on the hard bench beside her, my back against the wall. I took off my useless shoe. My stockings were ruined, the feet shredded and huge ladders running up my legs. I pulled them off and balled them up and stuck them in my coat pocket.

"But there weren't any communists," said a thin-faced woman pacing by the bars. "How will they sort us out?"

"Oh, they're sure to let us all go," the first one said, comfortably.

"If they bring in a lot of politicals, they might let us go to make room," said one of the streetwalkers to the other. "That's happened before."

"What'll happen to you otherwise?" I asked, turning my useless shoe over in my hands and thinking again of Cinderella. What prince might find my other shoe and come seeking me? I didn't think of Sir Alan but of the handsome young man who had sung and incited the riot.

"Fine," the streetwalker said. "Ten shillings. Not so much. It's much worse losing business spending the night in here. You got a fag?"

I shook my head. "I don't smoke, sorry." It always made me cough.

A woman on the bench along the back wall obliged and handed around cigarettes to most of the women in the room. "If they'd been really worried they'd have taken our smokes," she said, sharing a light. "I wasn't expecting no trouble or I wouldn't have gone along, I just wanted to hear the bands and have a bit of a knees-up. That's all rallies have been for a long time now. I haven't been arrested at one since I was courting." She looked at me. "You never been to one before, have you?"

"Not since I was a nipper," I said. "My dad took me to one at Camden Lock once. Since then, no, but my boyfriend wanted me to come along with him tonight and it seemed like it would be a bit of fun."

"Thought I hadn't seen you before," she said, clearly satisfied.

Just as I was congratulating myself on how easily I had blended in with these women, the motherly one sitting next to me noticed my skirt. It wasn't true you could go anywhere in tweeds; Paddington Nick was obviously too rough for them. I had kept my coat buttoned so that they wouldn't see my silk shirt and cashmere sweater, but I couldn't help my skirt showing. Part of it was muddy where it had been trodden on. The woman reached out and rubbed the cloth between her finger and thumb. "Nice bit of stuff you've got there," she said. "Where'd you get that?"

"Second-hand stall at Camden Lock Market," I lied. "Hardly worn at all. It's my best skirt, my mum will skin me for getting mud on it."

She gave me a shrewd look as if she was summing up my hair, bedraggled as it was, and my raincoat, and not quite believing me. It was a relief when a policeman came to the bars and called out two names. The streetwalkers answered. "Letting you two go, this time," the policeman said.

"That's a relief," said a woman in turquoise, as soon as they had gone. "I didn't like being in the room with them in case I caught a disease."

Everyone else laughed, including the suspicious woman next to me. After a while, she offered me a barley sugar from a packet in her pocket, which I took gratefully. I was terribly hungry, and it was quite clear nobody was about to feed us. The sugar, or something, maybe just sucking the sweet, which I hadn't done for ages, made me feel a bit better. Dad used to like barley sugar. He'd buy two ounces in a twist of paper from one of the huge jars in the sweet-shop. They were golden like sunlight and terribly inclined to stick together. I don't think I'd had one since he died.

It was very cold in the room, so nobody questioned my keeping my coat buttoned. I chanced a look at my watch after a while, when nobody seemed to be paying any attention to me. Ten o'clock. I should have been in the Blue Nile by now—a real nightclub. Mrs. Maynard usually wouldn't let us go near them. If Betsy and Sir Alan had got away, he wouldn't have taken her to a nightclub, not with-out me. They'd have gone home. Mrs. Maynard would be terribly worried about me. I wondered what she'd do. She'd probably wait a bit in case I turned up, but after a while she'd be sure to contact Uncle Carmichael, in which case I might be taken out of here at any moment. I tried counting time and working out how long it would take for Betsy and Sir Alan to get home, and then for Mrs. Maynard to decide to get in touch with Uncle Carmichael, and then for him to find out I was here and come to get me. At least another hour, I thought.

I didn't want to ask for him, to say I was his niece, which wasn't quite true anyway. I thought it would be better to come from outside. I didn't entirely trust these bobbies to pass a message on to him quickly, and I didn't want to attract their attention. Besides, there was a chance they'd just let me go without bothering him at all. I could always tell them later if I needed to. It was like having an ace in reserve. I decided to keep quiet and wait. I sat still, my coat around me, and fell into a doze. I don't know how long I slept.

I was woken when another six women were pushed into the room. One of them had a huge red mark on the side of her face. Conversation turned to them and to the riot, which had apparently got completely out of control. The women had been at another police station, which was full, before being sent on here. "So whose side were you on, then?" a fat woman asked the woman with the mark.

"I wasn't on either side, as such," she said. "I was just trying to get away when I got clobbered. As for what they were saying, I liked the singing, but I didn't like hearing things said against Mr. Normanby. It's not as if it's his fault he's in his wheelchair, is it? Terrorists killed Sir James and they tried for Mr. Normanby, just like they'd kill us all if they had the chance."

"That lad did have a point though," said the woman next to me. "Mr. Normanby isn't a really strong leader, not when you compare him to Hitler."

I couldn't believe she'd be foolish enough to say this, after the riot, and sure enough the marked woman spat at her, after which the room erupted. Women who had been sharing cigarettes and sweets beforehand were clawing at each other and shouting names I hadn't heard for years. I cowered on the bench, my bare feet tucked up under me. The police had to turn a cold water hose on two women to get them to stop clawing at each other. When they separated us, I went with the woman who had seemed friendly. We were put in another cell, almost the same as the first, but with a thin high window on one wall, through which I watched the dawn coming. Every so often a policeman would call a name, and a woman would go off to be processed, then be brought back and another name would be called. At last I slept a little more. I was startled out of an uneasy dream to hear my name called.

It wasn't Uncle Carmichael, just an ordinary policeman, ready to process me as he had been processing the others. It must have been nearly midday by the light. The policeman made me walk in front of him down a badly lit corridor, then another policeman opened the door of a little cell. I stepped in, and had time to see dirty white tiled walls, a table, and two chairs before one of the men behind me pushed me hard in the middle of my back. I had to take a couple of running steps and then fell, banging my knee. I waited for a moment, on the ground, then got up slowly. "Sit down," the policeman said. It was then I realized it hadn't been an accident, he had quite deliberately given me a shove. I was furious.

"Why did you push me?" I demanded.

"Sit down, or do I have to make you?" he asked. He was quite a young man, red-haired. He sounded almost bored.

I sat down. It seemed like the best policy. He sat down on the other side of the table, and put my papers down in front of him, along with a file card. "Elvira Royston," he said. "Just eighteen. Resident in Kensington."

My papers had Uncle Carmichael's address, of course. "I'm staying with a friend in Belgravia," I said.

"What friend? Was he at the rally with you?"

"Elizabeth Maynard, and yes, she was," I said, stressing the pronoun.

He looked me up and down, quite obviously, not even trying to hide it. "So a pair of young girls went quite unaccompanied to the rally," he said, rolling his eyes. "Dangerous, that is, as you've seen."

"Her fiancé was with us," I said, stretching the truth. "Sir Alan Bellingham."

I had hoped that Sir Alan's name might mean something to the loutish officer, but he didn't twitch. "Is that right?" he asked, making a note. "How do you spell that?"

I told him, and he wrote it down. Then he looked up again. "So whose side were you on when the fighting started?"

"Neither. I was just trying to get away."

"And which side do you find more sympathetic? The singer, or Mr. Normanby?"

"I had no sympathies!" I insisted.

"You went with the British Power group when you fought in the cell," he said, looking down at his notes.

"That's just because—," I started, but I couldn't have told that cold cruel man about the barley sugar. "I have no sympathies," I repeated, but I saw that he noted down *BP* next to my name.

"Let's take you back, then," he said, getting out of his chair.

"When will I be released?" I asked, coming cautiously to my feet.

"When we're good and ready."

"With what am I being charged?"

"Nothing, just yet. We can hold you for twenty-eight days on suspicion. We could charge you with plenty, though, if we like. Riot, incitement to riot, conspiracy to incite riot, terrorism, communism, anarchism." He stepped a little closer, and I backed away, feeling the wall of the cell behind me. His hard eyes were green, and his eyelashes so pale it almost seemed as if he had none. "I wouldn't be so eager to be charged if I were you, Miss Royston. The Watch are very interested in finding out who caused this riot."

"I do hope they are," I said, deciding that it was now or never for playing my ace. "Chief Inspector Carmichael of the Watch is my uncle. He's probably wondering where I am. I expect he'll want to hear how I've been treated."

6

When Carmichael got back to the Watch buildings, the rain was coming down in stair rods. He ran up the steps towards his own door, which the guard helpfully opened for him as he came close. When the building was being designed he had deliberately asked for the rows of doors, dwarfed as they were by the huge pillars. In the Yard there was no way in or out except under the watchful eye of the sergeant on desk duty. Here, each department had their own exit and entrance, and although there were always guards on duty under the portico, keeping an eye on who came and went, Carmichael felt that the psychological effect was different. "Lovely weather for ducks," the guard said, and Carmichael favored him with a thin smile.

As he came down the hallway from the stairs, Carmichael removed his hat and skimmed it towards the heavy Victorian hat stand. It landed, as it did two times out of three, neatly on the top peg.

Miss Duthie was hovering outside his office. Normally she sat at a little desk in the capacious hallway, filtering his visitors, out of earshot when the door was closed and near at hand when he wanted her to make tea. Now she was pacing across the hallway. She looked very relieved when she saw him. "There's a rather strange thing, sir," she said. "They telephoned from Paddington, and spoke to me, and then to Mr. Ogilvie, and he wanted to go over there to deal with it but I said he ought to *wait,* as you'd be back so soon."

"Who telephoned?" Carmichael asked, beginning to take off his wet overcoat. Miss Duthie had no authority to give orders to Ogilvie, she wasn't in the chain of command. "Is this urgent? I'd love a cup of tea."

"I think it *is* urgent." Miss Duthie's brow was crumpled with distress. "The Paddington police telephoned. They said they had Elvira, that she'd been caught in that horrible riot."

"Good God!" Carmichael froze, one arm in and one out of his overcoat. "You did absolutely right stopping Ogilvie, Miss Duthie, thank you."

"I did think that as it was a *personal* matter, I might exercise my judgment," she said, looking much happier.

"Quite right," Carmichael said, shrugging his coat back on. "How did Elvira come to be— No, you don't know, you couldn't. I must go to Paddington right away." He pulled the notes he had made in the Prime Minister's office out of his pocket. "Give this to Mr. Ogilvie, and tell him to get on it."

"Yes, sir," Miss Duthie said, taking the paper. "Do you want to take Sergeant Evans with you?"

"No harm in it. Give him a call and get him to meet me out on the portico. Where the devil is my hat?"

"It's on the hat stand," Miss Duthie said, without looking, already dialing, her other hand patting her bun. "Paul? Chief Inspector Carmichael needs you to meet him on the portico immediately."

Paul, Carmichael thought as he walked briskly back the way he had come, settling his hat on his head. Miss Duthie was on first-name terms with all the sergeants and men, though she kept a strict formality with the officers, who she perhaps considered as her own social class. He had heard Sergeant Evans addressing her as Peg, though to Carmichael she was always Miss Duthie. If it hadn't been for the security check he wouldn't have known her first names were

Margaret Rose, after the princess. She might be a social oddity but she really could make tea. Besides, she wasn't likely to go off one day and get married and leave him in the lurch, not at her age, and not with those big glasses. And she had done just the right thing in this Elvira matter; he wouldn't have wanted Ogilvie going there and putting his big foot into what amounted to Carmichael's private affairs. However did Elvira come to be in the riot? She wasn't a little girl anymore. But what could have possessed her to go? And why on earth hadn't that fool of a Mrs. Maynard, who was supposed to be looking after her, told him she was missing?

He stopped, halfway up the stairs. Was she missing, or was this a terrorist ruse to get him out of the office in a predictable direction so they could blow up his car? He turned back. It was just the sort of thing they'd try, the BFG, the Scottites, any of the more violent freedom groups. He didn't really believe it, but he should check.

"Telephone Mrs. Maynard for me," he called to Miss Duthie as soon as he was sure she would hear.

"I tried her, but the maid said there was nobody at home," Miss Duthie said, dialing.

Carmichael snatched the receiver out of his secretary's hand and listened to the slow pairs of rings at the other end. It was picked up by the maid. "They've just this minute come in," she said, when he gave his name and asked for Mrs. Maynard. "I'll hand you over, or no, sir, here's Miss Betsy to speak to you now."

"Do you know where she is?" Betsy Maynard asked urgently, with no preliminaries. Carmichael's heart sank.

"When did you last see Elvira?" he asked.

"Last night, at Marble Arch. I got swept away from her in the crowd, and then I got my arm broken. They've been fussing over me and operating and it wasn't until just now that we found out that Elvira was missing. Mummy thought she'd have come safely home, but of course she hasn't, and we're frantic."

"I believe she's been arrested with the rioters," Carmichael said. "I'm going to Paddington now. I'll need to speak to your mother about this. She should have told me Elvira was missing."

"Mummy was at the Charing Cross Hospital with me all night," Betsy said. "Not that it's any excuse, really."

Carmichael was inclined to agree. "If you have a broken arm you'll need to rest," he said. "I'll speak to your mother after I'm sure Elvira is safe."

"Yes, do go and get her," Betsy said. "And if you wouldn't mind, could you let me know when she's safely with you? I'm terribly worried about her."

"I'll do that, Betsy," Carmichael said, and rang off.

"So she's really missing?" Miss Duthie asked.

Carmichael nodded. "I must get up to Paddington. Sergeant Evans is probably getting soaked to the skin waiting for me." He hurried off down the corridor again.

The guard raised his eyebrows when he saw Carmichael come out again so soon, but said nothing. Sergeant Evans was waiting under the portico, a capacious black umbrella under his arm.

There was a black police Bentley waiting outside, as there always was. This was another of Carmichael's improvements over the Yard, where getting a car was almost as bad an ordeal as being put up for a club. Carmichael nodded to the driver and then to Evans. "Is there room for us both under that thing?" he asked.

"Should be, sir," Evans said, putting it up and holding it more over Carmichael than himself. "Nasty day, isn't it. April showers!"

They hurried down the steps and into the waiting car.

"Paddington Police Station," Carmichael said to the driver. Then he looked at Evans, who was one of his favorite subordinates, being steady, intelligent, and with a sense of humor. He was also Welsh, and Jack had said once that he had the typical look of the British before the Romans came—small-boned, dark-haired, and clear-skinned.

"What's up, sir?" he asked.

"It seems my ward, Elvira Royston, Sergeant Royston's daughter, you remember, somehow got mixed up in the Marble Arch riot, and I need to bail her out. I'm just bringing you along for company, and in case we want to overawe the Mets with a uniformed presence."

"You should have brought Sergeant Richards for that," Evans said.

Carmichael laughed, despite his worries about Elvira. Sergeant Richards was six foot two. "You'll do."

Paddington Police Station, when they reached it, seemed a grim place in the rain. Carmichael gave his name to a stern-faced constable at the desk who checked his papers thoroughly, squinting conscientiously from the identity photograph to Carmichael's face. "Inspector Bannister wanted to see you, sir," he said, when he was confident of Carmichael's identity.

"I'm here to collect Elvira Royston," Carmichael said. He didn't want to waste his time talking to the Met. Bannister, he remembered from his reports, was one of Penn-Barkis's creatures, and Penn-Barkis's continued supervision over the Watch was one of Carmichael's constant irritations.

"Yes, sir. Mr. Bannister would just like a word first."

Carmichael frowned, and the officer quailed a little.

"Just in here, sir," he said.

Evans followed Carmichael into a little office as directed, where they waited for a few moments.

Bannister proved to be a redhead in his late twenties, and a middle-class southerner, as Carmichael learned the moment he opened his mouth. "Good afternoon, sir," he said, coming in, followed by a uniformed bobby. "This is extraordinary."

"Good afternoon, Inspector. I'd like to take Elvira home without wasting too much time," Carmichael said.

"Yes, certainly, but this is a very unusual situation. We're anxious to cooperate with you, of course, but there are certain formalities in the case of any arrest. And in this case, we're supposed to keep all the rioters and check on them thoroughly."

"Those are my orders," Carmichael said. "I hardly think they apply in this case. My ward was caught up in the riot by mistake."

"It doesn't look that way to me. Why did Elvira—"

"Miss Royston." Carmichael stressed her formal name. He didn't like hearing "Elvira" on Bannister's lips.

Bannister looked surprised, but corrected himself at once. "Why did Miss Royston go to the rally?"

"She no doubt went to the rally for the fun of it, probably never having heard of British Power until the fighting started." It would have helped, Carmichael thought, if he'd had any real idea why Elvira did go to the rally. He should have asked Betsy Maynard.

"Probably," Bannister said. "She said she was your niece. Now you say she's your ward?"

"She calls me Uncle, but she's my ward," Carmichael said, trying to be calm but knowing that the Lancashire was coming into his vowels as it always did when he was agitated. Bannister was trying to get him on the defensive, and he wasn't having it. He took a deep breath. "Bring Miss Royston in here immediately. We're leaving."

Bannister nodded to the bobby, who left the room. "He's just fetching her now," he said. "What are Miss Royston's political convictions?"

"She's an eighteen-year-old girl, she's about to come out, she doesn't have two political thoughts a year," Carmichael said. "She won't be old enough to vote for seven or eight years."

"A lot of the people we pulled in last night were young, the men especially," Bannister said. "And some of the British Power ringleaders move in debutante circles. The connections seem to go very high."

He was drawing breath to go on, but Carmichael interrupted, tired of all this. "No doubt there's a detailed report on all this on my desk at the Watch."

The bobby came back into the room with Elvira following him. She was limping and looked filthy and exhausted.

"Uncle Carmichael," she said, her voice wavering but determined not to cry, reminding Carmichael a great deal of how she had been when she was seven years old and had fallen down in the street outside her father's house in Camden Town. She looked at Bannister with loathing, and stood beside Carmichael, as far from Bannister as she could be in the small room.

"Soon get you away from this, Elvira," he said. "Do you have the papers, Bannister?"

Bannister hesitated. "I wanted to ask a few more questions," he said.

"Most Metropolitan officers find it to their advantage to cooperate with us," Carmichael said, silkily. "Or you might find the price of noncooperation is rather high. If you get on the wrong side of me you might end up spending the rest of your career directing traffic in John O'Groats, or something considerably worse." It would have given Carmichael no pleasure to ruin the man's career, but he had done a lot worse.

"Yes, sir," Bannister said, his face wooden. "But this isn't a Watch matter, is it? It's a personal matter. You're asking us to free Miss Royston unconditionally, not to transfer her into Watch custody. She looks to me like a crucial piece in the investigation. She and . . ." He peered at his notes. "Sir Alan Bellingham."

"I'll take her into Watch custody if it'll speed this up," Carmichael said. Once in Watch custody the bureaucratic procedures were under his own control.

"That's hardly proper procedure," Bannister said.

Carmichael loathed the layers of red tape and "proper procedure" that surrounded everything these days. "Transfer her to Sergeant Evans's Watch custody then. I assume that's all right with you, Evans?"

"Perfectly, sir," Evans said. He leaned forward and took the papers from Bannister's hand. "Where do I sign?"

"Give those back at once!" Bannister demanded.

Sergeant Evans held on to the papers for a moment, deliberately, then smoothed them between his fingers, scanned them, and signed at the bottom. "We've had about enough of your lip," he said, handing them back. "We're leaving."

Bannister handed Elvira's identity card to Sergeant Evans.

"Come on, sir, let's get out of here," Evans said, taking it.

Carmichael glowered at Bannister, who looked back impassively. "Come on, Elvira." He offered her his arm, which she took hesitantly.

"Tuppenny ha'penny Hitler," Evans said, as they left. "You were too soft on him, sir. Making himself important for the sake of it, trying to humiliate you because for once he had a bit of power. That's what's wrong with the country these days, too many men like him, sucking up when they have to and putting the boot in when they don't. Now the Watch may have its dirty jobs to do from time to time—"

"The Watch can be just as bad," Carmichael said, cutting him off.

"No, sir, there you're wrong, and I'll tell you why. It's because we're armed, and that means we don't need to push people around to show we can. Like the army. We know we can, and so we don't need to."

"That's an extraordinary theory, sergeant," Carmichael said. He knew Evans had rounded up Jews, and shot them too, when they'd tried to escape. It was impossible to escape brutality, in the Watch, but perhaps it really did seem to Sergeant Evans that brutality was better than petty humiliation.

7

I've never been so glad to see anyone in my life as I was to see Uncle Carmichael in that little office. I felt my eyes positively filling up with tears at the familiar sight of him. Not that he looked pleased to see me; quite the opposite. He had his official face on, but he was quite clearly furious. I didn't know if that was directed at my idiocy in getting myself arrested or at the red-haired Paddington officer who was clearly enjoying having the advantage on Uncle Carmichael for once. But controlled fury was a familiar mood of Uncle Carmichael's. It made me feel as if this was only a scrape and that I could smile and apologize and get out of it unscathed. Most things were like that. Indeed, there had only been three things in my life so far where I couldn't do that. The first was my mother walking out when I was six. The second was my father being killed when I was eight. And the third was Betsy getting herself into a mess in Zurich the year before, when we were both seventeen. Since my interview with the redheaded policeman I'd been starting to feel intimations that this arrest might be a fourth.

I went to stand in the corner of the office, out of the way. As well as the horrible policeman and Uncle Carmichael and a bobby, there was solid old Sergeant Evans, who was Welsh, and who loved horses almost as much as I had when I was fourteen. His wife, Jean, had taken a kind interest in me ever since my father died. Only the week before, Betsy and I had taken her for tea in the Ritz.

None of them looked at me while they squabbled over the papers. For a moment as he and the redhead bullied each other, Uncle Carmichael seemed his mirror image. I looked at him sideways as he made threats, wondering if I knew him at all. Then we left, the three of us stalking out with our heads held high, like a trio of affronted duchesses in a fish market. There was a police car outside, a plain black Bentley, the 1958 model with the silver grille. The driver didn't get out, and Sergeant Evans opened the back door for me. Uncle Carmichael sat in the back next to me, and Sergeant Evans in the front next to the driver.

"Where to?" the driver asked.

There was a pause. "Mrs. Maynard's?" I suggested.

"No," Uncle Carmichael said, abruptly. "Not yet, anyway. Betsy Maynard has broken her arm, and I need to have words with her mother. Severe words. Certainly not today. I need to talk to you."

"Is Betsy all right?" I asked. I could imagine all too easily how a bone could have cracked in that riot, and began to worry about how bad it was.

Uncle Carmichael looked perhaps a shade less annoyed as he turned his head to look at me, and his voice was certainly softer. Thinking of Betsy can have that effect on people. "I spoke to her on the telephone, and she was mostly worried about you. I expect she'll recover all right."

"How about going back to the Watchtower?" Sergeant Evans ventured.

Uncle Carmichael looked at his watch, and frowned. I glanced at my own watch reflexively. It was ten to four, which seemed preposterous, even though I knew about all the hours of waiting. I should have been with Betsy having our fittings for our Court dresses. "I noticed you were limping. Do you need a doctor, Elvira?"

"I don't think so," I said. "I lost a shoe, and then I banged my knee when that vile policeman pushed me. It'll be all right."

"Then home, I think," Uncle Carmichael said.

The driver pulled out into the traffic as if he and the car were one machine. I had plenty of opportunity to watch the excellence of his driving, as nobody said a word for the fifteen minutes it took us to make our way to Uncle Carmichael's flat. I was fretting about Betsy. An arm in plaster would put a damper on her coming out, and there wasn't really anything else for her. She could talk about being a secretary, but it wouldn't do, really. Her parents would never let her get away except in the approved fashion. I was so glad I'd decided to go to Oxford, and so lucky Uncle Carmichael and the Dean had let me.

When I was a little girl I used to think Uncle Carmichael was a rich man. He talked like a toff, or enough like one to fool my Cockney ear. I didn't know enough then to recognize the Lancashire that sometimes comes out in his speech. He was my father's superior, and as they often worked together, his boss. He was his friend as well, but Dad used to tell me to mind myself in front of Inspector Carmichael, not to take advantage even though he let me call him Uncle. Then, after my father was killed and Uncle Carmichael as good as adopted me and sent me to Arlinghurst, I came to think he was quite poor. After all, he lived in a flat with only one manservant, who did the cooking as well as valeting. A woman came in a few mornings a week to clean and do the rough, but otherwise poor Jack did everything. Since I'd grown up—for now, after my year in Switzerland, I felt myself quite grown-up—I'd come to realize that Uncle Carmichael's finances, relative power, and social position were far more complex than I had ever imagined.

His flat was spare and masculine. In my memory it was all maroon leather and mahogany and tweed. When I went there I was always surprised to notice the softening touches, the tassels on the green velvet cushions, the Victorian paintings, the Japanese teapot, the delicate china. There was a tiny bedroom there I called mine, where I kept a trunk full of mementos and old clothes, but it was rare for me to spend more than a day or so of any holiday there. It wasn't just that I found it claustrophobic, but that I always felt in the way. I didn't doubt that Uncle Carmichael was fond of me, as well as feeling me as an obligation, but even so, I never really felt comfortable staying in his flat. Every time I went into my room I remembered how I had wept the first night I spent there, so solitary and uncomfortable, and aware for the first time that not only my father but my whole life had been taken away from me. Home was a poky rented house in Camden Town, where I knew everyone and everyone knew me. The flat had never felt like home.

Uncle Carmichael nodded to the guard outside, who stepped aside to let us in.

"How do the other people in the building like him?" Sergeant Evans asked, as we trooped upstairs.

"They like the safety, mostly. They had to give him lists of their visitors, of course, so he can let them in, and some of them didn't like that; that's why we put in the intercom system so he can call up and ask if someone is expected. But if they really don't like it, they can always move."

Jack let us into the flat. I could see him looking at my dirty coat with surprise as he took it, but all he said was "I'll put the kettle on."

I went to the bathroom at once. I tidied myself up as best I could, and washed my face and hands, very glad of the hot water and lovely Pears soap. I couldn't help thinking how nice it would be to wear something I hadn't had on for twenty-four hours. I slipped into my little room and put on clean knickers, which was a great relief, and some nylons. There wasn't a skirt in my trunk that wouldn't have been well above my knee. I had grown, and fashions had changed. I brushed at the mud on my tweed skirt and got most of it off. Apart from that it wasn't too awful even after everything, so I kept it on. I brushed my hair and wished I could wash it. I'd have been very glad of a bath, too, but I also wanted the cup of tea Jack had promised, and I felt it was only fair to let Uncle Carmichael tick me off first. I left my face quite bare, as all my makeup had been in my bag, took a deep breath, and went into the sitting room.

Uncle Carmichael was just putting down the receiver of the telephone. "Betsy is relieved to know that you are recovered in one piece," he said. I would have liked to have spoken to her, and regretted the time wasted on hair-brushing.

"I'd better get back to the Watchtower," Sergeant Evans said. "You'll want these papers, sir."

Uncle Carmichael took them, and turned them in his hands. "Your identity card," he said, turning to me and handing it over. I took it and slipped it into my pocket.

"They didn't give me back my bag," I said, sitting down on the edge of the sofa.

"How much was in it?" Uncle Carmichael asked.

"Only a few pounds, and my makeup case, a few bits and pieces, but it's an Italian leather bag from Geneva and quite expensive." Then I remembered. "Betsy's pearls! They're in it! We have to get it back. Mrs. Maynard doesn't even know I borrowed them."

"Why did you borrow them?" Uncle Carmichael asked.

I squirmed. "Well, Betsy has a lot of jewelry, trinkets, you know, and I don't have any so when we were in Switzerland we got into the habit of sharing."

Uncle Carmichael looked away. "You should have told me you needed some."

"You have been so good to me already," I said. "I don't like to ask."

"I've always told you to ask for anything that makes you stand out as different from the other girls. Anything you needed like that."

"That was when I was in school!" I said. He had been really good about that. I had never lacked whatever that term's fad was, whether it was a pink tennis racket or a pin-striped dressing gown or a hamster. Uncle Carmichael had been to boarding school himself and understood.

"It still applies," he said, brusquely. "Evans, when you get back to the Tower, put through an inquiry to Paddington about Elvira's bag. You'll need the case number that's all over these interminable papers, so you'd better hold on to them for now. We may as well take advantage of the Watch custody nonsense to get hold of the bag— it's our evidence now. They can't have any claim to it. As soon as you get it, send it over here."

"Yes, sir. Shall I go and get on with that now?" he asked.

"Go on. And take the rest of these papers—Elvira will need her card, but all this can be filed."

Sergeant Evans winked at me as he slipped away, just as he used to do when I was much younger. I could have hugged him.

When we were alone, Uncle Carmichael turned to me. "What on earth did you think you were doing going to the rally? What possessed Mrs. Maynard to allow it?"

"Sir Alan Bellingham, who is a boo of Betsy's—"

"A boo?" he interrupted.

"That word has been around since the ark. A boo, a beau, a partner your parents approve of. In this case, her parents approve of him a lot more than poor Betsy does."

"Go on," Uncle Carmichael said, drawing his eyebrows together.

"Well, he offered to take us, and Mrs. Maynard didn't want to let us but I was fed up with her and so I said I wanted to go and so they let us," I admitted. "I see now that I was wrong, but I hadn't been to one since Dad took me to one when I was a tot, and I thought it would be more fun than the usual sort of deb evening out."

"As you see, it wasn't." Uncle Carmichael sat down on one of the easy chairs, as stiff as a ramrod.

"It was, though, until the riot started. The torches and the uniforms, the parade. The singing. There was an enthusiasm there, the ordinary people—I was having a good time until it all came to pieces."

Uncle Carmichael wasn't looking any less furious. "Mrs. Maynard should not have allowed it. She should have known better even if you didn't. And Sir Alan, having taken you there under his protection, should have looked after you."

"He was busy looking after Betsy," I said.

"That's precisely my complaint!" Uncle Carmichael riposted. "Damn the man for being such a fool anyway. It's no thanks to him that you even survived the experience."

"Did many people die?" I asked, remembering that horrible moment when I'd fallen and thought I'd be trampled.

"Nine people," Uncle Carmichael said.

"I can't believe I was such a fool," I said. "I'm very sorry, and I'll never go near one again."

"Did your father often take you to them?"

"Only once. And it was quite different, really." I remembered that long-ago day, the crowds, the parade, the sunshine. "Yet the same, too. The Ironsides expressing the spirit of the ordinary British people."

He winced. "Did you ever wonder why it was Switzerland I chose to send you to?" he asked, changing the subject entirely as far as I was concerned.

"It's a fairly ordinary place to go to be finished. With the chance to learn French as well as German. No, I admit, I never thought about it." I did now, though. What made Switzerland different from France and Germany? The Alps—my first thought, and quite the best thing about my memories of Switzerland—spilled over into both those countries.

Before I could think of anything, Jack came in with the tea tray.

He set it down on the coffee table. "This is the tea you brought us from Switzerland, Elvira."

Tea, China tea, especially unusual flavors, was always a safe present for Uncle Carmichael, who was impossible to find presents for, regularly causing me agonies at Christmas and birthdays. I usually bought tea for him at Jacksons of Piccadilly, who stock as many teas as wine merchants have wines, and talk about them in the same connoisseur's tones. I remembered buying the Swiss tea. I had nothing to do for two hours, while Betsy was under the anesthetic, and I had blundered out into the narrow streets of Zurich, catching glimpses through every gap of the blue lake, so much bluer than the sky. I had wandered with no idea of where I wanted to go, unable to sit down for more than a minute, so worried about Betsy and with everything out of my hands now. The little tea shop, with its brightly painted blue and gold tea caddy swinging above the door, had surprised me around a corner. Inside, it had been dark and tea-smelling, and the man who measured out the tea, using a little shovel, had been just like the assistants in Jacksons, although of course we spoke German together.

I poured the tea from the beautiful Japanese teapot into the waiting cups. Of course there was no milk or sugar on the tray, the way there would have been at Mrs. Maynard's, or even here, if there had been guests. I got up to hand Uncle Carmichael his cup. I would drink the tea, I thought, and then ask if I could have a bath.

"I don't suppose you saw how the riot started?" he asked, taking the cup.

"I did. I was right there."

"That's very interesting," he said. "Tell me about it."

So I did, and as I talked he made notes. He was especially interested in the British Power young man, and in the organization of those chanting for him. He wanted to know if Sir Alan was involved with him, which of course I couldn't tell him. Sir Alan had certainly steered us to that rostrum. Partway through, Jack came back with plates of delicious Welsh rarebit, the cheese melted just as I like it. I had forgotten about being hungry until I caught that smell, and then I could hardly wait to cut it up. We ate it in our chairs in the sitting room, with more tea, and Uncle Carmichael kept asking me about the riot and writing down what I said.

"In your interrogation in Paddington, they wrote you down as on the British Power side?" he asked.

"That's nonsense. I kept saying I wasn't on any side. But in the riot in the cell—," I began, and then we were launched into that, and into what the women had thought.

I don't know how long he'd have kept asking me questions, but we were interrupted by Jack coming in again.

"The guard called up from downstairs," he said. "Are you expecting a Mrs. Talbot? She said to say it was about the Eversley family. Woman in her fifties, he says, harmless and respectable-looking, no weapons."

"I'm not expecting her, and don't know the name. Lord Eversley would call me at the office—and if I wasn't there, Miss Duthie would call me here," he said. "On the other hand, it's just the kind of thing Lady Eversley would do, and you did say family."

"Could be an odd MO for another assassin," Jack said, glancing at me.

"I'm not a child," I said. "I know that policemen take risks doing their jobs better than most people." I knew how much some people hated Uncle Carmichael, too, because I'd met some of them, including one beautiful young man from Cambridge who said Uncle Carmichael was the visible face of repression.

Uncle Carmichael patted his pocket, where I knew he kept a pistol. "The guard already checked her for weapons. Eversley isn't a name I'd expect assassins to use. Send her up, but observe precautions," he said to Jack. Then he turned to me. "Elvira, go and have your bath. I'm not expecting any trouble, but it's better for you not to be here."

I stood up. My knee had stiffened, and I lurched for a moment and grabbed on to the arm of the sofa. I was exhausted. A hot bath sounded like the best thing in the world, even if there wouldn't be any perfume to put in it. All the same, I was curious about the caller, and lingered in the hall to see her coming in. Anyone less like an assassin you couldn't imagine. She was plump, had gray hair pulled up in a bun, and a dark gray coat with a white collar. She looked like a pigeon. I almost laughed as I went off into the bathroom.

8

Carmichael wondered what Lady Eversley could possibly want. It was just like her to bother him at home, probably for something entirely trivial. Yet there was something strange about this. He would have thought it a clandestine visit, but a terrorist wouldn't have allowed a weapons search, and the visitor hadn't given any of the Inner Watch passwords. He wasn't sure what to expect.

Mrs. Talbot turned out to be a stout woman in a severe dress. Carmichael guessed at once from her bearing and manner that she wasn't an assassin, and relaxed. He stood up and came forward to shake her hand, but she gave him a stiff old-fashioned bow.

"Mr. Carmichael," she said, and he could hear in her voice a slight trace of Westmorland.

"Do sit down," he said. "Would you like tea?"

"China tea will do very well for me," she said, surprisingly, and smiled at him almost conspiratorially. She sat on the sofa where Elvira had been until a few moments before.

"Has Mr. Normanby been gossiping about my tastes in tea?" he asked, uncomfortably. Jack raised an eyebrow and left for the kitchen.

"Not Mr. Normanby. I feel as if I know you from a different mutual friend. I once had the honor of being Lucy Kahn's governess,

and I have recently been editing her manuscript for publication."
Mrs. Talbot smiled as if this astonishing information was a bit of
cheerful gossip.

"Her manuscript?" Carmichael asked, dumbfounded. "Lucy
Kahn's manuscript?"

"She has written an account of what happened at Farthing the
weekend of Sir James Thirkie's murder, from her own point of
view, of course. She wrote it quite a long time ago, immediately after it happened, in fact, but only recently has there been any possibility of publication. She sent it to me to edit for style and consistency
and, well, certain other things."

"I see," said Carmichael, who didn't see at all. He remembered
poor Lucy Kahn only too well. She and her husband were the first
innocents he had betrayed.

"She talks quite a lot about you, of course. She mentions certain
things about you, such as your tea drinking and some of your . . .
other proclivities."

"How the devil did she know?" Carmichael blurted, entirely disconcerted.

Mrs. Talbot laughed comfortably. "Lucy always had an instinct
for that sort of thing."

"She can't go around making that sort of allegation based on her
instinct! She could ruin my reputation. There is still a law of libel in
this country." Carmichael drew himself up.

"There are a great many laws in this country, many of them excellent, and others of them perhaps less so," Mrs. Talbot said, not
moving, or looking at all intimidated, and continuing to meet his
eyes comfortably. "But Lucy's account couldn't possibly be published here in the present political climate. It's going to be published
in Australia and in Switzerland. We do expect copies will percolate
abroad."

"Are you attempting to blackmail me?" Carmichael asked.

Jack came with the tea tray and almost dropped it on hearing Carmichael's remark. The cups clattered and rocked on their saucers and a stream of tea from the spout of the teapot spurted onto the cloth.

"I resent that accusation," Mrs. Talbot said, her sharp eyes taking in Jack and the tray. "Indeed, if I didn't already know other things about you from Lucy's manuscript I might be inclined to leave without saying what I have come to say, which I think you will find worth the time it takes you to hear."

"I'm sorry," Carmichael said, stiffly. "Will you pour the tea?"

Jack gave him a look of inquiry as, having put the tray down, he turned his back on Mrs. Talbot to leave. Carmichael gave him a tiny nod of reassurance, though he was still by no means sure what on earth was going on. Mrs. Talbot poured the tea and Carmichael took his cup. He would have preferred a peg of whisky at this point, but something about the severity of Mrs. Talbot's clothes suggested that she would disapprove.

"In Lucy's account she explains how you telephoned Farthing so that they could get away in time," Mrs. Talbot said.

Carmichael stared at her. Someone else knew! He had somehow never thought of Lucy Kahn telling anyone, let alone writing out her account and having it published, though from her point of view he could see the utility of it.

"Naturally I have changed all the names and taken out that reference and the other references that might be damaging. I have also elided the help I gave her in getting out of the country."

"They got away safely, then?" Carmichael heard himself asking, as if from a long way away. "I've always hoped so, but never known for sure."

"They're in Canada, up in the north. David runs a little airline that connects the mining communities, and Lucy runs a school for the children of miners and Eskimos. Heaven knows what she tcaches them!" Mrs. Talbot smiled fondly at the thought. "They were in Montreal during the sack, but they got away that time too."

"I'm very glad to hear it." Carmichael sipped his tea.

"This isn't why I've come to you. So far I've just been presenting my credentials so that you'll listen to what I have to say. Also, so that you know I have kept your secrets all this time, and will continue to keep them. If I'd gone to an ordinary Watchman with this, I'd have been putting myself and my connections in considerable danger, yet I do want you to know. Mr. Carmichael, I am a friend." She paused, as if what she'd said was of great import.

It took him a moment to grasp the significance of what she was saying. "A friend? Oh, a Friend. A Quaker, you mean? The Society of Friends?"

"It isn't illegal to be a Friend, but since 1955 it has caused us to be viewed with a certain amount of suspicion. You were more lenient then than you might have been."

"You registered Jews as part of your congregations," Carmichael remembered. He tried not to think about 1955 more than he had to. "It isn't illegal to be a Jew either, for that matter, unless you're in the wrong place or trying to pass yourself off as something else. Between us now—you're not Jewish?"

"I do not have that honor." Mrs. Talbot looked as if she meant it. "My parents were also Friends. I was born in Kendal, where there is quite a large congregation."

"I'm from Lancashire myself," Carmichael said. "I've often noticed the Friends Meeting House in Lancaster, down the hill from the railway station on the way into town." That was in fact the only reason he knew that Quakers were called the Society of Friends at all. Quakers didn't tend to commit many crimes that would bring them to his attention.

Mrs. Talbot nodded, with just a touch of impatience at this geographical reminiscence. "Because I am a Friend, I am in contact with certain people who are in contact with other people who, well, move people around and procure papers for them. That is how I managed to get David and Lucy out of the country, and plenty of other people before and since."

"You're smuggling out Jews?" Carmichael sat right up and almost dropped his tea.

"Mr. Carmichael, you can arrest me if you want to, but I won't lead you to any contacts. We've all made sure of that before I came here." She stuck out her chin and looked ready to go to the stake.

Carmichael laughed, then hesitated. He should be cautious. She had no poison tooth, as members of the Inner Watch had, no protection against being made to talk. Yet he trusted her, and he had to make her see that she could trust him. He threw caution to the winds. "Mrs. Talbot, I have more desire to embrace you than to arrest you. My first question would be whether you could take any more. I do what I can in that way myself, but the problem is always having somewhere to send them."

Mrs. Talbot laughed in turn and turned quite pink. "Call me Abby," she said. "All my friends do. I apologize for not shaking your hand. You must be very discreet. I had no idea. Whoever would have dreamed of such a thing. An underground railroad in the middle of the Watch!"

"We send most of them to Ireland, where they take them in just to spite the English. It's so hard to find anyone who will accept them, and it's not as if there's a vast outflow of people from the British Isles to hide them among." Carmichael sighed. "We can issue false papers, of course, and we do, but there is oversight and we have to be careful, because if any of us were caught the whole thing would be over. And when it comes to expanding the operation, the problem is always of who to begin to trust."

"We used to send people to Canada, and sometimes to the United States, with cleverly forged papers, naturally. These days, of course, Canada isn't the haven we used to like to think it was, and America—well, President Yolen is doing his best just to hold the country together. He can hardly dare acknowledge that the rest of the world even exists." Abby sighed. "These days, we mostly send the Jews to Zanzibar. They have a thriving colony there. We have a company that exports Jews and imports spices and bananas. We have three ships that make the trip, and they never sail with empty places. If only we had another ship, we could take more people."

"Zanzibar. That's in Africa, isn't it?" Carmichael had barely heard the name.

"It's an island off the east coast of Africa," she said, and he saw how she must have been as a governess.

"Mrs. Talbot—Abby, forgive me—I can see there might be many ways we can profitably work together now that we've been fortunate enough to meet. But will you tell me why you came to me? Curiosity is overcoming me, especially since you really didn't know about the Inner Watch. I'd be happy to talk about how we can help each other afterwards."

Abby took a deep breath, set down her empty teacup, folded her hands, and settled herself more comfortably on the sofa. "My organization, unlike yours which stays aloof, is in touch in a vague way with a number of other organizations. We overlap, we have members in common, we know people. The Friends are strictly nonviolent, but sometimes a violent organization wants us to smuggle someone out of the country, or hide someone for a while. Likewise we sometimes need funds. When we hide fugitives we don't ask who they are or what they've done. You understand?"

Carmichael nodded, not at all clear where she was going, but following her so far. This overlap was why the Watch tried to infiltrate any opposition group, no matter how seemingly innocent; he was well aware of the theory.

"Through these channels I have heard certain rumors for a while now, but discounted them, largely because there are always rumors through such channels, and most of them nonsense. But this was a more persistent rumor than most, and coming from people who call themselves followers of Lord Scott, concerning support for their cause from the Duke of Windsor. Then, a few days ago, the parents of one of the children at my husband's school, respectable people, unconnected so far as I know with any underground activity, mentioned the British Power movement, within the Ironsides, and that the Duke of Windsor, who they called King Edward VIII, was involved in some way with it. Putting this together with what I have heard from friends with Scottite affiliations, I believe that the Duke of Windsor is going to attempt a coup d'etat, using both the Ironsides and the poor deluded Scottites. Bad as things are in Britain now, Mr. Carmichael, I believe they'd be considerably worse if that wicked man were to come to be in charge."

"Do you know him?" Carmichael asked, curious at her vehemence and the use of the word *wicked.*

"I have met him. He used to come to stay at Farthing in the early part of the thirties." Abby pursed her lips. "There's no doubt whatsoever of his fascist sympathies, or of his overwhelming vanity and sense that he deserves whatever he wants as soon as he wants it. He would have made an appalling king, and it's as well that there was an excuse to get him off the throne. I believe that was the best day's work Mr. Baldwin ever did. As king, as a legitimate and constitutional monarch, he might have sapped the will of the nation—but he couldn't really have done anything like the harm he could if he were to seize power illegitimately now."

"How could he be worse than Normanby?" Carmichael asked, cynically.

"Mr. Normanby has at least a fig leaf of constitutionality. He keeps Parliament in session. There are elections and an opposition. There is lip service at least to our traditions of freedom. Bad as things are, for most people they are very little different from how they have always been. And better the devil you know, Mr. Carmichael."

Carmichael stood up and paced the length of the sitting room. He stopped in front of a watercolor of a moorland landscape and stared at it, not really seeing the familiar pattern of browns and greens. "The real problem is that people mostly are perfectly happy with things as they are, or else too afraid to do anything. I sometimes wonder whether if things got notably worse it would be an improvement, because they'd have to take notice."

"And what would come of it if they took notice at that point?" Abby asked. "It would be too late for them to act. It is possible to make people brave, and clear-sighted, and open-eyed. I do it with my pupils. But I do it individually, and it's hard work that takes years. I don't know how to do it for a whole country, so that they'd look at what their government is doing in their name instead of ignoring it, and then throw them out instead of making excuses. But they have to have the power to throw them out if they do wake up to it. At the moment, the inertia and the institutions are still just about there. If we took them away, as they have been taken away in Germany, if we installed a king to rule over us by divine right, what would a waking-up avail but a massacre, as happened in Vienna two years ago?"

Carmichael had paced back the length of the room and found himself at the window; he turned back to her. "Every day I see men and women betraying their friends and families because they are afraid. It's easy for me to despise them, but I do my job for the same reason. I betrayed Lucy and David Kahn when I had proof that they were innocent, proof! But it wasn't enough when nobody would accept it, when I was threatened myself." He hesitated, wincing as he spoke, still bitterly ashamed ten years later and after all that had happened since. Not even to Jack had he talked about it this clearly.

"They knew I'd warned Lucy, they knew about what you called my proclivities, they threatened me, they threatened Jack, they cut me off so I couldn't have achieved anything by speaking out, and in the end I sold my soul to them."

"It wasn't the end," Abby said, twisting on the sofa to face him head on. "Your soul is still your own. You know how to be brave. Think what you have done since, how many souls are alive and free in Ireland instead of slaves or dead on the Continent. You failed a test, yes, that one and perhaps others, but you have never surrendered your soul. And I believe it's the same for the whole country."

"I think you are the most extraordinary person I have ever met," Carmichael said, walking back to his armchair and sitting down again. "I'll do what I can, and have the Watch do what they can, to stop whatever the Duke of Windsor is attempting."

"I felt sure you would, sure enough to come here even without knowing very much about you," Abby said.

He held up his hand for silence and picked up the receiver of the telephone that sat on the little table beside his chair. "Home Office, please. Who's that? Oh, Atkinson, good, didn't know you were taking the evening watch over there these days. It's Carmichael. Do you know about this Duke of Windsor business? Well, please take a message for whoever is dealing with it. Tell him with reference to the query he sent us about the Duke of Windsor, on consideration, the Watch feels it would be better if he were kept out of the country. Could you write that up as a memo and drop it on his desk, and also the Duke of Hampshire's desk for first thing in the morning?"

He listened to a few moments of polite wittering. As he listened he could hear, in his own flat, the sound of the bath draining. "Thank you so much, good-bye," he said, and grinned at Abby. "I wish it was all so easy."

Footsteps padded down the corridor. Abby raised her eyebrows. "My ward. She doesn't know anything about anything. If she comes in, don't say anything," Carmichael said. The footsteps passed the door and went on down towards the kitchen. "Probably looking for a cup of hot milk before bed."

"Well then, about Zanzibar," Abby said.

"Wait a moment. You said you needed money. I can put you on our payroll as an informer. You did just give me some very good information, and I can also explain your visit that way. What you do with the money, putting it towards paying forgers or buying ships to export Jews, is your business. Our budget for information is high."

Abby looked as if she almost disapproved, but after a moment she began to laugh.

9

The next morning, which was Thursday, I woke up in my bed in Uncle Carmichael's flat and for a moment had no idea where I was. The bed was narrow, and the room was narrow, and for a second I had the ridiculous fancy that I was in a cabin in a ship. The sun was quite high, so they'd obviously let me sleep. I stretched and yawned and got up, feeling a million times better than I had the day before. I riffled through my trunk trying to find something I could wear, but it was no good. I had grown and styles had changed while I'd been in Switzerland. I had clean knickers, and I found a vest, but had to put on the same bra and cashmere sweater and tweed skirt I had been wearing for what already felt like an eternity. I had taken the silk shirt off the night before, but I had no hope of getting it on again without help because it buttoned up the back. I made a mental note to find clothes I could get into without help before Oxford. I didn't want to take a maid to St. Hilda's, and I wouldn't have Betsy. Poor Betsy. I wondered how she was as I slipped the embroidered lavender bag she had made me back into my bra.

At the bottom of the trunk I found a pair of gym slippers that still fit, only because the leather was so soft, old bronze ones with rosettes on the toes.

It wasn't until I noticed my empty Ovaltine cup on the bedside table that I remembered what I'd overheard on my way to the kitchen. "It's my ward. She doesn't know anything. If she comes in, don't say anything." I hadn't thought anything of it. He was the head of the Watch, after all. But a few moments later, after she'd muttered something, I heard him say, "I can put you on our payroll as an informer. You did just give me some very good information, and I can also explain your visit that way. What you do with the money, putting it towards paying forgers or buying ships to export Jews, is your business. Our budget for information is high."

In the morning sunlight, as I brushed my hair with my old school hairbrush, it seemed like a dream. How could Uncle Carmichael be involved with anything clandestine? He was the head of the Watch! And if he were, how could I inform on him as I had been taught I should inform? Who could I tell who wouldn't immediately report it to him? And besides, I owed everything to him; without him I'd have nothing, no hope of paying my fees at Oxford, no money to pay Mrs. Maynard for my board. I'd have to go back to the gutter, and there was nothing there for me either. In any case, the very concept was ridiculous. I trusted him, had trusted him for years. The very idea of my turning him in was ludicrous, immoral even, no matter how much we were all exhorted to be alert. Even if he were involved in something wrong, I couldn't possibly do my duty and turn him in. But he couldn't have been doing anything wrong. Yet I remembered him threatening the redheaded policeman the day before, and shivered. He had been so different. Still, I must have misheard, or misunderstood. Though spending Watch money to pay forgers or export Jews was unarguable—unless he was leading her on in some way, playing her along so that he could find out more. Yes, that must be it. Relieved, I pulled the wooden brush quickly through the night's tangles in my hair and caught it back in a simple ponytail.

My makeup was in my bag and my bag was still missing, so I

couldn't put my face on. I went out in search of breakfast bare-faced like a little girl. To my surprise, Uncle Carmichael was sitting in his usual armchair. "Good morning," I said. "I thought you'd be in work by this time."

"Today's the day we had the date to go down to Kent to see the primroses and your great-aunt Katherine. I'd booked the day off. I've telephoned the Watchtower and checked that there are no urgent fires that need attending to, and I thought we might as well do as we'd planned."

"What a splendid idea," I said. I had almost forgotten about our plan, although we did it every year. The last few years I'd been bored by it, but today, with the sun shining, and after the events of the last few days, I was only too happy at the thought of going out into the countryside and breathing some really fresh air. "The only problem is that I have nothing to wear."

"Eh? What you're wearing looks fine to me," Uncle Carmichael said. He was a typical old bachelor, he never took the faintest notice of clothes. "And don't you have a trunkful of fripperies in your room here?"

"I have grown four inches taller since I left them here, and two inches broader across the chest," I said, baldly. "Worst of all, I have no proper shoes."

He had the good grace to look embarrassed. "Well, what you're wearing will do. The shoes look fine. It's not as if you're going to be presented this afternoon. Sit down and have some breakfast and then we'll get off."

With that, Jack emerged from the kitchen with a toast rack and two boiled eggs in eggcups. There was butter on the table already, and the Japanese teapot sat beside Uncle Carmichael. "Will you want more than this, Elvira?" Jack asked, smiling at me. "Bacon? Kippers? Porridge?"

"I'd love a kipper. Mrs. Maynard won't have them in the house.

And in Paris, you wouldn't believe, it was worse than Switzerland—nothing for breakfast but a croissant and a little dab of jam. They were scrummy croissants, admittedly, and good jam too, but that's not enough for a growing girl."

"Not enough for one who has grown four inches in the last two years," Uncle Carmichael put in. "Maybe you should keep off the kippers and stick to croissants in future."

We ate our breakfasts, bickering amicably, and finished off with more toast and marmalade. He was Uncle Carmichael; it was so unthinkable that he could possibly be any sort of traitor that I almost forgot about it, but it kept creeping back into my mind in the oddest way.

It wasn't until we were putting on our coats to go that I remembered Aunt Katherine's present. "We have to call in at Mrs. Maynard's first," I said.

"You look fine as you are," Uncle Carmichael said, impatiently. Jack had found time somehow to brush and sponge my coat and get the worst of the muck off it. It wasn't a disgrace anymore, it just looked like a much older coat than it was, and one that had been worn in the country.

"No, it's not that, though these shoes really won't do. I have a present for Aunt Katherine. I brought it from Switzerland."

"What is it?" Uncle Carmichael asked.

"You'll think it's terribly silly, but it's a cuckoo clock. It's just the sort of thing she'd love and think was really special."

Uncle Carmichael sighed. "If we call at the Maynards', you'll disappear off with Betsy and I'll have to give Mrs. Maynard a piece of my mind for the way she abandoned you, and half the day will be gone before we're out of London. Why don't you tell your aunt Katherine about it today and send it on to her by post?"

"Look at these slippers," I said, thrusting my foot out.

He peered at them doubtfully, then sighed. "We'll have to be very quick."

The car was waiting, a staid old black police Bentley. It always was, and I'd have been surprised to see anything different. This was just like the car in which Uncle Carmichael and my father had driven into Hampshire, on which drive my father had confessed to liking primroses and having an aunt who lived in Kent. I don't know why this had become so significant to Uncle Carmichael, because I could think of lots of things Dad liked more, such as a good pint of bitter, or a plate of steak and chips, or a sing-along at the panto. Uncle Carmichael always drove himself, and I sat in the front seat. When I was nine and we did this for the first time, I was quite excited about that. I remembered how my feet hadn't reached the floor. Now, I had to put the seat back a little to make room for my legs.

We wove our way through the London traffic to the Maynards' house, Uncle Carmichael muttering about wasting time and routes to Maidstone all the way. The funny thing was that I knew once we were out of London he'd cheer up, even though he always said he liked the north best.

"Do you want to move back to the Maynards'?" he asked, turning down Park Lane behind a big red bus. "You can stay at the flat if you prefer."

"Mrs. Maynard is supposed to present me next Tuesday evening," I said, remembering guiltily that I'd missed a fitting for my Court dress. "If I'm doing the whole deb thing and coming out, I have to stay with her. Besides, Betsy needs me."

A taxi cut in front of us; Uncle Carmichael braked hard. "I hate this London traffic," he muttered. "What do you want, Elvira? Do you want to be a deb?"

"Well, it's what girls do, isn't it? And I'm so close now, it would seem silly to stop at this point." I had already said that Betsy needed me, so I didn't say it again, but that's what was in my mind. She had looked so desperate. "What's really important to me, what

I'm really looking forward to, is Oxford, but that doesn't start until October. I may as well do this properly over the summer first."

"All right then," he said, pulling up in front of the Maynards' house. I jumped out and ran up the stairs to ring the bell. Goldfarb came and opened it, of course. "Miss Elvira," he said, unbending a little from his usual hyper-correct butler manner to smile. He remembered me as a child, of course. "I'm glad to see you're well."

"I'm very well," I said. "I'm going to run up to my room to get some things, and then look in on Miss Betsy if she's awake. Is Mrs. Maynard receiving? Because if she is, my uncle would like a word with her."

By this time, Uncle Carmichael had locked the car and was standing beside me. Goldfarb nodded to him. "Your card, sir?"

Uncle Carmichael handed Goldfarb a card, and I slipped in and ran upstairs to my room and shut the door. Olive or one of the other maids had hung up the clothes Betsy and I had left draped on the bed. I flung off everything, dropping it in neglectful heaps, and opened the wardrobe. Tweeds would be ideal for a day in the country, and fortunately I had another good set. The heathery ones had come from Edinburgh, and the mossy ones from Perth, but I'd bought them both in London. I looked at them, then thrust them back into the wardrobe. The sun was shining and I wasn't going to that kind of country. I took out a very simple dress I'd had made in Geneva the summer before, one of the few things Betsy and I didn't have to match. It was cream cotton, sprigged all over in a tiny pattern with little blue flowers. I'd fallen in love with the material and had the dress made up. It wasn't quite as long or as full as it should have been, for this year, but neither Uncle Carmichael nor Aunt Katherine were likely to notice. It felt cool and fresh and I put a blue ribbon on my boater and stuck that on top of my head.

I pulled on nylons and glanced at myself in the wardrobe mirror. I put my face on quickly; powder, eyes, just a dab of blusher. My favorite lipstick had been in my bag, so I had to use a redder one, but it looked all right. I took the cuckoo clock box out of the wardrobe. Then I couldn't put it off any longer and went down the corridor to Betsy's room.

I didn't knock, in case she was asleep, just opened the door and peered around it like a housemaid. Her arm was in plaster from shoulder to fingertips, and fixed in a kind of sling thing to support it. She wasn't asleep, but she wasn't doing anything either, just staring straight ahead at the pink cabbages on the wallpaper, or maybe at our formal Invitations to the Presentation that were propped on her mantelpiece. She looked over at the door when I slipped in, and her face just crumpled up with relief. "I'm all right, Bets," I said, slipping in and closing the door. "But how about you? You look as if you've been in the wars."

"Both the bones in the lower part of my arm are broken. The doctor said they made an *S* shape on the x-ray. They had to operate to get them back where they're supposed to go. This huge plaster is to keep everything in position." She looked dubiously at it. "It has to stay on for two weeks, then there'll be a lighter plaster probably for another month or six weeks, they say."

"You poor old thing." I kissed her cheek. "Does it hurt much?"

"Right after it happened it hurt like billy-o, and when I was in the hospital having it messed with, x-rayed and things, before they knocked me out to operate. But now it just aches, and kind of itches in a funny way. They've given me tablets, and stuff to make me sleep in this funny position, and that helps. But it's not so bad."

I perched on the chair at the side of the bed. "How did it happen?"

"Oh, I slipped and put it out to save myself and it just snapped. Sir Alan was very good, he got me to the car and to hospital. Then he phoned Mummy. But what about you? We thought you'd come home in a taxi. We had no idea you were missing practically until we got back."

I took a deep breath and gave her the summary. "I got swept up with rioters and they put me in a cell. It was pretty grim, but Uncle Carmichael got me out all right. The problem is, and I'm terribly sorry, but they took my bag, and your pearls are in it. I don't expect your mother is going to come in and check your jewelry box, but try to think of something if she does before I get them back."

"The pearls don't matter. Mummy won't check, and if she does I can say I was wearing them and they broke," Betsy said, airily.

"Uncle Carmichael says he can get the bag back, so don't say anything that would mean they were really lost. But I don't know how long it'll take."

"Don't worry about it," she said. "I'll say they slipped down the side of the sofa. More important is, we missed our fittings."

"Are we still going to be presented, with your arm like that?" I asked. "Couldn't we put it off until one of the later Courts? They go on until June, after all."

"Mummy said it would be hard to rearrange this late in the day, and that it isn't discreditable to have an accident and besides the sling might get me some sympathy attention." Betsy looked pale and miserable. "I begged her to put it off, actually, but she wouldn't have it. She thinks it isn't as important now to make a good impression. She seems to think Sir Alan will be bound to marry me now he's let me get my arm broken—and he really was very good and attentive during all the fuss."

"But you don't like him any better?" I asked.

"I do, actually, though not at all in a marrying way. He seemed much more human, fussing with doctors and trying to get hold of Mummy and all of that. He was really concerned about the x-ray. He didn't leave until after I'd come round from the anesthetic. I still don't find him the slightest bit attractive, that beard, ugh, but he made a marvelous buffer with Mummy during all the hospital stuff." She sighed. "It would be a terrible reason to marry someone, wouldn't it, because I liked them better than Mummy?"

"Do you think he likes you?"

"I don't think he has the slightest idea who I am," Betsy said, and bit her lip the way she does when she's afraid she might cry.

"Look, I have to go," I said. "Uncle Carmichael's downstairs talking to your mother. He's taking me to Kent to see primroses and give the clock to my aunt. I'll be back tonight, and we can have a proper chin-wag then."

She smiled a little at the old-fashioned word. "I'm so glad you're coming back. I was afraid your uncle would say we hadn't taken proper care of you."

"He did say that, but I said I wanted to come back anyway," I said. "Don't worry, Elizabeth, it'll all come out all right. Just don't let your mother know about the pearls."

"Never mind piglets, she'd have a whole pig," Betsy said. "But she won't know. Have you got the cuckoo clock there?"

"Over by the door. Even though it's silly, she'll love it. It's just the sort of thing that would appeal to her."

Betsy smiled, and I picked the clock up. "See you later," she said.

I wanted to reassure her again that everything would be all right, but I couldn't quite bring myself to it, so I just smiled and said good-bye and went off to find Uncle Carmichael.

10

As the car swept along the raised autobahn past Maidstone there was a moment when all Kent spread out before them like a banquet. Carmichael always looked out for that first glimpse, when the patchwork of fields, the hedges, the round stone towers of the oasthouses, and the incredible green of the English countryside in spring came together to make a vista. He remembered the first time he saw it like that, the year the autobahn was finished. Elvira had been twelve, and she'd said if it had been an ordinary sort of road they'd have put up signs and a stopping place for people to take photographs and a little stall selling whelks and ice cream. The autobahn permitted no such lingering; it forced you on at speed in a straight line from London to Folkestone and Dover, where boats left regularly for the Continent. They were talking about building a tunnel from Folkestone to Dieppe, but Carmichael didn't think anything would come of it. Besides, when he thought about his own escape from Dunkirk, it struck him as like digging a tunnel under the moat. Britain might be best friends with the Continent these days, but plenty of people hadn't forgotten 1940, or 1914, or 1810 for that matter.

They needed to leave the elevated road at the next exit, and Carmichael signaled to change lanes. "I'll be glad to be in the country rather than just looking down at it," Elvira said. "I saw it from on top when we came back from Paris last week. The oasthouses look like toys from the observation deck."

"I'll be relieved to drive a little slower," Carmichael admitted. He didn't often drive himself, and had found both the London traffic and the high speeds of the autobahn trying. "They didn't even have this kind of road when I learned to drive."

Elvira laughed. "You talk as if you're a hundred years old, Uncle Carmichael, and you're not even forty."

"How do you know how old I am?"

"I asked Jack." She giggled. "Servants always know everything."

Carmichael couldn't smile. Keeping his love for Jack hidden from Elvira had been a constant heartache since he took over responsibility for her. He dreaded her finding out and her affection for him turning to disgust.

They turned off the old Maidstone road down a country lane, between hedgerows of hazel and hawthorn. "Might be some primroses soon," Carmichael said. He stole a glance at Elvira. She was eighteen; not a child any longer but nor was she quite grown up. She looked summery and fresh in her pretty straw hat. She had come to mean a lot to him, the child he would never have, the last of Royston, and her own self, so clever, so pretty, so brave—and so young and innocent. It tugged at his heart that she had needed pearls and he had not provided them, and it distressed him past endurance that she had been thrown into a cell with Ironsides and could have ended up in a slave camp in Germany. He had established the Inner Watch out of his belief that it shouldn't happen to any innocent, but ten times, a hundred times more it shouldn't happen to Elvira. Elvira should have sunlight and pearls and primroses and a presentation to the Queen, and he would do everything in his power to see that she had them.

He looked at her again. She was smiling out of the window at a

village with a little inn and a duck pond. How little he knew her, after all, how little he could trust her. She had grown up in Normanby's
Britain. She took fascism so much for granted that she went to a
rally for a pleasant evening out. He had wanted to unburden himself to her the night before. He had started to ask why she thought
he had chosen Switzerland for her finishing school and not Germany
or France. But her look of complete puzzlement when he asked her
stopped him. He couldn't tell her about the Inner Watch any more
than he could tell her the truth about Jack. Her world didn't have
room for such things.

"Primroses!" she cried triumphantly, as she spotted the first of
the little yellow flowers in the bank of the hedge.

"Shall we pick some here?" Carmichael asked.

"No, let's go on to Aunt Katherine's and then pick some later,
deeper in the countryside. They'll have more chance of lasting to
get home. But let's stop here and smell them!" She was almost
bouncing in her seat as Carmichael indulgently drew the car to a
halt where the road widened at a white three-barred gate. As soon
as the engine was off, the country quiet swelled to fill their ears.
There was no sound but thrush song and the distant sound of running water.

Elvira got out of the car, disturbing the thrush for a moment
with the metallic clack. She knelt beside the car and thrust her nose
into the little clump of primroses growing where the hedge began
again after the interruption of the gate. Carmichael followed her out
but stood for a moment looking over the gate at the neat little pad-
dock in front of them. Two white horses were munching the grass
contentedly. There was a little spinney on the other side of it, oak
and beech from what he could see. He wondered if there might be a
fox. It looked like good hunting country. A crow in a nearby beech
tree let out a series of caws, puffing itself up like a bellows for each
one.

"Do smell," Elvira said.

Obediently he bent down to the tiny yellow flowers. The light sweet scent, indistinguishable from any distance, became intoxicating once he came within a few inches.

"I kissed my love and I made him mine, the taste of his lips was honey and honey and wine," Elvira sang, picking a little bunch of primroses.

"Honey and honey and wine?" Carmichael asked, teasingly, as he straightened up again. "Is that what they're singing these days? Honey once isn't enough for your generation?" It wouldn't be long now before she'd be singing songs like that in earnest; marrying and having children. What sort of a world would it be for them to grow up in? One with camps and fear, but also with primroses and pretty girls singing in the April sunshine.

"Choruses are supposed to repeat things. Honey and wine always makes me think of the scent of primroses," she said, turning the little bunch in her hand. "Isn't it glorious here? I think I'd almost forgotten how beautiful England could be. The Alps were splendid, of course, breathtaking in a way that this isn't. But this is special, even though it's just ordinary, maybe because it is, just a field and the green of newly unfolded beech leaves, and primroses, and a stream somewhere away down in that little wood."

"Your father felt the same about it," Carmichael said, remembering Royston. "I always thought he was a London man, and he was, London born and bred, but he surprised me one day talking about his Kentish aunt and the primroses." He stopped. "I don't want to bore you. I've told you all this before."

"You have," she said, smiling. "It's good to remember him happy."

"He'd have been so proud of you," Carmichael said. "If only he could see you now."

"I'd have been a very different person if Dad had lived," Elvira said, leaning on the top bar of the gate and staring off into the distance, frowning a little. "I wouldn't have had the advantages I've had. I wouldn't be going to Oxford. I'd be a Cockney girl, out at work by now."

"I've tried my best," Carmichael said, awkwardly. "Your father would have known what to do, and yes, done different things for you. I did the best I could do in his absence."

"You've told me how he was killed, but I've never been there, to Coltham. Do you think we could go there today?"

Carmichael hesitated, surprised. "The present Lord Scott, the son of old Lord Scott, lives there now. I don't think we could just turn up in his drive. If I send an official request we could go another day. I'm sure he'd understand. But there isn't anything to see, beyond the house, and the drive." He hadn't been back since the day Royston was killed. He could picture it now; the house, the roses, Royston's body splayed out and Ogilvie bleating on about dents in the car. He shook his head a little and deliberately looked up into the blue sky where a few tiny clouds seemed to be gathering.

"No, it doesn't matter," Elvira said, and opened her car door again. "Let's get on to Aunt Katherine's."

She was quiet for a while as they wound their way through the lanes, then as they came nearer to her aunt's house she began to exclaim at the silly names of the villages: Monk's Horton, Wormshill, Frinsted, Eltham.

Katherine Pendill, Royston's mother's sister, lived in an old stone farm cottage on the Coltham estate. It was picturesque; a single story, stone and thatch. The pump outside had seemed a quaint touch until Carmichael had realized it was all the plumbing the place had. The old lady was expecting them and flung the door open as the car drove up. "It's like a witch's cottage in a fairy tale," Elvira said. "I always think that when I get here." She jumped out of the car. "Aunt Katherine, how are you?"

"All the better for seeing you," her aunt replied. She was in her seventies, long-widowed, white-haired, and with a long nose and chin. "My, what a big girl you are. You have a look of your father now, though you have your mother's coloring, of course. And how are you, Inspector Carmichael?"

"I'm very well, thank you," Carmichael said, stretching as he clambered out of the car. He did not try to correct her use of his title. He had been an inspector the first time she had met him, and he would remain an inspector forever in her mind. He rather liked it, as he had liked being an inspector.

"Come in, come in," the old lady said. "I've scones ready, and I've saved the last pot of last year's elderberry jam because I know how much you like it."

Inside, the cottage was dark. There was a strong smell of baking in the air. A huge ginger cat was curled up on the best chair, and Mrs. Pendill scolded him until he jumped off and walked with offended dignity to curl up again next to the fireplace. On previous visits Elvira had rushed around examining everything; now she sat down and took a scone and jam and a cup of strong tea. Carmichael accepted the scone but couldn't bring himself to drink the tea.

After the scone, Elvira presented the cuckoo clock, to her aunt's delight and astonishment. It was hideous, Carmichael thought. It looked like a little wooden chalet, covered in fretwork, and the bird came out through the central door. The hands and numbers were scrolled brass, as was the key. Mrs. Pendill hung it in the pride of place over the mantelpiece, wound it, then they all waited for the cuckoo to tell them it was noon.

"Now what are you going to make of her?" Mrs. Pendill unexpectedly asked Carmichael as they waited.

"I'm sorry?" he asked.

"My great-niece. Elvira. She's well grown now, it's time she started a job of work, or settled down and got married. You're not planning to marry her yourself?" The old woman's blue gaze was penetrating.

Elvira blushed, and Carmichael felt his own cheeks heat. "Certainly not. I think of Elvira as my adopted niece," he said, stiffly.

"Good. I wouldn't really hold with that. But I did wonder if that's what you were raising her up for, the way I've sometimes heard about men doing. You're not an old man, and you never have married."

Carmichael had no idea how to answer this, so he said nothing. The cuckoo began to chime in the silence, startling them all. The ginger cat leapt up and ran outside, tail bristling. They all laughed.

"I'm coming out this summer, being presented to the Queen, Auntie," Elvira said.

"You'll meet the young Queen?" her aunt asked. "Well, that's an honor."

"Yes. . . ." Elvira looked tentatively at Carmichael, as if for help. He shrugged. "Then afterwards I'm going to Oxford in the autumn."

"And what will you do there?" her aunt asked.

Elvira looked surprised to be asked, as if to her Oxford was only a university and not a town. "I'll go to college, and learn, of course."

Mrs. Pendill sniffed. "Always a one for your books. But I thought you were finished with school? How can you go to the college? Isn't that for men, and for people of good family?"

"Women have been going to Oxford since the last century," Elvira said. "And you are supposed to be the child of someone who went, but Uncle Carmichael fixed that for me."

"And how long will it take? You're eighteen now; time to think about settling down. Switzerland and cuckoo clocks are all very well, but where's it going to leave you when you get old?"

"If I have my degree, I can always teach. Or I might go into journalism," Elvira said, raising her chin emphatically. "In any case, a degree is four years, and after that I intend to have a career."

The old lady's eyes met Carmichael's past Elvira, and suddenly they were complicit. "Don't you ever mean to marry and have children?" she asked.

"If I meet the right man. But with a degree I'll be able to earn my own living whether or not that happens." She turned to Carmichael. "I know I'm not a rich girl, even though I've been brought up like one since my father died. You've been very kind, as kind as a real uncle could possibly have been."

"Kinder than her own family could have hoped to be," put in Mrs. Pendill.

"I intend to see you properly provided for, Elvira," Carmichael said, taking a gulp of abominable cold tea in his confusion.

"Her idea is better," her aunt said. "Be independent, as so few of us can be these days. I'm seventy-six years old. I was born in the old Queen's day. I remember Queen Victoria visiting Coltham as if it was yesterday. Things have changed, with motorcars and airships and autobahns, but they haven't changed so much when it comes to how people live. I was a servant at the Court until I married. I worked in the stillroom. I know how gentry live. You'll meet the young Queen as I met the old one. Did I tell you what she said to me? She was walking in the garden and she saw me out by the kitchen door, picking parsley. She asked me my name, and I told her, and she asked what I did, and I said I was the stillroom maid. Then she said she'd liked my jam, and then she said, 'Keep on as you have been doing, Katherine, and you'll do very well.' Maybe the young Queen, Queen Elizabeth, will have something to say to you that you can remember all your life."

"Maybe she will," Elvira said. She looked pleadingly at Carmichael.

"I think perhaps we'd better be going," Carmichael said, rescuing her.

The farewells took a long time, and they heard the clock strike again before they emerged from the cottage. The clouds had covered the sun. "I hope it doesn't rain," Elvira said, after she hugged her aunt good-bye.

"It won't rain until tomorrow," Mrs. Pendill said, definitely. "All that education and they didn't teach you how to read the weather?"

Carmichael drove off, with Elvira waving beside him. After a moment she laughed, and he laughed too, and it reminded him of a hundred times with Royston when they had got through a sticky interview and back into the car where they could laugh about it. "You're just like your father," he said.

"I thought I was going to sink through the floor when she asked if you were bringing me up to marry me," Elvira said.

"So did I!" said Carmichael. "The idea had never occurred to me. I'd never even thought that other people might be thinking it."

"I'm sure they're not. Not anyone who hasn't spoken to Queen Victoria, that is." Elvira hesitated. "You know, she's right about it being an honor to meet the Queen. I'd been thinking of it as a ritual and a bit of a chore, but for someone like Aunt Katherine it is an honor, and it should be for us too. I don't know. Sometimes I have no idea what class I belong to or where I ought to belong, but she really is right about that."

"I've met the Queen once or twice," Carmichael said. "She's very nice from what I've seen."

"That's not really the point, is it? What's important is that she's the Queen. Mr. Normanby's the Prime Minister, but she's the one who really matters. He might run the country, but she *is* the country."

"It's next week, isn't it?" he asked.

"Next Tuesday. Poor Betsy will still be in plaster, but her mother wants to go ahead regardless. I don't know how she'll carry her flowers. Maybe they'll let her do without."

A few drops of rain spattered the windscreen. "We'd better get those primroses before they're all soaked," Carmichael said.

"It doesn't really matter about taking them back, not if it's raining. I've got this little bunch anyway. The important thing is that they're growing out here, that England's still here, so beautiful, so green. If it's going to rain, we might as well head back to London. Oh look! This little village is called Ospringe! Do you think it's pronounced like *offspring*, or like *orange*?"

Carmichael turned north at Ospringe, onto the Gravesend road.

11

When we got back to London, Uncle Carmichael took me to Cartier and bought me a string of pearls, much nicer than Betsy's, and the prettiest little lapis-lazuli-and-gold pendant. I thought he'd either forgotten what Aunt Katherine had said or forgiven it, but he insisted on the shop assistant, a frightfully superior young lady, doing up the clasps for me when I tried them on. I'd never thought of him in other than a fatherly way, and I couldn't, not even experimentally. There was some reserve about him that made it seem almost blasphemous. If he had been doing what Aunt Katherine suspected, which she must have got from some horrible Victorian story, I don't think I could have gone through with it. Though if he had, he'd have been a different person and I suppose it would have been different.

"Thank you," I said, as we got back into the car, me clutching the little velvet-lined pouch in its bag. "And thank you for everything, for looking after me since my father died. When I said I wanted a career and to be independent, I don't want you to think I'm ungrateful. It's just that I don't want to be dependent."

"I do understand," he said. "It's harder for a girl than a boy, but you're going the right way about things to my mind, wanting your own life. I'm just glad I can help you do what you want, this Oxford thing. As I said this morning, I think Sergeant Royston would have been very proud of you."

I felt different with him, somehow, as if he'd finally noticed that I'd grown up and wasn't a little girl anymore, and while that was terrific, it was a little bit sad too.

"Will you come to the dinner before the presentation?" I asked, as he pulled up in front of the Maynards' house.

"Next Tuesday?" He frowned as he pulled on the hand brake. "Next Wednesday is the opening of this idiotic peace conference, so every loon in Europe will be in London. I'll be run ragged. But I dare say I can manage dinner. Where is it, the Ritz?"

"The Dorchester," I said. "You're paying for it, you should know."

He turned towards me. "I dare say I am, but I don't argue with what Mrs. Maynard sends me. That's why she was so polite this morning, no doubt. She started to say that you should have stayed with Betsy, but when I pointed out that Betsy should have stayed with you she soon saw my point." He smiled, tightly. "Send me a card. But I'll see you before that. I'll be bringing your handbag over to return Betsy's pearls."

"Mine are much, much nicer," I said, and leaned over to kiss his cheek.

My banged knee twinged a little as I got out of the car, but I covered it, and waved cheerfully as Uncle Carmichael drove off.

Goldfarb opened the door to me. Only Mr. Maynard, as head of the family, had his own front door key. "There are flowers arrived for you, Miss Elvira," he said, as I took off my hat.

"For Betsy, surely?" I was surprised.

"For both of you. Miss Betsy's are in her room, and yours are in the drawing room. I believe Madam would like to see you in there when it's convenient." Goldfarb inclined his head a little in a very regal way.

"Do I have time to freshen up a little and look in on Betsy?" I asked.

"Miss Betsy is sleeping," he said.

I ran upstairs, used the lav and touched up my face, then put my little bunch of primroses into a bud vase in my room, before bracing myself to talk to Mrs. Maynard.

Mr. and Mrs. Maynard were both in the drawing room, along with the biggest bouquet since the Royal wedding. It was mostly carnations, variegated ones, but there were also dog daisies, roses, love-in-a-mist, freesia, and half a dozen other things. It was huge, more than a double armload. It was so big that it had been put in an urn that was normally only used in the ballroom. In April, it was beyond all dreams of extravagance.

"How are you, Elvira, my dear?" Mrs. Maynard asked, smiling one of her insincere smiles and actually getting up and taking my hand. "Sit down, sit down."

"I wasn't hurt, I'm just concerned about poor Betsy," I said, sitting on the sofa beside her.

"The doctors have fixed her up right as rain, don't worry," Mr. Maynard said heartily. "I'm only sorry that when we were so concerned over her we allowed your welfare to slip between the cracks."

I hadn't forgotten the time I'd spent in the police station in Paddington, but I didn't especially hold it against the Maynards. "It was natural that you'd be worried about Betsy. She was injured."

"But you were missing and anything could have happened to you," Mrs. Maynard said. "You shouldn't have separated yourself from Betsy and Sir Alan, that was most foolish. We're all fortunate that the police found you and restored you to your uncle. And apart from Sir Alan, unavoidably, who is practically a member of the family and will not tell, nobody else knows, and nobody else will."

I blinked for a moment at the way she emphasised this last part. Then I realized. I had been out alone and unsupervised overnight.

For a debutante, this was the equivalent of throwing my bonnet over the windmill or declaring open season on myself. My precious virginity could have been threatened, and just the rumor that it could have would be enough to ruin me. For a moment I was horrified. Then I remembered that Mrs. Maynard's poisonous whispers about my background would have ruined whatever chances I might have had in advance, and that I didn't care anyway. "Nothing like that happened," I said.

"Yes, so your uncle assured us. The police were looking after you all the time."

"That's right," I said, though it seemed to me a remarkably twisted view of my time in the cells, especially when I thought of that red-headed officer shoving me.

"Well, that's all right then," Mr. Maynard said, exchanging glances with his wife. "We'll say no more about it, and as far as anyone else is concerned, you were with poor Betsy the whole time. Now how about having a look at your note from Sir Alan?"

There was a sealed envelope among the flowers. I got up and took it. "Miss Royston," it said, correctly, on the outside. Inside it began: "My dear Cinderella." I rolled my eyes. "I'm more sorry than I can say that I didn't manage to get you home before midnight, and that you ran into some trouble. I'm glad to hear it's all sorted out, and, having been sworn to secrecy by Mrs. Maynard, shall of course tell no one. I'm sorry my choice of entertainment—and yours as well—turned so unexpectedly violent. I must assure you I had no idea whatsoever that things would get out of hand so quickly. Elizabeth told me you had taxi-money in your bag, and that in the circumstances would be sure to use it. Nevertheless, and despite her injury, it was very wrong of me to leave you alone in such circumstances. Please accept these flowers with my most sincere apologies, and permit me to hope for a dance with you when next we find ourselves in the same circles. Yours sincerely, Alan Bellingham, Bart."

"It's just an apology," I said.

"He sent a matching bouquet to Betsy," Mrs. Maynard said. "As I said, he's practically one of the family. He hasn't actually proposed, but we have very high hopes. . . ."

"How lovely," I said, smiling brightly. I was not about to steal Betsy's boo, nor betray her secrets to her parents.

"We didn't want you to think . . . ," Mrs. Maynard said, in another of her famous trailing sentences.

"Oh no, I'd never have let any such thought cross my mind," I assured her enthusiastically.

Betsy came down for dinner, looking awfully pale. Her freckles stood out like islands on a map. She didn't eat much, just pushed the food around a little with her right hand. Her father kept encouraging her to take something, but all I actually saw her eat was part of a bread roll and a few grapes. I wanted to show her my pearls and my pendant after dinner, but she said she wanted to sleep so I said I'd study, and in fact fell asleep almost at once.

On Friday morning Nanny woke me, looking sour. "Insisting on you both having your fittings, she is," she said, setting down a cup of tea on my bedside table and drawing back the curtains. It was raining.

"Our fittings?" I asked, yawning, then remembered. "For our Court dresses?"

"Miss Betsy with a broken arm and hardly able to sit up, but Miss Tossie insists that you both go off to have them. What's the sense in it?" Nanny was an elderly woman, with iron gray hair and a rigid deportment. She had been Mrs. Maynard's nanny, and come back to her for Betsy's birth. Betsy always said she had a very soft center and was wonderful with illness and small children. Everyone agreed that she was rather too inclined to continue to treat her erstwhile charges as if they were three years old, but precisely because they once had been, she continued to get away with it. In fairness to Mrs. Maynard, while I'd been delighted to learn that Nanny called her "Tossie," I should record that her baptismal name was Theresa.

"There's no use asking me, Nanny," I said, sitting up and reaching for the tea. "I hoped we'd put the whole thing off until Betsy was better." Nanny had known me for years and had seen my transformation from guttersnipe to young lady. These days she regarded me with a certain amount of limited approval, as if I were a puppy or a kitten Betsy had taken a fancy to and who had been house-trained more successfully than she had feared. She didn't necessarily like me, but she saw I was good for Betsy and that was enough.

"It's not Miss Betsy who's panting to get on with it," Nanny said.

"In a way she is," I said. "Our whole life for years has been leading towards this."

"Then why is she crying into her pillow this morning? And don't tell me it's the pain, she tried that one on me but I'm too canny for her."

"You're cannier than the whole family put together and you know it, thank you, Nanny," I said, jumping out of bed and making for the door.

"Slippers!" Nanny said, sounding thoroughly horrified that I'd contemplate going out of the room without them. I pushed my feet into them, snatched up my teacup, and was off down the corridor towards Betsy's room.

Betsy's room was twice the size of mine, but all the same it was absolutely dominated by the bouquet, twin of mine downstairs even to the urn. I was very glad they hadn't tried to put mine in my room. The primroses were much more to my taste.

Betsy was sitting up in bed, not exactly crying, but wiping her nose in her handkerchief and very red around the eyes. "What's wrong?" I asked. "Nanny is really worried."

"Did she tell you to come?" Betsy asked.

I sat in the bedside chair and settled my teacup on the arm. "Nanny wouldn't do anything so uncouth. She told me you were upset, knowing that of course I'd come. What is it?"

"Mummy had one of her little talks with me last night, and now I can't see how to get out of marrying Sir Alan," she said. "It wouldn't normally make me cry, but it just seemed too much along with the ache and the pills. I kept waking in the night every time I moved, and remembering."

"Your parents can't make you marry him," I said, as reassuringly as I could. "You have to agree. Just keep saying no. Be firm. I'll ask Uncle Carmichael about finding a job for you at the Watch, like you said."

"It's easy for you to say be firm. I realized last night that I'd been secretly hoping I'd meet someone during my season, someone possible—someone with enough money but not an eldest son and not caring a straw about my not being a catch. Someone nice. But now, dragging around this cast, there's no chance of that." Betsy buried her face in her handkerchief.

"You'll just have to tough it out and keep saying no. I hear that Oxford is full of men—eighty percent men. I'll find one for you, nice, and with a preference for redheads, and I'll lure him back here with stories about how wonderful you are."

She smiled, but her eyes were still spilling tears.

"Just keep saying no," I said. I knew how wearing Mrs. Maynard could be.

"Look at the flowers he sent. I almost persuaded myself in the middle of the night that marrying him would be better than living here with Mummy, beard and all." She looked desperate.

"He might be persuaded to shave. But if you don't like him it would be wrong to marry him. Besides, your mother might be counting chickens. He sent me a bouquet every bit as towering. And she explicitly warned me off him in the drawing room yesterday.

Why not have one of your painkillers and see if that helps you feel better about the world?" I smiled, but she didn't smile back.

"Would you draw him off?" she asked.

I almost choked on my tea. "I'll try if you really want me to, but good Lord, Elizabeth, he's a grown man, it's a terrible risk if I make him think I like him. Besides, I don't know if he'd draw. You're the one with the connections, and the settlement. His mother likes your mother, and all that. I don't know that he'd pay any attention to me except to be polite to you." He would though, I thought, remembering his eyes on mine and thinking of his note, but it wouldn't be at all safe. There *was* a funny kind of excitement in the thought. "He might think I'm the kind of girl you don't marry, and that really wouldn't be safe, you know."

"You wouldn't have to marry him, or even be alone with him, just so long as you drew him off me a bit," Betsy said. "And he would draw. He likes you. Mummy said he called you Cinderella in the note. He called me Miss Maynard. She might have warned you off; she was warning me about the danger of you."

"Then your mother read my note somehow, because I didn't tell her that," I said, indignant.

"She steams them open," Betsy said. "She thinks she's the Watch. But will you draw him off? It's the only thing I can think of that might work."

"Well, I'll try if you really want me to, but I'm not very comfortable about it, and if I signal you I want you to stick to me like a limpet!" I said.

"That's such a relief," Betsy said, and smiled her sweetest smile. "Now I'd better get up and have breakfast before we go off to have our Court dresses pinned onto us. Ugh, mint green for me and rose pink for you. I'll look like death warmed up and you'll look feverish. Do you think they'll do me a sling to match?"

"And our trains draped over our arms," I said. "I've only ever worn a train in dancing lessons. At least we know how to curtsey. There's an advertisement in *The Lady* for a place that offers to teach debs how, if they don't already know."

"They say if you smile at the Queen she always smiles back," she said. "Think how stiff her face must get with all that smiling."

"Do we actually get to talk to her?" I asked, thinking about what Aunt Katherine had said about Queen Victoria. It might sound utterly stupid, but before that I hadn't thought about being presented as a case of meeting the Queen, only as a ritual we had to go through.

"There's a hand signal we can give if we particularly want to speak to her. I believe that afterwards she summons those who have given the signal into her drawing room. Then after that she comes out and mingles, and she might come up to any one of us then, of course, when we're all mingling like mad. I don't think you could exactly have a conversation when you're curtseying. Think of everyone being in line behind."

"You're right. It's a funny ritual when you think about it. Your mother can present us because she was presented to Royalty, and so on back to what, William the Conqueror? And I'll be able to present my children, because I was presented, even though I'm not anybody."

Betsy rolled her eyes. "You're you, Elvira Royston, and you should stop being so idiotically diffident about the class thing."

"It does matter. It matters like mad to your mother." I shrugged. "Never mind."

"It won't matter to the Queen. Probably you'll do much better than I will. I always get so nervous at things like that. Still, once it's done it'll be over, and there's nothing but balls and dinners, and if I don't have to worry about evading Sir Alan I think I can endure it."

"I hope so," I said. "And we have a ball tomorrow night, in case you've forgotten; Libby Mitchell's party."

"That's where you can start drawing Sir Alan off," she said at once.

"I'll try, anyway," I said. "I'm a bit apprehensive about this, but oh well." Then I remembered. "Your pearls! I hope we have them back by then. Uncle Carmichael's doing his best, but I don't know how long it'll take."

"I can always wear Aunt Patsy's seed pearl thing, Mummy won't think anything of it. Probably." Betsy frowned. "Well, there's nothing we can do about it anyway. And I can't lend you anything anyway, because she will be there and she will notice."

"You don't have to," I said, pleased. "You were right. Uncle Carmichael took me to Cartier and bought me pearls and a pendant, so I have what I need."

"What are the pearls like?" she asked.

"Like a string of pearls. A single strand, well matched, a little bit pink." Betsy's were a little bit yellow.

"Then if the worst comes to the worst and Mummy insists it's a pearl occasion I can wear your pearls; she's not going to look at them under a microscope, after all."

"I suppose so," I said, somehow reluctant to lend them before I'd had a chance to wear them myself, and knowing this was rank ingratitude after all the times she'd lent me jewelry. I put my teacup down on her bedside table. "I'm off to dress, and then we can enjoy a couple of hours of having pins stuck into us."

"It'll remind me of a confidential chat with Mummy," she said, and we laughed as I went back to my own room.

12

The Watchtower was in a flap when Carmichael arrived in work at ten o'clock on Friday morning, much refreshed after his day in the countryside. Miss Duthie's desk was overflowing and she was pacing the hall awaiting his arrival.

"What's wrong?" he asked at once.

"Lieutenant-Commander Ogilvie wants to see you, and so does Lieutenant-Commander Jacobson, and Captain Hickmott called twice and the Home Office called *six times* for you yesterday, and the *Times* has been calling this morning, and the BBC, and the Prime Minister, and Mr. Penn-Barkis of Scotland Yard, and"—she lowered her voice—"the Duchess of Windsor, if you can believe it."

Carmichael did his best to hold on to his good cheer. "Oh, I believe it. Out of the office for twenty-four hours and I could believe all hell is breaking loose, never mind Wallis Simpson. Give me the list, Miss Duthie, and I'll take care of it. Do you know what any of it is about?"

"I think it mostly has to do with the conference opening, oh, and the arrests, of course." She looked flustered.

"Tell Jacobson and Ogilvie that I'm here, Jacobson first, please."

"Certainly, sir." Miss Duthie pushed back her hair and handed him a neat sheet of paper with a list of calls. "Oh, and today's watchword is *raven,* by the way. And there seems to be a lot of mail this morning, but I haven't opened it yet."

"Well, when you get to it, bring me whatever's urgent. But first, a cup of tea if you wouldn't mind, Miss Duthie?" Carmichael smiled at her encouragingly.

"I'll put the kettle on right away. I was just about to when you came," she said. "But is Elvira, I mean Miss Royston, is she all right?"

"She's perfectly all right, no harm done at all, don't worry. Her friend, Miss Maynard, broke her arm, which is why the Maynards didn't get in touch with us. But she's back there now and everything is fine, don't worry."

"Oh good, that's such a weight off my mind," she said, and disappeared down the corridor towards the kettle.

Carmichael went in and sat down, leaving the door open. He felt a little guilty that he had left her in a state of distress about Elvira all this time. He had thought Sergeant Evans would have told her the news. But then Evans had the discretion he expected in Watch officers.

He looked at his list. Normanby had to be first, regrettably. Hickmott probably wanted clarification on the Duke of Windsor business, and Wallis Simpson—imagine her ringing him!—the same. The BBC and the *Times* very likely wanted comments on something; no doubt Jacobson or Ogilvie would know what. As for Penn-Barkis, he had no idea what his old Chief wanted, but the Prime Minister came first. He picked up the receiver, and suffered through three layers of secretaries, during which time Miss Duthie came back with the tea tray, before Normanby came onto the line.

"Whatever anyone says, we hold our course," the Prime Minister said.

"Yes, Prime Minister," Carmichael said, considerably startled.

"That's all. Good." There was a click as the line disengaged.

Carmichael put the receiver down thoughtfully as Jacobson came in, grinning.

"Tea?" Carmichael asked, pouring his own.

"Not your dishwater, thanks all the same. I don't know how you can stand it."

"Would you like to sit down and tell me what's going on?" Carmichael sipped his tea and looked at Jacobson over the rim of the cup.

Jacobson closed the door and sat down. "Normanby's overstepped. The people are finally getting fed up with all this. It's like *Coriolanus*. The papers, the ordinary papers and the broadsheets, are all full of it. Arresting all those rioters was one thing, sending them off to the camps is another entirely. The *Telegraph* has even raised the question of why we have anything to do with the death camps in the first place."

"The *Telegraph*!" Carmichael said. It was the most conservative and right wing of the daily newspapers; generally, if anything, to the right of the government.

"I really do think he's finally overstepped and people are starting to be outraged at last," Jacobson said. "But why are you frowning?"

Carmichael put down his teacup deliberately. "Because I had news the other night of a coup from the right, led by the Duke of Windsor, to oust Normanby and install him as an absolute monarch, with backing from both the madder Scottites and the people who think Normanby is a moderate and soft on crime because he doesn't send gentile criminals to the camps until their third offense."

Jacobson's smile became a sagging jaw by the time Carmichael had finished his sentence. He closed it with a visible effort. "You think they're behind this British Power movement?"

"It certainly seems so. There is some good news, though. I've discovered a Quaker movement shipping Jews to Zanzibar, and we're going to funnel as much money and as many people their way as we can without being noticed. They're the ones who tipped me off to this Duke of Windsor business."

"That's wonderful!" Jacobson said, his whole face relaxing into a smile in a way Carmichael hadn't seen for a very long time. "That's the best news for months. Years. How many have they got away?"

"They have three ships, which make every trip full. We can help them get more. They've been doing this under our noses and we never had a sniff of it. They must be very good." Carmichael and Jacobson smiled at each other. "But for now we have to concentrate on putting out this British Power fire. I think we have to throw all our weight behind the Prime Minister and also stop the Duke of Windsor from coming into the country, so he can't do anything physically. We are the Watch, we may as well take what advantage we can of that. Better the devil we know. Normanby has a hold on us and a use for us; goodness knows who a new shower would put in, but you could rely on it that we'd be out."

"I had been hoping that this change of heart was the beginning of people stopping being afraid," Jacobson said. "I wouldn't mind being out of a job if that was the case. I could retire and go to the theater every night."

"I'd be delighted myself," Carmichael said.

"But how—," Jacobson began, as there was a knock on the door.

"That will be Ogilvie," he said, as Ogilvie put his head around the door. "Good morning."

"Good morning, Chief," Ogilvie said, cheerfully. "You picked a terrible day to take off, I must say, though not as bad as Lieutenant-Commander Jacobson here, who has chosen to take next Tuesday off."

"Next Tuesday? Why on earth next Tuesday, Jacobson, with the conference due to start on Wednesday?" Carmichael asked.

"Passover," Jacobson said, with a set jaw.

"Oh." Carmichael had only the faintest idea what Passover was, something to do with unleavened bread and the Last Supper? "Nothing wrong with that, Ogilvie, no need to be unpleasant about it."

"Oh, he's our model Jew, sir, we all know that." Ogilvie smiled at Jacobson unconvincingly. On one occasion in 1955 Carmichael had had to call Sergeant Richards to separate his two subordinates.

"Is there anything else, Jacobson?" Carmichael asked.

"A couple of minor things, but they'll wait until this afternoon," Jacobson said, getting up.

"I have the order for the procession ready for your approval," Ogilvie said. "I'm closing off Central London completely from the night before, tripling the security checkpoints so nobody can get in or out without us knowing who they are. Oh, and the Japanese are causing trouble, wanting to go to dodgy nightclubs and to see famous landmarks outside London. But there's a real problem about the Duke of Windsor."

Jacobson, who had been halfway out of the room, lingered in the doorway. Carmichael waved him away. "What about the Duke of Windsor now?" he asked.

"Well, apparently we changed our minds, is that right?" he asked.

"More like we took a little time to decide whether we had an opinion," Carmichael said. "And what we did decide was that we had enough problems without adding in that horrible little man."

"Yes, sir. The Palace apparently expressed the same sort of opinion. But we'd said we could cope at first, and the HO had gone with that, and he was already here before we said firmly enough that we didn't want him."

"Damn," Carmichael said. "Sorry. Go on."

Ogilvie looked down at his notebook. "Well, now his equerry, Captain Hickmott, is trying frantically not to have him deported, which is more awkward, as you can imagine, than not admitting him in the first place, and also the Duchess wants to join him."

"She telephoned me," Carmichael said. "Keep sending a firm no on that one. And as for the Duke, we want a squad on him at all times. I want to know every contact, every word. Get him six of our men as honor guards and a whole surveillance team, I don't care what you scant to get it. I don't want him to drop a crumb on his trousers without us hearing about it. If he so much as orders a whisky, I want to know which."

"Yes, sir," Ogilvie said, making a note. "Why, if I may ask?"

"I think he's tied up with this stupid British Power thing," Carmichael said. "I haven't told the PM yet, and I don't have any proof that would stand up against a Royal Duke, an ex-king for God's sake! But I'm pretty sure he's at the bottom of that one, not any singer from Liverpool."

Ogilvie looked surprised. "I didn't get so much as a sniff of that from the report I did on them."

"I have an informer," Carmichael said.

"Are you sure you can trust him?" Ogilvie asked. "I'm not questioning you, but there has been a tremendous amount of fuss about the deportations, at high levels too. It's somewhere we'd have to be very sure before acting if we didn't want to provoke an outcry."

"Quite. That's why I'm asking you to keep a close eye on him, so that if he does anything at all, we'll know and can stop him right away. I'll have the PM's backing on this. I'd have spoken to him already if I'd known the Duke was in the country."

"Bad day to take off, as I said, sir," Ogilvie said. "Oh well, these things happen. I'll put a squad on him right away, and let you know any developments."

"Where is he, exactly?" Carmichael asked.

"He's staying at the Dorchester Hotel. He has a suite," Ogilvie said, all the details at his fingertips as always.

"If he makes any overt British Power connections there or anywhere, arrest him right away. Throw him in the Tower, that's the procedure. I don't suppose anyone will be really sorry." Carmichael leaned forward. "This is really important. I want it to be your priority."

"Yes, sir."

"Anything else? I do have some other calls I need to make."

Ogilvie hesitated, then said, "Big Wheels won't like this, but we couldn't find the Liverpool singer. He's disappeared completely."

"Damn. Keep looking."

"Yes, sir. We are. One more thing, is it all right if the Jap prince goes to Salisbury?"

Carmichael raised his eyebrows. "I suppose so, but why on earth does he want to?"

"He wants to see Stonehenge. The Japs came up with a whole list of things they want to see, all tourist stuff, but that's the only one that's in an easy day's range of London. No accounting for foreigners, is there, sir?" Ogilvie shook his head in wonder.

"I suppose if you and I went to Japan we'd want to see, well, temples and palaces and things. Stonehenge should be safe enough. Make sure there are people watching him—and the same if they go to restaurants or nightclubs or whatever. He's pretty powerful at home, isn't he? And haven't they sent some general, too?"

"That's right. They've sent very powerful people, because these negotiations are very important to them—all the business about the border, and the proposed buffer states in what used to be Russia." Ogilvie shrugged.

"Well, give them the go-ahead on Stonehenge, but make sure we don't lose track of any of them. They're having dinner with Her Majesty one day soon, they won't run off before that," Carmichael said. "Anything else?"

"If I can leave the procession list with you, I think that's all that's urgent. The total clampdown beforehand begins on Monday night. I thought it best to let no Jews at all in Central London that day. I'll issue our friend Jacobson a special pass for Wednesday, assuming he's back from Passover by then. Pass, Passover, get it?"

"Very funny," Carmichael snarled. "Go and get on with it."

He looked at his list as Miss Duthie came in with the mail. He nodded to her, and she left the neat pile on the corner of his desk. "Any priorities?" he asked.

She smiled. "You should look at all these today, sir, but I don't think there's anything really urgent. Mostly reports. Do you want another pot of tea? You look as if you could do with one."

Carmichael looked down with surprise and saw that his cup was empty. "Yes, thank you," he said, and she scurried off. He should speak to the press, but first to Captain Hickmott, and certainly to Penn-Barkis. He picked up the receiver and dialed the Yard.

Of all the people in the world Carmichael could be said to hate, Chief-Inspector Penn-Barkis of Scotland Yard came second only to Mark Normanby. It had been Penn-Barkis who had personally forced Carmichael to betray everything he believed in. Though these days he was almost as powerful as his old boss, Carmichael still braced himself when he had to speak to him.

"You left a message for me, sir," Carmichael said, when he got through.

"What do you think you're playing at with this Paddington business?" Penn-Barkis said, without pausing for pleasantries. "I have a complaint about you, went straight up through the Met and ended up on my desk. Taking away a suspect into Watch protection who turns out to be your niece or some such nonsense. And now you want to get hold of confiscated property."

"Sergeant Royston's daughter Elvira got caught up in the riot through no fault of her own and I was retrieving her," Carmichael said. Penn-Barkis couldn't resist any opportunity to needle him; he knew that was all there was to it and kept his voice deliberately even. "The so-called suspect property the thugs at Paddington hung on to was her handbag, which contains nothing more suspicious than her purse, lipstick, and a string of pearls. The boys in the Met will have to cut back on their graft this time. We want it back."

"Innocently caught up doesn't seem like half of it. It seems as if she was taken to the rally by one of the chief organizers of the British Power movement."

"Sir Alan Bellingham?" Carmichael put in, inquiringly. "Yes, we're certainly investigating him. The connections are running into some very odd corners. But my ward barely knows him, he's the sweetheart of an old school friend of hers. I'd regard it as a favor if you'd look out for her property, and anything I find out about Bellingham that might have significance to your operation I'll share with you at once—though at the moment it all seems tiresomely political and thoroughly in the Watch's bailiwick. I quite agree that our services should cooperate at the top levels when it's relevant."

Penn-Barkis grunted, and Carmichael smiled to himself. He'd taken the wind out of his sails. "I thought everyone arrested on the British Power side was being sent off to the Continent," he said. "The papers are full of complaints about it."

"Elvira wasn't on the British Power side," Carmichael said.

"Not what it says on the papers on my desk," Penn-Barkis said. "You have her in Watch custody, don't you? Is she in the cells?"

"No," Carmichael said, flatly.

"Well, do you know where she is, who she's seeing?" Penn-Barkis asked impatiently.

"I know exactly where she is. She has nothing to do with anything. I'm intending to release her from nominal custody today." *Bellingham,* Carmichael wrote on his pad.

"I wouldn't do that," Penn-Barkis said. "Not while there's a chance she's important."

"It is the business of the Watch to take care of political—"

"Allegations of corruption in the Watch are something we take

very seriously in Scotland Yard's role of watchdog on all Britain's police forces, including the Watch," Penn-Barkis interrupted. "And
while we're on the subject, there is also the matter of detainees escap-
ing to Ireland, which some allege takes place with Watch connivance."

Carmichael ground his teeth. "You're trying to push me beyond
where I will go, sir," he said. "There is no corruption in the Watch.
Any occasional escapes of detainees, which do happen despite all we
can do, are a red herring. We're talking here about my ward. If I
can't protect my own people, what is my position worth?" I sold out
my integrity for this, you bastard, he thought, at very least I should
be able to protect those I care about.

"No doubt you know best," Penn-Barkis conceded. "But keep her
in custody on the books, and do keep an eye on her. She seems to be
caught up with some very funny people. Who are these Maynards?
Why did she have pearls in her handbag anyway, rather than around
her neck? It all looks suspicious. Watch corruption . . . well. The allegations have been made. We certainly can't let you have the handbag back until we're sure about her. And do let me know if you get
any more on Bellingham."

"Certainly," Carmichael said. "And you should know I'll be
speaking to Mr. Normanby about this."

"You do that," Penn-Barkis agreed silkily.

Carmichael put the phone down. As soon as the heavy black receiver was back on the cradle, he picked up the internal telephone.
"Jacobson?" he said. "If you have a minute, could you get me a dossier
on an Alan Bellingham, Baronet. Anything known, you know the
drill. My ward knows him, and I've just had a tip-off that he might
be one of the British Power boys. Also a friend of his called Sir Mortimer, surname not known, and Mr. and Mrs. Maynard of Belgravia."

"I'll get someone on them right away," Jacobson said. "Reports by
Monday morning?"

"The sooner the better," Carmichael said.

"While you're on the line, what was that about the Duke of Windsor, sir?" Jacobson asked anxiously.

"He's in London. But we're keeping a very close eye on him. Ogilvie's putting a team on him, don't worry. He won't be able to sneeze without us hearing about it."

"Thank you. I'll get the reports up to you as soon as possible, sir," Jacobson said.

Carmichael hung up, took one long breath looking at his Grimshaw print, thought about the papers and the BBC, and decided not to make any more calls until he had had another cup of tea.

13

The fittings took longer than any sensible person would believe possible. The dressmaker managed to simultaneously cluck over Betsy's arm and reassure her that she'd be the most beautiful deb ever. Then she said the same thing to me, while sticking a pin into my hip and warning me not to do without my beauty sleep. I suppose I still wasn't properly caught up after my night in the cells. Her assistants fussed around tacking on drapes of fabric. It took half the morning just getting the trains the right length. It would have been much quicker to have had them made in Paris when we were there anyway, but it wasn't the done thing so naturally we hadn't done it.

We spent the afternoon resting and after dinner played checkers decorously with Mr. Maynard. Life seemed to be resuming its normal pattern.

On Saturday morning, as I looked in vain for the *Times* on the breakfast table, I realized I hadn't seen the papers for days. Usually Betsy and I skimmed the front page and looked at the society pages for pictures of ourselves or our friends "enjoying a joke" the night before. I sat down and buttered myself some chilly toast from the toast rack. I was alone in the breakfast room, save for the disapproving be-ruffed gaze of some Tudor Maynard ancestors. Mr. Maynard had finished eating already and left for whatever it was he did at his office. Mrs. Maynard never came down to breakfast, and Betsy was having a tray in her room. Goldfarb happened to pass through the dining room on his way to do something butlery and mysterious, so I asked him. "Where are the papers, Goldfarb?"

He didn't meet my eye. "I don't think they have been delivered today, Miss Elvira."

"Why ever not?"

"You'll have to ask Madam about that," he said, and glided off noiselessly on his errand. I stared after him in disgust and took the silver cover off the bacon dish.

When I asked Betsy about it later she said that her parents were probably keeping the papers from us because they would be talking about the riot. It seemed quite unnecessary to me. I wanted the gossip pages, not the news. "Anything actually interesting will be in the *Tatler* on Wednesday," Betsy said philosophically. "What can I possibly wear to the ball?"

In the end she wore her blue backless dress, because it was sleeveless as well, which was necessary with her arm in a cast. Nanny insisted she wear her one kid glove on her other hand, and fussed and fussed over the flowers standing up in her hair. Red hair is so very difficult. Every time I saw Betsy going through this kind of thing I felt grateful for my own mousy locks. She ended up with two yellow carnations and a dog daisy. Her mother, fortunately, didn't say a word about her choosing the seed pearl pendant. The backless dress made the most of her figure, and if it showed rather a lot of freckles, that couldn't be helped. Anyway, the sling covered a lot of them.

My own hair swept up rather nicely, for once, and I put one of Sir Alan's pale pink roses in it, one the color of may blossom. I wore my cream silk Parisian dress and my lovely new pearls. I put talcum powder into Betsy's single long glove, and both of mine, and helped her pull hers up. "Sometimes I think dressing to go out is the best part of the evening," she said, frowning at herself critically in the long glass behind her bedroom door.

"You'll enjoy it once you get there, you won't want to come home," Nanny said, in exactly the tone she would have used to a four-year-old reluctant to go to a nursery party.

I spent the early part of the evening rather bored. Even though my season hadn't formally begun, I'd already been to half a dozen balls since I came back from Switzerland. This was only to be expected, because thanks to Mrs. Maynard's formal sponsorship, I was on the 1960 List. The balls were all very similar. They started with a dinner party—well, a number of dinner parties, really, groups of people going to the same ball who were dining together in tens and dozens. Dinner was either at the Maynards' or at one of the other debs' houses, or in one of what my father would have called the posh hotels—the Ritz, the Dorchester, Claridge's, and so on. The good thing about this from our point of view was that the men who came to our dinner party were pretty much obliged to dance with us, which meant, at the beginning of the season when we didn't know anyone, that our cards weren't such an appalling blank as they otherwise would have been. I don't know what the advantage was from the men's point of view. A free dinner, I suppose. In Switzerland I read a German book about an anthropologist spending time with the Hottentots and observing their peculiar customs. I sometimes wondered, as I moved under the chandeliers of another ballroom, what a Hottentot observer would make of ours. I'd picture him sitting tucked up in the corner, black and nearly naked and with a bone through his nose, scribbling away in a notebook. Sometimes I wished he really was there so I could go up and talk to him. I felt that we'd have a lot in common. I didn't really belong here either. I just had better camouflage.

Anyway, after dinner we all went on to the ball, crammed four or five together in black taxis, trying hard not to crush our dresses, timing it carefully to arrive after it had properly started—nobody wanted to be first—but while the hostess was still receiving. Nobody wanted to be late, either. Later in the season Betsy and I would give our own ball, in the Maynards' ballroom, which was being turned out for the purpose. Goldfarb, who had been with the Maynard family since before the War, said it hadn't been used for a ball since Mr. Maynard's youngest sister Diana came out in the glittering season of 1943. I was dreading it, especially standing there shaking everyone's hand as they came in and having to remember all their names.

The balls were all pretty much the same. The rooms were decorated in some way supposed to be thrilling and novel, which never managed to carry it off properly. We'd be formally greeted by the nominal hostess—the deb—and her mother. Then we'd go off to the cloakroom and check our faces and our hair. Usually there'd be a maid there to help with hair, and pin up any hems that had come loose or anything like that. Lady Avril Bellamy once famously trod on her hem dancing and her dress tore right up to her thigh, and the cloakroom maid managed to tack it back up so she kept on dancing all evening and eventually married a marquis. It just goes to show, Nanny said when she told us this story, though she didn't go on to say what it showed. I hope Lady Avril had tipped the cloakroom maid pretty well for that, is all I can say. I always made sure to take half crowns to tip them. It must have been a horrible job. Early on the cloakrooms would be full of debs chattering away nineteen to the dozen, all trying to get the maid's attention. But we could go into the cloakroom at any time, as of course the toilets were in there, and the poor maid often looked frightfully bored if I popped in mid-evening.

After the cloakroom visit we had to go back to the ballroom, where there would be a series of numbered dances, interrupted by one break for refreshments mid-evening, usually at about eleven o'clock. These things went on until one o'clock at least, and later in the season we'd be expected to go to one every night. We were being eased in at the shallow end by going to one or two a week before we were presented.

The dances were grim. There was usually a band butchering the tunes in the corner, though I did go to one ball where they spelled them with a gramophone. You had to find partners for at least some of the dances, and for the refreshments as well, or the evening, for you anyway, was considered a failure. You could be considered a failure too, for that matter. If you spent the evening sitting by your chaperone or hiding in the cloakroom people started calling you a wallflower, and once you got a name as one it was hard to lose it. To succeed as a deb, you had to be able to get men to dance with you. They had to ask you, of course; you couldn't possibly ask them even if they were standing right there. Viola Larkin supposedly asked a man to dance once, a generation ago, and look what happened to her.

Usually, Betsy and I were pretty good at finding partners. We could dance fairly well, because years and years of lessons do eventually pay off. We were also a good team, passing off partners to each other, and generally looking after each other when we weren't dancing, rather than hanging around with Mrs. Maynard, who generally sat against the wall with some of the other chaperones, knitting and talking to her friends. We'd been told in Switzerland that staying with your mother was one of the ways to keep yourself a wallflower, and we'd soon been able to observe this for ourselves. We were lucky that there were two of us. There were some other pairs of sisters or cousins or friends being brought out together, and we always had the advantage. Some of the singleton girls had come up from the country and knew absolutely nobody. Their families were county gentry and they were utterly naïve. If they hadn't been to school or been finished, and some of them hadn't, then they'd never met strangers in their lives, and now they were expected to deal with the haut monde without any training at all. There was one girl we met in the cloakroom of a ball crying her eyes out who had spent pretty much her whole life up to that point doing nothing but breeding dogs and riding to hounds. Mary Carron said (bitchily, but it made us laugh) that it would have been kinder to have left her on her pony and let her marry a groom.

Of course, while you had to be able to get men to dance with you, you weren't supposed to be too friendly with them. You weren't supposed to be "fast," and heaven help you if a rumor got around that you weren't a virgin. You weren't even supposed to have more than two, or at absolute most three, dances with the same man unless you were engaged. You could take refreshments with them, but you weren't supposed to leave the ballroom otherwise. We heard stories about people sneaking off to nightclubs with men and coming back before the end of the ball without their mothers noticing, but if anyone really did and it had been found out, it would have been a total scandal. I think all those stories were from the twenties and thirties when things were more relaxed. (They say Unity Mitford once brought a ferret to a ball hidden in her handbag.) In 1960 we were far more formal and such goings-on were quite beyond the pale. Debs certainly did go to nightclubs, but they didn't sneak out of balls to go to them without their chaperone knowing where they were, unless they wanted to ruin their reputations.

Betsy's broken arm caused a sensation as soon as we arrived. Everyone wanted to commiserate with her and hear all about it, all the girls at least. Libby Mitchell—another Elizabeth, a very pretty and popular deb, our hostess—spent at least ten minutes asking her about it, with the line building up behind. Of course, Betsy couldn't really be expected to dance, and either I'd only been dancing at balls before because men put up with me to dance with Betsy, or everyone thought I'd naturally want to keep her company. I had my dances of obligation with two of the three young men from dinner, neither of them anyone I cared two pins about. The third, Tommy Charteris, said he'd take me down for refreshments instead. There was no sign of Sir Alan, rather to my relief. It had occurred to me that it was going to be hard to pretend to like him while avoiding being alone with him. His friend Sir Mortimer was there, dancing with all the more sophisticated and prettiest debutantes. He opened the ball with Libby Mitchell, who was looking absolutely radiant. He looked very light-footed for such a fat man.

Tommy Charteris did show up to take me down to supper, which was nice, as he was the heir of a marquis, and after all he couldn't help the buck teeth. Once I was sitting down and had my champagne and ice cream he buggered off and talked cricket with Jumbo Wilson, ignoring me entirely. Betsy was on the other side of the room with one of the Farnham twins. One of the chaperones, seeing me there alone, came up to me. She was gray haired and wearing a rather splendid diamond waterfall on a mauve and lace ball dress in the style of about ten years before. "Do you mind if I sit here and join you while I eat this ice?"

"Not at all," I said. "I'm rather glad to have someone to talk to, as the boy who brought me down would rather talk to his old school friend than to me."

She gave them a rapid glance. "Oh, young Charteris? My grandson was at Harrow with him and he tells me he plays for the other team." Seeing I didn't follow this expression, which indeed confused me entirely, she glossed this. "He prefers men to girls. Well, a lot of men do, I suppose, but I mean in bed, not just to talk to in the ballroom."

I looked sideways at Tommy, who wasn't five feet from us in the crowded room, but he hadn't heard because of the general noise level caused by everyone braying at each other. He didn't look any different from the way he had at dinner or when I'd taken his arm to let him bring me down to the supper room. It was hard to imagine him and Jumbo doing whatever it was men did together. They looked so ordinary, bellowing away about England's chances in the Ashes. I knew what girls did together, of course, nobody could go to Arlinghurst without finding that out. Men, though, were still pretty much a mystery to me. I'd had my chances in Switzerland, but unlike Betsy I'd not taken advantage of them.

"You're Mrs. Maynard's protégé, aren't you?" she went on. "I'm Lady Malcolm, Heidi Harnesty's great-aunt. My husband and I are here with Heidi tonight because my niece, her mother, is feeling a little under the weather."

"So early in the season?" I asked.

Lady Malcolm laughed loudly, causing one or two people to look over at us and then away. "I suppose it does grow a little wearing," she said. "So you're bored with all this tiswas? Heidi is thoroughly enjoying all the attention, the little beast."

"Lady Heidi's very popular," I said, truthfully. She was one of the debs whose picture was always appearing in the papers. She was to be presented with us the following week.

Lady Malcolm snorted. "What a waste of time this all is. I came out in 1910, and all this nonsense has hardly changed a bit. Pairing up, two by two, checking the bloodlines. Just like breeding livestock, when you think about it. But you seem a sensible little thing. What's your name?"

"Elvira Royston," I said.

"Oh, of course. I've heard of you. Your uncle is something in the Gestapo, the Watch that is, Bertie always calls it that and I always pick up his bad habits. Sorry, my dear."

"That's quite all right," I said, politely, though I was seething. I always hated it when people called the Watch the Gestapo. "My uncle is Watch Commander, and my father was a policeman, and I suppose you think I'm here under false pretenses, not having the right ancestors."

"Nothing of the kind," she brayed. "Our class has always re-
newed itself with bringing in new blood. Good for you is what I say.
Wasn't your father some kind of hero? I'd positively encourage my
sons to marry you, except that they're both married already, the id-
iots. Would you believe I have five grandchildren?" She smiled dot-
ingly. "They're still a little young for you yet. But this isn't what I
was going to say. I saw you sitting here and I thought perhaps you'd
do me a rather odd favor."

"It depends what it is," I said, cautiously.

"There, I said you were a sensible girl," she said, patting me on
the knee. "You're a pretty girl, and just the type my husband always
went for. You wouldn't believe the grief he's caused me in forty years
of marriage, falling in love with lovely young brunette after lovely
young brunette, but most of them meaning nothing, and in any
case, always coming back. I've got used to it, it's just his way. And
now—he's fifteen years older than me, which didn't seem so much
when I was eighteen and he was thirty-three, but now I'm fifty-eight
and he's seventy-three it does tell. He's in a wheelchair these days,
you know, poor Bertie. Gout. The pain makes him cry out sometimes. I wouldn't wish it on a dog. And he has a dicky heart too, the
doctors say he could just keel over at any moment."

"I'm very sorry to hear it," I said.

"No you're not, and why should you be? Bertie's nothing to
you," she said, and laughed unexpectedly. "But I wanted to ask you
if you'd be so good as to go over and flirt with him a little, if you
find yourself with any spare slots on your dance card. Flirting gal-
lantly is all he can do now, but it does cheer him so much to do it.
After all these years of making myself miserable whenever he had
a new girlfriend, now I can't see how I was ever so foolish. Now I
know I don't have much more time with him, I find I'm prepared
to do whatever it takes to make him happy. What did it take from
me, after all, that he loved them too? He always came home." She

dabbed at her eyes, quite unself-consciously. "So am I asking too much of you, Miss Royston, or would you be a dear good girl and allow a very old man to flirt with you for a minute or two, behind my back, so he can have something new and happy to dream about?"

I don't know what I would have said, but Sir Alan came up behind us before I could answer. "Cinderella," he said. "I was hoping I'd find you here. Oh, Lady Malcolm, how lovely to see you. And how is Lord Malcolm?"

"As well as can be expected," Lady Malcolm said. "I'll leave you with your boo, but do think about what I've asked," she said, getting up and pushing her way through the crowd.

"How are you?" Sir Alan asked.

That was when I wished Betsy hadn't asked me to draw him off. Naturally, I'd have replied that there was nothing wrong with me but that Betsy had a broken arm and was on the other side of the room. With a brief to be nice to him, I couldn't, and my hesitation was immediately apparent. "I'm fine," I said.

It came too late; Sir Alan had decided that I wasn't fine at all. "Would you like to dance, or are you all booked up?" he asked.

"I'd love to dance," I said, emphatically, putting down my champagne glass and getting up. Tommy didn't notice, the pervert, but Betsy gave me a thumbs-up sign from across the room.

Sir Alan took me back to the ballroom and onto the floor. The band were playing one of the newest tunes, a jaunty thing called "Way Up North in Hitlerhavn." We started to waltz decorously enough, though he held me very close. I noticed Mrs. Maynard watching with narrowed eyes as he whirled me around. I looked back at Sir Alan, who was looking at me. I found the way his eyes were precisely at the same height as mine quite disconcerting.

"Your ordeal wasn't too much for you?" he asked. "I was horrified when I heard you'd been taken by the police. One hears the most awful things about them these days, they're quite out of control, it should be looked into."

"Mrs. Maynard says it was fortunate I was looked after by the police," I said.

He laughed. "Did they ask you about me?" he asked.

"I mentioned you. I thought perhaps the title might impress them, but it didn't seem to. I had more luck mentioning my uncle."

"Your uncle?" he asked. "I thought you were an orphan."

"I believe Mrs. Maynard told your mother all about my family," I said, quite sharply, because I was sure he knew.

"Oh, but I never listen to a word my mother says," he said, charmingly, steering me quite expertly around Mary Carron and a great clumping Guards officer.

"My uncle is Watch Commander Carmichael," I said.

Sir Alan missed a step, so it must actually have been a surprise to him. "Good gracious," he said, quite lightly, but his expression was very hard to read. "It seems I have been worrying about you needlessly. They surely wouldn't have held on to someone with such highly placed relatives."

"No," I said, with some satisfaction.

14

As the Caravan Club enclosed them, Carmichael couldn't help wishing that he were anywhere else. The air was blue with smoke. The band were playing the inevitable Cole Porter. The walls were hung with red fabric held in place with golden cords, meant to evoke tents, Morocco, and the mysterious world of the Arabian Nights. Curtains were drawn across most of the alcoves, which offered a certain degree of privacy, but sounds escaped and were not quite drowned by the band. A few couples, all men, were shuffling around the tiny dance floor. Others clustered at the bar. Some were dressed as hideous parodies of women, others were disguised so well Carmichael would hardly have guessed they were men, save for their hands. Most were dressed in ordinary male clothes, respectable enough in their hats and waistcoats, if not for the look in their eyes. Where did they go the rest of the time? Carmichael wondered. Could these men who simpered on Saturday night in the club spend their daily lives as ticket-sellers on the railway, office clerks, shop-keepers, schoolteachers, policemen, like everyone else? Some of them, he knew, would be married. Two men, having negotiated at the bar, went off into one of the alcoves and drew the curtains across. Would their wives, smelling the cat-house perfume on their collars, suspect infidelity and leap to the wrong conclusions? Could they have any lives outside this room, the only place he ever saw them, and could they have imagined that he did?

It wasn't that Carmichael didn't want to make Jack happy. He did. It was just so difficult. Once, when they had been in the army, they had dreamed of having a flat together in privacy where they could close the door to everyone else. They might appear as master and man before the world, but in their own space they would just be Jack and P. A. In their dreams, that had seemed enough, and to Carmichael it was still enough. He was still thankful for the miracle that had brought him Jack. He regretted that they couldn't go out like other people. He would have liked to take Jack to good restaurants, and to Elvira's dinner, to be open before the world like the couples he saw holding hands as they walked down the street on a warm summer evening. But if he couldn't have that, he didn't want this tawdry alternative, the half-life of the bars and clubs where homosexuals gathered furtively, almost all of them speaking mincingly and miming effeminacy in their every gesture. It set his teeth on edge. He didn't identify with them; indeed they repelled him utterly. He would have avoided them even if it had been safe to associate with them. As it was, he would have shunned them like lepers, if not for Jack.

Jack greeted friends and made for the bar, Carmichael staying close behind. Jack wanted to go to Greece and Turkey and he had to deny him. Jack wanted their life to be more open as it became ever more closed. Jack wanted fun and excitement, and the world denied him much of it and Carmichael most of the rest. The Caravan Club, long established and as safe as any such establishment could be, was their compromise. Carmichael came with Jack because otherwise Jack would come alone, as he sometimes did when Carmichael had to work long hours. "I was only having a drink with my friends. I can't sit at home waiting for you every minute with no knowing when you're going to deign to turn up," Jack would say, and every time Carmichael's gorge rose at the thought that Jack might have gone off into the alcoves for a tryst with some of those "friends." He loved Jack, and he trusted him, but Jack felt none of Carmichael's distaste; he felt he belonged among the patrons of the club.

Jack ordered drinks, a cocktail for himself and a whisky and soda for Carmichael, as usual. "Bottoms up!" Jack said, and the barman laughed shrilly, though surely the joke must have worn as thin for him as it had for Carmichael, who sipped his whisky morosely. If they were raided, he thought, it would be best not to run but to hold on to Jack and go out of the front and simply overawe the police presence there with his card. He was almost sure it would work. The Watch were feared even by the Metropolitan Police, usually, until it got to high levels. Penn-Barkis—he didn't want to think about Penn-Barkis, so he downed his whisky and bought another.

"This is nice, isn't it, P. A.?" Jack cajoled.

"Lovely," Carmichael said, resisting the urge to say that they had better whisky at home, and better music too. The band were sawing their way through "Anything Goes." A man dressed quite convincingly as a woman caught Carmichael's eye. It was interesting how men looked older in women's clothes. Seen as a man, Carmichael would have guessed his age as perhaps twenty-two, but as a woman he looked every day of thirty. He wondered if the reverse were true.

"Dance?" the man asked Carmichael. His voice was Cockney and masculine, even though he was consciously trying to lighten and raise it.

"No, thank you," Carmichael said.

"How about you, then?" he asked Jack.

"Do you mind, P. A.?" Jack asked.

"Doesn't own you, does he?" the man asked.

Carmichael wanted to reply that he did, that Jack was his, every square inch of him, but he was here to make Jack happy, so he smiled and said that Jack could certainly dance if he wanted to. He leaned against the bar and watched them. They could have been a conventional couple, and if they were, he would have described them as a forty-year-old man with a thirty-year-old woman, not married, but both very much of the same class.

Class would always come between them, Carmichael knew. Jack's parents kept a fish and chip shop. Jack had left school at eleven and worked in a factory. He had gone from that into the army at the beginning of the War, and become Carmichael's batman. He had almost no formal education, but he loved to read. In the years they had been together he had read far more than Carmichael, who liked to read Maugham or Forster now and then. Jack had no time for fiction, he liked only serious books. He had become almost an expert on Byzantium. But still he felt comfortable in this bar, with people like his new dance partner. He wanted to campaign for homosexual rights, and would have gone on a march once if Carmichael hadn't explained to him the likely fate of the marchers. Carmichael knew what happened if you stuck your neck out. Jack dreamed of utopias. He had risen in the world, but resented the fact that he was stuck where he was.

Carmichael's own family were country squires in the north of Lancashire. His brother looked after his tenants and his sheep with very much the same attitude to all of them. He had married a girl from Carlisle who had a little money from a share in a biscuit factory, so they had more spending money than the family had when Carmichael was a boy. His nephews were at Shrewsbury School. It gave him pleasure to think that he had been able to send Elvira to Arlinghurst, which was better than Shrewsbury—indeed it was widely considered to be the girls' equivalent of Eton. Such distinctions didn't mean much to Jack, but Carmichael couldn't help noticing and adding up the tiny gradations of school and class and income.

It was possible to rise in the world, if you started early enough. Elvira, born the daughter of a sergeant in Scotland Yard, was being presented to the Queen. She could marry a Duke, or become Dean of a great Oxford College. But it was too late for Jack. Yet Jack would never be content with what he had. Carmichael earned a good salary as Watch Commander. He was not rich, and educating Elvira had cost a great deal, not that he begrudged it. What he had he considered as much Jack's as his, but Jack would not see it that way. He had made a will leaving everything between Jack and Elvira, including his insurance policies. He expected to live for years, yet, but you never knew. There had been assassination attempts, after all.

Just as Carmichael was finishing his whisky and growing morbid, Jack came back from the dance floor, smiling. Carmichael bought him another drink, wincing a little as he pronounced the ridiculous name. Did anyone else still drink cocktails? Jack was getting a little drunk. He put his arm around Carmichael's neck. "Shall we dance?" he asked.

If it wasn't for Jack, Carmichael thought—as he thought at a certain point every time he visited this club, or one of the others like it—he would have had no way to find a partner, ever, without resorting to a place like this. He felt ridiculous as they moved onto the dance floor, conspicuous and pathetic. Jack led, and he stumbled through the steps of the dance, remembering dancing classes in the upstairs room of the Farmers Arms in Lancaster and the pink cheeks and protruding pigtails of fat Lottie Cunningham, who had always been his partner. The dance floor at the Caravan Club was as formal and chaste as those long-ago dance lessons. Except for the gender of the participants it would have been acceptable at any church social evening. "Let's misbehave!" crooned the singer, moving into a new song. Jack winked, and Carmichael tried to smile. It was ten o'clock. In another two hours they could go home.

More people were dancing now, and Carmichael didn't feel quite as if he stood out so conspicuously. A man in a bright pink sweater trod on his foot, and apologized profusely. Carmichael noticed an Oriental dancing with one of the less-plausible-looking men dressed as women. "Just like in Shanghai before the War!" he overheard as they swept past him.

The tune ended, and they stumbled back to the bar. The barman produced more drinks. Carmichael had a beer this time, which came in an old-fashioned pink china pint mug. "I didn't know there were any of these left!" he said. "The last time I saw one of these was when—" He cut himself off. "It must have been about ten years ago in Bethnal Green." He and Royston had been investigating the supposed Irish communist Guerin who had turned out to be an unemployed fitter from Liverpool called Brown. It had been part of the Farthing case. But he wouldn't have talked about it in the bar whatever case it had been. Nobody here knew who he was, and he wanted to keep it that way.

"I've got a *friend* in Bethnal Green," the barman said, stressing the word emphatically.

"Lots of nice pubs down that way," Carmichael said. "Though it's years since I was there. London's like that, isn't it, you keep to your own patch?"

The barman agreed, and explained that he came from Sunderland, where people were much friendlier and got around more, but that he'd been in London since the War. "I was too young for the forces, so I became an ARP warden, they were taking them at seventeen. I trained at home, then they sent me to London because of the Blitz. I spent night after night really thinking we were all going to be blown to bits. I got interested in London, the buildings and districts, because of saving it from burning down, which is funny when you think about it. When Thirkie made the peace in 1941 I took the first job here I was offered, and I've been here ever since. I can still remember how relieved I was that the Blitz was over and the War with it. I couldn't believe I was going to survive to grow up. I remember walking around London with one of my friends, a French boy he was, one of de Gaulle's men who went off to Canada later. He was crying, but I just felt this incredible sense of relief."

"It's much the same for me," Carmichael confided. "I was in the army, and so was my friend." He glanced at Jack, who seemed happy enough talking to a listening coterie. "They kept us in uniform for a while, in case, and then we came out at the same time and I found a job down here. I'm from Lancashire originally."

"I'd have guessed that from your voice," the barman said. "What's the scene like over there?"

"The scene?"

"You know, this sort of thing. Places for people like us to meet. That's one thing where London has Sunderland beaten hollow, if you ask me. That's the other reason why I stayed. There's nowhere homely like this, almost in the open. This club has been here since 1930. It's practically an institution. Oh, we get raided now and then, but the peelers know we don't put up with any rough stuff, or young boys. You need to be a member to get in, and we don't let anyone join who doesn't already know a member. Almost like a real London gentry club." He looked around at the little dance floor and wall hangings proudly.

"There's nothing at all like this in Lancaster as far as I know," Carmichael said. "There's a pub where men are supposed to meet, it's called the Ring O' Bells. Even the communists have their meetings there, can you believe? It's a funny place. Good beer, and a nice garden outside, but if men do meet there, I didn't meet any when I was there. But I was young." It had only been one illicit visit, after he had heard the rumors about it, and the whole time he had been terrified his father or his brother would come in and read his purpose on his face. He had hardly dared look at the other customers in case they were, or were not, interested in him. He had been eighteen and had just left school, where the rules had been different and everyone had been more or less queer.

"You didn't understand how it was done, I don't suppose," the barman said. "But there, I shouldn't be talking to you about this. Your friend will be getting jealous."

Carmichael turned to Jack. He had become the center of a group of enthusiastic talkers, all telling jokes and keeping each other in stitches. Carmichael took his place in the circle, tried to listen, tried to smile in the right places. He sipped his beer slowly and tried not to look at his watch too often.

When he was ready to scream with the sheer tedium, he waited for a pause and leaned over and asked Jack if he wanted to dance again. They were playing a lively tune, one Carmichael didn't know for once. He took Jack in his arms and led—he was better at leading than following—and even though the dance floor was quite crowded they managed to revolve several times before the song came to an end.

"Shall we dance again?" Jack asked.

"If you want to," Carmichael said. All the curtains across the alcoves were drawn, and couples waited at some of them for those inside to be finished so they could go on. The Oriental gentleman came out with a sailor, or perhaps a man half-dressed as a sailor, and they made their way to the bar. The room was filled with more smoke than air, and the red drapes on the walls seemed to pulse in time to the music.

Jack put his hand on Carmichael's cheek, then kissed him.

"Happy anniversary," he said.

15

Really," Sir Alan said, looking at me in a considering way.

Now this bit is going to be hard to explain and I hope I don't make too much of a hash of it. Before this I'd been aware that he had a certain interest in me, and one that was different from the interest he had in Betsy. There were girls you married and girls you didn't, and he'd always looked at me as one of the girls you didn't. There was a sexual element in his attitude that simultaneously attracted and repelled me—that beard!—but now his whole expression changed. He looked very assessing and calculating, and he didn't say anything after that "Really" for what felt like quite a long time, while we carried on dancing quite automatically. Of course, I didn't realize all this entirely at once, on the dance floor. In fact I didn't work half of it out until afterwards when I was talking to Betsy about it. He held me a little bit tighter and said very quietly, "Do you like brandy, Cinderella?"

Of course, I thought he was suggesting we sneak away to a nightclub. "Sir Alan! I can't possibly leave the ball!" I said, in a shocked tone, but not too shocked because I was still trying to draw him off.

"Not before midnight," he said, playfully. "But we wouldn't have to leave the ball. I happen to know there's a bar set up in the card

room, where Sir John Mitchell is sitting, and where most of the gentlemen, and more than a few of the young ladies, have been with-
drawing for a few moments for a little liquid refreshment. I saw you
drinking champagne downstairs, so I know you're not a teetotaler."

"Certainly not," I said. Nobody had ever suggested that I was
a prude. "I suppose I could drink brandy, though I never have." I'd
had it with lemon in tea when I had colds and thought it very nasty,
but I didn't think that should count. At least it wasn't beer.

"Come along then," he said, and steered me off the dance floor and
through an archway into another room, which had lovely eighteenth-
century white molding but was empty. The Mitchells certainly had a
lovely house. We went on through a heavy paneled door into another
room. There were four green baize tables set up for bridge, three of
them occupied. The players were all men—all fathers, I would have
thought from their ages. Lord Malcolm was among them, and I gave
him a smile as we went by. There was a proper bar, on wheels, with a
servant standing behind it, bartending. A handful of younger men,
the kind who were my usual dance partners, were gathered around it.
It might have been true what Sir Alan had said about most of the
young ladies coming in from time to time, but at that moment there
was only one other female in the room, Christine ffoulkes, who I knew
only slightly. She was a hag—not literally! I mean she was a debutante
who has been out for two seasons without getting married. Sir John
Mitchell, who was dummy in one of the bridge games, looked up at
us and smiled as we walked over to the bar together.

"A pair of burning brandies," Sir Alan said to the barman.

The barman, who was probably a footman or something in every-
day life, raised an eyebrow slightly. He took down two little straight
glasses, set them on the bar before us, and filled them to the brim
with pale brown brandy. Then he flicked a cigarette lighter and lit
them both. Little blue flames danced over them. "It's just like Christmas pudding," I said. "Of course, that's brandy too!"

"You are so charming. Now, you mustn't hesitate, you have to down it all at once, or you burn your mouth," Sir Alan said. He picked up his glass and demonstrated, tipping it straight down his throat.

I was afraid, actually, if you want to know, but I didn't hesitate. "Cheers," I said, picked up mine, and tossed it down the same way. It did burn, going down, but I think that was the alcohol more than the flame. I spluttered a little, I couldn't help it. Christine laughed. She sounded drunk, and I noticed that one of the young men had his arm around her waist.

"Well done!" Sir Alan said, encouragingly.

"I'm eighteen, you know, I'm not a child," I said.

"Are you indeed? Well, how about a glass of champagne to cool your throat now," Sir Alan said.

"Are you trying to get me drunk?" I asked.

"Certainly not; nobody could get drunk on one brandy and two glasses of champagne," he said, sounding so surprised that I absolved him, though most boys who were interested did their best to ply the debs with alcohol, as one of them was doing with Christine right now. That had been Betsy's downfall with Kurt, so I'd always been very careful about it. "I just gave you the brandy because I wanted to confirm what I thought about how you felt about taking risks."

The barman poured two glasses of champagne, in flutes, not in the wide flat glasses they were using in the supper room. "Let's sit on the windowsill," Sir Alan said, leading the way across the room.

It wasn't a windowsill but a proper padded window seat, in a deep paneled recess. The window was open at the top, letting in some valuable cool air, but the faded velvet curtains were closed, so I couldn't see out. There was plenty of room for both of us to sit. We were perfectly well chaperoned by the card players and by Christine and her friends at the bar, but nobody could overhear us.

"Now, it seems I should have been listening to my mother for once," Sir Alan said. "You won't mind if I speak frankly, will you, Cinderella? There isn't any other way to say this, and I know you're brave and sensible."

"Certainly, say whatever you like," I said. I might have been a little affected by the alcohol, because I felt friendly and expansive. I liked him calling me brave and sensible, though I knew I wasn't really either of them.

"Mrs. Maynard told my mother that you were a nobody, and I'm afraid I've been treating you rather as if that were true, as if you were, well, a very attractive nobody."

"She said I was *not quite* . . . ," I said. "I overheard. That's what I was doing when you caught me on the stairs with my shoes off."

"Not quite . . . ," Sir Alan echoed. "How vile of her. That's much worse than saying you're of no family, which is true. But you're certainly a lady."

I was pleased that he understood so quickly and felt as I did, though I wasn't really sure he had thought I was a lady before that moment in the ballroom.

"Very well," he went on. "But it seems your uncle is Watch Commander Carmichael, which means she's entirely wrong, you are quite suitable, you're not a nobody after all, whoever your parents were. Now, Mrs. Maynard and my mother would like me to marry Miss Maynard, because they're friends, and because, frankly, she's not going to be that easy to marry off. I have some money, and she has the right sort of background, and I've been letting them go ahead with thinking that, because I do want to marry somebody. I'm twenty-nine, and there is the title to think of, and Rossingham. It is time to think about settling down, and while he *is* having money problems, Maynard still looked as if he could be useful to me. I wasn't at all attracted to Miss Maynard, I think you know that."

He paused and waited for a response, looking directly into my eyes. "Betsy and I are both quite aware of that," I said, drawing myself up and a little away from him.

His eyes widened a little, but he went on. "Now it seems to me that you and I could perhaps help each other out."

I thought he was about to suggest the same thing to me that Betsy had, that I should appear to draw him off so that they could disentangle themselves.

I nodded for him to go on. He leaned a little closer and spoke very quietly so that I had to strain to hear. "This is an awkward thing to say. But it seems I may have slightly overstepped with this British Power thing. I wasn't expecting everything to blow up. I don't expect to be in any real difficulty over it, but you never know. Your uncle's friendship could make a great difference. And as time goes on, who knows, his friendship could be a very valuable thing to a man like myself."

"I'd be happy to introduce you," I said.

He smiled. "You little innocent, you don't have the first idea what I'm talking about, do you?"

I sipped my champagne and tried to look grown-up. He laughed.

"I am under no obligation to Miss Maynard, I have made her no offer, nor has she led me to believe one would be welcome. In so far as her parents think chivalry demands that I propose because to some degree I endangered her at the rally, exactly the same applies to you."

Now I understood him, and he saw immediately that I did.

"How would you like not just to introduce me to your uncle, but to make him one of the family?" he asked. "I want a wife, and you'll suit me personally a great deal better than Betsy Maynard ever would. Would you care to be Lady Bellingham, Cinderella? Would you do me the honor of accepting my hand in marriage?"

"I can't possibly get engaged before I'm presented," I said. Even as I was saying it I knew I didn't want to be engaged to him, or married to him, or to anyone. The thought of being married in my first season and one of the first of the year to be engaged was enticing, and the thought of being Lady Bellingham and taking precedence of Mrs. Maynard was tempting, but none of it would have been compensation for being married to Sir Alan instead of going to Oxford. Oxford lay before me like a vision of punts and green willows and dreaming spires—and more importantly books, and talk about books, and young men who were interested in the same things I was and really liked me. Every girl is supposed to be swept off her feet at her first proposal. We'd even been taught how to deal with it, in Switzerland. But like a lot of Leni's teaching, it wasn't as much practical use as it might have been. There hadn't been anything about how to deal with a man laying things out and making as baldly self-interested an offer as this.

"We could certainly wait a week to make the announcement," Sir Alan said, encouragingly.

"Sir Alan, I'm quite taken aback. I must have time to think," I said. I almost said "This is so sudden," the way girls are always supposed to. It really was sudden, and I really was taken aback. "I don't think I can agree to this. No. I really must decline your very kind offer."

That last sentence was what Leni had told us to say.

"I'll certainly give you time to consider," Sir Alan said. "You don't know what you're saying now, that's clear. Talk to your uncle about it—talk to Miss Maynard if you like, though I'd prefer for obvious reasons that you didn't talk to Mrs. Maynard."

"I wouldn't give her the time of day," I said, without thinking. It was a Cockney expression, and it made him laugh.

"Oh, Cinderella, we could suit each other very well, you know," he said, coaxingly.

"Why do you always call me Cinderella?" I asked. "I don't believe you know my actual name."

"Miss Royston," he said, but I could see from his rueful look that I'd caught him out.

"What's the rest of it?" I pressed. "Good gracious, Sir Alan, do you often propose to girls whose names you don't even know?"

"Ellen? Elspeth?" he ventured. "No. What is it? I always think of you as Cinderella. And you call me Sir Alan, so formal."

"Elvira," I said. I wasn't actually cross about that at all, I thought it was funny, but I was further from agreeing to marry him than I ever had been.

"Elvira, of course. How could I forget something so uncommon?"

"I can't marry you," I said.

"We'll talk about it next week, after you've been presented, and when you've spoken to your uncle," he said. "I hope to take you up on your promise to introduce me to him, whether you accept or not."

"I think you ought to take me back to the ballroom," I said.

"Before midnight, of course, when your carriage turns back into a pumpkin," he said, smoothly.

"Thank you," I said.

"I won't kiss you, as you haven't agreed," he said. "But let me do this." He took a piece of string out of his pocket and before I had any idea what he intended, he took hold of my left hand and used it to measure the circumference of my ring finger. Then he kissed the back of my hand, like d'Artagnan. I'm afraid I just stared at him. My hand tingled when he let it go. Everyone in the room was looking, which I'm sure was what he intended.

"Should I congratulate you, Alan?" Sir John called.

"Not just yet, Sir John," Sir Alan said.

Christine giggled. I stood up and left.

Sir Alan escorted me back to the ballroom without speaking, and took me back to where Mrs. Maynard was sitting. Betsy was sitting by her mother. He bowed to both of them, and moved on. "Why, Sir Alan!" Mrs. Maynard said, but he was gone.

I gave Betsy a look, and I'm sure my cheeks were heated in any case. We ducked out to the cloakroom. We surprised the maid, who was sitting down reading a battered copy of the old scientifiction novel *Nineteen Seventy-Four.* I'd loved that book when I'd found it in the school library, and I'd have loved to have talked to her about it, but she whisked it under a cushion and stood up as soon as she saw us.

I was a little inhibited in the maid's presence, but Betsy didn't seem to notice her. "What happened?" she asked. "You drew him off ever so well."

"A bit too well," I said, powdering my face, which needed it. "He proposed."

"No! Did you accept?"

"I turned him down, and he said he'd ask again after we were presented. I'm not going to marry him! I only drew him off because you asked me to. But if we let him carry on thinking I might until next week, I don't think he could possibly propose to you after that. He practically cut your mother just then."

"Oh, wonderful!" Betsy said, kissing my cheek, and looking as pretty as she ever did. "Thank you so much. I don't know how you did it, but it's simply splendid."

"I want to tell you all about it, when we get home," I said, with a glance at the maid, who was pretending to straighten some cotton-wool tufts in a box. "Couldn't you tell your mother your arm was aching and you needed some medicine so we could get away?"

16

Carmichael had always hated giving press interviews, even when the press only really consisted of newspapers and he had information on a case to give them. Now that the press included the BBC, and what he had to give them was so often propaganda, he hated them ten times worse. Nevertheless he had agreed to go to their Central London location on Sunday evening to be interviewed for the prestigious *This Week* television program. The Prime Minister liked it, and what Normanby commanded, Carmichael did, especially this week. They needed each other.

He sat back in the chair with his eyes closed and allowed the makeup girls to dab at his face with a powder puff, trying not to think about what a fool it made him look. They fussed with him quite impersonally, as if he were a doll. "What do you think, Muriel, a bit more number two under the eyes?" He tried to relax. At least he used to be able to glare at the press and answer or ignore their shouted questions. He could leave when he wanted to leave. Now they had him over a barrel, and before the nation. "Right, sir, that's you ready, do try not to rub your face if you can help it, but we can always touch you up right before you go under if you do."

He opened his eyes and got out of the chair. Jackie Hardcastle, Mr. Bannon's assistant, was waiting. "Oh good, you're ready,

Mr. Carmichael," she said. "Now it'll be going out live, as usual, you're used to that, aren't you, you won't let the camera worry you? The other men this week will be the Japanese general—we couldn't get the prince, and he doesn't speak any English anyway—and the Home Secretary, and the Duke of Windsor. Now we're expecting the focus of the program to be on the peace conference, but the question of the riots is bound to come up, people would wonder otherwise, so be prepared on that one as well."

"The Duke of Windsor!"

"It'll be his first television appearance anywhere," Jackie said proudly. "Quite a coup for Antony."

Who had authorized that? Carmichael tried to smile, and felt the makeup caking his face. "Well, thank you, Jackie, you're very efficient as usual. I don't know what Mr. Bannon would do without you."

She looked down modestly. "I've been with him so many years I really do think he'd have trouble getting by without me now," she admitted. "I've been with him ever since he was an actor manager, you know, long before he got into television."

"I was at *Hamlet*," Carmichael said. He remembered meeting Jackie then, a younger Jackie, but just as efficient and no less harried.

"Oh. Yes, of course you were. Well, you know all about it then. He's never acted since, you know, but he made himself this whole new career. Do try not to be angry with him if he gets the teensiest bit sharp with you about the question of the riots." She looked at him imploringly. "It doesn't do any good with the viewers if you're angry. It doesn't play well."

"You mean Mr. Bannon is going to lacerate me about the riots on camera," Carmichael said. "Thank you for the warning. I know it's not your fault, and I'll cope, don't worry about me. I'll be calm."

Jackie looked dubious, but moved on. "You'll all be sitting there, and you'll all get one introductory question, which after you've answered he won't reply to, so don't make your response a question. Then he'll chat with each of you in turn, but bringing in the others as seems appropriate. The idea is to give the illusion of a quite natural conversation, but if you want to say something when it isn't your turn, signal Antony so the cameras can be ready. Now I can't let you see questions in advance, because he prides himself on being quite spontaneous," she said, glancing down at her notes. "I'm sorry, he hasn't quite decided on the order for today, but you'll probably be first after the opening speeches. Remember, he might ask you something at any time—you can't sneak away after he's done with you. In any case, you have to sit there and remember you might be in view in the back of a shot."

"Of course," he said.

"Come and sit down then, while I go and collect the others," Jackie said. "We've got five minutes if you want a cup of tea or to pop into the lav, but that's all we've got."

"I'm as ready as I'll ever be," Carmichael said, and went obediently through the swinging doors onto the brightly lit set.

The studio was huge. In the center was a rectangle set up to simulate a sitting room, with a Turkey carpet, five wing chairs arranged companionably, and a low table with a pot plant. Around this oasis of supposed normality were huge lights and lines marked with tape. Huge wheeled cameras, each with their operator riding on the back, hovered at all angles. The operators kept shouting to each other in a language that seemed to be largely composed of numbers. Carmichael made his way between them, feeling like a very small David amid an army of hostile Goliaths. Great boom microphones hung in the air above each chair. "And that's the last of the sound checks!" echoed across the room to scattered laughter.

Three of the chairs in the center were empty, but one was occupied by Tibs Cheriton, the Duke of Hampshire and Home Secretary, and another by the Japanese gentleman Carmichael had seen the night before in the Caravan Club. Carmichael blinked and wondered if it really was the same man or if he was being taken in by all Orientals looking alike. "Tibs, General," Carmichael said, quietly, so as not to disturb the sound checks. The General gave a nod that was half a bow. "Nakajima," he said. "And you must be Carmichael. I'm pleased to meet you," he added, in an American drawl. "I think I saw you last night, didn't I, but we haven't met properly."

Carmichael smiled as best he could. "Yes, how nice to meet properly at last. What excellent English you speak."

"I was at Princeton," General Nakajima said.

"Carmichael," Tibs said, beckoning him closer. Tibs had aged well. He, like Carmichael, was known as a confirmed bachelor. As a younger man he had seemed willowy and slightly effeminate, but middle age had given him dignity, and the active life he led, hunting and breeding racehorses, had kept him fit. "I do hope they're not going to interrogate you about the arrests after the riot. It seems to have caused a remarkable amount of difficulty."

"Yes," Carmichael said. He was already sweating under the heat of the lights. "The Prime Minister feels very strongly about it."

"Didn't like being called a cripple," Tibs said, succinctly summing it up. "He shouldn't be so sensitive. Mark is a cripple, he was crippled in a perfectly honorable way. Nothing shameful about it. He should milk it, not try to hide it."

Carmichael thought it would be indiscreet to say anything at all in response to that.

"Anyway, if he does press you, take the law and order line and if necessary I'll help you out," Tibs went on.

"Thank you," Carmichael said. He took his own seat, as indicated to him by one of the hovering directorial assistants. As he sat down, he noticed a huge clock on the wall in front of him, one with a sweeping second hand. Just then Jackie came out from the other side of the set, a smallish dapper middle-aged man beside her. Although he had seen his profile on stamps and his picture in the papers, it took Carmichael a moment to recognize the Duke of Windsor. He took a seat, leaving the large central seat for Bannon. He exchanged wary nods with Tibs, but ignored the others.

Antony Bannon was no less vain as a television personality than he had been as an actor. His hair was silver, and he had a potbelly— he must have been sixty—but he glided into the room with moments to spare as if he were Romeo about to win his Juliet. The director looked at his watch, nodded to Bannon, and started the countdown as Bannon took his place.

As the director's hand fell, Bannon stepped onto the stage, beamed confidently at the camera, and began to speak. "Hello, and welcome to *This Week,* with me, Antony Bannon. And this week, on this Palm Sunday, we have with us four very special guests. Please welcome his royal highness the Duke of Windsor, back in England after a long absence, General Nakajima, head of the Japanese delegation to this week's peace conference, the Home Secretary, his grace the Duke of Hampshire, and the Commander of the Watch, Mr. Carmichael." Carmichael tried to smile when his name was called, knowing the cameras would be pointed in his direction, trying not to pay attention to their movements and angling.

Bannon seated himself gracefully, and turned to the Duke of Windsor.

"So, Your Highness, how does it feel to be back in England after all this time?" Bannon asked, turning his beam full on the Duke.

"Very good. Very good indeed. Nowhere is as green as England in the spring, you know, nowhere in the world. I'm very pleased to be here, I've missed it a great deal. There are a lot of changes, of course, some for the better, and some, well, some adoption of Continental ways that I have to say has surprised me. But I'm certainly very pleased to be back in my own country."

Carmichael thought he sounded more as if he thought he owned the country, but that could have been because he knew about the plot.

"General Nakajima, this is your first visit to England. How do you like it so far?"

"The countryside is mighty pretty," the General said, in his American accent. "And London sure is entertaining. I'm here for the peace conference. The wars are over, at long last. Maybe all the wars are over. We have the Atomic Bomb now, to keep the peace. We've lived through the era of Total War. Maybe now we're entering the era of Total Peace."

Bannon blinked, but kept his composure and turned to Carmichael. "Commander Carmichael, the Watch hasn't been very popular this week, has it?"

Carmichael braced himself to look resolute. "Not very popular, perhaps. It isn't our job to be popular; it's our job to keep the country safe."

"And how do you feel about that, your grace?" Bannon asked Tibs. "Do you feel, as Home Secretary, that the Watch has overstepped itself this week?"

"As Mr. Carmichael said, the Watch acts to keep us all safe. And the Watch acts under political oversight, mine and the Prime Minister's. If there's any chance of them overstepping the line, we rein them in as soon as we can."

Thanks for that vote of confidence, Tibs, Carmichael thought. Bannon turned to him again.

"Rioting in Central London isn't what we've come to expect, though, is it?" Bannon asked. "Windows smashed in Oxford Street, nine deaths, numerous injuries—how did that happen?"

Carmichael hoped his sweat didn't show, as all the huge blind eyes of the cameras seemed to turn to him. "The Ironsides rally had all the proper permits. Such rallies have been taking place in London since 1931, and the last time we had any real problem with violence or rioting at one was in 1952. We had no reason to expect anything would be different last Tuesday. The Metropolitan Police granted the permits without hesitation. These rallies and torchlit parades are a normal part of London life. We believe that what happened was a small number of agitators—who have been dealt with severely—worked quite hard to turn a peaceful happy event into a riot."

"So this was an aberration caused by agitators?" Bannon asked, smiling and looking quite friendly.

"I believe so, yes, probably to cause trouble in advance of the peace conference." Carmichael smiled at the General, who smiled back. "Order was restored quite quickly, and the agitators dealt with."

Bannon smiled again, sharklike. "But the way those agitators have been dealt with has also been causing problems, hasn't it? Many people say those arrested were not agitators but ordinary British people, their families and friends, who were caught up by mistake. They don't want them sent off to the camps on the Continent like criminals."

"Then their relatives and friends shouldn't have crossed the law," Carmichael said. "Innocent people were arrested in the heat of the moment, certainly, and we have screened and are screening the suspects very closely to separate the sheep from the goats. By now, most of the sheep are back on the streets of London. Only the goats are getting what they deserve."

"The scapegoats," the Duke of Windsor interrupted. Cameras abandoned Carmichael and swung around to catch him. "One of the things that surprised me on my return was that England was resorting to shipping off her criminals and her Jews to the camps on the Continent; often, as in this case, without even a trial, instead of dealing with them ourselves at home. Is this in our great tradition of justice?"

"Would it be all right if I answered that, Mr. Bannon?" Tibs asked, giving the cameras time to come back to him. "We in Her Majesty's Government also have some concern about the ethics of sending our criminals off to work camps on the Continent. The idea of prison camps seemed a much more humane idea than hanging, or even life imprisonment, and when the Reich first offered to let us use their facilities we jumped at the chance. We inherited prisons that were unsanitary and overcrowded, and once someone had become an offender they were able to contribute nothing more to society. In the camps they work until they die. But as the Duke of Windsor has suggested, there was something a little un-English in shipping them off overseas. This was always intended to be a temporary solution. So we have been building our own facility, at Gravesend in Kent, which will be finished by the end of this year, which we expect to be able to meet all our needs, and to be just as efficient as any other such camp."

Tibs beamed. Bannon and the Duke of Windsor looked rather taken aback. "So we'll have our own concentration camp?" Bannon asked.

"That's right. We invented them, you know, in the Boer War."

"Well, well," Bannon said. "That was something of a bombshell. And speaking of bombs, General Nakajima, do you really expect the Atomic Bomb to keep the peace? So far it seems to have devastated Russia."

"Parts of the former USSR will glow in the dark for many years to come," General Nakajima agreed. "But now that the bomb has been used, it'll never need to be used again. The threat is enough. Nobody would be foolish enough to risk annihilation by going to war with a nation that has it, and very soon all nations will have it. We're entering the era of Total Peace, as I said before."

"But for now, only the Third Reich have it," Bannon said.

"You're wrong there, Mr. Bannon," the General said. "Imperial

Japan has it, and I'd be surprised if the Great British Empire doesn't have it too. Isn't that so, Duke?"

Tibs, appealed to, blinked. "I'm afraid I can't answer that," he said. "Classified information."

"No, you're making a mistake there," the General said, leaning back in his chair comfortably. "The thing with the Atomic Bomb is to be perfectly open about having it, so that everyone knows what they're dealing with. Now say just for example that we wanted to capture Singapore, or Hong Kong. If we know you have the bomb, why then we might well hold back in case you dropped it on Tokyo. Likewise if you wanted Shanghai or Manila, you wouldn't just snap it up if you knew we could take out London."

"There could still be wars between smaller powers," Bannon ventured.

"There certainly could, until they all develop their own atomic program," Nakajima said, smiling. "And there could be wars between the greater powers and the smaller powers, just as long as spheres of influence were clearly understood so that nobody accidentally trod on the toes of one of the other great powers. That's one of the things I expect we're going to be talking about at this peace conference, spheres of influence. That's one of the reasons it's so important, and why the Emperor has sent his son so we can make binding agreements. That's probably the most important thing we're going to be discussing after settling the borders. For instance, how would Great Britain feel if we were interested in, say, Hawaii? Or San Francisco? The East-Asian Co-Prosperity Sphere trades a great deal with the west coast of the USA. The United States have been at war with us and with you in the last generation. We both beat them, but let them survive. They're weak. President Yolen can't keep proper control. Maybe it's time to carve them up between us, as Russia is being carved between us and the Reich. Or maybe not. That's the kind of thing we're going to be discussing." He beamed.

Bannon turned to the Duke of Windsor. "Your Highness, you're here for the peace conference too; do you feel the same way?"

"I know that Britain has always been great, and always will be great. The way she rules the waves may change, new technologies arise—we don't still use the weapons of Drake's day, and new weapons always mean new tactics. But we will always rule the waves. When I was a baby, a photograph was taken of Queen Victoria, who was my great-grandmother, holding me in her arms. On either side of the chair stood my father and my grandfather, the future George V and Edward VII. That picture represented four generations of England's monarchs. We've been here a long time, and we've been great for a long time, and we'll carry on being great. The world has been devastated by war, but we've stood firm. Now we may be entering a new era, as the General here says. I don't know. But I do agree with him on one thing. The world needs strong leaders. Too often great countries wither away because they're led by women and weaklings. Compromises get made. That must never happen to us. Britain must stay strong, must remain Britain, must keep her place in the world."

"Well, this has all been very interesting, and it's about time to wrap up now," Bannon said, with a rapid glance at the clock and the gesticulating director. "Thank you everyone, you've given us all a great deal to think about. I don't know if we really are entering a new era, but I'll be here again next Sunday with another selection of guests, so that's all from *This Week,* until next week."

The red lights on the cameras went off, and so did the brightest of the overhead lights, leaving the room seeming almost dark. Bannon mopped his face. "We haven't had as many revelations as that on the show for some time," he said. "Thank you, everybody."

17

Mrs. Maynard was sleepy, so she wasn't at all reluctant to leave the ball. She looked down her nose at me as we got into the car, but I was used to that. When we got home, Nanny helped us undress, then Betsy and I talked half the night. What we decided was that I couldn't keep on saying no without Sir Alan believing it, but that it had probably already gone far enough to stop him being able to propose to Betsy. She was delighted. I, on the other hand, was confused. I didn't want to marry him for the triumph of it, or even to be a lady, but I was thrilled he'd proposed, that I'd had the possibility of all of that. I would have fallen asleep in Betsy's room, which I had plenty of times before, but she shooed me out because of her arm. Even in my own bed I slept badly. I kept waking out of complicated dreams in which one of us was getting married, or being crushed in the riot, and sometimes both at once, walking up the aisle and slipping and being trampled and "Here Comes the Bride" turning to the pretty song the British Power man had sung.

I woke ridiculously late. They usually let us sleep in on days after balls, only waking us if there was a luncheon party. I got up slowly, yawning, and smiled at my little vase of primroses as I pulled on my nylons. I was much too late for breakfast, and as I buckled my watch on I realized I was only just in time for lunch. I rushed downstairs and took my place at the table. Betsy wasn't there. Mr. Maynard grunted, and Mrs. Maynard glared at me. I wasn't aware of having done anything extra awful, so I ate my lunch quietly—roast lamb and mint sauce, since it was Sunday. "How's Betsy?" I asked over the apple crumble and custard. "I haven't seen her this morning."

"She's still sleeping," Mrs. Maynard said.

"We both missed church then," I said, thinking that I had worked out what was making her so unreasonably cross. "We'll have to go to evensong."

"There's a very nice sung evensong at St. Luke's," Mr. Maynard said. "I might stroll down with you myself before dinner."

Mrs. Maynard did not stop glaring, and Sunday morning church wasn't obligatory in London anyway, not for people like us, so it couldn't have been that. I found out what I'd done when we moved into the drawing room for coffee. Another enormous bouquet had arrived for me from Sir Alan—and on a Sunday! This one consisted entirely of roses. He did have the good sense to have made them mixed colors, to make the message slightly less unsubtle, but even so it was an unmistakable declaration. The card, which I knew Mrs. Maynard would have seen already, read "To my dear Cinderella, after the ball. I am waiting with your slipper. —Alan." She glared at me while I read it.

"Did Sir Alan send Betsy more flowers too?" I asked.

"A posy of anemones," Mrs. Maynard said. That was far more the usual kind of floral tribute.

I wasn't going to sit there and be glared at all afternoon, so I went back to my room and sprawled on the bed to read. I couldn't settle to any of my serious books for Oxford, so I reread Alice Davey's *Beau Homme Sans Merci*. Betsy came in just as I was getting to the part with the wild drive through the night to the Kentucky border. I put it down with hardly a pang and got up to hug her. "I think I don't have to draw him off anymore," I said. "He's sent me a huge thing of roses and you a little posy, and your mother is fuming."

"She also wants to know where my pearls are," Betsy said. "Nanny told her they were missing."

"Do you want mine, quickly?" I asked, going over to the little Cartier box where I was still keeping them.

"She might know the difference if she was already suspicious, and Nanny certainly would. I told her I lost them in the riot, that they were in my pocket and fell out, and she's scolded me for that and for the Sir Alan thing. She accused me of not making a push for him and letting you grab him under my nose."

"Well, you didn't make a push," I said. "You knew it would upset her."

"It's just so uncomfortable when she is upset . . . ," she said.

We went to evensong at St. Luke's with Mr. Maynard, who talked on the way back about the singing and about other church choirs he had heard. We dressed for dinner. I chose a subdued mauve dress with a scalloped hem. At dinner I tried to keep the choir subject going, asking Mr. Maynard about choirs in school and at Cambridge—he was a Trinity man—but although we did our best, it was anything but a sparkling conversation. Mrs. Maynard glared at me throughout, and Betsy looked as if she might be about to burst into tears.

After dinner, I decided to have it out with Mrs. Maynard. She couldn't hurt me the way she could hurt Betsy—after all, she wasn't my mother. The thought of my own mother, with, according to Aunt Ciss, improbably hennaed hair and painted fingernails, and probably at that moment pulling pints while swapping vulgar stories with her customers, was unexpectedly cheering.

"Mrs. Maynard, have I done something to displease you?" I began. "I couldn't help noticing your disapproving glances."

Mr. Maynard cleared his throat meaningfully.

"Nothing significant, I suppose," Mrs. Maynard said, still glaring, but now at my roses. "I did speak to you about our hopes for Sir Alan in this very room, but it must have slipped your mind in the excitement. . . ."

In this very room, on these very chintz chairs with their lace antimacassars, witnessed by these very flowers, I thought. "I think you have misunderstood," I said.

Mrs. Maynard turned to Mr. Maynard with a dramatic gesture. "We know you're to be Lady Bellingham," he said, embarrassed. "I was at my club this morning and the news was all over." He looked awkwardly at his wife. "I should like to congratulate you on such a splendid match. Sir Alan is a friend and a business associate of mine. And you, of course, being such a close friend of Betsy's and with Mrs. Maynard bringing you out, are almost like another daughter to us."

Mrs. Maynard continued to glare. Betsy was smiling to herself.

"I am not engaged to Sir Alan," I said. "He proposed and I declined."

"Now that's not very likely," Mrs. Maynard burst out.

"Nevertheless, it is the case," I said.

"You'll change your mind," Mr. Maynard said, in a fatherly tone. "Sir Alan is very confident."

"I don't know how you could do this to Betsy!" Mrs. Maynard said.

"Theresa!" Mr. Maynard reproved his wife. "There was no understanding between Betsy and Sir Alan."

"I didn't like him," Betsy said.

At that moment, just as both of her parents were drawing breath to speak, Goldfarb knocked and glided in with the salver. "Some members of the constabulary to see Mr. Maynard and Miss Royston," he said.

I was relieved at the interruption but I couldn't think what they could possibly want with me on a Sunday evening. It wasn't Uncle Carmichael's style to send Watchmen around on his personal errands.

"Send them in," Mr. Maynard said, his eyes flicking to me and then away.

There were three of them, all in uniform; the horrible redhead from Paddington and two others. The redhead's gaze rested on me for a moment, before briefly looking over Betsy and Mrs. Maynard. I felt suddenly quite sick to my stomach, and my throat spasmed. I hadn't thought about the man from Paddington at all; I'd quite deliberately avoided thinking about him ever since I'd been able to get away. "Mr. Maynard, Miss Royston, we believe you might be able to help us in our inquiries. Would you accompany us to the police station?"

"Is this really necessary?" Mr. Maynard asked. There was something strained about his voice, usually so assured. "Can't we answer whatever questions you have here?"

"It would be more convenient if you accompanied us," the redhead said.

I guessed that my ace card had been trumped this time, but I played it anyway. "My uncle, Commander Carmichael of the Watch, will be sure to take a close interest," I said.

"Oh, we know that," the redhead said, and grinned at the older of his two companions.

"We're taking a close interest in him, too," the other man said.

"Commander Carmichael . . . ?" Mr. Maynard asked, as if he didn't believe what he'd just heard.

The policemen didn't reply, just smiled to themselves.

"Are you arresting us?" Mr. Maynard asked. Mrs. Maynard gave a little gasp. I could just see Betsy out of the corner of my eye sitting as still as a statue, with her hands folded as they had been before the policemen came in. "Do you have a warrant?"

"I don't need a warrant to arrest you under the Defence of the Realm Act," the redhead said. "I'll arrest you if you insist, but if you accompany us voluntarily and satisfy us as to your answers then that won't be necessary. Miss Royston is, of course, still technically in custody."

"In Watch custody," I said, thinking of dear old Sergeant Evans. I stood up. It seemed inevitable that we'd have to go, and arguing was only going to make it worse. "I'll come with you, of course. I have nothing to hide."

I wasn't afraid at all. Betsy was, I could tell. She'd gone so pale that her freckles were standing out. Her father kept babbling about his office and my uncle, and I wondered if he was afraid too. Mrs. Maynard just looked frigid, which was one of her ordinary expressions around me, as if she could detect the faint smell of stale fish. The policemen took us out to the car. It wasn't a Black Maria this time, just two ordinary police cars. They put Mr. Maynard into one, still full of bluster, and me into the other. The redheaded policeman from Paddington was in my car. He looked indecently triumphant.

I was expecting them to take me to the notorious Finsbury in Muswell Hill, the huge square jail built especially to receive political prisoners. Instead they drove south, to Scotland Yard. Nobody spoke as we drove. It seemed incongruous that it was light, as it sometimes does when one comes out of a matinee. Arrests were supposed to take place in the darkness, at midnight, not in the early evening.

The car drew up outside the building. We'd lost the other car, the one with Mr. Maynard, somewhere along the way. I hadn't been paying attention. The red-haired man opened the door and as I got out took hold of my elbow. He drew me up the stairs. I found myself remembering something Sergeant Evans had said once, about taking prisoners down into the interrogation cells of the Watch building. "They never see the sky again." I looked up, frantically, at the patch of mackerel sky above, cut by the crenellated rooftops of London. I remembered leaning out of Sir Mortimer's window at sunset a few days before. Then he tugged me on, and I was inside.

The desk sergeant was sitting in a glass cubicle, looking very quaint and postwar. He nodded to my escort. "Royston?" he said, to him, not to me, and made a mark on a paper. "I've seen the warrant. Up to the Chief first."

"Thank you, sergeant," the redhead said, and pulled me, unresisting, towards a lift at the back of the lobby.

The lift went up. Sergeant Evans had been talking about the Watchtower, of course, where a lot of things were underground and bombproof, if there was such a thing as bombproof anymore, after those Atomic Bombs that wiped out Moscow and Miami. I still wasn't really afraid. Everything seemed a little dreamlike. "They never hold out on us," Sergeant Evans had said. "Everyone talks in the end. You don't need to torture them, torture's counterproductive, because they get so desperate they'll make things up to tell you if they think that's what you want to hear. But everyone tells everything in the end."

The lift doors opened, and I wanted to laugh at myself, because there was a huge glass window and a great expanse of sky, with all London below us. The clouds, lit from below by the setting sun, were furrowed like a plowed field. I didn't notice the Chief or the room at all, at first, until he came forward. He was completely bald, rather plump, and had thick eyebrows like a pair of white caterpillars. "Elvira Royston," he said, in a sorrowful tone common to all headmistresses everywhere when one is on the carpet. I put out my hand, but he didn't take it. "I'm Chief-Inspector Penn-Barkis. I remember your father. Very sad, what happened, but line of duty, I suppose, what he would have wanted. At least he didn't live to see this day."

I wanted to giggle, as I had always wanted to giggle in the head-mistress's study back at Arlinghurst. It's partly nerves and partly the over-the-top pomposity of that kind of sentiment. But I was eighteen, not twelve, so I controlled myself. "I have done nothing," I said.

"Belonging to a seditious organization is very far from nothing," he said. "Being engaged to one of the leaders of that organization is very far from nothing. But perhaps you didn't know that?"

"What?" I asked, genuinely confused.

"Come and sit down," he said, in a much gentler voice. I walked over to the desk and sat where he indicated. The redhead sat beside me, and Penn-Barkis sat on the other side of the desk. "Perhaps you didn't know that the British Power movement, also known as the Britain First movement, was a seditious organization?"

"Not until the riot," I said. "But I'm not a member."

"Are you the member of any Ironsides group?" he asked.

"No," I confessed, as if it was a failing.

"But you went along to the rally." Again, his voice took on that "more in sorrow than in anger" tone.

"I already went through all this at Paddington," I said, looking at the redhead, who looked back blankly. "I went to the rally thinking it would be good clean patriotic fun."

"At Paddington you said that Elizabeth Maynard was engaged to Sir Alan Bellingham," the redhead said. "Now we know you are engaged to him yourself. Can you explain this?"

I must have looked horribly guilty, because of course I couldn't explain it sensibly. "I'm not engaged to him," I said. "He did propose to me, but I haven't given him an answer. For one thing I wanted to talk to Miss Maynard."

"Sir Alan certainly seems to think you're engaged. He hasn't put an announcement in the papers, but he's been telling everyone at his club," Penn-Barkis said.

"I don't intend to marry him," I said, which is what I should have said in the first place. I decided to be honest. If everyone talks in the end, why wait? "The fact is that Betsy, Miss Maynard, didn't want to marry him either, and she asked me to lead him on so that he would stop bothering her. I was doing that. Neither of us want to marry him."

Both men looked extremely skeptical. "And why would that be?" the redhead asked.

"Because we don't like him," I said.

"Could you expand on that a little?" Penn-Barkis asked, leaning forward and folding his fingers together. "Why don't you like him?"

"He has that beard," I said. "And besides, there's something I just don't like about him."

"Would that be his connection with British Power?" the redhead asked.

"I don't like that either, but I meant something more subjective."

"You're very anxious to distance yourself from him," Penn-Barkis put in.

Clearly, I thought, Sir Alan was right when he said he might have got in too deep with the British Power thing and need protection, but any protection Uncle Carmichael might have offered would have come too late. "I'm telling the truth," I said.

"So how did you and Miss Maynard come to be associated with him, if neither of you like him?" the redhead asked.

I looked at him incredulously. "Her parents like him. They pretty much insisted she spend time with him. We didn't have much choice in the matter."

"And why do her parents like him? Would that be for his political connections, or for his financial ones?" Penn-Barkis asked.

"I think Lady Bellingham is a friend of Mrs. Maynard's," I said. "And Sir Alan does something with Mr. Maynard, probably financial. I don't know. I expect Mr. Maynard is explaining it all to someone even now."

"No doubt," Penn-Barkis said, steepling his fingers again. "Well, and what is Commander Carmichael's connection with British Power?"

"None," I said. "He was asking me about it after the riot."

"What did he ask you?"

"What you asked me. Why I went, how the riot happened, that kind of thing."

"When the riot began, you were right in front of the rostrum. Why were you there, exactly, rather than somewhere else?" Penn-Barkis asked.

"Sir Alan said that the best music would be there. And he was right, the singer was awfully good, before he started inciting the riot." I thought that might have been the wrong thing to say, because they exchanged significant looks.

"Had you heard him sing before?" the redhead asked.

"No, never." I was sure of that.

"Not in a nightclub? He used to sing in the Blue Nile from time to time," he persisted.

"I've never been to the Blue Nile," I admitted, and I really did feel guilty, because I hated to sound so unsophisticated. "Sir Alan had offered to take us there after the rally, but that never happened."

The two men exchanged a glance. "To return to your so-called uncle, your guardian, Commander Carmichael," Penn-Barkis said. "Do you know of any seditious or criminal activity of his?"

I immediately thought of Mrs. Talbot and the words I'd overheard. "No," I said, quickly, hoping he couldn't read my face.

"And how long have you been aware of his homosexuality?"

"What?" I asked, absolutely flabbergasted. "Uncle Carmichael? Homosexuality?" But in all the years I'd known him I'd never seen him with a woman, or heard so much as a hint of one, I thought. I'd always assumed he was married to his job. I thought of his embarrassment at Aunt Katherine's question, and how absolutely wrong it had felt.

"He and his servant have an intimate relationship," Penn-Barkis sneered. "You didn't know?"

"No," I agreed. "I had no idea." Jack. It made sense of all kinds of things. I was revolted. I screwed my face up, feeling as if I had a bad taste in my mouth.

"So what criminal or seditious activities were you in fact aware of?" Penn-Barkis asked, while my lip was still curling.

18

Drink, Carmichael?" Tibs said, as they wiped the makeup off. The Duke of Windsor had been whisked away, and General Nakajima swallowed up by a group of other Japanese. He sounded quite different speaking Japanese; no longer relaxed and American but vehement and Oriental. "I could certainly do with one."

"Yes, a quick one," Carmichael said. "Somewhere round here? Or I've got a car waiting."

"There's quite a nice pub just down by the river, one with a garden where we could sit outside and watch the boats," Tibs said. "It's one of Guy's haunts, I've been there with him. Poor Guy. His wife's having an affair, you know, and he's dreadfully cut up about it."

"Poor Guy," Carmichael agreed.

"At least we'll never have that kind of problem!" Tibs said, with a conspiratorial smile.

"I suppose not," Carmichael said, wincing inwardly, and wishing he hadn't agreed to a drink.

Tibs led the way out of Broadcasting House and down along the Embankment. "On the whole, I think that went quite well," he said. "Lots of surprises, but we more than held our end up."

"I'm convinced the Duke of Windsor is in with the British Power lot. He made my skin crawl to listen to him," Carmichael said.

"Women and weaklings," Tibs said, as they reached the pub, the Moon Under Water. "That won't go down well with Mark. I hope you're keeping a close eye on him."

Carmichael stopped just outside the door of the pub. "I thought we were," he said. "But I don't know who authorized him to appear on that program. Oh, I don't doubt Bannon asked him in all innocence, I know Bannon, but it would have needed approval from the Ministry of Information, and they should have asked us. The problem is that he has a lot of friends and we don't know how long he's been planning this."

"He's a bit prominent to arrest on the off chance," Tibs said. "Hold on a minute while I get them in."

The interior of the pub was dark after the evening sunlight outside, and Carmichael blinked for a moment as Tibs made for the bar. "Just a half for me," he called. It seemed a nice enough place, quiet on a Sunday evening, some old men playing dominoes in one corner and a few younger men standing by the bar.

"Guy!" Tibs said, delighted. "I half wondered if you'd be here."

"Tibs!" Sir Guy replied, with equal enthusiasm. He sounded drunk.

"Sir Guy," Carmichael said, warily, coming up to the bar and putting out his hand. Sir Guy Braithwaite was the Foreign Secretary, a position he had held for the last two years, since the death of the previous Foreign Secretary, Richard Francis, in a hunting accident. He had been knighted the year before in the Birthday Honours, and was widely seen as a rising star. The Farthing Set tended to be close-knit and didn't give many opportunities to rise. Sir Guy was fast on his feet and made himself useful. Carmichael had done his background checks and knew he had the right background, Eton and Cambridge, but not much money or influence. His father had been no more than a diplomat, not even rising to ambassador.

"Commander Carmichael," Sir Guy said, shaking his hand.

"How nice to see you off duty. I assume you're off duty, as you're in a pub."

"I've been in pubs often enough in the line of duty, but I am off duty tonight," Carmichael said. "Tibs and I have just been on the telly."

"And we need a drink!" Tibs said. "I'll get them, and let's sit outside."

"Is it warm enough?" Sir Guy asked, draining his glass. "I don't normally sit out until June."

"It's a mild night," Carmichael said.

Sir Guy got up and led the way out to the little garden, which was deserted. "Nobody else thinks it's warm enough," he said, sitting down on a chair with his back to the water. "Leave room for Tibs where he can see the boats, that's why he wants to be outside. If he can't look at a horse, he wants to look at a boat. He's always been the same."

"Have you known him a long time?" Carmichael asked, taking another chair. The Thames was very low, and nothing was visible on it at the moment except a little lighter moored on the south bank.

"I was his fag at Eton," Sir Guy said. "I didn't know him much after that, until we were both in politics. He was older than me, and it seems to matter so much more at that age. At Cambridge—well, at Cambridge we were all ready to make a new world. This isn't quite the world I signed on for, if you want to know, but you have to make the best of what you've got." He stared vacantly at nothing. "My tutor at Cambridge was a wonderful chap," he confided.

Tibs reappeared, carrying three large whiskies, which he put down on the table.

"I said a half," Carmichael said, and sighed ruefully.

"You deserve a proper drink after all that," Tibs said.

"Did Bannon put you through it?" Sir Guy asked, sympathetically. "He really grilled me the last time he had me on. It's worse than taking questions in the House!"

"The Duke of Windsor was on with us, and I'm not sure he wasn't talking sedition," Tibs said, sipping his whisky.

"I think he was," Carmichael said. "I don't have any proper evidence, or he'd be in the Tower, but it's a pattern of things, how he was talking, what he's been doing, that riot."

"What did he say?" Sir Guy asked.

"He said that some great countries became less great when they were run by women and weaklings," Tibs said. "Mark won't like that."

"Mark won't like that at all. There are people slowly starving in the death camps of the Reich for saying considerably less than that." Sir Guy shook his head. "Still, he was the King, you know, even if he wasn't crowned. We can't just pack him off to be made into soap like Joe Bloggs."

"We can't just let him go around saying whatever he wants, either. Carmichael thinks he's involved with a conspiracy."

"Do you?" Sir Guy looked at Carmichael intently, suddenly seeming almost sober. "Why?"

Carmichael couldn't tell them about Abby. The trouble with knowledge, he thought, just like power, was applying it in the right place with the right degree of force. "He's supposed to be under tight watch by the Watch," he said. "How did he come to be on *This Week* without anyone asking me, or even telling me? Then is it a coincidence that we have a riot at an Ironsides rally just before he arrives? He has connections with this British Power thing. I'm sure of it. He was saying the same things the British Power spokesman said. And the thing that worries me the most is that he *is* the Duke of Windsor, he *was* the King of England, even if only for five minutes, never mind all that old nonsense about Queen Victoria. The fact is that he knows people and has old connections and we don't know where they run. A lot of people will agree to do things for him because of who he is. He knows top people in organizations. I'm not saying they're traitors, even if he is; I'm saying they're his friends, and they'll do him a favor."

"I put a bit of a spoke in his wheel by mentioning the new Gravesend facility!" Tibs said, and giggled. "British death camps for British Jews!"

"Oh honestly, Tibs," Sir Guy said, disgustedly. "Do grow up. Three of the most powerful men in the country ought to be able to have a serious conversation without one of them giggling like a girl."

"I'm glad you agree we need to clamp down on the Duke of Windsor," Carmichael said, in the awkward silence. "Do you think one of you could talk to the Prime Minister about it?"

"I will, tomorrow," Tibs said. "And as soon as this peace conference nonsense is open, we'll pack him back off to Bermuda. Wednesday, isn't it?"

"The procession is Wednesday—and we're essentially shutting off Central London for it, nobody will be able to be there who hasn't been checked six ways from Sunday," Carmichael said. "The actual conference opens afterwards, with a speech from Her Majesty, followed by formal speeches from the major delegations. The whole thing's being televised."

"I hope the Jap general doesn't come out with the kind of thing he was spouting tonight," Tibs said, taking a large gulp of his whisky. "Britain and Japan should divide America between them. I didn't know where to look."

"Not such a bad idea," Sir Guy said. His glass was empty.

"Maybe worth consideration, but not to say it out loud and frighten the horses! And he said he knew we had the bomb."

"We can't keep that secret forever. The Germans already know," Sir Guy said. "I told you those Japs were trouble. We want a pretty big buffer zone there, I think. They'd be taking it all if they could, Burma, Malaya, India even. We need as big a Scythia as we can talk them into."

"He was certainly talking as if he had no discretion at all," Tibs said.

"Shall I get the other half?" Sir Guy asked.

"I really should get home," Carmichael said.

"Wife waiting for you?" Sir Guy asked. "My wife, Marjorie, she doesn't like it when I'm late. Wonderful woman, Marjorie. I have two sons too, Philip and Benedict. Wonderful boys. At Eton now, of course."

"Commander Carmichael is a confirmed bachelor, just like me," Tibs said.

"Lots of you buggers in politics. But there's no need to rush off then, Carmichael, stay and have the other half," Sir Guy urged.

"I do have somebody waiting at home," Carmichael said, standing. He had said all he wanted to say to these men. He wanted to be home, to be shut away from the world, away from conspiracies and innuendos and the problems of power.

"Well, then," Sir Guy said. "Nice chatting with you like this. Doesn't make any difference if it's a man or a woman, I suppose, keeping them waiting."

"How unbearably tolerant you are," Tibs said, and rolled his eyes at Carmichael, who stood.

"I'll see both you gentlemen soon, no doubt," he said. "Goodbye, thanks for the drink, Tibs."

He walked back to where his car was waiting. "Home," he said to the driver, luxuriating in the word.

The guard at the door of his flats looked uncomfortable. "Any problem, Mike?" he asked.

"Not here, sir, but I'm hearing reports of riots at different places around the country. Bristol, Liverpool, Newcastle."

"That's all we need," Carmichael said. "Thanks, Mike, I'll check into that."

"Yes, sir, thank you, sir," Mike said, and opened the door.

Carmichael took the stairs two at a time. He felt overheated and exhausted. Jack greeted him at the door with a whisky. "I saw the program," he said, and hugged him.

"How did I look? Not making a frightful fool of myself?"

"You did very well, I thought," Jack said. "Do you want this, or should I make you a cup of tea?"

"I had a whisky with Tibs and Sir Guy, after. It was ghastly. I'd love some tea, though. Thank you, Jack. You drink that whisky, now you've poured it."

Jack went off to the kitchen, and Carmichael went into the sitting room and sat down with a sigh. He was just taking his shoes off when Jack came back with the tea tray. "That was quick!"

"I had it ready too," Jack said. "Mrs. Maynard phoned. Twice. The second time she sounded very agitated."

"I don't suppose she said what was wrong?"

"No, just asked for you and asked if you'd call her back urgently."

Carmichael sighed, and dropped his shoes onto the carpet. "The stupid woman didn't call when Elvira was arrested in the riot, and now she wants me urgently and it's probably something ridiculously trivial about dinner on Tuesday or what flowers Elvira's going to carry to be presented."

"I think you'd better call her, P. A.," Jack said, hovering in the doorway. "She really did sound bothered."

"She always sounds bothered," Carmichael said, but he was reaching for the receiver even as he grumbled. All of the things that might have happened to Elvira went through his mind as he dialed, from falling through ice, unlikely on a mild evening in April, to being burned up in a fire.

Mrs. Maynard snatched up the phone on the first ring. "Commander Carmichael?" she asked. "Oh, I'm so glad you called. The most ridiculous thing has happened. Elvira has been arrested again, and so has my husband. They came and took them away just after dinner."

Carmichael heard himself making reassuring noises as if at a long distance. This had not been one of his imaginings. He listened to Mrs. Maynard, assured her he'd leave no stone unturned. "And she's got herself engaged to Sir Alan Bellingham, too . . . ," she said, reproachfully and almost as an afterthought.

"I'll do what I can, and let you know if there's any news," Carmichael said, and put the phone down.

"P. A.?" Jack was still in the doorway. "What's wrong? You look as if you've been struck by lightning."

"They've arrested Elvira again," Carmichael said. "And they've arrested Mr. Maynard. And I think this has to be aimed at me. But they left Mrs. Maynard and Betsy there, so they know I'll be told. I mustn't do whatever it is that they want me to. Oh, and Elvira seems to have got herself engaged to some idiot baronet who may be mixed up with this nonsense."

"Who's *they* in all this?" Jack asked, coming forward into the sitting room.

"I'm not sure," Carmichael said. "Not Normanby, for once, I don't think. It might be the Duke of sodding Windsor's lot. But if it is, her blasted baronet ought to be able to help her."

"Would Normanby help us if it is them?"

"I'll ask. But I don't know if he can. I don't know what he'd risk for me. Not much. I'm a useful tool, he could get another."

Jack put his arms around Carmichael. He was still standing, and Carmichael sitting, so his head was pressed to Jack's belly. The warmth and the closeness and the familiar smell of Jack made him feel safer, and he embraced him back tightly, arms around his waist. "What does Elvira know?" Jack asked. He loosened his grip, moved away a step, and sat down on the footstool.

"Nothing," Carmichael said. "She doesn't know about you and

me, or about the Inner Watch, none of it. I asked her if she knew why I'd sent her to Switzerland rather than France or Germany and she had no idea. She went in all innocence to an Ironsides rally as a fun evening out."

"If she doesn't know anything, they can't get anything out of her. And you have an organization—two organizations. You can get her away." Jack looked very earnest. "Or do you think it's time to get out?" His eyes went to the wall where a safe was hidden underneath a watercolor of Hagia Sophia. "We have the passports and the money. We could get away if we need to."

"It's not that bad yet," Carmichael said. "You're right. I have two organizations. I can get her away one way or the other. It might just be bureaucratic incompetence somewhere. And if not, we can get her away too." He reached for the telephone again. "Thanks, Jack."

"I hear Turkey's very nice at this time of year," Jack said.

"More Byzantine ruins than South America, certainly," Carmichael said. "But let's find out who's got her and what's going on before we panic." He dialed the Watchtower. "Carmichael here. Have any news on Elvira Royston, who was at home but in Watch custody?"

The night sergeant grunted. Carmichael could hear him turning the pages of the log. "Yes, sir, routine demand from the Met, looks like. Four o'clock, or sixteen hundred I should say. It got passed on to Sergeant Evans, who was the arresting officer, and he gave it the nod at seventeen-ten. It was all over before I came on at six."

"Thank you, sergeant," Carmichael said. "The Met are treading on our toes again. Don't let them have anything else without consultation, however routine it looks."

"Yes, sir. You give them a rocket, sir."

Carmichael put the receiver down and stared straight ahead. Jack got up and poured the tea. "Did Sergeant Evans by any chance try to reach me earlier this evening?"

"No," Jack said, handing him a cup of tea. "Are you sure you don't want that whisky?"

"I need a clear head," Carmichael said.

"Why did you ask about Sergeant Evans?"

Carmichael sighed. "You never quite get used to your subordinates selling you out, no matter how often it happens. I wonder what they have on Sergeant Evans?"

"You can't blame him—"

"I don't blame him. I don't have the standing to blame him. When it comes to it, there's always something you care about enough that they can use it against you. For me that was you. For Evans, I don't know. There's not even much point talking to him about it. But we know the Met have her."

"If the Duke of Windsor is attacking Normanby through you, then surely Normanby would help you stop him. It would be a coup," Jack said.

"I'll try that if I have to," Carmichael said. He dialed the number for Scotland Yard, and waited while it rang. "It's Watch Commander Carmichael here," he said, when they picked up. "Can I have a word with the Chief?"

"At this time on a Sunday night, sir?" The desk sergeant sounded dubious. "I'm afraid I can't help you. Shall I ask him to call you in the morning?"

"Then can I speak to whoever is on duty and in charge of the Elvira Royston case?"

"I don't know who that would be, sir," he said.

"Is Mr. Bannister there?"

"I'll see, sir. Hold the line." There was a pause. Carmichael sipped his tea. "I can't get hold of Mr. Bannister for you now, sir. Shall I leave a message to call you in the morning?"

"Yes, please, sergeant," Carmichael said. He put the receiver down. "Bannister's the man from Paddington," he explained to Jack.

"If he wasn't there, the sergeant would have said no straight away. He's there. What in heaven's name do they think they're doing? This has to be a move on me, but if so, why aren't they here?"

"Is it worth you going there?" Jack asked. "Or would that be putting your head in the lion's mouth?"

Carmichael glanced at his watch. "I'm going to call Normanby," he said. He took a deep breath as he reached for the receiver.

19

Now I know what you're thinking I did next, but nothing could be farther from the truth. Even if he was a poof, I knew he wasn't a traitor. It was impossible. He was *Uncle Carmichael,* he was practically the definition of integrity. These men, who I didn't like and didn't trust, were in some way out to get him. It's true that I'd been told for years it was my patriotic duty to report anything I happened to come across, and I'd paid lip service to that—literally, chanting it at Arlinghurst the same way I chanted prayers in chapel. But under that was an older code, one learned in childhood on the streets of London, a code that said you didn't rat out your friends no matter what. Uncle Carmichael had been a friend to me. He had come into Paddington to rescue me. I knew he'd be trying to rescue me again the moment he knew where I was. I knew it wouldn't make any difference to him what I'd said, and that made me more determined not to say anything at all. Besides, that meeting with Mrs. Talbot was such a little thing, and probably perfectly legitimate Watch business. If there was ever going to be a moment when I'd have thought it right to have ratted on him it would have been right then, when I was shaken up, but even then I knew better.

"I don't know anything," I said. "I don't believe he has any seditious activities. Don't you know he's the Commander of the Watch?"

The redhead looked at Penn-Barkis. "You haven't observed anything that made you suspicious?" Penn-Barkis asked, in a kindly, almost fatherly way.

I knew that what came next was being asked all these same questions in a more uncomfortable way. And I knew that everyone talks in the end. "Nothing whatsoever," I said, in my best supercilious Arlinghurst manner.

"Yet he took you in all this time about being a homo, I suppose he could have hidden it from you," the redhead said, in skeptical tones.

I just stared at him. It wasn't like the thing with Sir Alan where I really did feel guilty about my behavior, or the riot, where I really had been in the wrong just by being there. Nothing they could say about Uncle Carmichael made any dent. I even tried to tell myself that they could be lying about the homosexuality bit, except that it explained such a lot and fitted so well.

"Well, it's getting late, Inspector Bannister," Penn-Barkis said, looking at his watch. Outside the sky was darkening. London looked far away below us. "Shall we leave it until the morning?"

"Yes, sir, if that's what you think best." I was very pleased to have a name for the redhead at last.

Penn-Barkis looked at me. "We'll have to keep you in overnight and talk to you again in the morning, unless you have any more to say now."

"Have you arrested Sir Alan?" I asked.

"If you're not engaged to him, I don't see why that's any of your business," the redhead, Bannister, said.

"I just wanted to ask you because if you had and you'd be seeing him, that you could make it clear to him, that when I said no, that's what I meant," I said. "If he's been telling people at his club he could ruin my reputation, make me seem a frightful jilt."

Now this was all true, but the reason I was asking about it was to see what chance they thought I had of getting away afterwards. If they laughed at the thought of my reputation mattering, it would mean I wouldn't survive. If they gave it some thought, it meant I had a chance. They didn't give me anything though. "We'll be sure to tell him," Bannister said. "Now come with me."

Penn-Barkis shook his head, more in sorrow than anger and more like a headmistress than ever. I could hardly believe they thought their charades would fool anyone. I suppose most of the people they had to deal with were awfully stupid. My dad used to say that villains were, mostly.

Inspector Bannister took me down in the lift, holding my arm in a precautionary way, but not very tightly. I could have broken away and run, except that it wouldn't have done me the least little bit of good. I'd still have been in New New Scotland Yard with no way to get out. It might have gained me thirty seconds, that's all. I thought about it, because thirty seconds of freedom might have been all there would ever be, in which case it would make a better memory. I decided not to, because it was so futile, and because there was still a chance of getting released at the end. I didn't think they'd be able to arrest Uncle Carmichael, and I knew he wouldn't give up on trying to get me away. The more I behaved like an innocent person— which I absolutely was—the better my chances of eventually being released. I hadn't done anything wrong, after all.

The lift opened onto a dingy corridor painted dark green to the dado line and pale green above. Bannister didn't say a word, just led me off to the right, where the corridor widened and there was a desk with two bobbies sitting behind it. "Royston," Bannister said.

"Yes, sir," one of the bobbies said, getting up and coming forward. The other one ticked something off on the ledger on the desk. "Complete search, sir?"

"Yes, sergeant," Bannister said.

They took me into a little bare room, with pale green walls and a tiled floor, like a bathroom. They made me take off absolutely all my clothes, while the sergeant read out what they were and the other bobby wrote them down. The other bobby seemed thoroughly bored and droned out the name of each item as he got to them. "One mauve dinner dress. One underskirt, silk. One brassiere, French. One sachet, embroidered with an *E*." Bannister watched all the time, smirking. I just stared over his head. It wasn't any worse than showering with Lavinia Wooton-Smythe, in fact, not as bad, because he just smirked, he didn't make comments. It was surprising how much my experiences under arrest reminded me of boarding school, actually.

At last I was absolutely starkers and all my clothes and possessions had been listed, including my Swiss watch, which I knew I'd never see again, any more than poor Betsy's pearls. The sergeant came up to me, looking embarrassed. "Bend forward, miss," he said. Then he poked his finger gingerly into my bottom, ugh.

I knew this was meant to humiliate me, as well as search for anything I might have hidden. I'd never have thought of hiding anything up my bottom, or in my fanny either, where he poked next, but I could see how clever terrorists might, though it must be frightfully uncomfortable. The funny thing though was that the sergeant's embarrassment and calling me "miss" served to make it all seem much more like going to the doctor. It would have been much worse if that horrible Bannister had done it.

When he'd quite finished poking at me, the sergeant gave me a paper smock. It was made of thick gray paper; it went on over my head and came down to my thighs. There were no sleeves. "Cell eighteen," he said, and led the way out of the tiled room and down the corridor. To get to the lift, I'd have had to go past the desk, but there was a chance both men would be checking in another prisoner. The real difficulty would be getting past the sergeant in the glass booth upstairs, because in this gray thing I'd be horribly conspicuous. At least it didn't have arrows printed on it, as I'd heard prison clothes did. I'd also be cold, I realized as I walked down the corridor. The tiled room had been heated, but I started to feel chilly as we walked.

"Do you want the toilet, miss?" the sergeant asked. "Because once you're in your cell, you won't come out until morning."

I decided the sergeant was a good man, despite his having done unspeakable things to me. He was probably kind to children and animals and loved by his family. "Yes, thank you," I said.

The toilet had no lock, more and more like Arlinghurst, but they didn't actually watch me while I was in there. There were no windows, and no way of escape. I took a handful of toilet paper and stuffed it inside my smock. It was the hard scratchy kind, and I thought I might be able to use it to write a message. I hadn't thought what I'd use to write—I think I really just took it because they'd taken everything I had, and it gave me some control to have something they didn't know I had, even something as small and silly as that. I drank a little of the tap water while I was washing my hands. There was nowhere to dry them, so they stayed wet, which made me feel even colder.

Bannister shoved me into the cell, when we got to it, but this time I was expecting it and managed to stay on my feet with two or three running steps. The cell was gray. It had a shelf about as long as a bed, but with no blanket or pillow. There were no windows, and the fluorescent light was way above my head out of reach. The door had a barred window to the corridor. It was cold. Bannister followed me in, and leaned on the wall. The door shut behind him with a clang, and I found myself wanting to call out to the nice sergeant to come back.

I sat down on the "bed." Bannister told me to stand up. I stood up, raising my eyebrows as if it was the most ridiculous request but I was complying to be polite. He asked me all the same questions he'd asked me upstairs, varying the order, and sometimes being very precise and sometimes very vague. I was cold, and after a while my legs started to tremble with the cold and being tired. I don't know how long it went on for. They'd taken my watch. He didn't touch me, but he wouldn't let me sit down and he never stopped asking me questions, the same questions, over and over, about the riot, about Uncle Carmichael, about Sir Alan and British Power.

Eventually the sergeant came back and asked if everything was all right, and Bannister said he was finished and would come back in the morning. He went off, and I was alone for the moment. I took the toilet paper out of my armpit, where it had been scratching me the whole time, and sat on it. The bed was as hard as concrete, and very cold. I was shivering all over, big shivers that shook me. The muscles in my calves were cramping, and I rubbed them as best I could.

I was doing that when the sergeant came back and let himself into my cell. He had a blanket, which I took most gratefully and wrapped around myself, even though it was gray and woolly and itchy. "Oh, thank you so much, sergeant," I said. When I got up to take the blanket, I'd dropped one of the pieces of toilet paper, and the sergeant saw, but he didn't say anything, just handed it back to me.

"I knew your father," he said. "I remember you when you were a nipper, too, Elvira. Do you remember me? I'm Sergeant Matlock. Constable Matlock then."

I didn't remember him at all, but it seemed rude and ungrateful to say so. "I think I do," I said. "It was a long time ago."

"And Sergeant Royston had a lot of friends," he said, not seeming at all hurt. "Some of them he might have been better off keeping away from, as things are. It pains me to see a nice girl like you in a cell for nothing more than knowing someone who's been causing trouble. What could you know about it, I asked them. You're what, seventeen, eighteen years old?"

"Eighteen," I said. "Nineteen in May."

"Just two years older than my eldest, Rosie," he said, sitting down on the bed beside me. "You wouldn't know anything about Commander Carmichael's misbehavior. You're too young."

"Can you get me out of here?" I pleaded. "I don't know anything, and I'm so cold and tired and I'm afraid of Inspector Bannister."

"You poor little scrap," Sergeant Matlock said. He put his arm around me, which I welcomed for the comfort as well as the warmth. "But I can't let you go, it's more than my job's worth; I'd be in here myself if I did that, or more likely off on a transport with the detainees. That's what'll happen to you if you don't give them something, you know."

Off on a transport, off to the work camps of the Reich where I'd be fed on starvation rations and worked literally to death. It was what terrified me—what terrified everyone, what kept us all quiet and living in fear. I started to cry. "I don't have anything to give them," I said, in despair.

"Then why don't you cooperate? Tell them what you do know, about your uncle's visitors and that? About anything you might have wondered about? It's no harm to you, and if he's innocent there's no harm to him either. It's just that Inspector Bannister thinks you're holding something back, so he's going to push you until he finds out what that is. It's probably nothing important, but if you tell him, he'll have something to go after, so he'll leave you alone, and let you go home."

"There's nothing that would satisfy him," I said, moving a little away from the sergeant so I could wipe my eyes with the toilet paper.

"Why don't you tell me, and I'll see what I think?" he asked. He looked patient and reliable, like my father, like Sergeant Evans, like the men I had grown up with.

A shadow fell across the wall of the cell. I looked up, and saw

Inspector Bannister outside the door. He came back about thirty seconds too soon, because I had fallen for the whole thing and was about to tell Sergeant Matlock all about Mrs. Talbot and what I'd overheard. Now I sprang to my feet, dropping the blanket. "You're working with him!" I said.

"Of course I am, but that doesn't mean that what I say isn't true," Sergeant Matlock said, taking a step towards me.

"Get away from me," I said.

"Come out, sergeant, it isn't going to work," Bannister said. "Let's leave her until morning. Check on her every fifteen minutes, would you?"

"Yes, sir," Sergeant Matlock said, stolidly, not looking at either of us. "Do I leave the blanket?"

"No, I don't think so, not unless there's been any cooperation."

Sergeant Matlock picked up the blanket and folded it, then went out of the cell. I was a little warmer than I had been, which was partly the blanket and the sergeant's arm, and partly rage.

I tried to sleep. I curled up on the freezing cold slab and shut my eyes. The light stayed on. Every fifteen minutes either Sergeant Matlock or the bobby who had recorded my possessions came into the cell and shook me awake, to "check on me." I did sleep for a few moments here and there. Eventually the bobby escorted me to the toilet, and when I returned to the cell there was a cup of hot sweet tea and some cold porridge on the slab, which I ate. I assumed by this that it was morning. I expected them to come to take me back upstairs at any moment. The tea warmed me and I did some Swiss calisthenics, which warmed me even more. They left me alone for long enough for me to begin to wonder if they'd forgotten me, and to regret not having tried to sleep again.

20

O n Monday morning Carmichael was in the office before Miss Duthie arrived. He had an appointment with Mark Normanby at ten, and he wanted to set wheels in motion before that. He went down to the records office himself, walked past the duty clerk, and snatched up the report on Alan Bellingham, Bart.

Sir Alan was born in 1929, which made him thirty-one, surely much too old for Elvira, who was only eighteen. What could the Maynards be thinking? Carmichael realized he was grinding his teeth, and stopped. Sir Alan inherited his title at the age of ten, when his father, Colonel Sir Ulger Bellingham, 1889–1940, was killed fighting in Belgium with General Gort's forces. He had also inherited Rossingham Manor, in Cambridgeshire, and a small amount of money. Death duties were high in 1940, and the family had needed to struggle to keep the house. Young Sir Alan's trustees—his mother, Lady Prudence nee Arden, and his uncle, Oswin Bellingham—had sold off a lot of family treasures in those years. Nevertheless they had contrived to send Sir Alan to Eton and to Jesus College, Oxford. After Oxford, which he left with a first in Mathematics, Sir Alan had gone into the City—an unusual choice, in 1951, even for a mathematician. He had done well, parlaying his small fortune into a large one and even managing to buy back the treasures his trustees had squandered during his minority.

The list of his investments was long and thorough, doubtless gleaned from Inland Revenue sources. Carmichael skimmed it. Most of his holdings were in Britain and the Commonwealth, with a substantial fraction in the Reich, and shares in one very profitable uranium mine in Italian Libya. He seemed to be good at guessing how the market would move—either that or he had a lot of inside information. His clients loved him, and Carmichael didn't blame them. He turned the page. Politically—here Sir Alan seemed to be all over the map. He knew people with affiliations in all directions, it seemed. He had class C contacts with suspected communists, with Scottites, with the Ironsides, and with impeccable Conservative, Liberal, and Labour members of Parliament. There was nothing beyond class C—and the Watch could rate you a class C contact by being at the same dinner party as someone. "This is meaningless," Carmichael muttered.

"I'm sorry, sir?" the clerk interjected, looking up. "Can I help you find something?"

"No, no problem," Carmichael said. "I have what I need." He turned the page again. Here was the report he had asked for, on Sir Alan's British Power connections. It could mean anything or nothing—Sir Alan evidently knew a lot of people. Some of those people were, or seemed to be, or to have been at one time, involved with British Power. He had several times been to a nightclub where the Liverpool agitator had sung. He had visited the Duke of Windsor's yacht when in Capri. It all depended how you squinted at it. Carmichael wanted to meet the man.

The next page was Criminal—no record, no arrests, but, to his surprise, several suspicions. Unlike Scotland Yard's records, the Watch recorded suspicions. Sir Alan had several times skated close to the thin edge of the law in his financial dealings, and had once been warned by his firm and once had his taxes investigated. In 1955 he had transferred money to the United States for a Jewish client and then turned the client in to the Watch. Nothing illegal about that, though it was enough to make Carmichael decide to forbid the banns if it ever came to that. This was not a man he would like to have marry Elvira. The Jew, after his arrest and before his deportation, had claimed that Sir Alan had previously helped several of his friends successfully remove their assets, and the friends had subsequently left the country without any problem. The emigrated friends' names were listed, and there was a note in the file to watch Sir Alan for any more of this kind of behavior. There had been none, and someone had penciled "Probably spite?" against the report.

Carmichael shut the folder and slid it back into place. "Thank you," he said to the clerk, who stared after him as he stalked off down the corridor.

Miss Duthie was sitting at her desk outside his office. She took one look at his face and jumped up. "Today's word is *hammock,* and I'll bring tea right away," she said.

Carmichael grunted and went into his room. It was nine o'clock. He telephoned Scotland Yard. "Can I speak to the Chief now?" he asked.

"He's not in yet, sorry, I'll get him to call you. Commander Carmichael, isn't it? I already have a note here for him to call you."

"Thank you," Carmichael snarled, and put the phone down.

Miss Duthie sidled in with the tea. "The kettle was just on the boil," she said, putting it down.

"Anything urgent?" Carmichael asked.

"Riots all over the place, and a strike in Edinburgh," she said. "But you've probably seen in the papers."

"I haven't looked at the papers. Penn-Barkis, or someone, has pulled in Elvira again. I'm meeting the Prime Minister at ten. Hold all my calls. If there's anything about the conference that absolutely needs an instant response, give it to Ogilvie, and if it's about the riots, give it to Jacobson. Send him in when he comes. He's in today, isn't he? It's tomorrow he's out for his whatnot."

"Yes, sir," she said, and poured his tea. "Why did they arrest Elvira?"

"It's hard not to see it as a power move on me," he said, and then regretted it as Miss Duthie seemed to shrivel under the thought. "But it might be because she's become engaged to some jackass who is closer to British Power than he ought to be. Which reminds me." He picked up the internal telephone. "Ted, could you take a couple of men and arrest Sir Alan Bellingham of Rossingham Manor, Cambridgeshire, and the Albany, W1? If you can find him, bring him here for interrogation and hold him under the Defence of the Realm Act. It's possible the Met have him, but they're not talking to us today."

Miss Duthie was still hovering when he looked up. "Is there anything I can do?" she asked. "Besides hold your calls, I mean. Anything to help Elvira?"

"Miss Duthie, you help inestimably by doing your ordinary job," Carmichael said. "If there have been riots, it's going to be chaotic, and you and Mr. Jacobson are going to have to deal with it this morning. That's already more than two people's work on your shoulders."

"Very well," she said, pushing up her glasses resolutely. "But if there is anything else, please just let me know." She left quietly.

Carmichael took a sip of his tea. He admired her loyalty. It was refreshing. He thought about speaking to Sergeant Evans, and decided to wait. He had slept very badly. He kept thinking that Penn-Barkis no doubt had relatives, and Bannister undoubtedly did, and the Watchtower had deep cells and officers far more practiced in interrogation techniques than the Yard. He didn't believe they'd hurt Elvira, but he hated to think of what he could do if they did. What he would do. He drank his tea and tried to stay calm. If they had anything against him he wouldn't be sitting here now, in control of the power that was his.

Jacobson came in. "Miss Duthie said you wanted me," he said. "Have you heard about this round of riots?"

"Not really. British Power?" Carmichael asked.

"No. Well, some of them, it seems like, but lots of them seem to be spontaneous. They're protesting about the protesters being sent off, and against the camps. There were signs in Leeds calling for the Gravesend facility to be closed before it's even opened. They don't seem to be any one organized thing, just people taking to the streets for whatever's coming into their heads. The local police don't know what to do about them, when they're peaceful, and respectable people are among them the marchers. In Swansea someone even called for civil rights for Jews, apparently." He smiled. "Maybe people are waking up at last, the way we always hoped they might. Maybe it only took a poke."

"They've arrested Elvira again," Carmichael said.

Jacobson's face collapsed from a smile to dismay. "That's terrible!"

"What's worse is that nobody will talk to me about it, they're giving me the runaround. I'm seeing Normanby at ten, but I don't know if he'll help. I don't know where he is on all this, or how useful I am to him. If he won't help, we're going to have to get her out. Us, the Inner Watch. I've thought about it, and the only time it would be possible is when they move her."

Jacobson's face went through a number of contortions, from dismay, to horror, then it tightened up into something unrecognizable. "We've always said we wouldn't try to get individuals," he said. "It's just too dangerous. We've always agreed about that."

"But this is different," Carmichael said. "It's Elvira. Dammit, Jacobson, it would be the same if it were your daughter, or your niece."

"They're all my nieces," Jacobson said.

"I know you feel that way," Carmichael said, awkwardly. "But this is Elvira."

"The difference between us, Carmichael, is that you don't really believe you could be the one being shipped off. Oh, you *know* you could be, but you don't *believe* it. You think if you keep on doing what they want and keeping your nose clean and selling little bits of your soul every time you're required, and keep everything else out of sight, it'll keep you out of that boxcar. I don't think that. I don't have the luxury."

Carmichael stared at him, hardly recognizing him. "But will you help, if we have to do it?" he asked.

"Have you thought it might be a trap, to get you to try it, so they can see what we've got?" Jacobson asked, furiously. "I can't believe you're willing to risk everything this way, just when things were looking up."

"I can't believe you won't help me rescue Elvira," Carmichael said.

"Oh, I'll help. Of course I will. What choice have I got?" Jacobson paced to the limit of the little office and then back.

"I don't understand," Carmichael said. "Look, we might not have to do anything. I'm going to see Normanby—" He glanced at his watch. "I'd better get off to see him now, or I'm going to be late. We'll talk when I get back."

"I'll be here," Jacobson said.

"Do whatever you want about the riots, for the time being," Carmichael said. He went out into the hall and took his coat and hat from the stand.

"Good luck," Miss Duthie said. "I'm sure Mr. Normanby will do the right thing."

Carmichael wished he was sure. He didn't understand Jacobson. The Inner Watch had rescued thousands of Jews, and now he didn't

want to help rescue Elvira? It was more risky when it was one partic-
ular individual, and in London, but he had absolutely meant it when
he said he would have done the same for Jacobson's family. Of
course, he didn't need to, because they were safe in Nova Scotia, all
but his wife who refused to go. Maybe he should have sent Elvira to
Canada or New Zealand years ago.

There was a car waiting, as always, and Carmichael swiftly found
himself turning down Downing Street and getting out at Number
10. One of the policemen on duty saluted him, and the other checked
his papers conscientiously. "The Prime Minister is expecting you,"
he said as he handed them back.

Carmichael usually saw Normanby at the House of Commons.
Number 10 Downing Street, with its hall full of portraits of former
prime ministers, intimidated him. He was ushered into a downstairs
office where Normanby sat, as usual, in his powered wheelchair.
The room had comfortable leather chairs and a huge portrait of Pitt
the Younger on the wall. An Alsatian barked once and got to its feet
as Carmichael came in. "Down, Fang," Normanby said, absently,
and the dog settled itself reluctantly back on the tartan rug, still
growling.

Most people who had met the Prime Minister seemed to find him
charming. Most people who hadn't met him seemed to adore him.
They thought of him as a God-given saint who came at the right moment to save the country, martyred by the bomb that put him in the
wheelchair, but miraculously still present. Miss Duthie, Carmichael
knew, kept a silver-framed photograph of Mark Normanby on her
bedside table, beside those of her dead parents. Normanby encouraged this worship by, for instance, making photographs easily available and signing them when asked, but he didn't think Normanby
particularly enjoyed the thought of spinsters all over the country
resting their eyes on him. Hitler, who Carmichael had met twice,
once when he saved his life and once when he was given a medal,

seemed to thrive on such things. Normanby encouraged them in imitation, because he knew they worked. Carmichael suspected that, left to himself, and if it had been equally effective, Normanby would have preferred to have had everyone loathe and fear him, as Carmichael did.

"All right, Carmichael, sit down and tell me what's so urgent that you had to call me at home in the middle of the night?" He waved at a chair, and Carmichael sat.

"My ward, Elvira Royston, has been re-arrested by Scotland Yard, and they refuse to give me any information. Sir, I think this is an attack on me, and on you through me. I think British Power are involved." Carmichael had been thinking how best to phrase this half the night.

Normanby frowned. He had a tartan blanket tucked over his useless legs, and he absentmindedly fiddled with the fringe. "What I heard is that she's engaged herself to one of these British Power people and they think she's tied up with them. They're afraid you might be. Penn-Barkis didn't want me to be alone with you in case."

"That's nonsense!" Carmichael said.

"I know," Normanby said, smiling. "Here I am with you, so you can see I didn't believe a word of it. Guy tells me you think the Duke of Windsor is in with these British Power people, and that he might have connections that go anywhere."

"Yes," Carmichael said, cautiously. "I'm very worried about that, and I was even before they arrested Elvira."

"They're only doing their job, there, you know. They have to check up on you, see if you are involved. It does look suspicious, you must see that." Normanby put his head a little on one side and studied Carmichael. "You and I might know that you're loyal, but it doesn't hurt to have it checked. They won't harm your little ward. They'll let her go in a day or two, as long as everything really is above board."

"She's entirely innocent of anything, and she shouldn't have to go through this. She's a debutante, for heaven's sake. She's due to be presented to the Queen in a few days! You can't—"

Normanby raised a hand. "Would you have preferred that we pull in your man to check on you?"

Carmichael bit his upper lip, drew in a long breath, and only then realized he was snarling. Normanby laughed. "There's no need for you to check on me at all. You know I have been loyal to you ever since you put me in this position," he said, evenly.

Normanby shook his head slowly. "But this Bellingham looks like a bad egg. And she's close to him, and she lied about that, and she's close to you."

"Bellingham may be a bad egg himself or he may be a man who knows a lot of people and some of them bad ones. I'd like to talk to him."

"I'm sure you would. I'm not sure it would be a good idea. The Yard have him. Look, Carmichael, I do have some sympathy for your position. You're quite right about this Duke of Windsor business. I want you to deal with that—isolate him, stop him from seeing anyone at all. He'll have to be in the procession now, too late to stop that, but apart from that keep him under house arrest in his hotel. Then on Friday—Good Friday, eh!—we'll toss him back out of the country. He won't be able to organize any more riots from there. And these riots—I want you to clamp down on them. People are grumbling about all sorts of things they've been perfectly happy with for years. Get that back under control. You've plenty of Watchmen. And I was thinking, you have always been loyal, and it's about time we did something for you in the Birthday Honours. You've got that German gong, and we gave you a George Cross for that too, but there hasn't been anything since then for all these years you've been getting on with doing your job. Wouldn't you like to be Sir Peter?"

"I'd much rather have Elvira back right now," Carmichael said. "That's much more important to me. I don't give two pins about a knighthood." For the first time ever, now that he was reduced to offering him a bribe, he saw Normanby as pathetic.

"I can't do that," Normanby said. "They think she knows something and she's holding out on them."

"For God's sake, she doesn't know anything!" Carmichael shouted. "There's nothing for her to know. Probably she doesn't want to tell them Bellingham kissed her at a ball, or some other childish secret. What are they doing to her?"

The dog erupted off the rug, snarling, and went for Carmichael. The attack was so unexpected that he couldn't do anything to stop it. "Stop, Fang!" Normanby said, just as its jaws were about to close on his throat. It stayed where it was, but did not bite.

The door opened and a guard looked in. "Everything all right?" he asked.

"Everything's fine, thanks, Clement," Normanby said. The door closed again. "Down, Fang." The dog obediently slipped down from Carmichael's chest and slunk back to the rug. "Isn't he well trained?"

"Yes," Carmichael said, shaking a little. "Does he always do that if someone raises their voice?"

"If he perceives a threat to me," Normanby said. "Much like you and Penn-Barkis really, and much like Penn-Barkis he sometimes perceives a threat when there isn't really one there. But when my dogs overreact, I can call them off and apologize, and there's no harm done."

"What are they doing to Elvira?" Carmichael asked, quietly.

"Nothing that will do her any harm as long as she cooperates. She's in the Yard, and they'll be taking her to Finsbury today. As soon as she's told them whatever it is they think she's holding out on, she'll be back with you. And it isn't about Sir Alan, it's about you, whatever it is. She'll tell them soon. You've approved the methods at Finsbury yourself."

Carmichael wanted to say that he hadn't approved them for Elvira, for an innocent girl, but the words wouldn't come out of his mouth. He had approved them, and if he had approved them he had approved them for her, for anyone, for everyone. "She's probably guessed about me and Jack," he said, through the lump in his throat. "That's probably her secret that she doesn't want to tell them."

"No, it isn't that. She didn't know that. I'm afraid she does know now, which is a pity considering that you seem to have been able to keep it from her. You must have been very discreet. I can't imagine how you managed it all these years. Though of course she was away at school, wasn't she, and in Switzerland?"

Carmichael felt his hands tensing. The pleasure of strangling Normanby would be almost worth being hung, if it wasn't for what they'd do to Elvira. The dog growled menacingly. "Let me have her back, now," Carmichael said. "There is no secret she knows, I assure you. I've always been loyal, and I always will be. I'll deal with the Duke of Windsor, with the riots, whatever you want. I don't need any recognition. I won't even object to being on television to be vilified. Just let me have her back."

"You'll do all that anyway," Normanby said. "I'm not going to interfere with my subordinates doing their job. If there is any secret, they'll get it out of her. And then, if it's trivial, you'll have her back, probably even in time for her to make her curtsey to the Queen on Tuesday. Now go and get on with your job. Fang, show him out."

Fang rose, took hold of Carmichael's trouser leg between his teeth, and began to move towards the door.

21

I combed my hair with my fingers, as best I could. I did some more calisthenics. Eventually I gave in and tried to sleep again, and I think I did sleep, but not for long, it was too cold.

I don't know how long it was before they came for me. It wasn't Bannister or Sergeant Matlock, it was two strange constables. One of them told me to stand up and the other unlocked the cell. Then the first one told me to walk forward, and when I did he handcuffed my wrists behind my back. Then they made me walk down the corridor, not as far as the desk and the tiled room, and into a different cell. This one was painted green and had two chairs in the middle and a little desk and chair at the side. It wasn't as cold as my cell. Then a different man, a dark-haired one with bushy eyebrows and a big jaw, came in. He made me stand there in handcuffs, which is terribly awkward and uncomfortable, and he asked me all the same questions, and a few more, about things I knew nothing about, like Sir Alan's investments and Uncle Carmichael's education. The two bobbies stood behind us, leaning on the wall, and another man, a clerkly type, came in and sat at the desk and made notes of what I was saying.

After a while, I don't know how long, they let me go to the toilet. They uncuffed me for that, and to drink a cup of tea. It was awful tea, strong and sweet and milky. I'd have turned my nose up at it at any other time. Right then it was like nectar. They all drank tea. I wanted to laugh, because there we were in a torture chamber, or the next thing to it, and they were interrogating me, and we were having a tea break, just like anyone doing their job. Of course, they were just doing their job. There was no animosity in it. I could tell that. But as soon as we'd all finished our tea and one of the bobbies had collected the cups, they were at it again, Bushy Eyebrows asking questions and me answering and the clerk writing it all down, over and over.

I think it's true that everyone breaks in the end and tells everything they know. I was very close to it several times. I kept thinking about Mrs. Talbot and what I'd overheard, and how if I told them they'd leave me alone and let me sleep, and maybe even let me go. "We've let Mr. Maynard go home," Bushy Eyebrows told me. "He cooperated. He told us what he knew, and now he's safely back with his family. You're supposed to be a clever girl, Elvira, down for Oxford they tell me. The clever thing to do would be to tell me, and then you could go home too." He'd alternate that kind of thing with bullying me, shouting, making me stand up and sit down senselessly.

He cuffed me again for a while, then took them off for another tea break and toilet break. I was getting hungry and wondering if we'd have a lunch break. The bobbies went off shift, or something, during the second tea break, and were replaced by two different bobbies. The same clerk stayed though. He had his sleeves rolled up and he never looked at me. I could see him out of the corner of my eye, writing away, looking bored to death, from time to time pushing his hair out of his eyes. I was bored, myself. I was starting to think that as I was bound to give in eventually I might as well tell them now.

Then, after an interminable amount of time—I hadn't seen daylight since the day before—Bannister came back. "Any progress?" he asked.

"Not a sausage," Bushy Eyebrows said. "Elvira isn't cooperating, are you, dearie?"

"I'm doing my best," I said.

Bushy Eyebrows raised his eyebrows, and Bannister snorted. "All right," he said to Bushy Eyebrows. "I'm going to take her over to Finsbury, where they really know how to make people talk."

I felt sick—I was hungry really, because it had been a long time since that porridge, but my stomach turned over at the thought of Finsbury, and what they might do to me there. I'd been congratulating myself on holding out, and at the same time knowing I couldn't keep it up forever, not when I was so tired and hungry, and now I knew I couldn't hold out against something worse. The fact that I had no idea what they did at Finsbury or how much worse it was didn't help at all, in fact the opposite; because it was unknown it was much more terrifying.

"Finsbury it is. Unless you're ready to tell us what you know about Commander Carmichael's disloyalty," Bushy Eyebrows said. "Come on, Elvira, you've held out all this time, you've been very brave, but you know, everyone tells everything in Finsbury. They'll make you glad to tell them over there. You might as well save yourself a lot of time and trouble and tell us now."

"All right," I said, and sat down without him having said I could, but he didn't shout at me. My legs were shaking, and so were my hands, so I wrapped my arms around myself. I felt thoroughly ashamed of myself, and not at all as if I was doing the right thing, but also so terribly frightened. "It isn't anything much. You might not think it's anything at all. The day after I was arrested the last time, I was in the flat, and a woman came to see him, a Mrs. Talbot. I was walking down the corridor, and I heard him say that he could put her on the payroll as an informer. Then he said she'd given him some good information, and he could use that to explain her visit.

He said what she did with the money was her business, and that she could use it to pay forgers or buy ships for Jews. Then he said his budget for information was high. That's all, honestly it is."

"Mrs. Talbot?" said Bushy Eyebrows to Bannister.

Bannister shrugged. "What was she like?" he asked.

"She was like a pigeon," I said. "All in gray. Middle-aged, plump, with a chest like a pigeon."

"How tall?" he asked, sounding very unimpressed with my description.

"Not as tall as me," I said. "Average height?"

"Hair?"

"Gray, and pulled up in a bun."

"Gray hair. Eyes?"

"I didn't notice," I confessed.

"Age?"

"About sixty, I should think. Maybe less."

The clerk's pen kept scratching. The two men looked at each other. "Clothes?" Bushy Eyebrows asked.

I tried to picture her in my mind and found it all came back clearly. "Gray coat, with a white collar, and black buttons all the way down, and a very plain gray hat, the kind widows wear to church. I don't know what she had on under that, I didn't see her after she'd come in and taken it off. She had flat black boots, practical, not chic." I looked back to Bannister, hoping that was enough. It was such a relief to be talking about it at last, not to keep holding it back.

"Town or Country?" he asked.

"Town, but not London," I said. "I don't know what gives me that impression."

"A clever girl like you can pick up a lot about someone by how they look," Bushy Eyebrows said. "And what profession would you say her husband was?"

"I have no idea!" It seemed a ridiculous unfair question. "I don't even know if she was married. She might have been a widow."

"Well, what was he then, if he was dead. A builder, say, or a clergyman?"

"Oh, a clergyman." Too late I realized that this was a question about class. "I'd say she was respectable but not well-off, certainly not from the laboring classes. She didn't talk like that either, she talked like an educated person."

"What did you hear her say?" Bushy Eyebrows asked. "You've only said what you heard your uncle say."

"I couldn't catch what she said," I admitted. "She was talking too low. But that in itself gives the tone of a voice. And I heard her say good evening before, when she went in."

"Did Carmichael send you out of the room when she arrived?" Bannister asked.

"I was going to have a bath," I said. "He did send me out, though. He didn't know who she was, and he was worried she might be an assassin. I went to have my bath, and then to go to bed, and he must have thought I was in bed, but I went to the kitchen to have some cocoa. That's when I overheard. The passage from the bathroom to the kitchen goes past the swing doors to the sitting room. It isn't a large flat."

"Why did he let her in at all if he thought she was an assassin?" Bannister sounded very dubious.

"She was a woman, and alone, and she let the guard search her and she had no weapons. Also she used Lady Eversley's name."

"Lady Eversley?" Bannister sounded really surprised. "What did she have to do with Lady Eversley?"

"I don't know," I confessed. "I have no idea."

"The Eversleys are all right," Bushy Eyebrows said.

"As far as we know," Bannister confirmed. "But I'd better speak to the Chief about that."

"Talbot's a common enough name," Bushy Eyebrows went on. "What's to prove you're telling the truth?"

"Nothing, except that I am," I said, indignantly.

"So what did you think when you heard this?" Bannister asked.

"I thought maybe I should tell someone, but then I thought it was Watch business, and he must have been saying it to deceive her," I said.

"When did you start thinking it might really be treason?" he asked.

"When you started asking me five million questions about his seditious activities," I said.

"Forgers? Jews? You thought that was Watch business?" He sounded terribly skeptical.

"I thought he might have been leading her on to entrap her."

"Did he sound as if he was?"

"No, he didn't," I admitted. "He was laughing. He sounded relaxed and happy about it. That's what was so strange. She was laughing too."

"And is that all?" Bannister asked.

"Yes, that's really all! Can I go now?"

"Your uncle didn't discuss her with you the next day or anything like that?"

"No, he never mentioned her again."

"Did you think that was strange?" Bushy Eyebrows asked.

"No, he never discussed work. I know more about his work from his friends than from him." I realized as I said this that I felt a little bitter about it. It was as if he thought I was a child.

"And that's the only time in all these years that you've ever come across him doing anything suspicious?" Bannister asked.

"Yes, it was. The absolutely only time," I said.

"And when was it exactly?" he asked.

"I said, the day after I was arrested. Wednesday evening last week."

"And you don't believe he was expecting her?" Bushy Eyebrows asked.

"He didn't even know who she was. He only let her in because she used Lady Eversley's name."

"Are you sure it was Lady Eversley?" he asked.

I frowned, trying to remember exactly. "It was the Eversley family," I said, triumphantly. "She said it was business connected with the Eversley family, and Uncle Carmichael said Lord Eversley would have telephoned or caught him in work, but sending someone round without any warning was just like Lady Eversley."

"How did you see her, if you were sent away?"

"I hung around in the hall to see her, out of curiosity," I said. "She didn't look anything like the way I imagined an assassin, so I went to have my bath."

"What would you have done if she had been an assassin?" Bannister asked.

"Screamed for the guard, I suppose," I said. "But Uncle Carmichael was armed, so I wouldn't have needed to."

"How did you see her hair if she was wearing a hat?" Bushy Eyebrows asked.

"She was taking it off when I saw her," I said.

"You didn't speak to her?"

"No, I just saw her and went off to the bathroom. Then later I heard them talking." I felt like a fool. "Can I go now? That's everything."

"If that's all, why didn't you tell us before?" Bushy Eyebrows asked. "I've been at you for hours, and before that Bannister asked you last night. If that's really it, why didn't you let us know right away?"

"I love my uncle," I said, and to my disgust started to cry.

"What do you think?" Bushy Eyebrows asked Bannister.

Bannister shrugged again. "I think that's probably it," he said.

"It's hard to be sure, but it holds water, and she's very naïve, no tricks at all."

I wiped at my eyes with the back of my hands. "You believe me? Then can I go? You said I could go home if I told you. Can I go?"

"Go?" Bannister asked. He laughed. "Certainly you can go. But I'm surprised you're in so much of a hurry. I'll be taking you to Finsbury right now."

22

"Can't you see it has to be a trap?" Jacobson asked. "They won't hurt her. They want you to try to get her, because they're suspicious. They want you to reveal the Inner Watch. That's what this is about." The office door was firmly closed. Jacobson was calmer than he had been earlier, but no less definite.

"They're going to take her to Finsbury," Carmichael said. "For God's sake, Jacobson!"

"We have never done this kind of operation, and there's a good reason why we haven't. It's just too dangerous. And if she vanishes on the way, they're going to know you've got her."

"But at that point, I'll have her. I can hide her—we have enough safe houses." Carmichael was frantic. "They'll know I took her, but they won't be able to do anything about it."

"In that case, go and get her with the power of the Watch, go down sirens blazing and guns visible and tell them to stuff their law. That would send a message about not messing with you. I'm sure Normanby doesn't want us to be at open war with the Mets and the Yard. What it wouldn't do is give everything away and ruin everything we've been trying to do for the last ten years." Jacobson started pacing again, though the office wasn't big enough.

Carmichael considered his suggestion. "There are enough Watchmen who know her and who'd come along on something like that. I needn't use anyone from the Inner Watch. Though I have some of our people watching the streets already, to let us know if she moves."

"You could just order them to do it. And if they want to make you desperate enough to step outside the law, it's better if you do it openly. Otherwise it's a clear admission of guilt, and you'll probably be lucky enough to swing for it while I'll end up as a bar of soap."

"They think she knows something," Carmichael said. "Normanby said so. He said she's holding out on something, and it's something about me."

"They're lying, to get you to try exactly what you want to try." Jacobson was at the end of his pacing space, with his back to the desk. He sounded impatient.

"I've been trying to think what she could know. I've been very careful. But there must have been something sometime that made her suspicious. I don't know what it was or when it was. We've never talked about anything like that. I've tried to keep it all from her, the work side of my life. I wanted her to grow up with advantages. She's going to Oxford, you know."

"She won't be going to Oxford if she's in hiding. She'll be going to Ireland, or maybe Zanzibar." Jacobson came up short against the desk and stopped.

"She wouldn't have to stay in hiding. Just for a day or two, until the Duke of Windsor is gone and everything has calmed down. That reminds me, hang on a moment. . . ." Carmichael reached for the phone and dialed. "Ogilvie?"

"Yes, sir," Ogilvie said. "There are reports of more riots this morning, sir, and the press want to know what we're doing."

"Jacobson's managing the riot situation," Carmichael said. "What I wanted to say was, from now on, house arrest for the Duke of Windsor, Prime Minister's orders. No visitors, no leaving the hotel except for the procession on Wednesday and the opening of the conference afterwards, and then closely escorted. No telephone, no outside contacts."

"We haven't turned up anything suspicious," Ogilvie said. He sounded dubious.

"Prime Minister's direct order," Carmichael said.

"Yes, sir, right, sir. About the riots, are you sure—"

"Jacobson has that in hand," Carmichael said, firmly. He put the phone down and looked at Jacobson. "I take it that's correct?"

"I suppose so," Jacobson said.

"What are you doing about them?"

"I've instructed local units to break up any that mention British Power or insult the Prime Minister, and arrest along the same lines as the Marble Arch riot, and otherwise to let peacefully demonstrating people alone. I've told the press there's a difference between the affair in Sandwich, with broken windows and looted shops, and the peaceful business in Lancaster where people marched through the city center chanting 'No British camps' and 'Free the Hyde Park martyrs.' Quite honestly, we don't have the manpower to clamp down on all of them, and it makes sense to leave the peaceful ones alone, especially when it does look as if people are finally getting unhappy about what's going on."

Carmichael hesitated. He wouldn't have treated them quite like that. But he had given Jacobson the authority, and besides, there were more pressing problems. "All right. I'll calm Ogilvie down about it later, after we've got Elvira safe."

"You'd do much better to wait until they get tired of testing you," Jacobson said.

"If she does know something, anything, and tells them, it could ruin everything. We have to get her out now." Carmichael couldn't understand how Jacobson could be so calm about it, not sharing his urgent need to act that made it difficult for him to sit in his chair as if everything was normal.

"If she knew something, why wouldn't she have told them already? There are posters on every street corner telling you to dob in your neighbors because anyone can be an anarchist." He rolled his eyes. "She'd probably have told them before this, and certainly when they asked. Everyone talks, after all, that's why we have the teeth, and why we make sure anyone only knows so much."

Carmichael touched his jaw automatically, on the left side, where the poison tooth was. He always worried that he would set it off by mistake, though he knew that to release it he had to press his jaw hard and bite down at the same moment, and then once released he had to bite it again to crack it and let out the poison. It was supposed to kill in seconds. "Elvira doesn't have a tooth. And she's an innocent eighteen-year-old girl, maybe she's been to the pictures and seen the brave Nazis holding out against the evil commissars one too many times."

"Much more likely that they're lying," Jacobson said. "She's probably tucked away in a comfortable cell while they wait for you to incriminate yourself. Why else would Normanby out and out tell you they're moving her to Finsbury?"

"I have to get her away. If she does know something, we have to find out what she's told them. We could all be in a lot of danger if she does know something and she talks."

"All right," Jacobson conceded. "But will you at least do it openly, as it's going to be clearly traceable to you anyway?"

"Yes. I'll put together a scramble team. I'll have to use our network of safe houses though, to put her in. But that doesn't matter. As far as they're concerned, I have her and she's vanished. Then, when it's safe again, she can reappear."

Jacobson frowned, but said nothing for a moment. "Don't take any more risks than you absolutely must," he said at last.

"You don't need to come. Aren't you getting off early today?"

"I need to be home for sunset, but that's after seven at this time of year. You shouldn't go to rescue her yourself. Send someone reliable. Send Sergeant Richards."

"I need to go in case someone needs to be overawed with authority," Carmichael said. "And to tell you the truth, I need to go because I'm useless here; I can't think about anything else and I can hardly keep still."

"I hate to see you taking risks like this that endanger everything," Jacobson said.

"I'll be all right," Carmichael said, reassuringly. "You go and look after your riots."

"My riots instigated by agitators and my completely separate peaceful marches for change," Jacobson agreed. "Good luck."

He closed the door quietly behind him. Carmichael took a breath and looked at his Grimshaw print, the street fading off into the twilight, the solitary figure. Then he reached for the telephone again. "Miss Duthie? Send Sergeant Richards in to me."

"Yes, sir," she said. "There have been a lot of calls, but nothing on your list."

"Just send Sergeant Richards, then," he said.

His list that morning consisted of the Prime Minister, Penn-Barkis, and the Home Secretary. Miss Duthie's hesitation sounded clearly over the line. "You don't want to speak to Sir Guy Braithwaite, then? He sounded urgent."

"I'll give him a call, thank you, Miss Duthie. Just send Sergeant Richards in as soon as he comes."

He put down the receiver and took up the receiver on the other telephone. "Can I speak to the Foreign Secretary?" he asked. He gave his name, and waited for a moment, then heard Sir Guy's plummy voice.

"Ah, Carmichael. Lovely having that drink with you last night. Pity you had to dash off. Maybe we could get together and have the other half sometime, eh?"

"Certainly," Carmichael said. The door opened and Sergeant Richards came in. He came to attention. Carmichael waved him to relax and wait. He indicated a chair, but Sergeant Richards ignored it and stood at parade rest.

"Splendid, splendid," Sir Guy was saying. "I just wanted to say, well, how about tonight? This evening, the same place? We can talk about the parade nonsense and all that."

"Certainly," Carmichael repeated. "That's very nice of you, Sir Guy, I'll look forward to it."

"No, no, my pleasure," Sir Guy said.

Carmichael exchanged unaccustomed parting pleasantries, and put the receiver down. He didn't understand the exchange at all. His dealings with Sir Guy were usually strictly business. Was this a covert offer of support? Or no more than it seemed, an offer of a drink from a man who drank a lot? He looked up at Sergeant Richards, and kept looking up. He was a huge man, well over six feet tall, and broad shouldered in proportion. He had come to the Watch from a Guards Brigade, and he had never lost his military manner.

"Sergeant Richards," Carmichael said.

"Sir," Richards said.

"I want you to put together an armed scramble team, enough to stop a van transferring a prisoner from New New Scotland Yard to Finsbury. I'll be coming with you. Get it ready to go at any moment, on my signal."

"Yes, sir. How many men, sir?"

"Use your own discretion. I'm not expecting to have to fire, and in the first instance any shots should be aimed over heads. I'd like to have sufficient force with us that it doesn't come to that. I want to look intimidating. They have a hostage, and we want them to hand her over." Looking up at Richards, Carmichael felt anyone would be sufficiently intimidated.

"Yes, sir. Do we know their route?"

"We don't. But we will have warning when they move. I have men in place." Carmichael glanced at his third phone, the one he rarely used, which connected to the walkie-talkies his men used on operations.

"Might be better to be out there ready, rather than starting from here. Can we get the move signal on the radio, sir? If we take a radio car?"

"We could, sergeant, that's a very good idea," Carmichael said. The thought of going into action, of actually doing something, being able to move, was a tremendous relief. "Get that organized, call me when you're ready, and I'll come up. Tell the radio operator the number of our radio car so that she can route the call there."

"Yes, sir," Richards said, and turned to go. "It'll be about ten minutes, sir."

"Miss Duthie!" Carmichael called, as Richards opened the door. Miss Duthie appeared in the doorway, hesitating on the threshold.

"You called me?" she said, tentatively.

"Yes, I did. When Sergeant Richards calls, let that through. Keep holding everything else. And is there any chance of tea?"

"Oh yes, certainly, right away," she said, and scurried off.

Carmichael could not bear the thought of starting to work on anything. He picked up the *Times.* "Revelations on Television" he read, and moved on. He glanced through the reports of the riots, which did seem to be much as Jacobson said. "What Has Brought the People to the Streets?" the headline asked, over a picture of a smartly dressed blond woman pushing a perambulator with a sign pasted to the side reading FREE THE HYDE PARK MARTYRS.

Miss Duthie returned with the tea, and a plate of custard creams.

"I didn't know if you'd eaten anything," she said, putting them down.

He hadn't, and he couldn't face anything now, but he appreciated her kindness. "That's very thoughtful of you," he said. "I'll be going out with Sergeant Richards. I don't know if I'll be back in today, but you can tell everyone I'll definitely be here tomorrow."

"I will," she said. "I hope you don't mind, but I've been praying for Elvira. I keep thinking of how she was when you first started bringing her in, before we had this building, when we were still on Jermyn Street. And she's grown up to be such a young lady. I do hope she's going to be all right."

"She will if I have anything to do with it," Carmichael said, as cheerily as he could manage. "But you keep right on praying, Miss Duthie—who knows, it might help."

"One feels so helpless," she said, pouring the tea, and not looking at him. He realized she was blinking away tears.

"One does," he said, gently. He took the tea.

"I suppose," she said, "these people, these protesters who want to free the people arrested at Hyde Park, they feel the same as we do about Elvira. It's always been criminals, before, or people associated with outrages, bombs and sabotage. But anyone could be caught up in something like that Hyde Park thing, someone's daughter, or husband, or friend."

"You're right," Carmichael said. "I expect that's just what they do feel."

"Do you think dear Mr. Normanby might be persuaded to change his mind?" she asked.

Carmichael sipped his tea and burned his tongue. "No," he said, thinking of Normanby and the dog Fang. "I think he's afraid to change his mind, in case he looks weak."

"But it would be an act of strength, to admit to a mistake," Miss Duthie said.

"You might see it that way, but he wouldn't."

"He ordered them sent off because the agitator called him a cripple, didn't he, and that hurt him and made him angry. That was a mistake, and I suppose if he admitted that, he'd have to admit why he did it, and he'd have to face up to being hurt and angry about being crippled. I think it would be very brave to do that. And he is a brave man, a man who has done so much for the country over the years. I'll pray that his eyes are opened by all these protests and that God gives him strength to face what he has to do."

Her serene faith in both God and Normanby shook Carmichael. "Let me know when Sergeant Richards calls me," he said.

She went back to her post, and he drank his tea and read the *Times* article about the delegates coming for the conference from so much of the world. At last, the telephone shrilled. "Everything's ready, sir," Richards said.

"I'll be right up," Carmichael said.

He put on his hat and coat, nodding at Miss Duthie in what he hoped was a resolute way. "Good luck," she said. "Oh, the very best of luck!"

He ran up the stairs and found what seemed a procession waiting. There was a radio car, an armored van, two marked police cars, and one plain black Bentley. "How many men did you decide on, Sergeant Richards?" Carmichael asked.

"Enough to do the job properly, sir," Richards replied. He was wearing a flak jacket, and he held one out to Carmichael. "Bulletproof, sir?"

"Thank you, sergeant." It wouldn't fit over his coat, so he put it on underneath, like a waistcoat.

The convoy drove off and waited in Russell Square, on the most likely route. The wait was interminable. Every half hour, the radio car contacted the Watchtower briefly, to make sure everything was still in working order. Carmichael sat beside Richards in the Bentley, wishing he'd waited in his office. The flak jacket dug uncomfortably into his side. Passersby looked at them curiously, and one man walking a dog scurried off down a side street rather than pass them. "We're not inconspicuous, sergeant," he said.

"No, sir. Did you want to be, sir?"

That was unanswerable. "I suppose not," he said.

Later, Richards asked, "When we have secured the hostage, where do we take her, sir? Back to the Watchtower?"

Carmichael started. "No, that won't do. I'll take her. But you'll have to stop them following me."

"Yes, sir." Richards got out of the car and walked along the parked convoy, giving or adjusting orders. "That's sorted, sir," he said when he came back. "Constable Black will be moving up to be your driver, and I'll stay and direct the operation. He'll keep his eye out for anyone following."

"Not Black," Carmichael said. "Can I have Collins?" Black was driving one of the marked cars and Collins the other. The only real difference between them was that Collins was a member of the Inner Watch.

"If you prefer, sir," Richards said. "I'll tell them. Now when it happens, sir, if you don't mind, you just stay in this car. You don't need to get out unless I signal you, or anything happens to me."

"Very good, sergeant," Carmichael said. "I won't come across you, this is your operation."

"Yes, sir."

Richards got out and went over to Black, and then Collins. He went to the van and had a word with the men inside. Carmichael didn't see how many were in there, but they looked crowded. Then Richards came back and folded himself into the driver's seat beside him. "That's all sorted, sir. Collins will drive you."

"Well done, sergeant," Carmichael said. They settled down again to wait. It was some time before a signal came from the radio car.

It all went with strange dreamlike precision, as the Yard van drove up Great Russell Street. It came on without hesitation, and as it came alongside the convoy, almost before Carmichael was aware what was happening, the Watch van skewed across the road in front of it, forcing it to a stop. The two marked cars immediately flanked it, and all of them were instantly bristling with armed Watchmen. Sergeant Richards got out of the Bentley, which hadn't moved. "We want your prisoner," he called. "Hand her over and nobody gets hurt. This is a Watch operation. Everybody out."

Bannister got out of the Yard van, followed by three bobbies in uniform and Elvira, in a prison paper dress and with her hands cuffed behind her. He felt a huge wave of relief on seeing her. He felt hot tears prickle at the back of his eyes and blinked them away fiercely.

"Let me see your papers," Bannister said, taking a step towards Sergeant Richards.

"You're seeing our guns, matey," Richards said, though Carmichael had given no orders against showing papers. "Now unless you want to see them a lot closer, like inside your head, stop right there and hand her over. We're the ones who ask to see papers. Nobody messes with the Watch."

Carmichael felt proud of him, of the Watch, of all of them. Not a gun barrel hesitated. Bannister looked around, then said something in a low voice to one of his constables, who gave Elvira a little push towards Richards. Richards didn't take his eyes off Bannister. Constable Collins came up and put his jacket around Elvira and led her over towards the car where Carmichael was waiting. A huge snarl of traffic was building up behind them.

"I'll take her papers. And the keys to those cuffs," Richards said.

"We don't have the keys, they're standard transfer cuffs," Bannister said. "As for her papers, this is what I have." He held out a packet to Richards, who nodded, and another constable took it.

Elvira looked pale and cowed. "Uncle Carmichael," she said, as he opened the car door.

"I'm so glad you're safe," he said. The constable with her papers handed them to Carmichael, who tucked them inside his coat. Elvira collapsed against Carmichael's side, shivering and crying. He put his arm around her.

Collins got into the driver's seat. "Where to?" he asked.

23

At first I hadn't the faintest idea what was happening. Nothing was further from my mind than the idea of rescue. From the time when Bannister had said they were investigating Uncle Carmichael, I'd assumed he wouldn't be able to help me, and as time had gone on and on I'd come more and more to believe that he wouldn't be able to. I'd resigned myself to torture, or anyway extreme methods, as Sergeant Evans discreetly put it, followed with being shipped off to the knackers. In that van, on the way to Finsbury, with my hands cuffed and Bannister beside me, I almost felt as if I was already dead and forgotten. When it suddenly screeched to a halt, I fell forward and bumped my chest into the side of the van. Then Bannister got out, and I could hear confused shouting. I couldn't think about running or anything, because there were two bobbies in the van with me, as well as the driver, both keeping a close eye on me. Then Bannister opened the door and told us all to get out. He didn't sound surprised at all by what was happening, so I still didn't realize. One of the bobbies gripped the top of my arm and I stepped out.

They'd given me back my shoes for the trip, but no stockings, so the wind hit my legs hard. The daylight—quite ordinary April afternoon daylight, sun filtered through clouds—seemed terribly bright.

I stood there blinking for a moment. We were outside the Russell Hotel, where I'd once been taken for tea years before with Elizabeth Mitchell and her grandmother. The road was full of cars and flashing lights and Watchmen and rifles, all pointed in my general direction. I felt like a grouse on the Twelfth, and it was only then I realized that they weren't attacking me, they were here for me, to rescue me. I recognized Sergeant Richards, a great giant of a man, and several of the others. One of them winked at me. I couldn't believe it.

I should have known Uncle Carmichael would have been able to come for me, I thought, feeling terribly guilty that it was too late. Bannister exchanged some conversation with Sergeant Richards, and then the bobby holding my arm let me go, and a Watchman put his jacket around my shoulders, and took my elbow, quite gently, and just like that I was walking away, out of that ring of guns and eyes towards an ordinary black Bentley with Uncle Carmichael in it.

"Uncle Carmichael," I said. I was feeling quite stunned. It was all so abrupt. I got into the backseat beside him. My hands were still cuffed behind my back, so it was hard to get in properly. The jacket slipped down off my shoulder.

"I'm so glad you're safe," he said. One of the Watchmen passed him something, and the other got into the car. I started to cry, and Uncle Carmichael put his arm around me and just held me.

I didn't think at all about what Penn-Barkis and Bannister had said about the beastliness and all of that. I just cared that he was my beloved uncle and he had come for me. "Make sure we're not being followed, and then make for Ambrose Gardens," he said to the driver.

"Yes, sir," the driver said. "Is this Inner Watch business?"

"As soon as you're sure we're not being followed it is. If Sergeant Richards asks, I gave you directions and you took us to somewhere behind Claridge's. Thank you, Collins, that was very well done."

"Nothing, sir," Collins said. "Can't have them snatching Miss Royston like that." Yet as far as I knew, I'd never seen him before.

"Where are we going?" I asked, through my sobs. "And what's the Inner Watch?"

"Sorry, sir," Collins said.

"The Inner Watch is an organization within the Watch that helps innocent people who might otherwise be in trouble," Uncle Carmichael said. I couldn't see him, because I was tucked up under his arm, but I could feel him tensing as he spoke. "Did you know about it before?"

"No," I said. "You mean they were *right*? You really are doing something seditious and criminal?"

"I suppose so," Uncle Carmichael said, tightly.

I didn't know what to think. I'd only half believed it about Mrs. Talbot. "Why didn't you tell me?" I asked. I pulled away from him and sat up.

"So you couldn't tell them," he said. "The less you know the safer you are. This should never have touched you."

"Why do you do it?" I asked. I couldn't believe he had put me at risk this way.

"You're not the only innocent girl ever to be swept up by the system," Collins said, looking at me in his mirror. "Your uncle rescues a lot of people who never know who to thank. You shouldn't be accusing him, miss."

"Thank you," I said, stiffly. "Where are we going?"

"We're taking you somewhere safe, where you'll be passed along to another safe place, where you'll have to stay for a few days until it's all right for you to come out again. You'll be in some of our Inner Watch safe houses," Uncle Carmichael said.

"I'm being presented on Tuesday night," I said, absurdly.

Uncle Carmichael laughed. "Don't worry about that now," he

said. "Do you have a cuff key, Collins? She'll look funny being presented to the Queen with the handcuffs as accessories."

Collins snorted, and the next time we stopped at a red light he handed back a key on a chain, which Uncle Carmichael used to undo the handcuffs. I rubbed my arms, where they were sore from the cuffs, and my chest where it had bashed into the van. This made me realize I was still wearing the paper dress and Collins's Watchman's jacket. "I need some proper clothes," I said.

"They'll have something where you're going," Uncle Carmichael said.

"It might be better if she put your coat on, sir," Collins suggested. "It's long and it'll cover her up. Nobody would pay any attention to a girl in a macintosh, and what she's wearing is very conspicuous, even if she's only on the street for a minute."

Uncle Carmichael took off his coat and handed it to me. I put it on. It was much too big in the shoulders, of course, and I'd never normally wear a beige coat, but the height was just right to be fashionable. I buttoned it up and belted it around my waist.

"Why did they arrest me now?" I asked.

"There really is a plot against the government, by the Duke of Windsor, and British Power is part of it. They thought you being at the riot was suspicious, since apparently Sir Alan is a part of it."

"They asked me a lot of questions about Sir Alan," I confirmed. "And I think he is involved. He was hoping you could help him."

"He can keep hoping," Uncle Carmichael said. "What possessed you to get engaged to him?"

"I didn't," I said. "It was all a mistake. A misunderstanding. I never said I'd marry him."

"Thank goodness for that. He's a cad, and I refuse permission."

I wasn't sure whether he could refuse permission for me to marry, but it didn't seem like a good time to have that argument, as I didn't want to marry Sir Alan anyway. "So they were afraid he was involved with British Power, and I was, and therefore you were?"

"That's about it. But also, Penn-Barkis took you to see what I'd do, Elvira, and I wasn't prepared to put up with it. When he sees that I won't, especially as he must know by now that I have nothing to do with British Power, then it'll all be all right again. If not, well, if not then you and I will have to get out of the country. But if it comes to that, I have plans, don't worry."

"There's nobody following us now, sir," Collins said. "If I go round the block to Ambrose Street, I can drop you at the curb."

Uncle Carmichael looked at me. "We're going to drop you at a clothes shop. Ask to speak to Mr. Ambrose. When they say there is no Mr. Ambrose, say you want to buy some green flannel pajamas. They'll take you through to the back, give you some clothes, and someone will take you on to a house where you can stay until it's safe for me to collect you. Stay there, Elvira, or wherever they send you on, because otherwise I won't be able to find you."

"Yes," I said. I was still bewildered. The car drew to a halt, and Uncle Carmichael leaned over and opened the door for me.

"Go safely," he said, and kissed the top of my head. "I'll see you soon. Here, you'd better have these, but don't use them."

I took a packet from him, and pushed it into my pocket. "Goodbye," I said, getting out. "And thank you, and thank you too, Mr. Collins."

The clothes shop was in front of me. It was called Ambrose Clothes and Stores. The slogan across the window was GOOD QUALITY CLOTHES IN QUANTITY. There was yellow cellophane in the windows, to protect the clothes inside, and I saw school blazers and summer dresses on display. It looked like the kind of place where a respectable but impoverished mother of a large family would shop. I went in. There was a counter across the room, dressmaker dummies displaying summer cotton dresses, racks of patterns, and bales of cloth. There was a young woman behind the counter, and another older woman attending to a customer—she had two different sprigged cottons spread out before her and was clearly debating their merits.

"Can I speak to Mr. Ambrose?" I asked the young attendant. Without conscious decision, it had come out in my Cockney voice, which felt more natural for this shop.

"Mum!" the young woman said. "Someone asking for Mr. Ambrose."

"I'll deal with this," her mother said. "You help Mrs. Tenant with the cottons, Flo." The two of them changed places. "Now, there's no Mr. Ambrose here, miss," she said to me, giving me a penetrating look. "Is there anything else I can help you with?"

"I want some green flannel pajamas," I said, feeling absurd, like the time I'd had to play Celia in the school play and I felt as if people would laugh at all my lines except the funny ones.

"You'd better come through to the back," she said, and opened a flap in the counter and ushered me through, behind the bales of cloth and through a solid door, which she shut behind us, into another room. It was piled up with boxes and boxes, all brown, and all written on in neat black handwriting. "What are they thinking, no warning, and on Erev Pesach," she said. "What do you need, love?"

"I need somewhere to stay for a few days, until it's safe, and if you don't mind, some clothes, because I only have this coat." I opened it and showed her the prison dress underneath.

She tutted, and immediately started fumbling around in the boxes. "You'd be about a thirty-four?" she asked.

"Thirty-six-C," I said, embarrassed, but she must not have meant bra size because she pulled out a navy blue polyester dress, some knickers, and after some more fumbling a cream woolly sweater. "And a bra, I haven't forgotten," she said.

She opened another box and whistled to herself. "Here you are, I hope beige is all right," she said. "Now put those on, and I'll pop round with you to Paula's. You'll be safe enough there, and she doesn't have anyone there at the moment."

"Do you help a lot of people?" I asked, pulling off the prison dress, which tore, and putting on the bra and knickers as fast as I could.

"Sometimes we might go a week or two without anyone, other times ten people in a week," she said. "They give us money; don't worry about paying for those clothes." I started, and missed the hooks on the bra, because I hadn't even thought about it. I had no money, as of course they hadn't given me my bag back. "They got you out of prison, did they?" she asked, picking up the dress and crumpling it into a ball. "I'll burn this."

"They were taking me to Finsbury," I said.

"Don't tell me anything, what I don't know I can't tell," she said. "We've been doing this nearly ten years now, and never any trouble."

I pulled the navy dress on. It wasn't long enough, and it felt cheap and scratchy. I was cold, so I put the sweater on over it—it wasn't wool—and then Uncle Carmichael's coat over that. She handed me another two pairs of knickers, which I stuffed into the coat pocket. Then she gave me a hairbrush, which I used right away. "Is that your natural color?" she asked.

"What, my hair?" I asked. "Yes, it is."

"You should try lightening it up with some highlights, if you get the chance," she said. "Looks less Jewish, like, and you've got the skin for it."

"I'm not Jewish," I protested.

"What are you here for, then?" she said, skeptical. "Have you been passing? Well, you needn't try that on me."

I didn't argue, but put the hairbrush in the pocket of Uncle Carmichael's coat, along with the packet he had given me. I glanced at it, and saw it was my identity card and papers.

The woman led the way out of the back of the shop and down the road to the corner, where we waited at a bus stop. We got onto the bus, and she paid both fares. After a long ride through parts of London I didn't know at all, we got off at another corner. In one way this was all terribly tedious and I couldn't wait for it to be over so I could sleep, but in another way it was all marvelous that London was so big and so full of people and red double-decker buses and houses, and I wanted to hug all of it for being there and normal and not a little cold room with someone asking me questions.

I trudged with her up another long street. The houses were all built in terraces of red brick, sharing walls with one another. They had little square gardens outside, some of which grew a few brave flowers. She didn't talk at all while we were walking, and I didn't feel I could start a conversation. I was getting more and more tired as we went. The little squares of grass in the gardens started to look as if they'd make comfortable beds. At last she stopped, opened a gate, took two steps up the garden path, and knocked on a door. She used an odd knock; two raps and then two more.

The door was opened by an elderly woman in a pink dress. "Oh, Mrs. Berman," the shop woman said. "Is Paula here?"

"Where else would she be?" Mrs. Berman replied, and then bellowed down the passage, "Paula!"

Paula Berman was a pretty middle-aged woman with brown curly hair and a pleasant smile. She looked quite athletic, as if she could run a mile or swim fifty laps without breaking into a sweat. I felt relieved to see her somehow, as if she'd be able to organize everything now. "I'm sorry to bother you, and today of all days, but this little one needs a place for a day or two," the shop woman said.

"It's Pesach," Mrs. Berman said.

"All the more reason to take her in, Mother. Dan and Becky will just have to go home to sleep, that's all, and we can squeeze another one in around the table." She spoke cheerfully, and smiled at me.

"Now I'd love to have you come in properly, but that won't do, so you'll have to come around the back and up inside. I'm sorry to do this when you're so tired."

"I'm all right," I said, though I was ready to drop.

"Pesach kasher v'sameach," Mrs. Berman said, or something like that, and the shop woman echoed her. We left, calling good-byes, for the benefit of the neighbors, and walked around the block and down an alley that ran behind the row of houses. Each house had a back garden and many of them had sheds. The shop woman took me to one of the sheds, and looked both ways to make sure nobody was watching. Then she stepped inside, and beckoned me to follow. Once inside, she took a spade off the wall, and pulled the hook where the spade had hung, which opened a trapdoor.

"You go down those steps, and along the passage, and you'll come up in Paula Berman's kitchen," she said. *"Mazel tov!"*

There was a huge cobweb across the steps, which I gingerly edged around. The shop woman closed the trapdoor, and at once a little light came on. The passage was stone-flagged but the walls were earth. It bent to the right, and then there was another turn and another flight of stairs. Paula Berman was standing on them, with light pouring down behind her. "We never get around to cleaning in here," she said. "Maybe I should sweep it out now. Apart from this, everything was done yesterday."

"That's all right," I said. "It's very kind of you to have me."

"Our pleasure, my dear," she said. "It's a good day for taking in strays. Now are you hungry? Tired?"

"Both," I said, following her up the stairs and into the back kitchen.

Now whatever you may have heard, it isn't true that Jews are dirty. Apart from the passageway, I didn't see as much as a speck of dust or dirt anywhere in Paula's house; in fact it was spectacularly and notably clean. Even the oven was spotless. "We're going to be eating late, of course," she said, leading me out into the proper kitchen. "It's five o'clock. There's two hours until sunset. Would you like something to keep you going, and then a nap?"

"Yes," I said. "Thank you." I sat down at the kitchen table—the kind of table that's called a "scrubbed" table, and this one was scrubbed to within an inch of its life. A fat servant with a thick accent brought us a pot of tea—I declined milk and sugar—and after a moment a plate of new potatoes, cooked with mint. I'd never eaten anything so delicious in my life, and I said so. Paula sat down with me and drank tea, which was good, too, stronger than I like, but very good. While I was eating, Mrs. Berman came in and started fussing away at things, setting timers on the stove, and then just when I was finishing, two children erupted into the kitchen, a girl and a boy of about eight and six.

"These are my children, Ben and Debbie," Paula said. "Children, this is our cousin Hava."

I looked at Paula and raised my eyebrows as the children shook hands with me and went dashing off out of the room. Mrs. Berman followed after them. "Hava?" I asked. It had a long *A,* in fact it sounded just like "harbor" except with a *V.*

"I should have told you," she said. "I haven't asked your name, though you know mine. I always call all our visitors my cousin Hava, or my cousin Michael, that way if the children babble in school it doesn't sound like anything. I hope you don't mind the name."

"It's very pretty," I said. "I haven't heard it before, is it a Jewish name?"

She looked at me with her head a little on one side. "Are you not Jewish?" she asked.

"No, I'm not," I said.

The servant sniffed. Paula laughed. "Well, I think we won't mention that to my mother-in-law. She's a little old-fashioned. It doesn't make any difference to me. We help anyone who needs help. We've had people who weren't Jews before, occasionally, but they've always been men."

"I see," I said, though I didn't.

"Everyone knows I'm Jewish. It's on my identity card, after all. Hava certainly is a Jewish name, and if anyone wants to know details about my cousin Hava, I can say that's her Hebrew name, and her real name is . . . one of my real cousins from Manchester. It's just a safety precaution, more for when the children were younger than now."

"You've really thought about this," I said, but what I was thinking was how brave she was, taking this extra risk, when being Jewish was risk enough for anyone.

"You look exhausted, let me show you to the spare bedroom. I'll send Debbie up to wake you before we start," she said. "I hope you don't find it all too confusing."

"I'm sure it'll be all right," I said. My eyes were closing. She showed me out into the hallway and up a flight of carpeted stairs into a little room with a bed. I took off my shoes and lay down and was asleep before I could even start to think about what was happening to me.

24

It was half past four. Time to get back to the Watchtower and cover whatever needed to be covered. Everything had been done in the open, except for the very end. If Penn-Barkis, or even Normanby, took it as a challenge, he had better be where they could get hold of him to shout at him. But shouting was all they could do—they needed him, and he'd just shown them that the Watch would follow him.

"Back to the Watchtower now, Collins," Carmichael said.

"Yes, sir." Collins changed lanes sharply. "I'm sorry if I spoke a bit out of turn, before."

"Not at all, thank you for saying it. She needed to hear it. I don't know what she's going to think about all this in the end, but at least she'll be safe to think about it. I've been so worried." It was only as he said this that Carmichael realized how worried he had been. He was still worried, and would be until she was back where she belonged, but she was safe in the hands of the Inner Watch.

He started to relax as Collins drove him into more familiar streets and at last drew up in front of the Watchtower steps. "Don't forget, if they ask—," he began.

"Dropped her behind Claridge's, then took you back to the

Watchtower," Collins said. "And if they ask, I'll let you know, or Mr. Jacobson."

"That's right," Carmichael said. "Thank you, Collins. Good job."

Miss Duthie looked up as he came down the corridor. "Where's your coat?" she asked.

"I gave it to Elvira," he said. "She's safe, we got her away."

"Oh, thank God," she said, fervently.

"I'm going to go home a bit early, but I'll look at anything urgent first," Carmichael said, opening his door.

"Your telephone has been ringing off the hook, but Mr. Ogilvie and Mr. Jacobson have dealt with most of it. Mr. Ogilvie said to tell you he's gone out to Heath Row with the Duke of Hampshire to meet Herr Hitler."

"Good," Carmichael said. "Bring me some tea and whatever is most urgent."

"Right away," Miss Duthie said. "I'm so glad about Elvira, really, it's a great load off my mind."

"Mine too, Miss Duthie," he said.

As soon as he sat down at his desk the external telephone rang. He answered it. "Carmichael here."

"What do you think you're doing?" It was Mark Normanby, absolutely furious.

"Protecting my own, since you wouldn't help me," Carmichael said, calmly. "No harm done."

"Good God, man, do you think you're above the law?"

"Yes, I do. And so do you, and so does Chief-Inspector Penn-Barkis. And we're all right."

"Hand her back, Carmichael." Normanby sounded furious.

"No. She's innocent and she knows nothing. She's my ward. She's not even engaged to Bellingham. There is no dangerous connection. I have her safe and I intend to keep it that way."

"I gave you the Watch and I can take it away," Normanby raged.

"You need me," Carmichael said, secure in the knowledge that it was true. "Of course you can replace me, but you know that I am loyal. You have a hold on me, you always have had. You don't need to threaten my family, that was going too far. You wanted to see what I'd do, and I'm showing you I won't stand for that."

"I don't know who you think you are," Normanby said, and slammed the receiver down so hard that Carmichael winced. He put his own telephone down and smiled to himself. It was so good to be able to speak to Normanby without cringing, to use some of the power he had.

Miss Duthie came in with the tea and a pile of papers, all of which she set down carefully on the desk. "These are the most urgent," she said. "Should I put all your calls through now?"

"Yes, go ahead."

"I told most people to catch you tomorrow, so I don't expect there'll be much," she said.

Carmichael looked at the pile and sighed, then pulled it reluctantly towards him. The paper on top dealt with the house arrest of the Duke of Windsor, which had gone ahead as ordered. The next four pieces were vehement protests from the Duke, handwritten, addressed to Sir Guy; Mr. Blair, the Director General of the BBC; Air Vice-Marshal Harris; and Winston Churchill. Carmichael smiled as he read them. Under these was a note from Ogilvie to the effect that the Duke believed that correspondence dropped into the slot in his room would automatically be posted, but in fact it was all being collected by the Watch. Under this was a letter from the Duke of Windsor to the Duke of Hamilton, ordering him to go ahead with all the BP plans in his absence, and signed "Edward R." That was probably sufficient to constitute treason. A note from Ogilvie was clipped to this, saying laconically, "Duke of Hamilton arrested 3 P.M."

Nothing else in the pile was as interesting. There was a brief note confirming that the Yard had got to Bellingham first, a lot of information about the procession and the peace conference, including the positioning of snipers on possible rooftops in case of assassins, which Carmichael blinked at in wonder. Ogilvie really was very thorough, and had been working hard. He was the one who deserved a knighthood. There was just one note from Jacobson saying briefly not to worry, the riot situation was under control and Ted McMaster would be handling it tomorrow when Jacobson was out.

Carmichael got up and collected his hat. "I'm going home a little early. You can go now too, Miss Duthie. You've done a good day's work. I'll see you tomorrow."

He'd get home early and surprise Jack, he thought, looking at his watch. He should be home before six, which was very unusual. He waved over a car. "Home, please," he said to the driver. He shut his eyes as the car began to weave through the traffic. He'd slept badly, wondering what they were doing to Elvira. But now she was safe, hidden away, and he had time to go home and see Jack and perhaps eat something before meeting Sir Guy later. Then when he'd found out what that was about he'd go home and have an early night.

The guard on the door nodded as he opened it for Carmichael, and Carmichael nodded back. He went up the stairs two at a time, eager to tell Jack that Elvira was safe, but his door stayed closed, and he had to take out his key to open it. "Jack?" he called, going in, but he already knew the place was empty. Jack wasn't expecting him home so early. In fact he had said that morning that he might be late. He fought down his disappointment. Jack had every right to go out, whether he was running errands, visiting the library or even the Caravan Club.

One of the books he'd bought Jack the week before, a new translation of the *Chronographia*, lay on the coffee table, face down, though it was festooned with bookmarks. It wasn't like Jack to be so careless. Carmichael put a bookmark in where it was open and closed it carefully. The Byzantine mosaic princess on the cover seemed to sneer at him. He walked through the flat looking for signs of Jack. In the kitchen, some teacups waited to be washed. In the refrigerator were two fat pork chops wrapped in butcher's paper, a cabbage, and a bag of mushrooms. In the bedroom, the bed was neatly made and a parcel of clean shirts from the laundry waited to be put away. Nothing indicated where Jack was or how long he might be. He put his head around the door of the little box room they called Jack's dressing room, next to the kitchen. The spartan single bed was made up but strewn with Jack's clothes. The bed in Elvira's room was stripped, and her chest pushed back into the corner.

Carmichael wandered back into the sitting room, defeated. The bookshelves bulged with Jack's Byzantine books. He turned on the television, and was rewarded by a pair of teddy bears grinning at each other. He stabbed savagely at the button. On the other side was an old war film, the heroine melting into the hero's arms. He sat down to watch, but as she sped away across the Steppes on skis he realized he had seen it before. He pushed the button again and caught the news.

"There have been more protests today in almost all parts of the country," the announcer said. Scenes of protest flickered across the little screen. Maybe Jacobson was right, if so many people were taking to the streets. "Huddersfield, Blackburn, Glasgow, Wolverhampton, Cambridge. The question to the forefront seems to be the treatment of the alleged Hyde Park martyrs, but many other issues are being raised." To Carmichael's surprise the massed rioters were replaced by his own face, looking fatter than the way he saw it in the mirror. "Innocent people were arrested in the heat of the moment, certainly, and we have screened and are screening the suspects very closely to separate the sheep from the goats. By now, most of the sheep are back on the streets of London. Only the goats are getting what they deserve." He winced. The picture cut back to protesters. One had a banner reading FREE THE SCAPEGOATS!

"Watch Commander Carmichael wasn't available for comment this afternoon, but Deputy Jacobson had this to say." Jacobson looked nervous. His hand fumbled with his tie as he talked. "People are taking courage from each other. We can't arrest the whole country. Maybe mistakes have been made and we are certainly looking back carefully. For the time being, while we investigate nobody is being deported." Carmichael wasn't sure if that would calm things down or have the opposite effect. "And the Gravesend camp?" the interviewer asked. "The Gravesend facility isn't yet open," Jacobson said, which was nothing but the truth. They hadn't even finished building it. The camera cut to a picture of Hitler descending from an airship plastered with swastikas. "The Fuhrer arrived today in advance of the peace conference, due to begin on Wednesday. He will dine with Her Majesty this evening, and tomorrow visit Kew Gardens." Hitler paused on the steps to smile and give his straight-arm salute. Carmichael turned the television off in disgust. Where was Jack?

He thought about pouring himself a whisky, but remembered that he would have to drink later with Sir Guy. He wished he hadn't made the appointment, but curiosity alone would cause him to fulfill it. If Jack wasn't going to be back in time for dinner maybe he should go out and get something to eat, though the pork chops looked as if he meant to be home in time to cook. He walked over to the wall phone and called down to the guard below. "What time did my man go out?"

"He went out with a couple of bobbies at about five," the guard said, matter-of-factly. "They weren't quite dragging him, but it was a near thing. I was surprised, to tell you the truth. I mean I know servants steal, but he'd been with you for years, hadn't he? And always so polite."

"Bobbies," Carmichael repeated.

"Yes, uniformed bobbies. They had cards and everything, or I wouldn't have let them in. They said not to give him any warning. Did I do wrong, sir?"

"You were just doing your job," Carmichael said.

About five. Just after he'd spoken to Normanby. Jack knew everything. But Jack had a tooth, and Jack wasn't a coward. He'd been in action, in France, and he'd done his best to save Carmichael's life on the boat home from Dunkirk. If they started to press Jack, Jack would die rather than betray him. Carmichael realized he was still holding the receiver and put it down gently. The thing to do would be to get Jack out before they started to press him. But a straightforward attack wouldn't work if they were expecting it, and besides, he had no idea where they might have taken him. He felt strangely distant. He remembered Jack the night before, standing there so practical, helping him organize his priorities. First, he thought, he should see if there was anything to be gained by groveling.

The telephone was on the table next to his chair, so he sat down. Jack, he thought, and felt as if a part of himself had been amputated. He called Normanby and had to pass through two layers of secretaries. "Well, Carmichael, have you come to your senses?" Normanby asked.

"Yes, Prime Minister, I have," Carmichael said. "I don't know how I could have been such a fool."

"Neither do I," sneered Normanby. "You knew you had hostages. Now, give us back the girl and then we can talk about your . . . servant."

"Yes, Prime Minister," he said. I'm sorry, Elvira, he thought, remembering her in the car asking how he could put her in danger. Then he remembered that now she knew about the Inner Watch. "I can't get hold of her right away," he added, temporizing.

"Then we'll keep hold of Jack until you can," Normanby said.

"You won't hurt him?"

"You're very anxious for his welfare, belatedly. I don't believe he'll come to any harm. How soon can you get the girl?"

Carmichael took a deep breath. He felt as if he wasn't getting enough oxygen even so. "Sir, you said this morning you'd give her back in a day or two. And you've made your point, you've made it very clearly indeed. Is this really necessary?"

"You're the one who forced the issue by laying hands on her," Normanby said. "*Is* this just a power play, Carmichael, or is there really something you've been getting up to? Something beyond the obvious, that is?" He laughed.

"I'll have her in the morning," Carmichael said.

"Get in touch with Penn-Barkis when you do, and he'll sort out the details," Normanby said, and the line went dead.

Carmichael stared at the cross-eyed Byzantine princess on Jack's book. Jack would die rather than reveal anything. Elvira would tell them about the Inner Watch, as well as whatever else it was she might have known, which he'd forgotten to ask her about. He could get hold of her through the shop on Ambrose Street. If Normanby knew about the Inner Watch they were all as good as dead anyway. Jack had wanted to run last night, and they should have. If Carmichael left Elvira where she was, she was safe. They'd get her out, to Ireland and maybe beyond that to Canada. It wouldn't be what she was expecting, but she'd be alive and free, and so would the other people the Inner Watch could carry on helping. If he left Jack to die. Left Jack to die, the thought was impossible, ridiculous. Jack might be dead already. But he couldn't sacrifice Elvira for Jack, because Jack wouldn't be safe in any case. The only chance would be if there was time to get away, after they gave him back Jack and before Elvira talked. Only that morning the thought of Elvira being tortured had seemed the worst thing in the world, now he was coldly calculating how long she could hold out if he betrayed her to it. He groaned.

On the wall opposite hung the picture of Hagia Sophia, undis-
turbed. There was money behind it, and false identity cards and passports. Jack hadn't had a chance to use them. Carmichael opened the
safe—the combination was 1453, Jack's choice. Everything was
painful, everything reminded him of Jack. He took out the new iden-
tities for Elvira and Jack too, and the other thing the safe contained,
his old Farthing notebook. He took his black coat from the peg and
stuffed the whole lot into the pockets. He would go out and have the
drink with Sir Guy and find out what that was about, and after that
he would decide what to do. At least he could walk. Movement might
help him feel better, or at least more capable of making a decision.

He walked all the way to the river, and along the Embankment to
the Moon Under Water. It was mizzling, so the garden was empty.
He ducked his head and went inside, where Sir Guy was at the bar
again, although it was still early. "Carmichael," Sir Guy said. "Pint
of bitter?"

"Thank you," Carmichael said.

"You look dreadful. I'm not surprised, considering, but you do.
Have you eaten?" Sir Guy looked concerned.

"No," Carmichael admitted. "But I don't think I could."

"Let me get you a terrible ham sandwich and a packet of crisps,
which is all this place rises to. The beer's good, though."

The barmaid smiled at him and put a curling sandwich onto a
plate. "Salt and vinegar or cheese and onion crisps?"

"Salt and vinegar," Carmichael said.

"Make that two pints, and two whiskeys," Sir Guy said. "Let's go
over into the corner." He indicated the darkest part of the pub, far-
thest from the door and also from the other customers. They settled
onto the uncomfortable chairs, and set their beer down on the table.
"Cheers," Sir Guy said, taking a swig of his own beer.

"Cheers," Carmichael echoed, cheerlessly, following suit. "What's
this about?"

"Well, what I wanted to say this lunchtime is pretty much redundant by this time. I didn't think you'd be setting the Thames on fire all afternoon. I wanted to tell you that Mark was gunning for you and to lie low, because it would blow over."

"You could have told me that on the telephone," Carmichael said.

"Eat your sandwich," Sir Guy said.

Carmichael took a bite. The bread was dry, the lettuce limp, and the ham too salty.

"I wouldn't give you the time of day on the telephone, not yours and not mine. You probably record your own, and I know you record mine, and I suspect you're not the only one recording both of them. I didn't want it getting back to Mark that I was warning you. I didn't even give the name of this place, if you remember, though as Tibs knows it isn't very safe."

"You sound as if you've had a lot of practice at this kind of thing," Carmichael said, through a mouthful of sandwich.

"More than you'd imagine," Sir Guy said, looking a little sad. "Though not recently. But that's all moot. Look, have you been home?"

"Yes," Carmichael said.

"Then they've been following you. I told them if you came here to leave you alone, to bugger off and go home, that I'd take care of things from here on. But be careful when you go, all the same, in case they weren't listening properly."

"They snatched Jack," Carmichael said.

"Well, I'm sorry to have to tell you this, but he's dead," Sir Guy said, looking really sorry. Carmichael had known, almost known, been prepared for it, but all the same the news was more than he could bear. He felt his mouth opening wide as if to scream. Sir Guy handed him a whisky. "Knock it back, it's the best thing. The only thing, really."

Carmichael knocked it back, choked and spluttered. Sir Guy

handed him the other whisky. "Why are you doing this?" Carmichael asked.

"Common bloody humanity," Sir Guy said. "Not that that's a thing there's much of these days. I told you yesterday this wasn't the world I signed up for. I was being literal. This morning, I wanted to tell you to keep your head down. Now I'm telling you to get out. Leave the country. Don't stop. You seem like a decent chap."

"Did Jack tell them anything?"

"No, of course he bloody didn't. As I understand it, as soon as they started asking him about you, he offed himself. Hollow tooth, was it?"

Carmichael nodded. He couldn't quite believe that Jack was really dead and gone forever. One part of his brain still thought he could go home and tell Jack all about it.

"I thought so. I have one too."

"You have one? Why?" Carmichael sipped the second whisky.

"My masters in Moscow gave it to me, not long after I started to work for them. But as they're radioactive dust and ashes now, I suppose I don't need it as much as I did then. What happens when you're a sleeper for an organization and the organization vanished? What do you do then?"

"I don't know," Carmichael said. "You were a communist? Really? When you're Foreign Secretary?"

"They kept on telling me to keep my head down, do what Normanby wanted, get in with the Farthing crowd, let things get worse so they could get better," he said, taking a long pull of his beer. "And I did what they told me until they lost the war and my contacts ran away, or started to pretend they didn't know anything about anything. Now, I'm not sure what to do. I've realized that Stalin wasn't the right answer to the questions I had in Cambridge, any more than bloody Hitler was, but the questions are still there, and getting louder."

"You shouldn't have told me that."

"You've got a tooth too, if your man had one," Sir Guy said. "You'd use it before you gave them my secrets. You're a decent chap."

"I'm not," Carmichael said. "I thought about turning in Elvira to get Jack back."

"You didn't, though," Sir Guy said, with impeccable logic.

"I betrayed David Kahn, when I knew he hadn't done it, when I had proof that it was Normanby and Angela Thirkie."

Sir Guy's eyes widened. "Proof?" he said.

"They killed my witnesses. But I had their testimony. Agnes Timms, a hairdresser from Southend, and the dowager Lady Thirkie. Between them they could have hanged Normanby. Penn-Barkis wouldn't listen to me." Carmichael finished the second whisky and put the glass down.

"Do you still have the proof?" Sir Guy asked.

"For what it's worth now," Carmichael said, bitterly. "In fact I have it right here."

"Will you give it to me?" Sir Guy asked.

Carmichael fumbled through his pockets and pulled out the notebook. Even in the pain of losing Jack the sight of the notebook made him wince. He had set everything down so plainly, all his evidence, and it hadn't been worth a farthing.

Sir Guy took the book. "Get out, go now, tonight, as soon as you've finished your pint. It isn't safe for you. Even if you're as innocent as the day is long Mark will never believe it after that tooth business. He doesn't know what you've got to hide, but now he knows you really do have something to hide he won't let you get away with it. No, don't tell me what it is."

"I wasn't going to," Carmichael said, finishing his pint.

25

When little Debbie came to wake me I was dreaming that I was in a grand ballroom dancing with a snake. The snake had Sir Alan's beard but talked like Bannister, and I had to stay there with it making conversation until my friends came back, and the lights were going out and it was getting darker and darker, so all in all I was very glad to wake up. I wasn't even confused about where I was. "Mum says it's time to wake you. Everyone's here, we're about to start the seder."

I sat up and yawned. I hadn't undressed to sleep, but the navy dress had stayed surprisingly uncreased. I supposed that was its virtue, to make up for its unpleasant texture, along with its cheapness, of course. I followed Debbie downstairs and into a room I hadn't seen before.

My first impression was that hundreds of people were crammed around the table, and all the men were wearing long white robes, almost like dressing gowns, but with suits underneath instead of pajamas. The women and children were dressed up, and wearing enough jewelry between them to put good taste to shame—Mrs. Berman looked like a Christmas tree. I realized from the odd way the tablecloth was falling that the table was on two levels—probably the kitchen table had been brought in and put next to the dining room table, which was extended as far as it would go. Chairs were crammed in around it, filling the room. Two of the men were even sitting in armchairs. On the table was a silver plate with indentations, filled with what looked like food oddments, an elaborate silver goblet alone in the middle, what looked for all the world like a plate of Ryvita, and a collection of wine bottles.

Paula got up, showed me to a chair between her and little Ben, and introduced me to the company as her cousin Hava. She told me who everyone was, but it confused me. I gathered that her husband was the man in the armchair on her other side, the other man in an armchair was her brother, the woman next to him was his wife. A bearded man smiling across the table at me was Paula's brother-in-law, Dan, also with his wife, and the others were apparently friends who worked in the neighborhood. There were a lot of children, some of them quite young. I never did get it straight who they all belonged to. I did eventually gather to my astonishment that the plump woman sitting on the far end of the table, nearest to the door, was the servant who had brought me the potatoes earlier, sitting down to eat with the family. Not that there was any food yet, except the odd things on the plate. I could tell that there was proper food somewhere, because I could smell delicious roasting meat, but none of it was on the table.

"Hava isn't observant," Paula said. "We'll have to explain as we go along."

"It's supposed to be about explaining," said Debbie, taking her own seat. "It's supposed to be about explaining to children, but I already know about it. I'll help explain to you, Hava."

"Cousin Hava isn't going to ask the questions, is she?" asked one of the younger children, anxiously.

"No, don't worry, you'll ask your question," Paula's husband said. I was deeply relieved, as I'd have had no idea what to ask. And after that, with no more ado, they started.

It isn't true that they sacrifice babies. And they're clean enough to put us all to shame. But their customs are very peculiar, and all their prayers are in Hebrew, and they wear robes and have strange rituals in their houses in the evening. I'm not surprised that people get nervous about them and wonder what they're up to. I felt nervous myself. First, everyone trooped off to the kitchen to wash their hands, using a special cup, and everyone making jokes about not praying while they did it. Washing hands in the kitchen seemed very strange to me, almost dirty, although the kitchen was so very clean. Then we went back to sit down again, crowding in around the table. There were a lot of jokes, and a lot of arguing. Frankly, I didn't understand what was going on even with the explanations.

Then we dipped parsley in salt water (for affliction, Debbie told me, confusingly) and Dan broke the Ryvita in half, and then Paula's husband read a piece of Hebrew, and there was a little silence.

"It's hard to think now of God always redeeming us from the hands of those who persecute us," Dan said, scrunching the edge of the tablecloth between his fingers. "Knowing what's going on in Europe, and with the news about them opening a camp here."

I just stared at him. It did indeed seem as if the Jewish God wasn't doing a very good job of looking after his people just at present.

"Well," Paula said, looking around the table at the children and the older people and especially at me. "We've been through times like this before, and we've always come out of them. No matter how bleak things seem now, God will save us from this too. Maybe not any of us as individuals, but as a nation we will still be around long after they are as extinct as the Pharaohs."

Then they went back to Hebrew and incomprehensible behavior. I didn't know why they broke one of the pieces of Ryvita in half, or why the children stole it and hid it. I didn't know why we had to keep drinking, or picking up and not drinking, glasses of sweet red wine—with grape juice for the children, and for me after the first glass. But however peculiar it is, it's all done in goodwill. I couldn't mistake that. And they were good people. They'd taken me in when they didn't know the first thing about me.

Most of the service, if that's what it was, went over my head. Even when they were arguing in English, I didn't really know what they were arguing about. Paula's husband would read something, in Hebrew, and then they'd all quibble about it, or that's how it seemed to me. It was interminable, and I was getting hungrier and hungrier. The little bits of odd food they passed around didn't help. The children were getting visibly tireder. They took turns asking their questions. When Ben asked his, in Hebrew, and clearly memorized by rote, he looked up at me proudly. I smiled back at him and mouthed, "Well done." It certainly seemed like a lot more fun than I'd ever had in Sunday school.

After a lot of this, and some strange things like flicking wine, or grape juice, from our fingers onto plates, apparently to represent the plagues of Egypt, and filling the cup in the middle of the table, which I suppose was some sort of chalice, because nobody drank out of it, we all trooped off to the kitchen to wash our hands again. The smell of the food was unbearable. This time we did have to say a blessing, in Hebrew. Debbie said it for me, and reminded me to wash each hand twice. Then we went back to the table and ate the Ryvita, which wasn't exactly Ryvita but definitely some kind of crispbread. We had it first plain, then with horrible fresh horseradish. "Be careful, it burns," little Ben warned me. Then we had it with a weird kind of chopped salad stuff, with apples and walnuts, to which we were, amazingly, supposed to add more horseradish.

Eventually, after we'd eaten these, the servant got up and went to the kitchen, and Paula got up to go to help her. "Let me help too," I begged, and she nodded, so I followed her out. The servant was putting dumplings or something into the soup, and Paula took a huge

piece of beef brisket out of the oven. It was late in the evening—
we'd been sitting around the table for hours. I could hardly believe
we were going to sit down to such a heavy meal at this hour, but it
seemed we were. I'd almost stopped being hungry and would have
liked to have gone straight to bed. I was put to stir the soup, which
was some kind of chicken broth, with dumplings fluffing up in it.

There was a loud knock on the front door. Paula and the servant
froze, staring at each other. "Who could that be at this hour?" the
servant asked, in her thickly accented English.

"Nobody we know, or they'd have given the special knock," Paula
said. Then she turned to me. "Into the passage," she said. "If it's safe,
Rivka will come and get you soon. If she doesn't come, get out
through the passage and run for it. It comes out in Dan's garden,
not ours, so it should be safe even if they're behind the house."

I followed her out into the back kitchen. She drew up the rug that
covered the trapdoor. "Shouldn't you all hide?" I asked.

"There's probably no need," Paula said. Fat Rivka was walking
towards the door, calling out that she was coming as fast as she could,
there was no need to knock the door down. "Besides, the lights are
on. If they see the table laid and no visitors, they'll wonder even
more. Probably you're just going to spend ten uncomfortable minutes before we all laugh about this." Paula handed me my coat, or
rather Uncle Carmichael's coat, which I'd left in the kitchen earlier,
and I put over my arm.

I went down the steps and she closed the trap above me. The dim
little light came on, and I heard her putting the rug back in place. I
waited, hoping she was right, hoping this was nothing, that it wasn't
Bannister and Bushy Eyebrows and their friends come to find me
again, even though I knew it was. I even tried to pray, for whatever
good it could have done. I'd been to church almost every Sunday of
my life, but I think the last time I'd really prayed from my heart had
been when Betsy was pregnant.

I heard bangs from above, followed by screams. I thought about going back up the stairs and saying I was there, they should leave everyone else alone, but I knew if I did they'd only take it as proof the Bermans and their friends were guilty. They were guilty, guilty of hiding me, guilty of being Jews, of terrible taste in jewelry, of wearing weird robes and chanting in Hebrew, of not eating until ten o'clock at night. I walked away up the passage towards the place where it bent, where the light was. There was nothing I could do for the Bermans, nothing at all. It was hard to see clearly through the tears in my eyes, so I kept wiping them away as I walked.

There was nobody in the shed at the other end of the tunnel. It was drizzling. I put the coat on and came out cautiously. There were men waving electric torches around in a garden a few doors down, but nobody in front of my shed. I slipped away down the alley in the opposite direction, not running, but walking as rapidly as I dared. There were dustbins and things in the alley, and I didn't want to bang into anything and make a clatter. At the corner where the alley intersected a cross-street I turned towards the Bermans' street. When I came to it I glanced down it, then looked away and went on along the street I was on. There were three police cars outside the Bermans' house and they were dragging people out in handcuffs. None of the neighbors were paying any attention. I suppose people don't. I wouldn't myself, normally.

I kept walking, with no idea of where I was going. It was late, I was tired, I couldn't go to the Maynards or Uncle Carmichael or anyone I knew, because they'd find me there. Obviously Uncle Carmichael was wrong about how safe I was. I looked through the pockets of my coat as I walked and found a ten-shilling note and half a crown tucked down at the bottom underneath a big striped handkerchief. I wasn't sure how much a room at a hotel cost, and I knew that respectable young ladies didn't ever stay at hotels alone in any case. But I wasn't a respectable young lady, was I? I wasn't sure what I was, walking alone at night through a strange part of London. I wasn't Elvira Royston, of Arlinghurst and Switzerland and soon to be presented and then go to St. Hilda's. I wasn't the Cockney child I had been, but I knew what she knew. If I went to a hotel in my cheap ready-made frock and good shoes and man's coat, they'd take me for a prostitute, like the ones I'd met in prison, and throw me out. So where did prostitutes go? There I could be safe, or at least inconspicuous.

I was glad I'd had that thought, because on the next street corner there was a policeman. This street was well lit and had traffic on it, and I could see the warm lights of a pub glowing nearby. The policeman looked at me suspiciously. I didn't cower away as I would have before. "Got a fag?" I asked him, in my London voice, just as the streetwalker I'd met in Paddington had asked me. Prostitution was technically illegal, of course, but they could hardly arrest every whore in London. I didn't look quite sufficiently a floozy, for one thing I had no makeup on at all, but I obviously didn't arouse any suspicions.

"Try the George and Dragon," he replied, bored and already moving on.

I went into the pub. I had to, he was still on the corner and might have been watching. Besides, it was brightly lit and full of people. It smelt horribly of beer, which reminded me at once of the one place I could perhaps go and be safe. People looked up as I went up to the bar, but they looked away again quite quickly. Only one man kept on looking. He was unshaven and beer-smelling, and shorter than I was. "You working, love?" he asked.

"Not tonight," I said. "Do you know how much it would cost to get a taxi from here to Leytonstone?"

"Haven't the faintest," he said. He didn't seem unfriendly. "I'd go on the tube, assuming I wanted to go, which isn't very likely in the first place."

"Where's the nearest tube station?" I asked.

"Just down the street to Golders Green," he said, jerking his thumb in the direction away from the Bermans'.

I went to the bar and bought ten du Mauriers, tipped, and a box of matches. I lit one as I went out of the pub, in case the policeman was watching, but he'd vanished in any case. I walked off in the direction the man had indicated, smoking and coughing. I came to the tube station eventually, when I was starting to think I'd missed it, because nobody could say just down the road and mean this distance. I bought a ticket to Leytonstone and as soon as the train came subsided into a seat in the corner of the carriage.

Golders Green is where the Northern Line dives underground, after running on the surface. I felt safe once we were buried, anonymous, underground, hidden. I could almost have fallen asleep. There was a very tall man sitting opposite me with an amazing carved face. He was reading the *Standard*. The headline was "Strike Spreads." I changed trains in Tottenham Court Road, and made it without incident to Leytonstone not much after eleven. It was enough after that when I walked into the Nag's Head, my mother told me they were closed, though people were still drinking up.

She hadn't changed a bit. She still had the dyed red hair, overpainted face, and mutton-dressed-as-lamb look she'd had ten years before when my aunt Ciss had taken me there and persuaded her to agree to let Uncle Carmichael have me. She didn't recognize me at all, and I could see her coming to the same conclusion as the policeman and the man in the pub in Golders Green. "Out," she said. "It's after closing time."

"Mum," I said. "It's me, Elvira."

She stopped still and went pale beneath her makeup. "You never," she said. "All grown-up. I thought they was going to make you into a lady."

"They have been," I said. "But I'm in trouble."

"Always the same," she said, with a look at my waistline. "And I'm the only one you could think of who could help? Well, how far along are you?"

"Not that kind of trouble," I said, blushing, thinking of poor Betsy.

She frowned, as if the other had been at least comprehensible. The man behind the bar raised an eyebrow and took a step towards us, and she waved him away. "Did your Auntie Ciss send you?"

"She gave me your address, so I could send a Christmas card," I said. "But she didn't send me."

"You always have remembered the Christmas cards," she said, unbending a little. "Even one from the Alps. Where's that our Elvira's got to now, Germany, I asked Raymond, and he looked at the stamps and said no, Switzerland."

"That's right, I was in finishing school there," I said.

"So what do you want with me now?" she asked. "What sort of trouble are you in, anyway?"

"Police trouble," I said.

"But your dad was police, and your new uncle too," she said.

"He's in trouble too," I said. "I just need somewhere to hide for a couple of days, Mum. If you have a room or anything. They won't be looking for me here."

"What have you done?"

"Nothing," I said, but she looked at me disbelievingly.

"What's he done, then, your so-called uncle?"

I didn't want to tell her he was involved with rescuing Jews. She was the one who had first told me they were dirty and ate babies. "Butted heads with another policeman," I said. "It'll all be sorted soon. Can I stay here?"

"Of course you can," she said. "I was just overset for a minute, that's all. Come on and meet Raymond." She took my arm and I followed her to the bar. Raymond was older than my mother, but unlike her made no attempt to disguise it. He had meaty forearms, a beer belly, and no hair at all. "Raymond, this is my little girl, my Elvira that I've told you about."

"Pleased to meet you," I said, putting out my hand.

"I saw the likeness as soon as she came in," he said, taking my hand and squeezing it enthusiastically. "She's not quite as pretty, Irene, but I can definitely see you in her." He seemed appallingly sincere.

"Drink up now!" my mother suddenly bellowed. "Let's have your glasses!"

"When they're gone, we can open a bottle of champagne for the prodigal daughter," Raymond said.

"And you can tell us all about being made into a lady," my mother added.

I yawned.

26

Carmichael stood outside the Moon Under Water looking down at the Thames, which was oozing along in its usual mud-brown way, under the light evening rain, taking the echoes of streetlights and neon lights and reflecting them back as a kind of diffused glow. There was nothing on the South Bank to catch the eye, except Lambeth Palace, the Archbishop of Canterbury's London pied-à-terre. A boat hooted mournfully somewhere out of sight. He might just as well throw himself in the river as carry on without Jack. He touched the side of his jaw. Throwing himself in the river wasn't the sure route to death his tooth could provide. Carmichael considered suicide calmly for a moment. He could break out the tooth and die like Jack, without betraying anyone, without, or so the doctor had promised, very much pain. There'd be no chance that he'd betray the Inner Watch, or anyone. Everything could go on without him. Or he could shoot himself. He had the little pistol in his pocket.

The only reason he could find that made it worth struggling on was Elvira. If he left London immediately he could get in touch with Jacobson and have him send her to join him. He might not be able to give her Oxford, but surely there were universities in Canada or Australia? He had enough money, in untraceable securities, to pay for her education. He couldn't imagine what he could do himself, how he would live, but he could give Elvira that, in return for having endangered her, and thought of sacrificing her. The education was what she cared about, and he could give her that, even if it wasn't Oxford. Besides, he was afraid to die, even if living offered nothing to go on for. He stared out across the river at the hazed jewels that marked the streets of the South Bank and loathed himself. After a while he started to walk.

The thing Carmichael and Sir Guy had both forgotten about getting out of London quickly was Ogilvie's extra restrictions around Central London for the procession and opening of the peace conference. Carmichael remembered them just as he was about to run into one of the checkpoints. His false identity cards were good, but he was afraid of being searched with so many of them on him. Besides, he might well be recognized by any random Watchman. He was probably safe for the night, with Normanby expecting a call in the morning about exchanging Jack for Elvira, but he wasn't sure he'd be safe trying to leave London. If he waited he could leave London on Thursday, when the extra checkpoints were gone, and take Elvira with him.

He turned away from the checkpoint and went by Underground to Victoria Station. He wandered out into the mean rundown sidestreets in the Pimlico direction. The houses there had once been grand eighteenth-century and early nineteenth-century mansions. Time had not been kind to them—they were shabby now and down at heel, their stucco peeling, either subdivided into lodging houses or eking out a living as rundown hotels. It was far easier to be anonymous here than in a flophouse, where he would be conspicuous because he didn't belong. Here he could be one more failing commercial traveler, one more gray man who nobody cared about.

Although London was bulging with delegates for the conference, most of these hotels had signs reading VACANCY. Carmichael knocked at a door at random. It was opened by a cheerless woman in a print pinafore. "Yes?" she asked, listlessly, pushing back a strand of pale brown hair.

"Do you have a room for a couple of nights?" Carmichael asked.

"Yes," she said, and stood aside. He took this as an invitation and followed her inside. The hall had a smell of old kippers and cabbage, and the room she showed him was half underground and painted dark gold. He paid her for two nights in advance, and she handed him the obligatory police form to fill in. She checked it half-heartedly against his false card, looking from the picture to him. She looked again, and showed a first faint flicker of interest. "Have you been ill?" she asked.

"Yes," Carmichael said at once. "My glands. I lost nearly a month of work, I'll never make it up, and I don't know how we're going to pay the doctor's bills."

"My sister suffers terrible with her glands," she said, handing back the card. "You want to drink hot milk and build yourself up."

"That sounds like a good idea. Do you have some?"

"Me?" she asked, sounding offended, and went out, leaving the door open. "Bathroom's down the hall, and the lav next to it, if you want it."

If he wanted it, he thought, outraged, and then the outrage, the pleasure of having convinced her of his illness, and the desire for hot milk all disappeared into the bleakness of being alive in a world that had no Jack in it. He sank down on the bed, and sat there staring at a picture of a cross-eyed cat without seeing it. After a long time, he got up and closed the door. He took his coat off, carefully folded it up, and put it under the thin pillow. Locking the door carefully behind him, he went down the hall to use the toilet. When he came back he locked the door again, undressed, and turned out the electric light, deploring without really taking in the gold-tasseled shade. He got into bed and lay there for a while in the darkness.

Eventually, he wept, and was shaken with a storm of silent weeping. At last he fell asleep, like falling down a well.

He woke with the dawn and lay watching the piece of window at street level, far above his head, grow gray, then pink, then begin to darken periodically with the feet of early risers. He used the bathroom, running into an Indian in the hall and muttering good morning. He wondered if the man was here for the conference. India was due for Dominion status next year, if all went well. He dressed, pulled on his coat, and went out to find a cheap greasy breakfast in a corner café. The shop on Ambrose Street wouldn't open until ten, so there was nothing he could do until then. He couldn't call Jacobson, it was his Passover, and he'd been told never to telephone on Saturdays or holidays unless it was an emergency. This wasn't an emergency, quite. Jack hadn't told them anything, and Elvira should be safe enough where she was for a day or two.

The appalling breakfast (tea strong enough to go into the wrestling ring, bacon as limp as a face-flannel, fried eggs swimming in bacon fat, a burst sausage, an oozing tinned tomato, and two slices of cold toast) nevertheless did him good. It reminded him of the time when he had been an inspector for Scotland Yard and had no more to worry about than solving a case. He ached for a case to solve, a puzzle, a mystery to fit together, Sergeant Royston at his side and Jack waiting at home to hear about it when it was over.

He walked to Ambrose Street, through the early morning streets of London. He saw shops opening their blinds, and pale office workers hurrying from the Underground to work. He saw queues at bus stops disappearing into scarlet buses, which simultaneously disgorged a load of passengers who scattered onto the streets. The sun was shining and the air was clear after the rain. He saw hurrying businessmen clutching their bowler hats as a breeze came off the river. A black taxi honked its horn impatiently. In Covent Garden, where the fruit and flower market was almost over for the day, he stood for a while and watched a juggler tossing five balls in a complicated pattern, and at last gave him half a crown when he moved on. London was all around him, the familiar, ever-changing kaleidoscope of London. And there, in the pattern, belonging, was a helmeted bobby walking his beat, in blue uniform and silver buttons.

Carmichael, who did not belong and did not want to be seen, ducked into a newsagent and bought a copy of the *Times*. He sat in another corner café to read it, among the costermongers of Covent Garden, who were having their lunch. He drank Earl Grey tea, and hid behind his newspaper.

"Protests Spreading" read the headline. "Fuhrer Arrives Safely in Britain." Carmichael read the paper carefully, but there was no mention of his fall, or Elvira's rescue, or Jack's death. He hadn't really expected that there would be. He was interested to read of a protest against death camps in France. Marshal Desjardins had responded that he would have to look into the question.

Carmichael folded the paper up and left it on the table. He walked on, through a city now thoroughly awake, to Ambrose Street.

Although he wouldn't be recognized, he knew the code phrases, and felt confident he could soon be reunited with Elvira. Then they would both have to wait until Thursday and then—the simplest way out of the country was to take the boat-train from Paddington to Ireland. From Ireland, which maintained a prickly nose-thumbing independence from the practice and policies of the rest of Europe, it would be possible to go farther. They could take ship, or fly, to Canada. Jack had wanted to go to New Zealand, Carmichael remembered, and stopped, caught between two strides by a gale of grief. He blew his nose, that acceptable English substitute for emotion, and kept walking. They should have gone as soon as they knew Elvira was arrested. He should have told Jack as soon as Elvira was safe, to give him the courage to hold on until he could have been rescued in his turn. He should have gone years ago, as soon as they had the false papers. Jack had persuaded him to stay, to keep on helping.

When he turned onto Ambrose Street he recognized the stakeout at once. The unmarked cars, the men waiting, inconspicuously watching the shop, were unmistakable. He kept on walking, not slowing his stride at all, right through and past them, and on, his heart beating hard against his chest. How had they found Ambrose Street? Had Collins talked? Had that been what Elvira had known and told them—though how could she have? It wasn't possible. Had they followed them, after all, yesterday? That was the most plausible explanation. How much did they know, how much had they found, was Elvira still safe, or in their hands? He kept walking, regrets replaced by unanswerable questions.

He could track Elvira no farther without help. He had never known the details of the safe houses, beyond Ambrose Street, the gateway. If Penn-Barkis had Ambrose Street he had a great deal, but not everything. They knew where to send people, they had a system of safe houses in London—these were lost, none of them could be considered safe any longer. But they wouldn't have the rest of it, the mechanism for getting them out of the country, the false papers, the connections with the Inner Watch, all of that would still be safe, unless Collins had talked, or one of the other Inner Watchmen. He needed to call Jacobson. It was an emergency now.

He walked on, quickly, trying to look like someone with somewhere to be, late for an appointment. He tried not to feel eyes on his back as he turned the corner and made his way into the anonymity of other streets. He walked past three red telephone boxes and went into the fourth, one of a pair standing outside the gates of a little park. He dialed Jacobson's number. He could see the rusting iron railings dividing the road from the trees, and the little square of grass. The telephone rang and rang, with no reply. At last he gave up and dialed again. This time it was picked up on the first ring, and he had trouble pressing button *B* and getting his pennies inserted in time.

"Jacobson, it's me, Carmichael," he said.

"Is this call urgent?" Jacobson asked.

"Yes, it is," Carmichael said. "Jack's been arrested, and he's used his tooth. And there's more, worse, I don't want to tell you on the telephone. Can you meet me?"

There was a brief hesitation. "I'll meet you this afternoon. Where are you?"

"I'll meet you in Green Park," he said. "By the tube station, on one of the benches. Three o'clock?"

"All right," Jacobson said.

For now, Carmichael thought, leaving the telephone box, he'd work on the other end of the problem. With any luck he and Elvira would be able to just buy tickets from Paddington to Rosslare, but as luck seemed not to be going his way, he wanted a backup plan.

He took the Underground to Waterloo, feeling every casual glance an assault. There was a pub here, beside the bridge, a red brick Edwardian pub with grubby stained glass in the windows and an Irish landlady, like hundreds of others all over London. Its name was the Duke of Wellington, and it was known as the Duke's Head. There was nobody watching outside it, at least nobody Carmichael could see. He walked past on the other side of the road, then crossed back and went in. It was just open, the fire in the grate was smoking and there were no customers. The landlady was wiping down the bar with a striped yellow cloth. "Morning, Breda," he said.

"Oh, it's you, is it?" the landlady replied, looking up. She was about Carmichael's own age, closing on forty, and he had known her for a long time. "Trouble? Or were you looking for himself? Because he's over the water, as you should know."

"He's not back yet?" Carmichael asked, casually. "I heard it all went well."

"Aye, that's what I heard too, and there's nothing to go wrong now, as he's doing nothing against the law on that side. He's just stopping on a day or two to see his sister's boy get wed." Breda stopped mopping the bar and straightened up. "Shall I pour you a drink?"

"I'd prefer a cup of tea," Carmichael said. "China, if you have it, but anything will do."

"I don't know what you want to go muddling up your insides with that stuff for" she said. "Beer's much better for you. But I'll put the kettle on. Give me a shout if anyone comes in and wants serving."

Nobody came in. Carmichael poked the fire, then took a seat at the bar. Breda came out with a steaming mug of tea. "Thank you," Carmichael said.

"No milk, that's right, isn't it? Do you want some lemon? I've got some cut up for putting in G and Ts."

"I'll have a slice if it's no trouble," Carmichael said. She passed him a slice and he dropped it into the mug. Breda settled down on the other side of the bar. "Now, as you've guessed, it's himself I wanted. I am in trouble, bad trouble, and maybe you'll have to go slow on all of this business and keep your heads down. In any case, you'll be seeing Mr. Jacobson and not me, because I have to get out."

"That is bad," Breda said. "Do you want to lay low here for a bit before you scarper?"

"I'd love to, but I don't want to put you at risk. What I might need is a ride to the Republic, for me and my niece. It might be safer that way."

"Well, you know he'd be glad to oblige, any time, but not this week. His nephew's getting married on Saturday, and of course he's staying over for Easter, so he won't be back until next Wednesday. I do have a friend who might be able to help you, though."

"Someone who helps you with all this?" Carmichael asked.

"Not exactly. He's an Irishman—" She hesitated. "He's someone I used to know years ago, before I got into this with you. In fact, my mother was his nanny, back before I was born, and I've known him since I was born and he was six years old. He might have his own ways in and out of England. I say might, but I know he does. He's a bit of a hell-raiser, to tell the truth."

"What does he do?" Carmichael asked, drinking his tea. "Smuggling?"

"A bit of that, a bit of the bombing, anything with a risk to it. When I think of all the narrow escapes he's had! But that's why he might be useful now. He likes something with a bit of a dare to it." Breda tutted. "But you might want something safer, and if you can hold on until next week, that could probably be arranged too."

"What's your fellow's name?" Carmichael asked.

"He's calling himself Jimmy, these days," Breda said. "He's staying here, though he's out this morning. You could catch him early this evening if you came back. Come and have a bite of dinner before we open, and I'll introduce the two of you. Maybe you can do business."

"Maybe we can, thank you, Breda." Carmichael smiled at her, glad to feel positive.

"We eat at five, because we open at six. I've got a nice bit of liver if you could fancy that. Or—"

"Liver would be lovely," Carmichael said. He wanted to tell her about Jack, about the pork chops that Jack had bought but would never cook, but he knew if he started to talk about Jack her sympathy would vanish to be replaced with horror and disgust. He applied himself to his tea, and just then a large group of men came in, joking and calling each other names.

27

It was Raymond who insisted I go to bed; I think my mother would have kept me up half the night telling her the highlights of my life history. Raymond was a very kind man, and no doubt this stood him in good stead as a publican. He seemed entirely sincere in finding my mother more beautiful than I was, though it would hardly have been unkind for a dispassionate eye to have described her as raddled. I had for years hated and resented him, without knowing him at all, for taking my mother away from my father and me. It was very hard to imagine, looking at him, how she could possibly have preferred him to my father, but I suppose there's no accounting for taste. My father was a busy man, and Raymond obviously adored her. Now, after my father had been dead for years, it was easier to see it as a second marriage—they had married, according to that infallible source of gossip, my aunt Ciss.

I was given the spare bedroom, and fell asleep under a striped bedspread, surrounded by hats—ghastly things with flowers and feathers—and wigs. I dreamed of missed trains, airships, lost cars, luggage, passports, and once, a lost child who was at once little Debbie Berman and myself, who was left behind on a platform as the train steamed inexorably away.

I woke staring at a particularly awful hat, which seemed to have a whole magenta bird fixed to the side along with a bunch of artificial dog daisies. Sunlight streaming in through the window had woken me; it felt as if I had slept very late.

I lay there for a little while, looking at the hat and thinking back over what had happened in the last couple of days and trying to work out what day it was. Eventually I realized it was Tuesday. I was supposed to be presented that very evening, to be formally introduced to the Queen and to society. Instead I was here. My life had been turned completely upside down and nothing made any sense. This was another one of those awful things that couldn't be put right and one couldn't get back before they happened. I wanted to. I wanted to be waking up on Saturday morning again, in my comfortable bedroom in the Maynards'. I wanted the Bermans to be safe in their home. I couldn't bear to think of where they were instead.

I sat up and combed my hair with the plastic brush the shop woman had given me. It was far more tangled than usual. I would have liked to have washed it but I didn't know if there was any hot water. I didn't know what time it was. They had kept my beautiful Swiss watch, just like they'd kept Betsy's pearls. They were the criminals, really.

There was a tentative knock at the door. "Come in," I said, pulling the covers around me, in case it was Raymond.

"It's only me," my mother said, putting her head around the door. She looked even more raddled in daylight than she had the night before. I swore I would grow old gracefully and never even think about dyeing my hair. "I thought maybe I should wake you, since it's two o'clock and we're just closing for the afternoon. Raymond thought you should have your sleep."

"Two o'clock!" I said. "I've only just this minute woken up."

"Well get dressed and come down and have a bit of breakfast, and tell us what's going on," she said, and thankfully went off and left me to dress.

I put on the navy dress again. It remained remarkably uncrumpled, but no nicer. The white sweater was lost, left in the Bermans' spare bedroom.

The stairs led down to a friendly kitchen I vaguely remembered passing through the night before on the way to bed. The fire was burning brightly and a copper kettle was singing over it. I remembered the kettle from my childhood. My mother smiled and poured the boiling water into a brown teapot as I came in. "I remember that kettle," I said.

"It was my grandmother's," she said. "It's one of the very few things I took. You must think I was awful, abandoning you like that, and you so small, but you don't know what it was like. Raymond would have had you too, he wanted to, but your father was that fond of you."

"It was a long time ago," I said, awkwardly, standing on the bottom step. "It hurt terribly at the time, but worse things have happened since."

I took another step down into the kitchen, and she handed me a cup of tea, in a proper cup and saucer with pink roses all over it, clearly her best china. I was touched. "It means a lot that you came to me, when you needed someone," she said, not looking at me. "Raymond made me see that last night."

"I hope I haven't brought trouble with me," I said.

"Well, you'd better tell us what you have brought. Raymond!" she called, raising her voice. "Come in here now!" She lowered her voice again. "He thought we ought to have a minute on our own, first, but I want him to know all about it. He might know what to do. He's very clever, is Raymond."

"I can see he's been good to you," I said, sitting on the bench beside the kitchen table.

"He thinks the sun shines out of my arse," she said. "And to be honest with you, I think the same about him, though I'm not silly enough to let him know it. Always been that way, ever since we first met. I didn't mean to trample all over you and your father, but I couldn't let him go."

Raymond came in through the door from the bar. "Now, now, Irene, I thought you'd got that all out of the way," he said, catching the last of this.

"We have," I assured him quickly.

"Well," he said, sitting down and taking a cup of tea my mother handed him. "Are you ready to tell us what all this is about? Your eyes were about ready to cross last night."

"I was exhausted," I said. "Thank you for letting me sleep."

"I'll make some sandwiches," my mother said, getting up. "Go ahead, I can listen while I cut." They had no servants, I realized. She had to do everything herself. Perhaps a woman came in once a week to clean, and no doubt people helped them in the bar, but otherwise all the work of the house fell on her. I thought I should offer to help, but I knew she would decline, so I sat where I was.

I went through it all for them—meeting Sir Alan, the riot, Betsy, the proposal, the arrest, the rescue, the attack on the Bermans, the escape, and then coming to them. Partway through my mother put down a big plate of beef and mustard-and-cress sandwiches, the bread cut thickly and liberally buttered, and we munched our way through them as I talked. They were not wonderful sandwiches, but they were the sandwiches of my childhood. I talked on, with my mouth full. They interrupted often, asking questions and clarifications. When we finished the sandwiches my mother got out a plate of scones and a pot of jam. I was touched that she had thought me worth baking for.

"So you really could have married a lord," my mother said.

"A sir," Raymond corrected her.

"A baronet," I corrected both of them.

"But you'd have been Lady Bellingham?" my mother asked.

"I would, but I didn't want to be, and it's all immaterial now because he's certain to have been arrested too, and very unlikely to have escaped," I said.

"And you really have been accepted at Oxford?" Raymond asked. He sounded envious, and I wondered if university had been a dream of his at one time, like Jude the Obscure.

"I have," I said.

"Maybe she'll go to Oxford and then marry a lord afterwards," my mother said, proudly.

"I don't know if I'll be able to go at all." It hit me then. "I don't know what I can do. I have no idea. I need to find out if Uncle Carmichael is still free, and if he is then get in touch with him, somehow."

"You could telephone his flat," Raymond said. "Or better yet, I could, and see who answers. I could be anybody. I'll call from the pay phone in the bar."

I looked at him with respect. "That's a very good idea."

"I told you he was clever," my mother said, smiling at him loyally.

"Ask for Jack, that's my uncle's servant." I stuttered a little on the last word. I hadn't told them what Penn-Barkis had told me about Carmichael and Jack. "He'll know everything, if he's there, and if he is, I'll talk to him. If someone else is answering, you could say you were a friend of his. He could have any number of friends, he's bound to."

"Bound to," Raymond agreed. "Or I could just be the fishmonger ringing up to say I had a couple of nice trout."

We all got up and went into the bar, which looked sad and deserted now it was empty. It was a big room, full of wood and polished horse-brasses and smelling of beer and men. "This is a big bar," I said.

"Roadhouse, we are," Raymond said. "This is a big step up for us, we started off in a tiny little place, and the brewery keep moving us up because we do so well. It's your mother, she charms the customers." He smiled fondly at her. "Hush, now." He pressed a button on the till and it shot open. He took out two pennies. "Number?"

I told him the number, and he dialed. It rang and was picked up on the third ring. "Is that Jack?" Raymond asked. "I'm Tom from Tom's Fresh Fish, and I'm ringing to say I've got a nice couple of trout. That isn't Jack, is it? Well, who are you then? Oh. Well, tell Jack I've got the fish, if you see him in the next hour or two, after that it'll be too late." He put the receiver down and turned to me with a long face. "That was someone very anxious to know who was calling, and definitely not Jack. Police of some sort, I'd say. I think your uncle's in very bad trouble, my dear."

"He's not really her uncle," my mother put in. "She can stay here. Nobody'll come looking for her here."

It was true, and it was even tempting. I could stay there and get to know my mother again. If it was true that she was dreadfully vulgar, then it was also true that I was a frightful snob.

"No, I have a better idea," Raymond said, grinning, and shut the till with a snap. "Didn't you say it's tonight you're supposed to be presented to the Queen?"

"That's right," I said.

"Well, you should go. They won't be expecting you, so they won't be trying to keep you out."

"They will be expecting me," I said. "My name is on an invitation."

"Yes, the Queen's men will be expecting to let you in," Raymond agreed, almost bouncing in his excitement. "But the ones who are trying to get you, Penn-Barkis and that awful Bannister, they won't. It'll be the last place they'd look for you. They'd never think you had the nerve to show up there, just where you're supposed to be."

"I suppose not," I said. "But what good would it do if I went?"

"Why, you could tell Her Majesty about it, just like you've told us, and she'll see it's all sorted out. She needs to know about her uncle trying to grab power again, the so-called Duke of Windsor. And she needs to know what abuses are going on in the name of the law."

"But—," I said. I didn't know where to start explaining about the role of a monarch in a constitutional monarchy.

"That's right," my mother said. "You're surely not saying that she knows about all this, Elvira?"

"No," I said, faintly. "But—"

"Well, they're her government, aren't they?"

This was unanswerable. I nodded. "But—"

"It's been needing something like this," Raymond said. "Look at all these protests, round the country. People have had enough. People don't want this kind of thing. Death camps on British soil, that's more than enough. Normanby getting away with murder, locking up people for saying no to him. That's not what we voted for."

"You did vote for him," my mother said, slyly.

"I did the first time," he said. "After those terrorists at Farthing killed that Thirkie. I wanted a bit of law and order and decent sorting out. But now it's gone too far. Arresting young girls for dancing with the wrong men, what's the world coming to?"

"That's right," my mother said.

"And the thing is, we can't tell Her Majesty," Raymond said. "We couldn't walk up to her and say it, because her guards and people wouldn't let us near. And you can bet they keep it from her very carefully, make sure she doesn't get word. But you have this chance, this presentation, but you aren't like the girls she usually meets who don't know anything about this any more than she does. You know. You're one of us, but you've got an invite like you're one of them. And you should go and tell her."

"So I should," I said. I hadn't gone mad or anything, it was just that they both seemed so sure. I remembered Aunt Katherine talking about meeting the Queen, and I suddenly thought, why not? I'd been rehearsing and practicing for months to be presented, why shouldn't I make it mean something? The worst that could happen was no worse than could quite likely happen to me anyway. And if they dragged me away from a presentation it would at least be a scandal, people would at least know about that. It would be something I could do. Raymond was right, things had gone too far. "I can't just turn up as I am. They'd never let me in any more than they would you."

"I can lend you a dress," my mother said.

I did my best not to shudder. "It's not that. I have an invitation, but it's at the Maynards'. And Mrs. Maynard has to present me. That's on the list."

"Will she still do it?" Raymond asked.

"I don't even know if they're free," I said. "They arrested Mr. Maynard at the same time they arrested me."

"They don't keep people like that for long," my mother said. "One law for the rich and one law for the poor."

"There is one law for rich and poor alike, that prevents them equally from stealing bread and sleeping under bridges," I said. It was one of Uncle Carmichael's favorite quotations, and it came from Anatole France, and that's all I know about it.

"That's lovely," Raymond said. "Prevents them all from stealing bread and sleeping under bridges. I'd like to have that done as a sampler. You may think I'm a rich man—well, not by your standards, but I've done well for myself in the trade. I'm comfortable now. But I started at the very bottom, and I'm still an employee. I'd love to go into business for myself, that's our dream, isn't it, Irene, but we've never had the capital to take the risk."

"We could call the Maynards and see if they're there, and if they're going to see the Queen tonight," my mother said, reaching for the telephone.

"Not from here," Raymond said.

"But you said—"

"We've used this phone now. They could trace that the two calls both came from it. We need to go out to the pay phone on the corner."

"You seem to know a lot about this," I said.

"Just what I've read," he said, shyly. He took a handful of pennies from the till.

"Always got his nose in a book, he has," my mother said, proudly.

"And you should tell her to go out to another box and call you back, if she is there. They might be listening to her telephone, but they can't get every pay phone in London, and they can't tap it quickly enough."

"Her mother wouldn't let her go out," I said. "Not just like that."

We went out of the front door of the pub to a telephone box on the corner of the street. Across the road I could see people going in and out of the Underground station. "In that case, you should tell her to meet you somewhere, but somewhere that means something else. Like say the Dorchester but mean the Ritz."

"The Ritz isn't a bad choice, if I need to get changed," I said. It has the most enormous ladies' rooms, with huge gold-framed mirrors.

"But you haven't arranged beforehand to mean the other place," Raymond said. "Most codes need to be arranged in advance. You need to say something she'll understand and they won't, like the place where you dropped your hanky."

"All right," I said, my head spinning with all this.

"Now, what shall I say to get her on the line?" Raymond asked me.

"Ask for Miss Maynard, and say—" Invention failed me. "Say it's about the flowers," I said. "That should fetch her. Or if it gets her mother, I'll speak to her."

Raymond went inside the box and made the call. Then after a moment he beckoned, stepped out, and I went in. "It's her!" he said.

"Betsy?" I asked, picking up the receiver.

"Oh, thank God," Betsy said, fervently.

It was so strange to hear her familiar voice, exactly the same as it always was, as if nothing had changed. "I have to be quick—is your father all right?"

"Yes, they let him go on Sunday night, late. But they won't say anything about you—have they let you out? Are you coming home?"

"It's more complicated than that. But are you still going to the palace tonight?"

"Yes, Mummy insisted. I didn't want to go without you." She sounded as if she might be about to cry.

"Will your mother still present me, if I'm there?"

"Oh, Elvira, I can make her, but can you really be? That would be so wonderful."

The pips went, and I deposited another two pennies for another three minutes. Raymond had left a little pile of them beside the slot for me. He was making a thumbs-up sign to me outside. He was terribly common, but really the salt of the earth, as my aunt Katherine would have said. I felt sorry for having hated him all these years when I could have known him instead.

"Are you sure you can make your mother do it? Because if she won't, this won't work at all," I said, when the money had gone in and the pips had gone away.

"She'll do it. I promise." Betsy never promised if she wasn't going to deliver.

"Then I'm coming. I don't think I should risk coming to the house to get my dress and my invitation, but could you bring them?"

"Where?"

"To the place where we had tea with Jean Evans," I said. I knew she'd remember that, meeting Sergeant Evans's wife had been memorable. Mrs. Evans had loved the Ritz, the chandeliers, the little cream cakes, the glamour of it all. "Don't say the name! But come about an hour early. Bring my dress and my shoes and my flowers and my invitation."

"And will you come home with us afterwards?" she implored.

"I don't know," I said. "I'll see you there at six, Bets, all right?"

"All right," she said, and the pips went again, and we shouted good-bye at each other over them. I collected the rest of the pile of pennies and stepped out of the phone box.

"I'm going to see the Queen," I said to their expectant faces.

28

His immediate problem, Carmichael thought, as he made his way cautiously from the opposite end of Green Park, was that he was too conspicuous. Too many people knew what he looked like. His face had been so frequently on television. People often recognized him, and would continue to. And yet disguise wasn't the answer either; there were few amateur disguises that didn't look like disguises, especially to a trained eye. He had compromised by having his hair cut in a gentlemen's salon on Piccadilly. He'd have dyed it if dyed hair on a man wasn't so conspicuous as to scream for attention. His brown hair was streaked with enough silver that he could have justified it as vanity, except that he wanted to be inconspicuous. Jack had said his silver hairs were distinguished, he thought, and paused in his stride, as if the absence of Jack were a physical pain.

The trees in Green Park were greening up nicely, with the young fresh green that only comes in spring. The leaves on the beeches here were still tiny, no more than a mist of green, seen more clearly from the corner of the eye. Green Park was right in the middle of London, off Piccadilly, by the Ritz and the Royal Academy. In summer it was full of weary office workers eating sandwiches at lunchtime, but now on a chilly April day there were only a few brisk walkers, wrapped up in their own thoughts and raincoats.

Carmichael had taken what precautions he could by coming early and from the wrong direction, so the pattern of watchers stood out clearly when he was still far enough away among the trees that they hadn't seen him. He slipped away, wondering whether Jacobson was dead, in custody, or turned coat. The last he thought the least likely, considering that Jacobson was a Jew. It needn't be a betrayal. Perhaps they were only listening in to his home telephone. When he realized he was clutching the thought to him as a comfort, he bit his lip, hard. How could he reach Elvira without Jacobson?

He made it back to the Duke's Head before five without incident. He stopped in the railway station and bought a bunch of daffodils for Breda. The flower girl looked tired, and so did her flowers, but she gave a real smile when Carmichael paid with half a crown and waved away the change. It must be a terrible life, he thought, coming up from the country on the early train with a bucket of bouquets and standing on the station forecourt all day trying to sell them until they were all gone and you could go home.

Breda tutted at the flowers, but she turned from the stove to put them into a Dutch vase immediately. Their yellow trumpets cheered the kitchen, which was in a half-basement, like Carmichael's hotel room, and consequently rather dark. A pair of cats were curling around Breda's feet, meowing.

"Loy will be down in a minute, Jimmy that is," she said. "Get your legs under the table." She put down some food for the cats.

"Loy. That would be Aloysius? I knew a Loy once," Carmichael said, sitting down obediently. "Years ago. Part of a case. He's dead, though. Is it a common name in Ireland?"

"Not as common as Jimmy," Breda said, her eyes crinkling. "This Loy's dead too, in a way. He's been to see his own tombstone, he says it's very fine."

"How did that happen?" Carmichael asked, intrigued, but just then the man himself came into the kitchen.

Loy was in his forties, tall and athletic and tanned, although it was April. His dark hair was graying at the temples. Carmichael would have known him for an Irishman anywhere, and he looked as if he was a devil for women. He looked nothing like the other Loy. "I'm Jimmy," he said, putting out his hand and looking assessingly at Carmichael.

The name on Carmichael's false identity card was Walter Sprange, but he felt sure Breda would have let slip his real name, as she had Loy's. "Carmichael," he said.

"You don't have a first name?" Loy asked, shaking his hand.

"I do, and it's Peter, but nobody calls me by it. I go by Carmichael." He would never again hear Jack call him P. A.

Loy nodded, and sat. One of the cats jumped up on his lap and he petted it absently. "Beer?" Breda asked, from the sink. "Drop of whisky?"

"Maybe later," Loy said, and Carmichael echoed him. "So, I hear you might have need to get to the Republic in a hurry?"

"I might," Carmichael said. "First I have to find my niece. She's somewhere that should be safe, but I don't know where."

"Well, in any case nobody's getting in or out of London before Thursday. It's clamped down tighter than a nun's habit, excuse me, Breda."

Breda laughed, and began to serve them an Irish stew.

Loy pushed the cat down to the floor. "If I'm still at liberty on Thursday, and if you've found your niece, I'll be heading back to Ireland on a boat I have at Swansea. A thousand pounds each, and guaranteed I get you into the Republic without any checks at either end."

"A boat?" Carmichael asked. "A yacht?"

Loy laughed. Breda set down a loaf of soda bread and sat down at the third place laid at the table. "A motor boat," she said. "A fine grand one from Denmark, isn't it, Jimmy?"

"That's right," Loy said.

"Goes everywhere in it. All the way to North Africa." That explained the tan, Carmichael thought. What could he be smuggling from North Africa?

"You want me to say grace, Breda?" Loy asked.

"If you please," she said.

Carmichael put down his spoon. The stew smelled meaty and delicious. Loy gave a blessing in Latin. He and Breda joined in on the amen. For a while they gave their attention to the food. "This is excellent," Carmichael said to Breda. "Did you make the bread yourself too?"

"I have to, you can't get decent soda bread in this city," she said.

"So what's kept you here all this time?" Loy asked, mockingly.

"You know that," she said. "We'd have been away to Ireland years back if not for helping Carmichael and his poor deportees. The stories I've heard! They're families, lots of them. I couldn't turn my back on that, not and sleep at night."

"You're a good woman, Breda," Loy said.

"He's absolutely right," Carmichael agreed. "There are too many people who do turn their backs on it and seem to sleep perfectly comfortably."

"It looks as if they're waking up a bit," Loy said. "All these protests around the country—and spreading to France now. People are starting to think about it, about what they've let go on in the name of safety."

"I really hope so," Carmichael said. One of the cats brushed against his leg under the table.

"How many have you got away all together?" Loy asked.

"I don't know," Carmichael answered shortly.

"No, how many? Thousands? Tens of thousands?"

"Thousands this year alone," Carmichael said. "Tens of thousands over time."

"It's funny, I thought Ireland would go the way of all the rest," Loy said. "But no, she walks her own road, priest-ridden and super-stitious and corrupt, more authoritarian and leader-worshiping than I'd like, but at least steering a course away from all this madness of Jew-hating and murder. They don't exactly have an easy life in the Republic once they get there, you understand. There have been pogroms against them from time to time, and it's hard for them to find work that's not scrubbing floors. But at least nobody's putting them into cattle cars or taking them to gas chambers, and they're grateful enough for it."

"There's nowhere better to send them," Carmichael said, spoon-ing up his stew. "Well, there might be." He wasn't going to discuss Abby, whose organization was entirely separate, and so far quite safe from anyone's betrayals. "We'll see."

"Sometimes I get one or two of them into Palestine," Loy said. "It's risky, though."

"It would be," Carmichael agreed blandly, but his respect for Loy increased. The Palestine Mandate was under firm British control, and the policy not to allow any more Jews in was very strict.

"So all the time you've been the visible face of repression, you've been trying to alleviate excesses under the table?" Loy asked.

"Something like that," Carmichael said, awkwardly.

"Well, isn't that interesting," Loy said.

"So what brings you to London, Jimmy?" Carmichael asked, to change the subject.

"Bit of unfinished business," Loy said, looking cagey. "Years ago a friend and I tried something, and it didn't come off and he was killed. Now I have a chance to try it again and make it work this time. He'd have wanted that."

"This is the friend who's buried under Jimmy's real name," Breda put in.

"His girlfriend identified him as me. I don't know to this day if she did it to give me a chance to get away, because they weren't look-ing for anyone else, or if she did it because she was completely out of her head." Loy shook his head incredulously.

Carmichael found himself remembering the *Hamlet* bomb, and Viola Lark identifying the bomber's body as Sir Aloysius Farrell, her face rigid, her voice high, acting madness or really mad, walking a line he didn't understand, quoting from the play and admitting her guilt at the same moment. She had identified Loy's body while saying something about putting gold coins on his eyes. It was too much of a coincidence. "That wouldn't be Viola Lark, would it?" he asked.

Loy shot him a sideways glance full of cautious menace. His hands disappeared underneath the table. "How do you know that?"

"Now, Loy . . . ," Breda said, reproachfully.

"Just a guess," Carmichael said, evenly, keeping both of his own hands in sight.

"You were there, weren't you? You were the one who saved them." Loy didn't relax at all.

"It didn't hit me until afterwards that I should have just sat still and let it happen," Carmichael said, laying down his spoon beside his empty plate. "Though I'm not sure it would have done as much good as you thought it would, not then. It was too late. Everyone was already afraid. There wasn't any swell of protest against the government then, almost everyone was behind them. Normanby would have been replaced by Lord Eversley or someone else just as bad."

"You have to try," Loy said, one of his hands emerging and scrap-ing up the last of his stew.

"And you're trying it again?" Carmichael asked.

"Not a bomb this time. I'm going to shoot them as they come through the streets," he said, with his mouth full but not taking his eyes off Carmichael.

"Ah. I don't suppose I'll be able to take you up on your offer of transport to Ireland, then. They've taken excellent precautions against snipers."

"Do you know what they are?" Loy asked.

"I've seen the plans," Carmichael said, cautiously. "More useful than that, I know the order of the procession. Where were you hoping to do it from?"

"A rooftop on Whitehall," Loy said.

"I don't want to hear this," Breda said, getting up. Both cats immediately began to curl around her feet. "You know I don't hold with it."

"Not even Hitler?" Loy asked. "You know it's Hitler we're talking about. You wouldn't even kill him?"

"No," Breda said, tight-lipped. "Oh, he's a bad man all right, but what good would it do?"

"What would you do with him then?" Carmichael asked, curiously.

"You could marry him, and love him and try to teach him better," Breda said.

The two men laughed. "It must be nearly opening time anyway," Loy said. "We'll get ourselves out from under your feet. I'll be back later to sleep, is that all right?"

"Thank you for the dinner, it was delicious," Carmichael said, rising.

Loy looked at him cautiously. "Like to take a walk?" he asked.

"Certainly," Carmichael said.

Outside, they both turned their feet towards Waterloo Bridge. The businessmen were walking back across the bridge to take trains back home to Dorking and Leatherhead. A little wind had come up and was tossing their ties merrily over their shoulders. Nobody was walking north, except Carmichael and Loy, going against the flow. "Marry him," Loy said, and laughed again.

Carmichael shook his head, smiling. "Women."

Loy stopped about halfway across and leaned on the rail. There was a fine view looking east towards Saint Paul's and the Tower. Looking west, past the stream of cars crossing the bridge, lay the Palace of Westminster. Loy took out a packet of cigarettes and offered them to Carmichael.

"No thanks," he said. "I never smoke." Jack didn't like the smell. He swallowed.

"Well, if I'm going to shoot rather than marry, we're inside the security perimeter," Loy said, quietly.

"You've got a rifle?" Carmichael asked, hardly above a whisper. The businessmen passing them did not stop, or pay any attention to them.

Loy nodded, jerking his head back in the direction of the Duke's Head.

"And you're good?"

"I was a sharpshooter in the army," he said.

"The British army?" Carmichael asked, and then remembered. "Of course the British army, I remember. You're the hero of Calais."

"I was," Loy said, and tossed the butt of his cigarette down over the rail. His eyes stayed on it as it spiraled downwards. "For all the bloody good it does me. There's no place for old heroes in this world. But you can trust me that I'm a good shot."

"The Queen will go first, after the police motorcycles," Carmichael said. "She'll be in the Royal Coach, the one that looks like a pumpkin. Then Hitler, in an open coach draped with swastikas. Then Normanby, in another antique coach. Another open one, because of the wheelchair."

"Alone?" Loy asked quickly.

"Yes. I don't know about Hitler. He's almost never alone, and he's an old man now. But Normanby will be alone, except for the driver."

"Who comes next?" Loy had turned his back on the river and was looking over at Westminster.

"The Japanese. Don't shoot them, for heaven's sake, it would probably start a war."

"If there are sniper precautions, I'll probably only get one shot. I don't know if it should be Hitler or Normanby. I've been waiting to get another chance at Hitler."

"Normanby," Carmichael said, without even stopping to think. "As to the sniper precautions, they're putting men on rooftops. But that could be a good thing, if they think you're one of them. If you dress in camo and act as if you have a right to be there, they'll probably ignore you until it's too late. They're going to be on a lot of those rooftops."

"Is there a password, in case one of them tries to come onto my roof?" Loy asked.

"There will be, but I don't know it. It will be tomorrow's watchword, and they're issued daily."

"Can you get it?" Loy asked, lighting another cigarette. "Who issues it?"

"My secretary does. Or— I don't know, I expect she'll keep doing it for the time being. If she's still all right." Carmichael thought of poor Peg Duthie and her loyalty and bad typing. He hoped they didn't sack her, or worse, think she was complicit in what they'd call his treason. "They're bound to question her, but she doesn't know anything at all. No. I suppose she'd give it to me, but it would be too dangerous even to try."

"To you or to her?" Loy asked.

"To her," Carmichael said. "She changes it every day, first thing in the morning. I wouldn't want to jeopardize her."

"Do you have a recent password?" Loy asked, uninterested in Miss Duthie's fate.

"Yesterday's was *hammock,*" Carmichael said. "But it won't do you any good."

"*Hammock?*" Loy asked, incredulously, and began to laugh. "It's all so childish, isn't it?" he said. "Look at these poor sods walking over this bridge to get their trains home to their nice little suburbs and their nice little wives, as if they didn't have less freedom this year than last year and everything wasn't closing in on them. Do they realize how thin a line they're walking?"

"I don't think so," Carmichael said. "Look at them. They just go straight ahead, not looking up or down. They worry about Frank's new girlfriend and Emily's bad school report and if they're putting on weight and whether their wife's being unfaithful, while all the safety nets are cut away around them. Then something frightens them, and they look up and realize they're tightrope-walking over an abyss."

"You'd have liked my friend Devlin," Loy said. "He used to talk like that."

"The man who's buried in your tomb?" Carmichael remembered his wary boxer's face and his quick smile. "I did like him. I met him once at the theater. Casing the place, probably, but I didn't know that at the time."

"He'd have laughed at the thought of being buried in my tomb. I'm not sure some of my ancestors would find it quite so funny." He dropped another cigarette end into the river. The flow of businessmen was slackening now.

"What identity are you using?" Carmichael asked. "With your own being lost to you?"

"I change them from time to time," Loy said. "I have a good one for the time being. German, not Jewish, a respectable young businessman from Vienna, party member. It's real, solid. He died in unfortunate circumstances, and all I had to do was replace the photograph."

"Can you *sprechen*?"

"Well enough," Loy said.

"The Gestapo have their own people here. I don't know anything about their procedure or precautions, so I can't help you there."

"I'll watch out for them. It would be a sight easier with a password, though."

Carmichael looked at him evenly. "Whatever else I might have betrayed, I'm not turning over a loyal and innocent woman to them, even if she would be fool enough to give the word to me."

"Worth a try," Loy said, blowing out smoke. "Well, I should get on back and calm Breda down. Marry him! She's always been a pacifist. She wouldn't have me around except that I'm like a big brother to her. Her mother was my nurse. And you probably have things to do."

"Not really," Carmichael said. "I'm just keeping out of sight until I can get out of town. I'm hoping I might be able to make contact with someone who can help me find my niece, but it won't be tonight." He'd have to approach Jacobson very cautiously indeed.

"Well, thank you for the information, it might help a lot," Loy said.

"Good luck. Get the bastards," Carmichael said.

"I thought you were one of the bastards until tonight," Loy said.

"There are probably a lot more decent people around than anyone knows, going along with things for whatever reason of their own. The only problem is we can't recognize them because they don't want to risk breaking their cover."

Loy nodded and ambled back across the bridge.

Carmichael kept on walking across the bridge, along the

Embankment, down long Victoria Street, passed all the way by red buses and black taxis, until he came to Victoria Station, Pimlico, and his seedy little hotel. After the long walk he was ready for a rest, and it seemed almost more of an insult than an injury when he felt a heavy hand fall on his shoulder and a voice call out, "I've got him, sarge!"

29

Betsy was waiting alone in the foyer when I got to the Ritz. She was looking around in an anxious way. There was no sign of Mrs. Maynard, or Nanny. She was wearing her mint-green Court dress, with the train looped over her broken arm, which was held in a matching mint-green sling. She had a dress bag over her other arm. She almost didn't recognize me in Uncle Carmichael's coat. I'd spent the afternoon washing my hair, and fighting off offers from my mother to lend me a brightening rinse, or a set of curlers. "Betsy," I said. "Elizabeth. It's so good to see you."

"I'm supposed to be having dinner in the Dorchester right now," she said.

"Well, so am I, for that matter," I said. "Come on, let's go to the cloakroom and get me changed."

"Whatever are you wearing? Is that a man's coat?"

"It's my uncle's coat," I said. "Wait until you see the frock I have on." I undid the buttons on the coat as I walked.

"Don't show me any more of it, I think I'm going to have to burn it!" Betsy said, and giggled. We were giggling as we went into the ladies' room. Betsy fingered the frock. "What is that made of?"

"Polyester," I said. "It doesn't crumple, it really doesn't."

"I don't think it will ever catch on," she said. Safely inside I took off the coat and navy blue frock and put them on one of the spindly little gilt chairs. "That bra is beige!"

"I know! But it's very comfortable."

"Where did you get it?" she asked.

"Ever such a nice little fat Jewish woman who kept a shop. I don't know if she's all right. The people I was staying with were arrested. I managed to get away, but they didn't." The thought of the Bermans sobered me.

"Jews?" she asked.

"Yes," I said. "It's not true, what they say about them. They're actually ultra-clean, and while they do funny things, they're very nice. And they had the sweetest little children, and they could all speak Hebrew, even the tiny ones."

"You sound as if they'd quite converted you," Betsy said, taking my presentation dress out of the bag, all pink satin and white lace. "But I've always been quite sure they weren't as awful as people said. I mean nobody could be. Besides, I remember in the parade they looked just like anyone, only having things thrown at them. That poor little girl with blood on her face."

"You're a much nicer person than I am," I said. "Where are the flowers?"

"Mummy has them in the car. She said she wasn't coming in here in case, she's waiting outside. She really didn't want to do this, I had to threaten to run away. And I was thinking, if they might have been listening about where we were going to meet, on the phone, then won't they know you mean to go to the palace?"

I hadn't thought of that. "I don't know. That wasn't in Raymond's book."

"What book? Who's Raymond?"

I was halfway through stepping into the dress, and I hesitated. "Raymond's my stepfather," I said.

"Your what? I thought you were an orphan." Betsy was looking at me as if I'd sprouted wings.

"I'm only half an orphan and the other half is an abandoned child. My mother ran off when I was six, then two years after that, my father died. My mother didn't want me, or I was always told she didn't, but she was alive. I never mentioned her in school because, well, she keeps a pub in East London, and who would. I never told you because you already thought I was an orphan, and it seemed too complicated to explain."

"Did you visit her?" Betsy asked.

"No, but my aunt Ciss kept me up to date with the gossip about her. I always sent her Christmas cards. And I thought of her when I escaped, because I knew nobody knew about her, she had no official connection with me, but she'd take me in. And she did. And Raymond, who's her second husband, reads Dennis Wheatley and spy books and knows what to do, or thinks he does. They're frightfully sweet, actually. Do me up?"

Betsy came around and started on the row of hooks and eyes that fastened my dress. It was hard for her with one hand, and went slowly. "Why do you want to go, anyway? Didn't you say it's all pointless? And especially now."

"There's something I want to tell the Queen," I said. "I know it sounds idiotic, but she is the Queen, it is her country in a way, and she should know. There's a plot to do with the Duke of Windsor, and there are people out there who arrest people like me just because they can, just because they want to."

"It isn't idiotic at all," Betsy said. "I've always felt like that, but I've never felt as if I could say so."

"It was my mother and Raymond who made me see it like that," I said. "She is like that to them. And I can speak to her, and I should."

"Whether or not it's in Raymond's book, might they be waiting at the palace to arrest you again?"

"They might," I said. I shivered at the thought, and Betsy hugged me, crushing my dress and hers.

"Was it very awful?" she asked.

"Simply unbearable," I said.

Someone came in to powder her nose then, and I don't know what she thought when we sprang apart guiltily. Betsy finished doing me up, then we both did our own faces, from Betsy's makeup bag, with towels over our dresses. After our faces were on, we did my hair—Betsy's was already up, and sprayed with so much lacquer and stuff that it felt like a butterfly's wings. I just put mine up normally. People came in from time to time, some of them girls we knew who were dining at the Ritz before their presentations. In a moment when we were alone, Betsy put on my pearls, and I put on my lapis-and-gold pendant. Betsy had brought them both in her makeup bag. "But doesn't your mother know about your pearls?" I asked.

"I don't care what she knows; I want to wear yours," Betsy said.

"You are the best friend I have ever had," I said.

I pulled on my long gloves, and helped Betsy on with her single glove. Then we looked at each other in the mirror, a perfect pair of empty-headed debs, or so you might think. Despite Betsy's sling we looked all right, and at the higher end of all right, come to that. We shrugged at our reflections and went out to where Mrs. Maynard was waiting.

The car crawled up the Mall towards Buckingham Palace, flanked by other cars full of debs all with the same destination. Mrs. Maynard didn't say a word to me all the way, and hardly more to Betsy. At last we came to the ceremonial guards, the pair of beefeaters in their scarlet uniforms and big black bonnets. With them were a couple of Watchmen. One of them peered into the car, and I saw it was Sergeant Evans. I shrank back in my seat, my heart hammering.

"Mrs. Maynard, Miss Maynard, and Miss Royston," Mrs. Maynard said, handing over our papers and invitations. The driver was having his own papers checked out of the front.

"Why, Elvira!" Sergeant Evans said. "I'm so glad to see you're where you ought to be."

"Is there a problem?" the other Watchman asked, handing the driver his papers back. He was a stranger to me.

"No, just greeting an old friend," Sergeant Evans said.

"Give my regards to Jean," Betsy said, naturally friendly.

"Thank you, Sergeant Evans," I said, making my stiff tongue move in my mouth at last. To this day I don't know for sure whether he was supposed to arrest me or not, but I suspect very much that he was.

We drove on. Before very long, we came to the palace, where we got out of the car, which went off somewhere to wait. Mrs. Maynard handed us both our flowers, which were posies we had to carry, and went in to an anteroom. We had our invitations checked again there by a very superior female secretary, and then we were told to stand in line in the corridor. The line was very long. "I've been told you can wait two hours," Betsy said. "And they don't let you go to the toilet."

Mary Carron was in front of us, with her mother, so her sharp comments kept us entertained as we moved very slowly forward. "I'm sure I've forgotten how to curtsey," Betsy said.

"You're lucky, if you do anything wrong they'll just blame it on your arm," Mary said. "Have you ever seen anything as hideous as that Grecian urn?"

Eventually we inched into the Throne Room. It was enormous and very splendid and eighteenth-century, with a painted ceiling and huge pillars. The Queen was sitting on the throne, very formal. She was wearing robes and a small crown, and she sat straight-backed and still. I was surprised how young she looked, and how pretty. She also didn't look the faintest bit bored, though it must have been incredibly tedious. Ambassadors and people like that and girls who had already been presented that night were standing around the walls, in Court dress, which meant uniforms or knee breeches and tights for the men. Some of them had rather good legs, but it was very revealing of those who didn't. Nearly all the debutantes were in white, or cream, or very pale pastels, and the men were in dark colors or black, and I understood for the first time why the conventional comparison for debutantes was to blossoms. All together like that, in little clumps along the wall, there really was a resemblance.

There was a carpet we had to follow. We inched forward along it. Mary Carron's mother took her forward, gave her name, she went on alone, curtseyed, smiled, backed away, and retreated. Mrs. Maynard went forward, and we went with her. You have to be presented by someone who has themselves been presented, it's as if it was a real introduction—though of course, Mrs. Maynard would have been presented to George VI. Betsy's turn came. She looked very pale. She touched my pearls with her good hand and gave me a wan smile. She went forward, swept a very good curtsey, rose up, backed away—you're not supposed to turn your back on the Monarch, and this backing away is the bit they spent the most time rehearsing, because it's harder than it looks. Betsy managed it all very creditably, and then, of course, it was my turn.

I was hardly aware of my name being called and my advance. I curtseyed, of course, but I don't know if I managed to smile. As I rose I gave the hand signal that meant I wanted to talk to the Queen, and she nodded, and looked at me a little more closely. I backed away, and an equerry in knee breeches came up to me and checked my name—he had it right—and said that Her Majesty would summon me later. I went to stand beside Betsy.

Mrs. Maynard was almost quivering with disapproval. I don't know what Betsy had had to threaten to get her to agree to do it in the circumstances, but it must have been dire. "I have been presented," I said to her.

"Indeed," she said.

"Nobody can deny any longer that I am a lady," I said.

"Nobody could ever have a moment's doubt that you are a guttersnipe and a jailbird, and if they did, talking to you for five minutes would put them right," she said, and turned her back on me.

Betsy rolled her eyes at me. "It doesn't matter," she said, loudly enough for her mother to hear. "Ignore her."

"When I graduate from Oxford and start earning money, why don't you come and keep house for me?" I asked.

"Like the Ladies of Llangollen?" she asked, her eyes lighting up.

"Though of course, I don't know what's going to happen. I might still have to flee the country. I don't know where Uncle Carmichael is."

"If you have to flee the country, I'll come too," she said in my ear.

Debs kept coming in, curtseying and rising up and backing away with relieved expressions. Their mothers, or whoever was presenting them, also looked frightfully relieved. It really was all a mummery, but yet it did mean something. It was an affirmation of class, and an announcement of coming of age and marriageability. If my Hottentot anthropologist had been there he'd have pinpointed it that way at once.

At last the flow of debs ceased. I saw the equerry talking to Sir Guy Braithwaite, the Foreign Secretary. The Queen got down off the throne and went out through a little door to the side. Then the equerry moved through the crowd, collecting the people who had said they wanted to speak to the Queen. There seemed to be hundreds of us, but in fact it was fewer than twenty. He led us, and Sir Guy, through the little door and into a charming little drawing room, also with a painted ceiling, but with a fireplace and very good but ordinary chairs and sofas and dark stuffy oil paintings of dogs and fruit. The Queen was sitting on one of the sofas.

The equerry murmured to us that we should sit elsewhere and wait, and the Queen would summon us one at a time, and we should watch as the previous person left. She called someone up right away, and chatted for a moment or two. I sat beside Elizabeth Mitchell, and she complimented me on my dress and my pendant, and I complimented her on her dress and her flowers, which were lovely, dark anemones. Mine were white roses, very conventional. They'd probably been part of Sir Alan's bouquet. I wondered where he was and if he was all right. I didn't want to marry him, but I wanted him to be all right.

It seemed like ages, but it probably wasn't, but I still didn't have my watch so I couldn't tell. At last the Queen caught my eye, and I went up and sat beside her on the sofa.

I'd been thinking all afternoon about what I was going to say, but even so I'm afraid it didn't come out very well rehearsed but all pouring out as fast as I could go. "There's a plot against you, ma'am, led by the Duke of Windsor," I said. "And you should know that Scotland Yard are just locking people up if they don't like them, they arrested me and kept me without sleep all night and asked me questions and stole Betsy's pearls and my watch, and it isn't right, it isn't the right way to do things. And they arrested all the Bermans just before they were going to have dinner, and they hadn't done anything except hide me."

The Queen blinked, as well she might. "Tell me about this slowly," she said, and she led me through it all in detail. I don't know how long I was talking to her, but far longer than any of the others had been.

"And I think they've arrested my uncle Carmichael," I said, at last. "His man wasn't there to answer the telephone."

"He's always seemed a loyal man," she said, musingly. "But he's Normanby's creature. I have to have my own people around me, my own organization. I've never known him well, although he was head of the Watch."

"He probably didn't want you to. He was smuggling Jews out of the country under Mr. Normanby's nose," I said. "All this killing Jews, it isn't right, ma'am, begging your pardon, it isn't English."

"I'm rather inclined to agree," she said. "And all these recent arrests seem to have caught the country's attention."

"People are upset about it."

"They have been demonstrating against them," she agreed. "Would you say that was the true temper of the country?"

It was strange in one way, her asking me that, because how could I know? But I could see that it must be hard for her to tell, because what normal people did she ever meet? She was the Queen. "I wish you could talk to my mother and Raymond," I said, without thinking. "They have such a belief in you. And they're ordinary people, just trying to get along, but they're against all this, they think it's gone too far."

The Queen looked off past me, thinking her own thoughts. "I've been suspecting something like this for a long time, and waiting for more evidence, and to know what my people wanted. I needed to be sure before I made any move. Why did you come to me, Elvira? What did you hope I could do?"

"I wanted to warn you to watch out for the Duke of Windsor, and—well, like my mother said, they're your government, aren't they."

She was quiet, still staring over my head. "There's so little I am constitutionally able to do," she said at last. "I need more than this to act directly against the Prime Minister. The Duke of Windsor is under arrest, you need have no fears about him. I appreciate your warning; it has made me think more seriously about everything else you have said. I can at least give you a Royal Warrant, which does not mean you are above the law but that if you are arrested I will be informed at once. That should slow them down. And I shall ask that the Bermans be released."

"Could you do a warrant for my uncle?"

"I'll have to inquire more deeply," she said. "I will not let this go. Thank you for coming to me with it, Elvira." She waved her fingers, and the equerry came up. "Make me out a Royal Warrant for Miss Royston," she said.

"Yes, ma'am," he said. "Ma'am, Sir Guy wants to speak to you very urgently."

"I'll speak to him next," she said, and gave me her hand. I didn't know whether to bow over it or kiss it or what, but I just shook it and backed away. As I did, I saw Sir Guy bowing as he came up to her, an old notebook in his hand. "Your Majesty, forgive me for interrupting you, but I think you will want to see this," he said, as I left. I wondered what it was. The Queen looked at it very intently. I sat down again, but kept my eyes on her as she read and questioned Sir Guy. I felt wrung out. I was waiting for my warrant. As soon as I had it I would go back to Betsy. We'd go back to her parents' house and I'd telephone my mother and Raymond to let them know what had happened. I was presented, I was a lady, and soon I would be going to Oxford, and one day when everything was all right I'd have the chance to write about all this and get it all clear for myself and for posterity. I sat hugging that thought to myself as I waited.

30

Two of them grabbed hold of his shoulders from behind. At least he could die as Jack had died, he thought, loosening the tooth. Carmichael wasn't sure what he thought about death. He'd given up the angels on clouds idea as a boy. Death had always represented a huge question mark for him, one usually clearly marked with questions about motive and means and opportunity. There'd be no doubt about the means in his case, he thought, just as a third Watchman grabbed his lower jaw and forced it open. He struggled, but they gagged him efficiently, meaning he could not reach the tooth. Then they cuffed his hands behind his back and searched him, taking the pistol, all his money, and identity cards. He wished he'd left the money with Breda, who could have used it. They thrust him into the back of a car. He struggled to sit up, which they did not prevent, piling in one on each side of him on the backseat.

Cut off, at least for the time being, from his means of escape, Carmichael paid attention to the car's direction. He wanted to know where they were going, the Yard or the Watchtower. He wasn't surprised when it was the Watchtower. The hotel would have routinely handed over the forms in the morning, and only Jacobson could have identified his aliases. Walter Sprange wouldn't have rung any bells with the Yard. Jacobson must have betrayed him after all, but why? It didn't make any sense.

The policemen on either side of him held on to his arms as they drove along. Sooner or later they would have to loosen his gag, and as soon as they did he would use the tooth. He would betray nothing and nobody, never again. "In the end, I sold my soul," he had said, and Abby had replied, "That wasn't the end." This, when they took out the gag to question him, would be the end that would make up for all the earlier betrayals that started with the Kahns and went on with all the other innocents he had not been able to save, the ones who were names on lists and statistics he had handed over to Normanby. They had nothing to threaten him with or promise him now. Elvira would have to look after herself, but she could manage that. Everyone sells out in the end, but he would leave before that end came. Perhaps he had failed another of Abby's tests when he had thought he would sacrifice Elvira for Jack, but there were no more tests, nothing else that could be taken from him. He didn't know where Elvira was and Jack was dead.

At the Watchtower he was taken in through one of the entrances that led down to the interrogation rooms, as he had expected. He was strapped into a chair, which one of the technicians angled back. He called another to hold Carmichael's jaw while he began to loosen the gag. When Carmichael realized he meant to remove the tooth, he began to struggle. In the end they had to use all the straps and his mouth was bloody, but the tooth was out. They left him there for a moment. His tongue, uselessly free now, probed the tender place where the tooth had been. He waited. He was hoping for Jacobson, but not altogether surprised to see Ogilvie. Ogilvie looked shocked, for the first time in Carmichael's experience.

"Sir," Ogilvie said. "I mean—I mean what's going on? Is Jacobson telling the truth? He knew what name you'd be using, and I thought I'd better find you before the Yard did."

"Good work, Ogilvie," Carmichael said, wondering if he could possibly persuade Ogilvie it was all some undercover work and that Jacobson was trying to blame him for his own underground organization. No, too many people knew too much, and sooner or later Ogilvie would talk to Bannister or Penn-Barkis.

"He said you were working with some Quaker from Portsmouth to get the Jews away," Ogilvie said. "He said you tried to recruit him!"

That's right, Ogilvie, tell me all about it, Carmichael thought. Jacobson had betrayed him, and Abby, to save the Inner Watch. Well, that made sense at least. Or had Elvira betrayed Abby? That could have been what she knew. Carmichael found himself laughing.

"What's funny?" Ogilvie asked, looking completely perplexed.

"That I keep on putting things together even in this situation," Carmichael said. "I really was born to be a detective."

"But what's going on?" Ogilvie said, looking down at him, bewildered.

"The Yard picked Elvira up at the riot, and let her go into Sergeant Evans's custody. Then they picked her up again and tried to get her to tell them I was a traitor. I rescued her, and tucked her away somewhere safe. In retaliation, Normanby killed my man, Jack, who had been with me for years. I went underground."

There it was, simplified, and leaving out the Inner Watch entirely, and it might buy him enough time to let him talk to Jacobson, so they could both get their stories straight. After that, Jacobson could certainly be persuaded to help him die, before he betrayed him in his turn.

"That's more or less what Jacobson said," Ogilvie said, looking pained. "Penn-Barkis is asking for you, but I'm going to keep you here tonight."

"You'll be made Chief," Carmichael predicted. "There's nobody else. They couldn't have Jacobson for Commander, he's a Jew."

"Did you really just go down there with guns out and grab Elvira?" Ogilvie asked.

"Isn't there anyone you'd do that for?"

Ogilvie's flat face went blank. "Will you fight if I let you up to walk to the cell?" he asked.

"No, I won't fight, there's no point anymore," he said.

Ogilvie and a Watchman loosened the straps and let Carmichael up. He walked quietly between them down the corridor. "The cell's just down here, sir. I mean, the cell's just down here," Ogilvie said. "I have some things to sort out. I'll come back and talk to you in the morning."

"Is Jacobson here?" Carmichael asked, as if casually.

"He's still off for Passover," Ogilvie said, caroling the last word mockingly. "See you in the morning."

"I certainly won't be going anywhere," Carmichael said, as they opened the cell door and he stepped inside.

One wall was barred and open to the corridor and there was a little toilet cubicle, with a sink but without a door. There was a bed, which was considerably more comfortable than the bed in the hotel in Pimlico. Carmichael lay on it and thought, staring up at the blank gray ceiling. Jacobson would probably help him die, if he could get away with it without incriminating himself. All that was lost of the Inner Watch was the London safe houses, and maybe not all of them. He had to stay at the Watchtower and avoid being sent to Penn-Barkis for as long as possible. Ogilvie would make a wonderfully unimaginative Watch Commander; as long as Jacobson kept his temper he'd be able to run rings around him.

He slept, dreamed of Jack, and woke with tears streaming down his face. He got up and washed his face quickly before anyone saw.

They brought him breakfast after a while; a cheese roll from the canteen and a paper cup of tea. The guard who brought it didn't speak, and didn't answer questions. Carmichael lay on his side and stared at the bars. He was expecting Jacobson, or a summons to the Yard. If it was the latter, he'd just have to hold out as long as he could, stick to his story, or rather Jacobson's story, buy time for Jacobson to cover up, so that when he did incriminate him it wouldn't be believed. Jacobson must have felt very vulnerable, a Jew, and involved in the Inner Watch, with Carmichael taking risks. He would have expected to have felt furious, but he couldn't rise above resignation. Everyone has something they care about more.

A while later, more than an hour, he guessed, the taciturn guard brought him more tea, on a tray. It was his own tea, in his own Orange Tree teapot and cup and saucer, with a plate of chocolate digestives, and a lace-edged cloth on the tray. Miss Duthie, Carmichael thought, you've let me know very clearly that you know I'm here, but don't go and get yourself into trouble! He was deeply touched. He drank the tea and ate all the biscuits, every crumb. He stroked the side of the teapot. Jack had chosen the pattern. He counted the oranges, and admired the elegance of the black lines. He imagined walking with Jack down an avenue of orange trees, in Greece, to see some Byzantine ruin.

By lunchtime (more cheese sandwiches, and the removal of the Orange Tree tray) Carmichael had worked out why nobody was taking any notice of him, and how Miss Duthie had managed to get away with the gesture with the tea and biscuits. Today was the procession, and they were all too busy with that to have time for him. He wondered about Loy, with his out-of-date watchword and his rifle. Had he got Normanby? Would that chaos bleed into the procession chaos and leave him bored in his cell for even longer? He'd never approved of assassination. He wasn't sure it would do any good even now. He hoped the Duke of Windsor wouldn't be able to take advantage of the chaos to seize power. No, he was probably in the Tower by now. If he'd still had the tooth, Carmichael would have used it out of sheer boredom.

After lunch, two Watchmen took him down the corridor to an interrogation cell. There was a television high on the wall, two chairs, and a table. He was strapped to a chair facing the blank screen and left alone. After a moment, Jacobson came. "It's all right, I understand," Carmichael said quickly, as he let himself into the cell.

"Why do you have to be such a bloody coward?" Jacobson asked. "You endanger everything and then you don't even have the decency to kill yourself when you had every opportunity."

Carmichael gasped. "I do see that you must have felt vulnerable," he began.

"You don't give a damn about me, you never did," Jacobson said.

"I'm prepared to back up your story, if—"

Before Carmichael could finish asking for what he wanted, Jacobson advanced towards him, and he saw with a strange kind of relief that there was a knife in his hand. "I can't risk that," Jacobson said.

The door clanged open, and Ogilvie rushed in and grappled with Jacobson. Carmichael almost wanted to laugh, watching them. They were quite evenly matched. Ogilvie realized this too. "Sergeant!" he called, and two Watchmen rushed to his assistance.

"Take Mr. Jacobson to a cell," Ogilvie said, once they had subdued him. He looked at Carmichael in confusion as Jacobson was led away. "I'm— There's someone here to talk to you. But he wants you to watch the news first."

"The news?" Carmichael asked, in astonishment.

Ogilvie shrugged and turned on the television, then left while the set was still warming up.

"The body of the man who fired the shot that narrowly missed Herr Hitler this morning has been identified as Gunther Wald, a salesman from Germany," the announcer said.

Ah, Loy. Not such a good shot after all. He was getting old. And why had he gone for Hitler rather than Normanby? Carmichael felt a pang of regret for his death.

"The peace conference, opened by Her Majesty the Queen," the announcer was saying as Carmichael started to pay attention again. "And now we take you live to her televised address to the British People."

There was a moment of static, and then the camera steadied on the Queen, holding a sheaf of notes, sitting down.

She set down her papers and looked directly at the camera, at Carmichael. "Today I have opened a great peace conference, at which delegates from all over the world will meet together to determine the fate of the world, this new world in which we have so much to fear, and so much to hope for. Now I want to address you, the people of Britain, as your Queen and tell you that it is my constitutional duty to call an immediate General Election. There have been coups and attempted coups. My uncle, the Duke of Windsor, is under arrest under accusations of treason. Also under arrest this afternoon is Mark Normanby, the former Prime Minister. He is accused, on the highest evidence, of the murder of Sir James Thirkie, at Farthing House, in 1949, and of the dowager Lady Thirkie in Campion House in the same year, and using these to engineer his own attempt at power ten years ago. The whole climate of fear we have all lived in for the last ten years was, if not imaginary, at least exaggerated."

Carmichael thought he must still be dreaming. Her voice went on evenly.

"Mr. Normanby is under arrest, as are Lord and Lady Eversley, for complicity in this crime. There will be a General Election on May second, and for the time being the temporary Prime Minister will be the Foreign Secretary, Sir Guy Braithwaite."

"Good God!" Carmichael said. Guy must have used his notebook, he must have—it was almost beyond belief.

"I am Head of State, not Head of Government, and it is no part of my duties to approve or disapprove the government, nor even the form of government; my country chooses for itself. But it seems to me that this government was not chosen freely, or in full knowledge of the facts. They have arrested those accused of no specific crime and held them in detention for long periods without bringing them to trial, they have created a climate of fear, they have shipped off suspects to foreign prisons where they knew they could expect bad treatment. This is not in the tradition of which we, as Britons, can be rightly proud. There have been spontaneous demonstrations this week against this behavior, and I feel in speaking out on this subject I am speaking the will of my people. With the agreement of Sir Guy, all the so-called Hyde Park martyrs will be released. All Jews and others presently detained under the Defence of the Realm Act will be released. All future arrests will be subject to Home Office oversight."

Carmichael wiped away tears from his cheeks. And to think he had almost killed himself and missed this!

"When you go to the polls, I ask you to vote responsibly, with forethought, for those you feel will do their best to govern, those who will be the servants of the people and not their masters," she said.

"Good God," Carmichael said again.

The door opened behind him. He turned from the screen, which had cut to a view of cheering crowds. He wasn't entirely surprised to see Sir Guy in the doorway.

"I've come to say you can go," Sir Guy said. "I wanted you to see that."

"I saw it," Carmichael said. "It was astonishing. Did you write that speech?"

"She wrote it herself," Sir Guy said. "Her Majesty had a long talk with your little girl last night, before I took her the notebook."

"Elvira?" Carmichael said.

"She went to be presented, right on time. And she made Her

Majesty much firmer than I'd have dared to be. I'd never have suggested letting all the Jews go."

On the television screen, the crowds were still cheering.

"Nobody seems to mind," Carmichael said.

"No, not as far as I can see. I was too timid," he said, undoing the buckles of the straps that held Carmichael to the chair. "I wish I could offer you your old job back, but it wouldn't do. Too many people know what you did. Penn-Barkis is also in a cell, you'll be glad to know, and I won't be going by this afternoon to let him out."

"What about Jacobson? Will you let him go too?"

"He went for you with a knife!" Sir Guy said.

"He did it with the best of motives," Carmichael said gravely. "You should let him go. He and Ogilvie can manage the Watch. I never liked it anyway. It was never my idea of a good job."

"What will you do?" Sir Guy asked.

"I don't know," Carmichael said. "I need to talk to Elvira. I do wish Jack could have seen this."

"I'm very sorry it came too late for him," Sir Guy said. "Come on, walk out with me."

They walked together through the corridors of the Watchtower, past cells and cubicles and offices. "Maybe I'll go into business for myself," Carmichael said. "A private detective, something like that."

"That's very traditional," Sir Guy said. "Well, good luck to you, Carmichael, whatever you do. Keep in touch."

"Keep the country on an even keel," Carmichael said.

"Oh, I'll have to, or Her Majesty will turf me out too," he said.

"And hang bloody Normanby!"

"I fully intend to," Sir Guy said. "It's your evidence that will do it."

Carmichael shook his hand at the top of the stairs. The sun was shining from a sky dotted with puffy white clouds; it was another beautiful spring day. He supposed he could call for a car for the last time, but he didn't want to. He didn't know where he wanted to go. Home would seem very empty without Jack, even if England was taking her first tottering steps towards being free again. He waved to Sir Guy and walked away in the sunshine up the dirty London street.

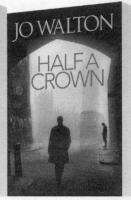